THE BURNING

THE BURNING

JANE CASEY

ISIS

LARGE PRINT

Oxford

First published in Great Britain 2010
by
Ebury Press
an imprint of Ebury Publishing

Published in Large Print 2011 by ISIS Publishing Ltd.,
7 Centremead, Osney Mead, Oxford OX2 0ES
by arrangement with
Ebury Publishing
A Random House Group Company

British Library Cataloguing in Publication Data
Casey, Jane (Jane E.)
    The burning.
    1. Serial murder investigation - - England - -
    London - - Fiction.
    2. Women detectives - - England - - London - -
    Fiction.
    3. Detective and mystery stories.
    4. Large type books.
    I. Title
    823.9'2–dc22

ISBN 978–0–7531–8880–4 (hb)
ISBN 978–0–7531–8881–1 (pb)

Printed and bound in Great Britain by
T. J. International Ltd., Padstow, Cornwall

For Philippa

The certainty of death is attended with uncertainties, in time, manner, places.

Sir Thomas Browne, *Urn Burial*

Bodies recovered from fires present similar problems of investigation to bodies recovered from water. In both instances the integration of information obtained from the examination of the scene, the examination of the body, and the history of the decedent, is particularly important.

Derrick J Pounder

She should have gone home with the others.

Kelly Staples stared at her reflection in the cracked and spotted mirror, trying to make sense of what she saw. Surely that wasn't her face squinting back. Mascara had smeared under her eyes, leaving shadowy smudges speckled with tiny flecks of black that wouldn't come off no matter how she rubbed at them. The remnants of her foundation were caked around her nose and across her forehead, where her skin looked dry. Her face was red and she had a spot on her chin that she was sure hadn't been there when she was getting ready to go out. Her mouth was slack and wet, and there was something on her top . . . With a huge effort Kelly bent her head to inspect the damage. Wine, she thought hazily. She had tipped red wine down her front. She vaguely remembered laughing hysterically, holding the wet material away from her, offering someone — a man she'd never met before — the chance to suck it, so as not to waste it, before Faye dragged her away from him, muttering crossly in her ear about behaving herself. But as Kelly had pointed out, or tried to, tonight was all about *not* behaving herself. Out with the girls for an evening of freedom, a pub crawl in Richmond. Dolled up, tanked up, ready for a laugh. It was getting near the end of term; they'd needed a break, all of them. Especially her, since she'd broken up with PJ three weeks before. Or, to be precise, he'd broken up with her. Two years they'd been together, and he'd thrown it all away to chase after Vanessa Cobbet, the fat slapper. A tear slid down Kelly's face, gliding through what was left of her make-up.

They'd started with white wine at home, getting ready, and Kelly had had a few glasses. Giddy with nerves, she'd needed it. And it had got the evening off to a good start.

The room behind her rocked and swayed. Kelly shut her eyes, leaning heavily on the sink as she waited to feel better. She had been sick already; she had thought it might help if she was sick. Behind her, a cubicle door banged. A bony middle-aged woman slipped past her with a sidelong look that said *you're too young to be in that sort of state*. Kelly thought, but wasn't confident enough to say, *yeah, well you're too old to be in here in the first place*.

The toilets were cramped, two cubicles and two sinks squeezed into a narrow corner of the pub, reeking of aggressive air freshener and the sour-sweet smell of vomited wine — that was Kelly's contribution. The fixtures dated the last redesign to the eighties if not before: pink porcelain fittings and pink-and-brown floral curtains that hung limply at the frosted window. The rest of the pub wasn't much better, though the dim lighting hid most of the damage at night. The Jolly Boatman had seen better days, as had most of the clientele, but it was busy nonetheless, crowded with

2

drinkers. The pubs by the river were all busy; it was Thursday night, the unofficial start to the weekend, and everyone was out to have a good time, including Kelly. But it had all gone wrong, somewhere along the way. The others had left, she remembered woozily, telling her to get a taxi when she was ready to come home. She'd been dancing with someone, a lad she didn't know, and Faye had tried to persuade her to leave but she'd refused. It had seemed to make sense then. It was her turn, her chance to have fun. They'd taken her at her word and left her. Kelly couldn't understand why she'd let them.

"I'm pissed," she said out loud, trying to make eye contact with the bleary figure in the mirror. "I need to go home."

The contents of her handbag had spilt into the basin in front of her. It seemed to take an extraordinarily long time to collect everything up again; her hands were clumsy and there were so many things — a pen, make-up, her keys, a bus ticket, some loose change — three cigarettes that had fallen out of their packet and were splotched with damp from the sink. The lid had come off a tube of lip gloss and as Kelly fumbled to pick it up sticky red goo smeared across the pink porcelain. It looked, for a moment, like blood.

The noise and heat hit her with a physical shock when she pulled open the door and she faltered a little, trying to remember which way she needed to go. The door to the outside world was to the left, she vaguely recalled, and set herself to push through the crowd. She was walking tall, acting sober, shoulders pulled well back and head up. It fooled no one except Kelly herself.

The crowd was thicker around the door, with smokers coming and going from the terrace that overlooked the water.

"Excuse me," Kelly mumbled, trying and failing to shoulder past a heavyset man who didn't seem to hear her or notice her cannoning into his back.

"Need a minicab, love? Let me give you a hand," said a voice in her ear as an arm snaked around her waist. "Time to go home, young lady."

Without consciously agreeing, she found herself making progress, guided skilfully and swiftly through the throng until they reached the chill of outside air. It was a clear night, still and cold, and the frost was already starting to bite.

She turned then, ready to thank her rescuer, and found herself looking at a stranger, a man her father's age or older. Kelly struggled to focus as the man's face swooped up and down in front of her. There were rimless glasses, and hair that was surely too dark to be natural, and a moustache over a mouth that smiled, that moved, that was saying *where do you live my cab is just around the corner why don't you come with me and I'll see you home it's no trouble it's not far I don't have anything better to do give me your bag that's the girl are these your keys I'll take care of you don't you worry. You don't want to be out on your own not at the moment not safe is it?*

Somehow, Kelly found herself following the man obediently. She wanted to take her bag back and find her own way home, but it seemed easier to go along with him. Her feet were hurting for one thing; the platform boots that had looked so glamorous before she left the house were pinching her toes and rubbing her heels, and the one on the right was squeezing her calf. They were far too high for a long walk home. And he was right; it probably wasn't safe to be out on her own.

The man was nice, Kelly thought hazily. He was polite, well mannered, thoughtful. Older men were, weren't they? They knew how to be gentlemen. PJ had never held her hand. PJ had never opened the car door for her and waited to close it after she sat down (a little heavily, truth be told, but then again he was a perfect gentleman and stared into the distance rather than at her skirt where it had ridden up). She usually got into the back when she took a taxi, but he'd opened the front passenger door and she didn't want to be rude.

He got in and started the engine, then helped her with her seat belt before he drove off. He revved the engine unnecessarily so the sound bounced off the buildings either side of the road.

"Mind if I smoke?" Kelly asked, pushing her luck, and was surprised when he nodded. The car smelled of mint and pine air freshener, two strong scents that didn't quite manage to disguise the tang of petrol, as if he'd spilt some on his shoes the last time he'd filled up. He wasn't a smoker, she guessed. But he'd agreed to it; he couldn't mind *that* much.

The only dry fag in the packet was the lucky one, the last one, the one Kelly always turned upside down when she opened a new pack so it stood out, a little white soldier standing proud beside the light-brown filter tips of the others. She fitted it between her lips and cupped her hands around the flame of her lighter, shielding herself automatically from a wind that wasn't there. She had the lighter turned up too high; it nearly took her fringe off.

"Fuck." She blinked a few times, dazzled, then shot a guilty look at the stranger. "Sorry. Shouldn't swear."

He shrugged. "Doesn't bother me. What's your name?"

"Kelly." She flipped down the visor and inspected herself in the mirror, fluffing her fringe. "What's your name?"

He hesitated for a second. "Dan."

"Where are you from, Dan? Birmingham?" It was a Midlands accent, she'd thought, but he shook his head.

"Round here."

"Oh yeah?"

He nodded, his eyes on the road. Kelly looked out too, peering at the shops they were passing. She frowned.

"This isn't the way."

He didn't answer.

"This isn't the way," she said again, embarrassed to be complaining when he was being so helpful. "You've gone wrong. It was left back there, not straight on."

"This is a better way."

"It isn't," Kelly said, nettled. "I should know how to get to my own house."

The only response she got was a change of gear as he accelerated.

"Hey," she said, warning in her voice as she braced one hand against the dashboard, the surface gritty with accumulated dirt. "Take it easy."

The car bounced down the road, going a little bit too fast for her liking. He looked nervous, she thought, blinking hard, trying to focus. His lips were chapped, and every so often he passed his tongue over them. It made Kelly's lips feel dry and she had to stop herself from doing the same. All of a sudden she felt cold, and cold sober too, the fog of alcohol lifting but leaving fear in its place. What had she done? All the times her mother had warned her not to trust strangers and here she was in a car with a man she'd never met before, going who knows where on a dark Thursday night. There was someone killing young women; she'd seen the headline in her dad's paper. Four girls dead, dumped and burned. Girls like her. The police hadn't a clue who the killer was, or how to catch him. He was on the loose, preying on vulnerable women out on their own. Even Kelly, who never paid much attention to the news, had heard about him. It wasn't late; there were still people out on the streets, but Kelly had never felt so alone.

"Listen, why don't you let me out here? I'd rather walk if it's all the same to you."

"Just relax."

The car purred to a stop at traffic lights. Kelly ran her hand over the door beside her, looking for the handle.

"It's broken," he said without looking around. "You can only open it from the outside. Now sit tight and stop making such a fuss."

"I want to get out." Her voice had risen, a raw edge of hysteria to it that made the driver wince.

"Calm down, would you. I'll stop and let you out if that's what you want." He turned into a narrow residential street that was lined with parked cars. "Nowhere to pull in. Let's see what's down here."

"Down here" was an alley between gardens, a dead end that wasn't overlooked, Kelly realised, her heart thumping. She felt as if it was going to burst out of her chest. The car slowed to a stop.

"What's going on? Why are you stopping?"

"I thought you wanted to get out. I'll let you out." He turned off the engine, then the lights, and the night closed in around them. Kelly could only see a silhouette beside her. Her nostrils flared, picking up the minty smell and the faintest whiff of petrol again, and she thought of the girls lying where they'd been dumped, of their bodies burning, of the newspaper headlines that talked about the Burning Man, and she heard him move and couldn't tell if he was reaching towards her in the dark car and without thinking, without even being aware that she'd moved, she reached down and slipped out the knife her little brother had given her, the one he took to school in case he got into a fight, the one that had been digging into her ankle for hours, the flick knife with the narrow blade and the wicked sharp point, and there wasn't even enough light to catch the edge of the blade as she swung with it in her left hand, aiming low, aiming for the soft part below the ribcage but above the belt, and he didn't have time to react at all before the knife was in him and out again and slipping back into him though he tried to grab the blade that time when Kelly pulled it out and the knife was dark now, and wet, and the man was whimpering, and she could smell him and smell blood — it was like a butcher's shop on a hot day, that sweetish reek — and he'd pissed himself and she was screaming, she realised, her heart pounding as loud as a drum so she couldn't even hear what she was saying. But she was still saying it as she scrambled over the seat into the back of the car and fumbled for the door handle and flung herself out, acting on instinct, her hands, all covered with blood, smearing along the paintwork, her knees buckling as she tried to run in her stupid boots, her sore feet forgotten. She was still saying it under her breath as she hobbled down the alley towards the houses, towards help, her breath sawing in and out of her lungs as if it was edged with rusty teeth. It was what she said to the woman who came to the door and screamed at the sight of her, and what she said to the police who responded to the 999 call, and what she said to the doctors and nurses later on at the hospital, when she was being examined. It was the one thing she was sure of, the thing that had kept her alive.

"Not me. I don't want to be the next one. Not me. Not me."

CHAPTER
ONE

MAEVE

I didn't know where I was or what I was doing when the phone rang; I didn't even know that it was the phone that had woken me. I came up from miles below the surface and opened an eye as one part of my brain tried to work out what had disturbed me and another part focused on how to make the noise stop. It resolved into a low rattle that was my phone vibrating crossly on the bedside table along with the high-pitched shrill of the most annoying ring tone I could have chosen. Fumbling for it in the dark, I sideswiped it and managed to push it off the table. It fell face down in the carpet, still ringing, the sound now slightly muffled. I'd winged it but not killed it. The bonus was that now it was a little bit harder to reach. I leaned out of bed at a dangerous angle, raking the carpet with my fingers, trying to get to it.

"Mmph!"

Most of the nuance was lost in the pillow, but I interpreted Ian's comment as "answer the fucking phone", which was pretty much what I was thinking myself. Along with *what time is it?* and *what does this eejit want?*

I got it at last and stabbed at the buttons until it stopped making a noise, trying to read the screen. LANGTON. Rob. I squinted at the time and read 03.27. Half past three in the morning and Detective Constable Rob Langton was calling me. I was waking up now, my brain starting to crank into gear, but my mouth hadn't caught up with the change of plans and was still slack with sleep. When I said hello, it sounded slurred, as if I'd been drinking for the last — I worked it out — three and a half hours instead of having some much-needed shut-eye. Three and a half hours. That made six hours of sleep in the last forty-eight. I squeezed my eyes closed and wished I hadn't added it up. Somehow, knowing the numbers made me feel worse.

"Did I wake you, Kerrigan?" I would have recognised the Manchester twang anywhere.

"You know you did. What do you want?"

I asked, but I already knew. There were only two reasons why Rob Langton would be ringing me at that hour of the morning sounding excited. One: there was another body. Two: they'd caught the killer. Either way, I wasn't going back to sleep any time soon.

"Got him."

"No way." I sat up in bed and put the light on, ignoring a groan from beside me and squinting as I tried to concentrate. "Where? How?"

"We had a bit of help. Nice young lady out on the beers with a bladed article didn't take kindly to being next on the Burning Man's list."

"He's not dead." My heart was pounding. If he was dead, that was it. No answers. No trial.

No justice.

"Nah, he's clinging on. He's in hospital. In surgery, at the minute. Two stab wounds to the abdomen; she lacerated his bowel."

"Ouch."

"Yeah, couldn't happen to a nicer person."

"Anyone we know?" I rubbed my eyes with the heel of my hand and tried not to yawn.

"Not known at all. Never been arrested before, and he hadn't come up in this enquiry."

I sighed. That wasn't great news. We hadn't even been close to catching him, then. We'd just been lucky. Though the girl had been luckier still. I wasn't a fan of people wandering around carrying knives, but I'd seen enough dead women in the past few weeks to think it wasn't such a bad idea.

"His name's Vic Blackstaff. He had all his documents on him — driver's licence, work ID. He's in his mid-fifties, does shift work for a call centre in Epsom. Lives in Peckham. Drives through south-west London to get home in the small hours of the morning. Plenty of opportunity."

"Older than we'd thought," I commented. "Shift work fits, though. Where did it happen?"

"Richmond."

"That's quite a long way out of the usual area. Up to now he's stuck to Kennington, Stockwell — nowhere as far out as Richmond." I was frowning.

"Yeah, but his usual area is flooded with uniforms. Makes sense that he would be hunting elsewhere, doesn't it?" Rob sounded confident and I gave a mental shrug; who was I to second-guess a serial killer?

"They're going through his car at the moment," Rob went on. "We're waiting at the hospital."

"Who's we?"

"Me and the boss. And DI Judd, unfortunately. We'll be interviewing the young lady as soon as the doctors tell us we can talk to her. She's still being checked out."

"How is she? Is she —"

I didn't want to fill in the rest of the sentence. Is she going to make it? Is she badly beaten? Is she burned? How far had he got?

"She's fine. Shaken up. Nothing wrong with her but we haven't been allowed in to see her yet. She says she's not ready." Rob sounded impatient, which nettled me. Why shouldn't she take her time before speaking to the police? She'd had a shock. What she needed was a sympathetic ear. And I was the ideal person to provide it. Energy flooded through my limbs, adrenalin pushing fatigue into a corner, to be ignored until I had time to give in to it again. Three hours' sleep was plenty. I was already out of bed, making for the door, stumbling on rubbery legs that ached as if I'd run a marathon the day before.

"Well, I'll be there soon. Maybe they'll let me talk to her." The perks of being the only woman in Superintendent Godley's inner circle were not legion, but now and then it came in handy.

"Why doesn't that surprise me? Nought to sixty in ten minutes, that's you."

"That's why you phoned me, isn't it?" I was in the bathroom now, and debated whether I could risk peeing while on the phone. He'd hear. I'd have to wait.

"I knew you'd want to be here." That was only half the story; it suited them all for me to be there. I could hear Rob grinning; he was a smug git sometimes, but I could forgive him, because when all was said and done, I did want to be there, and without a call from him, I wouldn't have known a thing about it until I'd seen it on the news.

"Which hospital?"

"Kingston."

"I'll be there in half an hour," I said before I'd thought about it properly. It was a long way from Primrose Hill to Kingston and I desperately needed a shower. My hair was sticking to my head. There was no way I was leaving with dirty hair. Not again. "Make that forty minutes."

"We're in the ICU. Phones off, so ring the hospital if you need us."

"Will do."

I flicked the water on before going to the loo, but even so, it wasn't even close to warm enough when I forced myself to step into the slate-lined shower area, wincing as the spray hit my goose-pimpled skin. The showerhead was the size of a dinner plate and pumped out rain-forest levels of water; it was just a shame that it never got hot enough for me. Style over substance, as usual. But it wasn't my flat so I couldn't really complain. I was sharing it, officially, but I felt more like a guest. And not necessarily a welcome one, at times.

I had balled my hands together under my chin, hugging body heat to myself, and it was an effort to unknot my fingers and reach for the shampoo once the water started to approach tepidity. Haste made me fumble the shampoo cap and I swore as I heard it skitter around the sloping tiles that led to the drain. I left it there, hearing my mother's voice in my head, *sure, it can't fall any further* . . . Two minutes later, I stepped on it and had to muffle a yelp in the crook of my elbow as a sharp edge dug into the arch of my foot. Swearing was a help. I swore. A lot.

I scrubbed at my scalp until the muscles in my forearms complained and rinsed my hair for as long as I could allow myself to, eyes closed against the lather that slid down my face. Bliss to be clean again, joy to know that the case was coming to an end. I wanted to stay in there for ever with my eyes closed; I wanted to sleep — how I wanted to sleep. But I couldn't. I had to get going. And by the time I got out of the shower, I was what passed for awake these days.

Back in the bedroom, I tried to be quiet, but I couldn't help rattling the hangers in the wardrobe when I was taking out a suit. I heard stirring behind me in the bed and bit my lip.

"What's up?"

I wouldn't have spoken to Ian if he hadn't spoken to me; that was the rule I observed about getting up and leaving in the middle of the night. Not that I was sure he'd ever noticed there was a rule.

"Going to meet a murderer."

That earned me an opened eye. "You got him. Well done."

"It wasn't exactly all my own work, but thanks."

He rolled over onto his back and threw an arm over his face, shielding his eyes from the light. He was in his natural position now, hogging the middle of the bed. I suppressed the impulse to push him back onto his own side and hauled the sheet up instead, tucking him in. *Look, I care about you. See how thoughtful I am.*

"Mmm," was the response. He was on his way back to sleep. I slipped the dry-cleaner's bag off my suit and balled it up, squashing it into the bin. I should have taken it off sooner. The suit smelled of chemicals and I wrinkled my nose, reluctant to put it on. The forecast was for a cold day, and rain. I thought longingly of jeans tucked into boots, of chunky jumpers and long knitted scarves. God, dressing like a grown-up was a pain.

I sat on the edge of the bed to deal with my tights, coaxing them over damp skin, wary of ripping them. My hair dripped onto my shoulders, cold water running down my back. I hadn't got time for this. I hadn't got time for immaculate. Slowly, infinitely slowly, I worked the material up over my thighs and stood to haul the tights the rest of the way. It was not the most elegant moment of getting dressed, and I wasn't pleased to turn and find Ian staring at me, an unreadable expression on his face.

"So is this it?"

"What do you mean?" I slipped on a shirt, then stepped into my skirt, zipping it up quickly and smoothing it over my hips. That was better. More dignified. The waistband was loose, I noticed, the skirt hanging from my hips rather than my waist. It took the hem from on the knee to over it, from flattering to frump. I needed to eat more. I needed to rest.

"I mean is this the end of it? Are you going to be around more?"

"Probably. Not for a little while — we've got to sort out the paperwork and get the case ready for the CPS. But after that, yeah."

If there isn't another serial killer waiting to take over from where the Burning Man left off. If nothing else goes wrong between now and Christmas. If all the criminals in London take the rest of the year off.

I was looking for shoes, my medium-heeled courts that didn't so much as nod to fashion but hey, I could wear them from now until midnight without a twinge of complaint from my feet. I could even run in them if I had to. One was in the corner of the room, where I'd kicked it off. The other I eventually found under the bed, and had to sprawl inelegantly to retrieve it.

"I hate the way they whistle and you come running." He sounded wide awake now, and cross. My heart sank.

"It's my job."

"Oh, it's your *job*. Sorry. I didn't realise."

"Don't do this now," I said, stabbing my feet into my shoes and grabbing my towel. "I've got to go. It's important and you know it."

He'd sat up, leaning on one elbow, blue eyes hostile under thick eyebrows, his brown hair uncharacteristically untidy. "What I know is that I haven't seen you for weeks. What I know is that I'll be ringing up Camilla to say you can't come to supper after all, and is that OK, and I'm really sorry if it's mucked up her seating arrangement. What I know is that your job always seems to come first."

I let him rant, towelling most of the water out of my hair and then dragging a comb through it, trying to get it into some sort of order. No time to dry it; it would dry on the way to the hospital. A few wisps, a lighter brown than the rest, were already curling around my face.

"Camilla works in an art gallery. She has nothing to do all day but rearrange the seating plan for her little dinner parties. It'll be a challenge for her."

He flopped back down and stared at the ceiling. "You always do that."

"What?" I shouldn't have asked.

"Put down my friends because their jobs aren't as important or as worthwhile as yours."

"For God's sake . . ."

"Not everyone wants to save the world, Maeve."

"Yeah, it's just as important to make it look nice," I snapped, and regretted it as soon as I'd said it. Camilla was sweet, sincere, a wide-eyed innocent that brought out the protective instinct in everyone who knew her, including me. Usually. The sharpness in my voice had been partly exhaustion and partly guilt; I *had* been thinking of skipping the dinner party she was throwing.

It wasn't that I didn't like Ian's friends — it was just that I couldn't stand the questions. *Any interesting cases lately? Why haven't you caught the Burning Man yet? What's the most hideous thing you've ever seen on duty? Do you wish they still had capital punishment? Can you sort out this speeding ticket for me?* It was tedious and predictable and I found it acutely embarrassing to represent the Metropolitan Police to Ian's friends. I was just one person. And traffic tickets were definitely outside my purview.

"Ian . . ."

"Aren't you in a hurry?"

I checked my watch. "Yes. Let's talk about this later, OK?"

"Can't wait."

I wanted to point out that I hadn't brought it up in the first place. Instead, I leaned across the bed and planted a kiss on the bit of Ian's chin I could reach easily. There was no response. With a sigh, I headed to the kitchen to pick up a banana, then grabbed my bag and my coat and ran down the stairs. I closed the front door with the key in the lock so I didn't wake the neighbours, though if they'd slept through my shower and relationship issues, they probably wouldn't notice the door banging. If they were at home, and not on a pre-Christmas shopping trip to New York or a winter break in the Bahamas.

I stopped for a second on the doorstep, head down, my mind whirling.

"What am I doing? What the hell am I doing?"

I hadn't meant to say it out loud, and I wasn't talking about work. I could handle work. My boyfriend was another matter. We'd been together for eight months, lived together for six, and from the moment I'd moved into Ian's place, the fighting had started. I'd fallen for a big smile, broad shoulders and a job that had nothing to do with crime. He'd told me he liked the dynamic, busy detective with long legs and no ulterior motives. I wasn't looking for a husband who could be the father to my children — yet. My eyes didn't light up with pound signs when I heard he was in banking. It was all so easy. We saw one another when we could, snatched hours in bed at his place or mine, managed dinner together every so often and when my lease came up for renewal, Ian had taken a chance, the sort of gamble that had made him rich, and invited me to move in with him in his ludicrously over-designed, expensive flat in Primrose Hill. It hadn't been a good idea. It had been a disaster. And I wasn't sure how to get out of it. After two months, we hadn't known one another, except in the biblical sense. We hadn't worked out what we had in common, or how we might spend long winter afternoons when the weather made going out an unappealing prospect. As it turned out, we stayed in bed or we fought. There was no middle ground. I started to stay longer at work, left earlier in the morning, popped into the nick over the weekend even if I wasn't on duty. The only silver lining was the overtime pay.

The night air was harsh and I shivered as I hurried down the road, my hair cold against my neck. I was glad of the coat Ian had bought me, full-length and caramel-coloured in fine wool that was really too nice for hacking about crime scenes, but he had insisted on it. Generosity was not one of his shortcomings — he was open-handed to a fault. Even allowing for the extra overtime cash, there was no way I could compete. We weren't equals, couldn't pretend to be. It was no way to live.

When I got to my car, parked where I could find a space the night before, which was not particularly close to the flat, I stopped for a second to fill my lungs with sharp-edged air and centre myself, letting the silence fill my mind. That was the idea, anyway. Somewhere an engine revved as a neighbour drove away; traffic noise was building already, even at that early hour. And I needed to be elsewhere. Enough of the Zen contemplation. I got into the car and got going.

My heels were loud on the tiled floor and Rob saw me coming a long way off. He was sitting on an upright chair with his legs stretched out in front of him, taking up most of the corridor outside the intensive care unit.

"Morning."

"Is it?" he said interestedly, handing me a cardboard cup with a plastic lid. "I thought it was still Thursday night."

"Nope. It's Friday. The twenty-seventh of November. All day, if that helps."

He grinned up at me, dark stubble bristling on his face, halfway to a decent beard already. Welsh forebears had given him black hair, blue eyes, pale skin and charm to burn, but he needed to shave twice a day to keep his five o'clock shadow in check. Rob never quite made it to groomed, but he was looking particularly rumpled, and I recognised his shirt as being the one he'd worn the day before.

"You didn't make it home."

"Nope."

"You've been sitting there for hours."

"Yep."

"How?"

"That," he said, wagging a finger at me, "would be telling."

I sat down on the chair beside him and took the lid off the cup, smelling the hot-metal steam of machine-brewed coffee. "How many of these have you had?"

Instead of answering, he held his hand out so I could see the tremors that made it quiver.

"God. No more caffeine for you."

"Aw, Mum . . ."

I sipped coffee, smiling against the edge of the cup, as Rob leaned his head back against the wall and yawned.

"You made good time. I expected it to take the full hour to get you from bed to here."

It should have taken me longer, but I had driven comfortably over the speed limit most of the way, and had thrown the car into a space in the hospital car park, leaving it without bothering to straighten up.

"You know me. Full of get up and go."

"Yeah, right. How's Ian?"

I hesitated slightly before I answered; I really didn't want to share the details of my domestic squabbles with my colleagues, but there was no point in pretending.

Rob had met Ian a couple of times and formed his own opinion of him.

"He was just delighted about being woken up."

"Sorry about that. I'm sure he understood it was important."

I let one eyebrow rise up slowly, expressively, as I took another sip of coffee.

Rob snorted. "Like that, is it?"

"What we should actually be discussing," I said quickly, "is what's going on with the case. Where's the boss?"

He jerked his head towards the double doors behind him. "In there, somewhere. He's doctor-bothering."

"They still won't let us speak to the victim?"

"Not much of a victim. I feel more sorry for poor old Vic. He's in recovery. Three hours of surgery, and apparently it was touch and go."

"My heart bleeds for him."

"Yeah, well, he could use the extra blood if you're offering. He nearly died on the way to hospital. She really did a number on him."

"Which is why she's alive to tell us about it," I pointed out.

Rob grinned at me. "Getting into the right frame of mind, Maeve? Starting to identify with her? Best mates by ten o'clock, is that the plan?"

"So what?" My coffee had cooled down enough so that I could gulp it. The caffeine was beginning to kick in. I wanted to be ready when they let us talk to the girl. I wanted to be on my toes. I wanted to get the answers we needed and bring them to my boss, Charles Godley, like a cat bringing in a dead bird as a loving present for its owner. I didn't mind the long hours, the total commitment that he demanded from his team. I knew how lucky I was to be in the inner circle. Sixty officers on Operation Mandrake, and most of them would never get to speak to Godley face-to-face. He had his system: orders cascaded down from the top, delivered by the police he trusted to their fellow officers who were allocated tasks and the manpower to achieve them and turned loose, not to return until they'd done it. He was running the investigation that had become the media story of the year, if not the decade, and he spent far too much of his time dealing with reporters to be able to manage every aspect of the case himself. He'd picked me out of the borough and added me to his squad, and I still didn't know why, but I was determined not to let him down.

"So nothing." Rob had lost interest in teasing me. He took out his phone and started scrolling through messages, yawning as he did so. I left him to it, happy to sit in silence for a minute or two. Waiting for a break in the case had been agonising, heart-scalding. Now that it was here, I could afford to be patient.

But I couldn't help fidgeting, all the same.

I didn't have to wait too long, because after a couple of minutes, one of the big double doors that led to the ICU opened. Rob and I both turned to see a nurse leaning out. She was young, with honey-coloured highlights through her hair and fake-tanned skin. I had to admire her commitment to glamour at that hour of the morning. She ignored me after one quick, assessing look that took in my damp hair and make-up-free face, then smiled warmly at Rob. *Here's one you charmed earlier . . .*

"Your boss wants you."

We both stood at the same time. Rob was a shade above average height and I was tall in my heels; we were eye-to-eye. Rob frowned.

"He wants to talk to me, not you."

"He doesn't know I'm here," I said sweetly. "He'd want to speak to me if he did."

"I'll tell him you're waiting."

"I'll tell him myself."

There it was. No matter how much I liked Rob, no matter how well we got on, when it came to competing for the attention of our boss, we were as mature and reasonable as children fighting over a favourite toy.

"Suit yourself." He slung his jacket over his shoulder and walked past me, pushing through the swing doors with a bang. He didn't wait to see if I was following him or hold the door open for me; not that I expected special treatment — it wasn't as if I made a fuss about needing to be treated like a lady — but I didn't expect outright rudeness. I abandoned my coffee cup on the chair and hurried through the door after him, practically clipping his heels. It wasn't my imagination that he sped up, determined to get there first. If I'd known where "there" was, I might have been tempted to compete, but as I didn't, I contented myself with being one step behind as he threaded his way through the ICU.

I somehow wasn't surprised to find that Chief Superintendent Godley had taken over one of the waiting rooms and made it his own. There were files open on the table, and a laptop that hummed quietly. Hunched over the screen was a thin, dark man with glasses and a pinched expression: DI Thomas Judd. That was no surprise: where Charlie Godley went, Tom Judd followed, and if I didn't like him much, I had to respect the way he'd organised the admin for the investigation so far. Godley was leaning back in a low chair, his arms behind his head, shirtsleeves rolled up, looking tired but focused. He had gone grey early — his hair was almost white — but it didn't make him look old: quite the opposite. The combination of silver hair and blue eyes was a bit of a winner, especially when Godley was also tall and broad-shouldered and altogether too photogenic for the media to be able to resist him. He was pale, though, and his eyes looked red and tired. I had to resist the urge to cluck sympathetically. Worship of the boss was not encouraged. He had no interest in commanding a cult following.

Rob tapped on the doorframe. "You wanted me, sir?"

Godley looked up, his eyes unfocused. "Yes. Good. And Maeve, you're here too. Excellent."

"Rob phoned me," I said from over his shoulder. I knew it would make him happy to get the credit. It might even take the sting out of the fact that Godley had smiled at me. But Rob didn't really need any help from me. He was carving out a reputation for himself quite competently.

Godley had snapped back to alertness by now. "Did you fill her in?"

Rob nodded.

"So you know we've got a suspect. And a witness."

There wasn't a chance in hell that I'd get within sniffing distance of the suspect. I had schooled myself not to want what I couldn't have. It would be the bigwigs who spoke to him, when he could talk to them. But the witness was mine. Smoothly, I said, "I'd like to interview her. The girl, I mean. Probably easier for me to gain her trust."

"We've been waiting for her to be willing to provide a statement, and to sober up. I'm sure you'll have a great rapport with her." Judd was still bent over his screen, tapping furiously, but he was never likely to miss an opportunity to put someone down. Particularly me. And just like that, the slight nerviness I always felt in the presence of the boss changed to outright anger directed at the inspector. I hadn't inherited my father's red hair, but there was no question that I'd got the temper that was popularly supposed to go with it.

"What's that supposed to mean, sir?"

"Exactly what I said." His tone was bland but there was a glint behind the glasses; he knew as well as I did — as well as everyone in the room did — that he had pretty much just called me a drunk. The same old rubbish all over again: of course I was a drinker, I was Irish. "Mine's a pint of Guinness — no, make that two pints with a whiskey chaser." Never mind the fact that my parents were both teetotal, that I hadn't tasted alcohol until I was twenty and that when I drank, I preferred red wine.

"You'll do fine," Godley said, ignoring the tension that was crackling through the stifling little room. "You can take Rob with you when you speak to her. I want to know what happened up to the point where she stabbed him. I want to know how he picked her up and how he got her into the car. What he did that made her panic. I'm working on the assumption that he did or said something that made her sure she was sitting in the car with our murderer, but I don't know what it was, and I don't want to talk to him without having her side of the story."

"Right." It wasn't rocket science. It should be straightforward.

Should be.

"This is an important witness," Godley said. "I don't want anyone putting her back up. Treat her with respect."

I was fairly sure this last comment wasn't directed at me. I didn't need to be told that and I hoped Godley knew it. Judd was a different story.

"When can we see her?"

"Straightaway. She's keen to leave. She's agreed to give us a statement, but my guess is she's halfway out the door. Don't hang about."

I turned to go, but stopped when Rob spoke. "Any news on the car, sir? Did they find anything?"

Judd answered, his lips thin. "Not so far."

"What?" I was genuinely confused.

"The car is clean. No evidence of any of the things we might have expected. No knife or weapon of any kind. No accelerant."

"Could he have dumped it? Done a Sutcliffe and hid the evidence when he knew he was going to be arrested? He was there for a while before they found him." It wasn't the first time the Yorkshire Ripper had been invoked in connection with our killer, but I was surprised at Rob for mentioning him. If there was one thing that annoyed Godley more than anything else, it was the comparisons between his investigation and the unwieldy, disorganised and ultimately futile hunt for Peter Sutcliffe, who was caught more or less by chance. And here was another parallel. It wasn't police work that had brought us Vic Blackstaff, and the media would be all over it. Godley's nostrils flared, but he didn't speak, letting Judd do the talking.

"We've been searching the alley and surrounding areas. But the doctors don't think he would have been able to move easily. He was unconscious when the paramedics arrived."

"So . . ." I said slowly.

"So you need to find out what really happened," Judd finished for me. "Because at the moment, we don't have the first idea."

It was the pretty nurse who showed us to Kelly Staples' room, or rather showed Rob, who was flirting pretty much non-stop. I followed along behind, mind whirling. This was a big moment for me. Ask the right questions. Get the right answers. Don't irritate her. Gain her trust. Don't assume you know what she's going to tell you. Listen. And listen to the things she *doesn't* say too.

Easy.

I pulled Rob to one side when the nurse had brought us to the door of the hospital room and wiggled off.

29

"You're taking notes, OK? No hijacking. I want to do the talking."

"She's all yours, love. Like Judd said, I'm sure you'll have a lot in common."

"That's not what he said." I couldn't help sounding defensive. *Not you too, Rob . . .*

"What's he got against you?"

"He's a racist, misogynist pig — didn't you realise? He's always making snide remarks about me."

"Seems like a good bloke to me."

I thumped him, then took a second to shake my head, as if that would clear my mind, rearrange the thoughts that were swirling in my mind into some sort of coherent pattern. "Got your notebook?"

"Always," he said, holding it up. "And a pen. And a spare pen, in case that one runs out."

"That's my little boy scout." Time to go. I rearranged my face into what I hoped was a calm and non-threatening expression, then pushed open the door.

The first thing I noticed about Kelly Staples was that she had been crying, the second that she was very young. She was sitting by the bed, wearing a patterned hospital gown. Her feet were bare, plump and pale, with scarlet marks where her boots had rubbed her toes and heels. She looked washed-out, her fair hair lank around her face. Her eyes were red and piggy with tiredness. She was overweight and uneasy in her flimsy hospital gown, pulling the hem down over her knees to try to make it longer. Her mouth looked raw, as if she had been chewing her lips.

30

I sat down on the edge of the bed, trying to look unthreatening, and smiled.

"Kelly? I'm Detective Constable Kerrigan. You can call me Maeve. And this is my colleague, DC Langton, who's going to take some notes for me."

Rob had folded himself unobtrusively into a hard chair in the corner of the room. She looked over at him, then up at me blankly. "Do you know when my mum is going to get here?"

"No. I'm sorry. I'm sure she's on her way."

"She's bringing my clothes. I ain't got no clothes. They took them."

"They'll need to do a forensic examination of your clothes," I explained. Never mind the fact that they would have been unwearable, covered in Vic Blackstaff's blood.

"I want to go home."

"Very soon." My voice was gentle, as if I was speaking to a child. Which was a good point, actually. "How old are you, Kelly?"

"Twenty."

Good. No need to wait for a responsible adult to be present. "And are you a student? Or working?"

"Student. Catering college." She looked a little brighter. "I'm in my last year."

"Do you want to be a chef when you're finished?"

She shrugged, looking baffled. "Dunno."

Enough friendliness. Back to the reason for talking to her in the first place.

"I'd like to talk to you about what happened earlier. We have a few questions, and then we'll let you go home."

She rolled her eyes and said nothing.

"Firstly, I'd just like to reassure you that you aren't in any kind of trouble. We're interviewing you as a witness, not a suspect, so please don't feel that you need to watch what you say. We just want to know what happened before you — er, escaped." Somehow, "escaped" sounded better than "stabbed a man in the stomach several times".

She stirred. "Is he dead, then?"

"No. He's in intensive care. But he's alive."

"Sorry to hear that." She lifted her chin defiantly, and I thought she was hoping to see shock in my eyes. If so, she was disappointed.

"Right. In your own words, then, can you tell me what happened? Start from the beginning. What time did you head out to the pub?"

I can't say that Kelly Staples was an easy interview. Fear made her bolshie. She battled me for the first few minutes, barely answering the questions I asked. But as the story of her night wore on, something seemed to take hold of her, and the monosyllables became sentences, and the sentences became paragraphs, and soon she was talking freely, the words running on like water into a gutter. I hoped Rob could keep up.

"So of course, I'm thinking a minicab will be cheap and I'll get home quicker. I mean, he was old. He was like my dad or something. Quiet, like. Just . . . helpful. I thought maybe I reminded him of his daughter and he wanted to see me get back safe. What an idiot. Total idiot. I should have run a mile, not that I could in my boots. I could barely walk."

"What happened when you got into the car?"

The words flowed on. His car, and what she'd noticed about it — a faint smell of petrol that had worried her, the more she thought about it. His refusal to take her home the way she knew. The alley he'd found, where he'd promised to turn the car. How dark it had been. How he'd stalled her, telling her the door wouldn't open from the inside. How he'd sweated. How it was wrong, and what he'd said was wrong, and she'd just known it was him, the Burning Man, so she'd got in before he could do her the way he'd done those other girls.

"I had this knife, see, in my boot. For protection. You can't be too careful these days, my little brother said." She gave a laugh, high-pitched with nerves. "Well, this just goes to show, doesn't it? I mean, if I hadn't had it, who knows where I'd be? On a slab, maybe."

Maybe, maybe not. I was beginning to feel edgy. "Go back to before you took out the knife, Kelly. What did he say or do to make you sure that he was a killer?"

"He stopped the car, and he said he'd let me out."

"And?"

"And nothing. As soon as he stopped the car, I just knew."

I waited. The only sound in the room was Rob's pen scratching across the paper. When it stopped, I said gently, "What did you know, Kelly?"

"That he was a killer. That killer. You know, the burning one."

I made myself look blandly understanding. But my mind was blank apart from one word repeating monotonously, over and over again. *Fuck . . . fuck . . . fuck . . .*

She finished off her story, telling us that she'd got to him before he could make a move on her, that he hadn't seen her coming, finishing up with, "And I've been stuck in this room for two hours and I haven't had a ciggie, so if you wouldn't mind, can I go now?"

"You'll have to hang on for a little while," I said, trying to sound pleasant. "You'll probably have to give another statement, I'm afraid. And the doctors haven't signed you out yet."

She looked as if she was going to cry. "I just want to go home."

"I know." I stood up, suddenly uncomfortable. I couldn't lie and say she'd be leaving soon; if I wasn't much mistaken, she would be arrested before too long. From her account of events, there was an obvious charge of Section 18, wounding with intent to do grievous bodily harm.

Kelly was rubbing her eyes, smearing moisture and the remains of her make-up across her pale cheeks. From behind her hands came, "I just want my mum."

I had got to the door and I yanked it open, pushing Rob out in front of me. "Thanks for your help, Kelly. We'll be in touch."

The sound of sobbing was cut off by the door swinging shut. Annoyingly, it was the kind of door you couldn't slam. I looked around for something to kick instead. Anything to vent my feelings.

"What a lovely girl."

"Don't be mean about her." I felt protective of poor, unlucky Kelly, even though I was furious with her as well.

34

"Who's being mean?"

"You are and you know it."

"I just said she was lovely." Rob blinked at me innocently. "Not the kind of girl you want to make a move on without fair warning, but sweet all the same."

"Blackstaff was up to something naughty. What was he planning to do with her?"

"We'll never know. And what we do know doesn't justify what she did to him, does it?"

I had to admit he was right. "By her account, he didn't do a thing. OK, he was a bit creepy — I'm sure she was right to be suspicious. Maybe he thought she was too drunk to know what she was doing and he could take advantage. But she completely overreacted. There isn't a shred of evidence linking him to the other murders, not one concrete thing that would confirm her story that he's the killer. And let's be honest, her story isn't going to stand up in court, is it?"

"She might have been right. Maybe he got rid of the stuff before we got there."

"What, a container of petrol and at least one blunt instrument? The stun gun? There wasn't any of that in the car, was there? Or around it. We're screwed. Completely screwed."

"Yep. And you're the one who's going to have to tell Godley."

"Don't think that hasn't occurred to me." I looked at him. "You don't give a stuff, do you? This is a total disaster and you're just not bothered."

He shrugged. "Nothing we can do about it now. Bad luck for Mr Blackstaff. But we're no worse off than we were before."

"Oh yeah, we're doing great. Four women dead and no leads. You're right, this is just a minor blip. Otherwise, we're gold." I closed my eyes and pinched the bridge of my nose, sighing.

"Headache?"

"Like you wouldn't believe."

"I'll see if Nursey can give me an aspirin or two." Rob patted me on the arm. "It's the least I can do."

"Don't get me started on what you can do."

"Oh, I know what you'd *like* me to do."

"Never in a million years, Langton."

"Nothing to be ashamed of, Kerrigan. You wouldn't be the first to fall for me. It's probably best if you don't fight it."

"Fight what? The urge to throw up?"

We retraced our steps along the corridor, bickering all the way. It was a relief, somehow. It took my mind off what I was about to say to Superintendent Godley. The chorus of bad language at the back of my mind had cranked up a notch, adding a little variety at least. *Shit bugger piss damn fuck* . . .

We rounded a corner, and in spite of myself I was laughing at something Rob had said, looking at him rather than where we were going, so it was only when his face slipped to neutral, uncertainly, then snapped into straight lines that I stopped grinning and turned my head. Godley and Judd were waiting for us, jackets on, grim expressions on their faces and I felt my own face mirror theirs. I was ready to let them know the worst.

"It's not him."

I stared at Judd, wrong-footed. "That's what I was going to say. How did you —"

"There's another body. Another young woman. He's done it again." Godley sounded drained. "Vic Blackstaff couldn't have done it. Best guess is that it happened in the last three hours. While Blackstaff was here, being operated on."

I nodded. "From Kelly Staples' statement, there was nothing to suggest that he was the killer, even if it does sound as if he was up to something he shouldn't have been. Unluckily for Victor, she got spooked and lashed out. She just got it wrong."

"She wasn't the only one," Godley said tersely.

DI Judd took over. "She'll need to be charged. We're not going to waste time dealing with it. I'll call the borough CID office and get the on-call DC to take over. You'll have to fill me in, Kerrigan."

I should have been grateful that he hadn't stuck me with letting borough CID know about their new case, but I managed to control my gratitude. It meant I had to talk to him, for one thing. I smiled brightly. "No problem."

"Then get going," Godley said. "I'll see you at the new crime scene."

And just like that, we were done with Kelly Staples; her fate was for someone else to decide. I couldn't help but think she was one more victim of the Burning Man, one more bit of fallout from his crimes.

We needed to catch him, and soon. But the fact that we were on our way to see another body proved that we weren't even close.

LOUISE

"Hi. This is Rebecca. You've got through to my voicemail, not to me, but leave me a message and I'll get back to you as soon as I can. Don't just hang up! Speak! After the beep! That would be . . . now!"

The voice filled my office, warm and lively, conjuring its owner so vividly for me that I could close my eyes and smell the faintest breath of her perfume over the sterile air-conditioning that kept my workplace at a steady 20 degrees, regardless of the weather in the streets. Outside, it was a cold and damp Friday morning in late November, dark and grey. Inside, my home-from-home was cosily lined with colourful files and folders and gently lit, as recommended by the ergonomic advisers whom my employers, Preyhard Gunther, had consulted when fitting out the London office. There are people who advise on the best conditions for keeping chickens to ensure maximum laying; at PG, if the associates were the chickens, billable hours were eggs and I was a champion layer who qualified for that unwanted status symbol, a foldaway bed under my desk. In a drawer, pyjamas and toiletries. On the back of the door, an entire outfit for a working day, ready to go at a moment's notice. Down the hall there were lavish bathrooms with power showers, and catering could be summoned up by lifting the phone any hour of the day or night. All designed to keep us happy, keep us working and, most importantly, keep us in the office.

And I had been good. I barely had a life. All weekend, every weekend. Evenings. Early mornings. In the last couple of years, I had made few arrangements to meet friends and broken those commitments I had allowed myself to risk. I had given away tickets to the theatre and concerts (all gifts to me from grateful clients, but still, it rankled occasionally when a thank-you email gushed about how it had been the performance of the decade).

I stared at the big phone on my desk, wanting to ring Rebecca's mobile again, just to hear her voice. I settled on calling her work number, letting it ring on speakerphone as I carried on crafting an exquisitely dull but effective email destined for my opposite number on the other side.

"This is Rebecca Haworth. I'm not at my desk at the moment, but please leave a message and I'll return your call as soon as possible. If your call is urgent, please press zero for the Ventnor Chase switchboard and ask for my assistant, Jess Barker."

Less lively, more polished, equally warm, very assured. My lovely friend Rebecca. My oldest friend. My least reliable friend, currently. But then, who was I to criticise her for that? I had missed emails from her over the past few months, losing them in the welter of work that pulsed into my inbox every minute of every hour of every day. If I didn't tackle the emails that day, they were gone for ever, pushed into obscurity and archived by the firm's inexorable system. Every hour was accountable; I didn't have time for personal email, I told myself. There was nothing to feel guilty about.

Except that now, when I wanted to talk to her — to her, not a machine — there was no reply.

The phone had beeped while I was thinking about Rebecca, and I found myself leaving a quick, half-mumbled message that she should call me, that I was thinking of her, that we needed to see one another soon, to catch up. I reached out and pushed a button to end the call, feeling my face burn as I thought back over what I had said, and how. Stupid, to be what anyone would see as a high-powered lawyer while lacking the confidence to talk on the phone. Ridiculous, to feel my heart jump every time it rang, to have to wipe my palms on my skirt surreptitiously before reaching out to answer it. I didn't like it, though. I didn't like how unguarded you could be on the phone. I didn't like how you could find yourself saying what you really thought. I had trapped people that way before, reading more than they knew into what they had given away to me on the phone. I had made suggestions that had won cases for the firm. I knew better than most that we were engaged in a highwire act that most days, everyone managed to perform. Now and then, someone fell.

A brassy head came around the door.

"Knock, knock. Want a cup of tea? You've got that meeting in five minutes. Have something first. Put a bit of colour in your face."

"I'm OK, Martine. But thanks," I said, looking up for a second before returning to the screen in front of me.

Martine, my secretary. Thirty years of experience, eight shades of red in her hair, an unlimited source of gossip, good humour and unsolicited advice. It wasn't her fault that I tensed up when she came into the room, or that I, alone among my colleagues, found her intimidating. She had seen lawyers come and lawyers go, and I was too young to be able to feel comfortable about asking her to do things for me. I thought she didn't like me and she certainly didn't rate me as a lawyer. It made me work harder, and buy her elaborate presents at Christmas or for her birthday. I did my own filing and photocopying; I bent over backwards to avoid giving her work to do. So Martine was bored. She devoted herself instead to being the company's unofficial social secretary, and my unwanted fairy godmother.

"You feeling all right?" She had come all the way into the room. "Only you look white as anything. Got a headache, have you? Want a painkiller? I've got some Nurofen."

I tried to ward off the pills with a quick shake of my head and a smile, but she was determined.

"I've got aspirin cos you're supposed to take that every day in case of strokes, at least that's what they say now but they'll probably say something else next week.

Let's see. I think there's some paracetamol in the first-aid kit. But you've got to watch that. Someone told me it only takes five tablets to *kill* you. Imagine!" Her face, impeccably made-up, was alive with delight at the very idea.

"I don't need anything, really."

"Someone else might have something. I can ask. One of the other girls might have Solpadeine. Do you take that, love? Or can you not have codeine?"

Somehow, Martine had got the idea that I was some sort of religious zealot. It was probably because I never drank at anything work-related, be it a lunch with colleagues or a night out with clients. The Christmas party was no exception. I only went because it would have looked bad to avoid it, and tried to fade into the background as much as possible, sipping a sparkling water until it was a reasonable time to go home. Martine found that incomprehensible and came up with a reason for it that made sense to her. I had never tried to explain it, after all. It seemed easier just to let her make up her own mind. But it involved me in futile, ludicrous conversations now and then.

"I can have codeine. I mean. I don't need it, but if I did, I could."

"Oh, so you'll have that, will you? *I* see." She looked arch, as if codeine was first cousin to cocaine, as if I'd managed to find myself a loophole and could spend many a happy hour hopped up on over-the-counter medication.

I was gathering up my papers for the meeting. "I'll just be off, then. I've got everything I need, thanks."

Then, thinking fast, "If my friend rings — Rebecca, you might remember her — can you get a number from her so I can call her back?"

Her eyes had gone straight to the picture of the two of us that was stuck to the wall above my desk, a picture from years ago, when I had been thinner, paler, even more quiet than I was now, and Rebecca had been at the height of her young beauty, flushed like a rose, yelling in triumph at the end of her exams. It wasn't a good picture of me — I was looking at Rebecca, not the camera, and the expression on my face was wary — but she was so very much herself in it, so very much alive, that I had always kept it as a reminder of how she'd been when I first knew her. As she grew older, she hadn't become any less beautiful, but her face had changed, refined a little, and her eyes, the last time I'd seen her, had been sad — so, so sad.

"Can't get hold of her?"

Martine's voice was sympathetic, and I found myself telling her that no, I hadn't been able to reach her, and what did she think I should do?

"Go round," she said instantly. "Knock on her door. You know where she lives, don't you? Too much time emailing people these days, ringing them, texting them — not enough face-to-face time."

It was one of Martine's favourite hobbyhorses, the isolation of modern life, and I slipped away to my meeting with a feeling of relief, but also with a renewed sense of determination. Martine, for once, had had a good idea. I did know where Rebecca lived, and what was more, I had a key. I would go after my meeting, I

44

decided, and sat down at the table with a light heart for the first time in weeks.

The good mood lasted me all the way from the office to her flat's front door. I had rung her landline on my walk from the station, so I had known she wasn't likely to be there, but when my key turned in the lock, dead air came out to meet me and I couldn't suppress a shiver. The flat was empty, I knew without looking. The question was whether she had left any clue as to where she'd gone, and if she had, whether I could find it. I had spent a lot of time tidying up after Rebecca, one way or another. Covering up. I knew things about her that no one else did — that no one else should. And she knew a fair bit about me.

Shaking myself out of my trance I closed the door behind me, took off my coat, and started to search.

CHAPTER
TWO

MAEVE

It wouldn't have been such a nightmare to get out of
the hospital if the press hadn't already picked up on the
fact that we had a suspect in intensive care. They were
on us like a pack of dogs as soon as the boss showed his
face outside the back door of the building. A babble of
shouted questions exploded from the far side of the
road, where the media had been corralled behind metal
barriers.

"Superintendent Godley! Over here, sir."

"Have you got him?"

"Is it true you have a suspect in custody?"

I slipped past the massed press, my presence
unremarked, heading for my car. I'd be on the news,
probably, but only my mother and her friends would
spot me. I went out of my way to avoid seeing myself
onscreen, as a rule. Untidy light-brown hair, a set
expression, hunched shoulders: none of these things fit
in with my image of myself, but undeniably they were
what appeared on the TV every time I stalked across a
cameraman's field of vision. My mother's voice was
ringing in my ears: *Ah, Maeve, if only you'd
remembered to stand up straight.* I bent my head,

looked at the ground and kept going, hearing the slap of Rob's shoes on the tarmac as he strode out to keep up with me. Not for the first time, I was glad to be out of the limelight, glad that Godley was the star of the show, even though he hated it. For such a high-profile senior officer, he wasn't the sort to court attention. His statements were businesslike, his press conferences orderly, and if he had nothing to say, he said nothing. But everything he said and did was news, especially at the moment. The level of interest in the Burning Man was nothing short of hysteria. Godley spent a great deal of time on the phone to newspaper editors and TV bosses, begging them for a bit of sensitivity and responsibility in the way they reported on the case. We needed space to work in, but if they had the opportunity, they dived straight in. All in the public interest, apparently — and if they meant that the public was interested, they weren't wrong. But I couldn't see how conjecture about our lack of success helped anyone.

Today, I doubted Godley had much he wanted to share with the press. Particularly today, when all the news was bad. An hour earlier, he would have been planning his speech at the press conference where we were to reveal the good news.

Don't worry, everyone. It's all over. You can get back to enjoying the run-up to the festive season. Don't mind us; we're off for a pint.

All of that was on hold, indefinitely. I couldn't help feeling cold at the thought of where we were going and what we were going to find there. Another body.

Another woman, brutalised and burned beyond recognition. And who he was — why he even did it in the first place — was as much a mystery now as it had been four bodies ago.

"You OK?" Rob had caught up with me at the pay station, where I was feeding an extraordinary number of coins into the machine. Surely I hadn't been there for that long. I excavated the last few coins from the bottom of my bag, disentangling them from an old shredded tissue and pushing them bad-temperedly into the slot. The machine burped. I stabbed the button for a receipt and managed a smile.

"Of course. All part of the job, isn't it?"

"It's me you're talking to, Kerrigan. You don't have to pretend."

"Yeah, well. Bit of a shitter, isn't it?"

"You're telling me. I thought we were done with this."

We both spoke lightly, but I knew he was feeling the way I was. Somehow, it made it worse that we'd had a break from the sick tension that was now pooling in my stomach and clenching my jaw, the tension that had been turning my days into marathons, stealing my sleep, keeping me at work. I'd done my best — we'd all been doing our best — to make sure this didn't happen again. And we'd failed.

"Je-sus. Good parking."

The car was skewed across two spaces. "I was in a rush, OK?" I unlocked the doors. "Get in, and less of the chat, or you'll be walking to — where is it?"

"Stadhampton Grove. It's somewhere behind the Oval cricket ground. Part of an industrial estate."

"Do you know how to get there from here?"

"Consider me your sat nav for the journey."

"Twat nav, more like," I muttered, shooting a grin at him before pulling out of my space. Well, spaces.

The traffic had built up in the time I'd been in the hospital, and the trip from Kingston to the Oval was torture. Rob got on the phone as soon as we were on the road, calling Kev Cox, who was at the scene already. He was head of the forensic team and had managed the last four crime scenes; if you wanted one person to keep everything under control, Kev was your man. I'd never seen him anything less than relaxed. I wasn't even sure it was possible to upset him.

"Who found it? Just walking past, was he? Did uniform get his details? Oh, he's still there? Good one."

I caught Rob's eye and tapped my watch. He got what I meant straightaway.

"What time was that, then?"

He had his notepad on his knee, balancing on a big London *A-Z* that was, I noticed, on entirely the wrong page. Some help he was. He scrawled "3.17" on the pad in big numbers, tilting it to show me. That settled it. Not that there had really been any doubt in my mind about Victor Blackstaff's innocence.

"No sign of anyone there, I suppose? Nothing left behind? Yeah, he's just not making any mistakes. How long is it since the last one?"

I could have told him that. Six days. And before that, twenty days. And before that, three weeks. Just over three weeks between the first and the second ones. He was speeding up, and that was bad news. The less time we had between killings, the more likely it was that more women would die.

On the other hand, he had to be killing more frequently for a reason. Maybe he was feeling agitated. Unsettled. Maybe he was losing control and he'd start making mistakes.

But he hadn't made any so far.

Rob was asking Kev about who else was at the scene but I tuned out, concentrating on the traffic. When he finally hung up, he turned to me. "How much of that did you get?"

"The important bits. Not the parts where you were finding out what the competition was up to."

He had the grace to look ashamed. "I just like to know who else I'm going to be working with."

"Bullshit. You like to know who else is going to be trying to get the boss's attention." *And I know that because I am exactly the same . . .*

"No sign of Belcott yet." He couldn't suppress a grin of triumph. Peter Belcott was one of the more irritating members of the team: ambitious, ruthless, awkward if you gave him the opportunity. Much too keen. Omnipresent, usually. There was some comfort in the thought that he'd been caught napping this time.

I tapped the map. "Come on. Concentrate. Where do I go from here?"

He peered at the street signs, then down at the page, flicking frantically as he realised he was looking at Poplar, not Vauxhall.

"Left at the lights. No, straight on."

"Sure?"

"Sure," he said, sounding anything but. I went with it anyway, and as far as I could tell, we didn't double back on ourselves more than a couple of times on the rest of the journey.

Unencumbered by the media, we got to Stadhampton Grove long before the boss arrived, and flashed warrant cards at the uniform on the cordon.

"At least we have a secure scene this time. That's something," Rob remarked.

I nodded, pulling in to park behind a police car. "I wouldn't like a repeat of the Charity Beddoes one."

That had been a fuck-up of epic proportions. It was the fourth murder, the body dumped in Mostyn Gardens, between Kennington and Brixton. The responding officers had seen the hallmarks of the Burning Man straightaway. Unfortunately, one of them had a nice sideline in tipping off a tabloid journalist, who had turned up with a video camera before the forensic team got there. Scotland Yard had to move very quickly indeed to prevent footage of the body and crime scene from being broadcast on the twenty-four-hour news channels; it was on the Internet if you looked for it, though we did try to get it taken down wherever it appeared. The forensic evidence was hopelessly compromised. A woman had died and we'd learned nothing that helped in the hunt for our killer. All because some plod had been partial to making a bit of extra cash.

It was easy enough to spot where we needed to be; the forensic team were already there, moving screens and lights into position around a patch of blackened grass on some waste ground about a hundred yards from where we'd parked. A tall, lanky figure in a boiler suit was stepping delicately around the area that they'd marked off, his attention focused on the ground where the body presumably lay.

Rob was looking in the same place as me. "Glen's here already."

"So I see. Godley will be pleased."

Glen Hanshaw was the pathologist who had examined all four of the other victims. He was also one of the superintendent's best friends. They were around the same age and had worked together for ever, including long hours on most of the cases that had made Godley's reputation in the first place. We had standing orders to summon Dr Hanshaw to every crime scene. He'd been in Cyprus for one of Godley's murders a couple of years ago and had come back on the next available flight, abandoning a family holiday with what appeared to be relief. I would not have been Mrs Hanshaw for any money, not least because I found the balding, beaky pathologist unsettling. He had a habit of looking past you while you were talking to him, as if whatever you were saying was so predictable and dull that he had already got to the end of the conversation in his own mind, long before you had stammered out your final question. I didn't like being made to feel thick, and Dr Hanshaw managed it every time. Presumably Superintendent Godley was more intellectually secure than me.

Dr Hanshaw's concentration was total, and he didn't look up as Rob and I walked towards him, following Kev Cox's instruction to keep to the common approach path the SOCOs had marked out through the lank winter grass. They'd put down a plastic platform where we could stand, the lead investigator had told us, and I stepped onto it carefully, feeling it flex under Rob's weight as he joined me.

There was no point in saying hello to Dr Hanshaw. We might as well not have been there. His assistant, Ali, was standing nearby, scribbling notes as he spoke.

"The body is lying face up in a shallow depression and shows signs of violence ante-mortem and post-mortem. It appears to be a female, but an estimate of her age will have to wait for the PM." He crouched. "Limbs drawn up and in towards the torso, but I'd suggest she was laid out flat originally; that'll be muscle-contraction from the heat. Look at the pugilistic pose, the claw-shaped hands. Classic characteristics of exposure to high temperatures."

The woman's skin was blackened and split, disfigured with patches of red and white where the lower layers of the skin had been exposed. The fire had burned her but not from head to toe; it was hard, the experts said, to make a human body burn without other sources of fuel, but you could certainly do a lot of damage. She was wearing what looked like the remains of an expensive dress. The dress had been black, long-sleeved, cut diagonally across the neckline and high on one thigh (— she wore no coat, though it had been a cold night.) The fabric was folded and twisted into a rose at the waist that had stubbornly refused to burn. It was a miracle of design and tailoring that would have flattered the slender figure in life, and still clung tenaciously to it now, even though the dress was in shreds, burned and stained. She had worn high heels, black patent, tiny straps. One had fallen off and was lying on its side beside her. There was dirt on her insteps, damage to the thin skin that stretched over her anklebones. The hands Dr Hanshaw had commented on were hooked and blackened, held just under the woman's chin as if she'd been trying to ward off the flames. I swallowed, my mind suddenly filled with fire, with fear, with pain. Ali — who was far too posh and pretty, you'd have thought, to be standing beside a dead body at that hour of the morning — was looking pale.

"Was she dead when the fire started?"

He took out a tiny torch and shone it into the body's mouth and nose, drawing down the jaw gently. "No sign of inhalation. I'd say probably, but we'll have to take a look at the lungs under a microscope."

The torch went into a pocket and his white-gloved hands stretched out, probing through the matted fairish hair on the victim's head, teasing out knots so he could feel what lay beneath. "Skull fractures," he said, matter-of-factly. "All at the back of the head. No trauma to the facial bones or tissue ante-mortem. Marks on the face are caused by scorching."

That was new. I leaned in, trying to see what he was indicating to Ali. The other victims had been battered

54

beyond all recognition before they were set alight. The Burning Man had done his best to obliterate their features, breaking bones, cartilage, ripping flesh, so they were hideous and somehow interchangeable. He made them into something they weren't before; he shaped them. Wanton destruction was part of the fun.

"Maybe he was disturbed before he could go through the usual ritual," Rob suggested.

"He still had time to set her on fire."

The pathologist twisted around and glared at us. "Speculation might usefully wait until after the examination, don't you think? Or would you like me to move out of the way so you can conduct your own assessment of the body?"

"Sorry," I said, embarrassed. Rob mumbled something beside me. The sound of feet approaching was a welcome distraction.

Hanshaw looked past us and his frown disappeared. He raised a hand and sketched a salute. "Charlie."

"Morning, Glen. What have we got?" The superintendent stood beside me, listening gravely as Dr Hanshaw ran through his observations. Ali was following him through the notes, ready to prompt, but the pathologist didn't miss anything out. He never missed anything.

"I'm going to presume you want me to compare this body to the others that we have attributed to your active serial killer," Hanshaw said, winding up. "Obviously, there are certain points of difference. Damage to the face is incidental. We also have no signs of restraint used on the hands. No ligature marks, no tape, nothing that he might have used to bind her. But we do have a mark from a stun gun — here." He lifted up her hair to show a small burn on her shoulder.

The stun gun was part of the Burning Man's signature; we had allowed that detail to be released just to warn potential victims. A jolt from a stun gun would be incapacitating, paralysing, and it was terrifyingly easy to do to someone. Easy, too, to get hold of one, even though they were illegal. We had circulated images of them, hoping that someone would recall seeing a man with a similar device.

We hadn't, however, mentioned in the press that the serial killer we were hunting had a distinctive way of tying his victims' hands, palms outward, thumb to thumb in front of their chests, using generic gardening twine that cut into their flesh. He took no chances that they might fight back. But this woman's hands were loose. He had been able to control this woman, whoever she was. He should have been finding it harder, not easier. He should have been coping with a terrified victim who knew what to expect, a woman desperate to escape certain death. The element of surprise — the hope of survival — should have been gone by now.

"Other things we might note: the position of the body. This is a much more organised disposal. The others gave the impression of being thrown to the ground — the clothing dragged out of position, grazes on the bodies and so forth. I'd guess that this one was laid out with some care. Face up as well — the previous two were prone."

Images flickered through my mind of splayed limbs, twisted torsos, blackened clothes and trees.

Hanshaw was completing his examination briskly. "No ID with the body that I can locate — no bag, nothing in the pockets."

"Signs of sexual assault?"

He shook his head. "Not at first glance. The underclothing is still in place. I imagine this one will be the same as the others."

The psychologists told us that the man we were looking for wasn't a conventional sexual predator. There was a thrill in what he was doing that was entirely titillating for him, but that didn't mean he wanted to rape the women he killed — the opposite. He despised them, we were told. He hated them and what they stood for. He channelled his rage into violence. None of the victims had shown signs of sexual assault. The appetite of our killer was entirely satisfied by blood, by breaking bones and charring flesh and leaping flames. It made it worse, somehow. It was one step further removed from anything I could understand.

Something else was bothering me. "He doesn't seem to have taken anything. Unless he took her coat."

"What?" Godley turned to look at me, blue eyes sharp.

"Both earrings are there." Gold knots glinted in her ears under the arc lights. "And her watch. Her ring." An amethyst and diamond eternity ring was on the woman's right hand.

"Maybe he took a necklace — a pendant or something," Rob suggested.

"No." Ali spoke at the same time as me, sounding sure. "She wouldn't have worn one, not with that neckline."

"She wouldn't have wanted anything else," I agreed, and smiled at the pathologist's assistant, grateful for the backup. I got a cool look in return. She wasn't easy to get to know, Ali, and I'd never managed any kind of general conversation with her. She was her boss's creature; her thinly disguised hostility matched his precisely.

Godley, who had been staring at the body as if he wasn't really seeing it, as if he wasn't really there, came to life. "No chance of fingerprints, I take it."

The pathologist peered at the withered, contorted hands and shook his head. "DNA identification, I'd say. Or we can match dental records if someone takes the time to report her missing."

But that would take days, he didn't have to say. The DNA would be quicker if she was on the database. I hoped she was. We deserved a break of some kind. The media would be savagely critical when they realised there was a new victim. It wasn't fair; we had worked for long days and nights analysing CCTV footage, interviewing sex offenders in the local area, talking to probation officers about people who were of concern to them, stopping and searching lone males on the streets. I had done hours of door-to-door enquiries myself and come up empty-handed. We had leafleted public buildings and local business. There had been roadblocks, appeals for witnesses, press conferences. And we had nothing.

58

Godley turned to us. "Right. Rob, I want you to go and talk to the first officers on scene. Maeve, can you speak to whoever found her? Find out if they saw anything useful. I'll finish up here."

"Right," Rob said easily, and turned to go. I paused for a second before following suit, knowing that I wouldn't get another chance to take in the scene before it was disturbed. Photographs weren't the same. And there was something off about this one, something that jarred me, even if I couldn't quite work out what it was.

After one last long look, I gave up, picking my way across the grass in my unsuitable shoes, wary of twisting an ankle. By the time I made it back to the cars, Rob was already deep in conversation with a couple of uniformed officers, taking notes. I recognised one of them; he had worked out of the same station as me in my first year on the street. I couldn't remember his name and settled for a brisk nod in his direction, glad that Rob had the job of talking to them rather than me.

"Where's my witness?"

The two officers jerked their thumbs in the direction of the police car that was behind them. A shadowy figure was sitting in the back with the doors closed so he couldn't escape.

"Did you arrest him?" I was puzzled.

"Almost," the one I knew said, and chuckled.

"You're in for a treat," the other officer said. "Never met anyone with less to say for themselves."

"How come?" I was interested.

"You'll see. Not the most forthcoming witness." He was old enough and experienced enough to have seen plenty.

"Deliberately obstructive?"

"You might have more luck than we did."

I frowned, not understanding why he thought that. "What's his name?"

"Michael Joseph Fallon, Micky Joe to you. He's an IC7."

"Oh." I was starting to understand. There was no official IC7 designation on the police national computer; it was cop slang for a traveller. "And you think he'll talk to me because . . ."

"You're Irish too, aren't you? Paddies always get on."

"Great," I said bleakly. My name was the giveaway — that and my wild hair, typically Irish, I'd been told. From the first day I walked through the door at Hendon, I'd been called Spud, or had to listen to jokes about how stupid the Irish were, or even fucking *Riverdance*, for God's sake. It was all too petty to make a formal complaint, but it bothered me. I'd grown up in England — I had an English accent — but I still didn't fit in and they made sure I knew it. I had been more than happy to live up to the reputation for having a fiery temper, but it got me in trouble and I was trying to keep it under control, so on this occasion I said nothing else.

Rob gave me a sunny grin that said more clearly than words *I'm glad I'm not you*. I resisted the urge to stick out my tongue and headed for the car.

Micky Joe Fallon was twenty-five, not wanted on any outstanding warrants, recently released from prison after a two-year term for burglary and clearly regretting whatever instinct of social responsibility had made him call 999 when he found a woman's body smouldering in the grass. I let him out of the back of the police car and leaned against the boot, trying to look friendly.

"Can you tell me in your own words what happened?"

"I don't know what you want with me, I've been straight with you," he muttered. He had a battered black cap pulled down low over his eyes, and in spite of the cold morning, he was wearing a short-sleeved shirt that showed off the flickering muscles in his arms.

"You've been very helpful, but I need to get another statement. It's normal procedure." He was edging away from me even as I spoke. "You're not in trouble. Just tell me what you saw and you can go." It was almost word-for-word what I'd said to Kelly Staples. This time I was reasonably sure I was speaking the truth.

He had been out early, he told me, because he was looking for his dog, which had gone missing.

"I saw the smoke first and came over to see what it was."

"Did you see anyone?"

He shook his head.

"What did you do then?"

"Had a look around. Once I saw what — it was."

"Had the fire been burning for long?"

"Don't know. It was smoking, though. I could smell it from over there." He pointed. "Thought it was a barbecue at first."

I wrinkled my nose in disgust, though in fact he was right. There was still the faintest trace of it in the air.

"And you didn't see any cars, or anyone else on foot?"

"Nothing." And even if he had, I wasn't going to get to hear about it.

"Have we got an address for you?"

He gave it to me again, his voice gruff. "Can I go?"

"I don't see why not," I said, resigned, and watched as he crossed the road and disappeared.

"Get anywhere?" It was one of the uniformed officers who had spoken, the one I didn't know, and I smiled at him though with gritted teeth.

"Not really. He didn't have much to say for himself. Even to me."

"Turns out a pretty face will only take you so far," the other one commented.

"What's that supposed to mean?"

"Nothing. Just that it's harder for some people to get on to murder squads than it is for others."

I felt my face flame; it wasn't the first time I'd had that sort of remark, but it usually wasn't so brutally put. The other officer laughed, covering it with a cough. There was nothing I could say in response, or at least nothing I wanted to. Ignoring it was the best option. But that didn't mean I had to be pleased about it, and I swore under my breath as I walked away, quickly.

"How did that go?"

I turned to glare at Rob, who had caught up with me. "Just fine, thanks."

62

"Funny, because you look like you're absolutely fuming."

"In what way?"

He scanned my face. "You're flushed. Your hair is all over the place. And when you get angry, you get this cute little white line across the bridge of your nose."

He reached out, as if to trace it, and I jerked my head back, out of range. "No touching, Langton, or I'll do to you what I wanted to do to that pair."

"And what's that exactly? You never know, I might enjoy it."

"Something that would be guaranteed to get me a reg nine if they made a complaint."

"Well, you don't need another one of those. I've never known anyone attract so many bullshit complaints."

"Tell me about it. It's nothing to do with the way I behave."

"I wouldn't dare suggest that it was." Rob looked over my shoulder and stopped smiling. "Here's trouble."

Trouble, in the stocky shape of DC Belcott. Peter Belcott, AKA Peter Belcock, his first name never ever shortened to Pete. Trouble because he had an absolute gift for getting up people's noses and a congenital inability to say the right thing. I turned to greet him without enthusiasm and was struck anew by how resolutely unattractive he was — small and square, with pouting lips.

"I hear you two have been having a busy morning. Got everything sorted now, have you? Suspect in custody?" He had a whiny voice that was even less appealing when it was edged with scorn.

"Fuck off, Peter," Rob said cheerfully.

"I know you wish I would. But the boss rang me personally." He rose up on his toes for a second and thrust his chest out, looking like a fat little pigeon mid-moult. "Asked me to come along and lend him my expertise. Apparently he doesn't have quite as much faith in the two of you as you might think."

I didn't believe him — not for a second. The man was a relentless self-promoter; if I took everything he said at face value, I would have been expecting him to be named as the new commissioner any day now.

"The boss said you would fill me in on this one. What do you know?"

I ran through it briefly. There wasn't much in the way of facts to tell him, but I had plenty of speculation to share. In spite of myself, I got absorbed in what I was saying. "You have to wonder, don't you, why he changed his MO. I mean, nothing seems to have been taken. Her hands aren't tied. This place isn't a park, not like the other ones." I looked around and shivered; it was a particularly bleak bit of ground, surrounded by high-walled industrial units and not overlooked. All the CCTV cameras I could see pointed inwards, at their own premises. We wouldn't get much from them.

Belcott shrugged. "His usual thing wasn't working for him any more. So what? They do escalate, serial killers."

"This isn't an escalation," I objected. "This is less violent, if anything."

"He's not a machine," Rob pointed out. "Sometimes things don't go according to plan. Even for killers who seem to have remarkably good luck."

"Don't talk to me about luck." Superintendent Godley had joined us, looking uncharacteristically irritable. "He has the luck of the devil. We don't even know who the latest victim is."

"And it's strange he's changed his MO. We might have expected him to get more violent, not less."

My words, spoken by Peter Belcott. I could have killed him where he stood. As it was, I was slightly surprised that he didn't burst into flames from the heat of my glare.

"Yes. That interests me too." The superintendent looked at me vaguely. "Can you hang on here until the body is moved?" Before I could so much as nod, he'd turned away. "Rob, I want you to find Tom Judd and give him the full picture. I sent him home to get changed and have some food — give him a call and see if he's ready to come back to work. If he is, you can pick him up. Peter, I'm heading back to the incident room. Come with me and we can discuss the differences on the way."

There was an extra spring in Belcott's stride as he walked off in step with the superintendent. I jumped as Rob's arm landed on my shoulders.

"You never learn, do you? Never share your bright ideas with Belcock. Not unless you're trying to get him a promotion."

I ducked out from under his arm. "What is it about 'no touching' that you don't understand?"

65

"Don't take it out on me," he protested, laughing.

"I can't believe I have to stay here." I shoved my hands deep into the pockets of my coat, shivering. Dawn had come but the sky was still steel-grey with heavy clouds that promised rain. "I'm going to catch my death."

"Try and keep warm," Rob said, walking backwards. "Light a fire or something."

"Very funny."

I watched him saunter off, wishing I was going with him, or Godley, or anywhere, in fact. But I had been told to wait, and wait I would, until the poor anonymous victim had been removed or I froze to death — whichever came first.

I was in a seriously bad mood by the time I got back to the incident room and the comparative comfort of my desk. No one had been eager for me to get back; no one had noticed I wasn't there. I had been forgotten during my futile vigil at the crime scene where the temperature had hovered around zero as the day wore on. My feet were completely numb, my face raw, and my stomach was in tight knots. I hadn't even had any breakfast yet and it was already getting on for two.

I'd stood and watched as a SOCO ran up, pink with excitement, to tell Kev Cox that he'd found a petrol can thrown into a front garden two streets away from the industrial area. I'd waited as the black mortuary van reversed into position, ready to retrieve the body from the dump site. I'd glared at the media as represented by a pair of helicopters that hovered overhead, almost invisible against the grey sky as they circled, and the camera crews that had hired cherry pickers to get a mobile vantage point. The rest of the press had been kept well back behind the cordon and it was the only thing that made my situation bearable. The one conclusion I had come to as I stood there was that we weren't going to be able to make much sense of how our victim had died until we found out how she lived. As with all the Burning Man's murders, we had arrived at the end of the story. We needed to fill in the rest of it to understand what had happened — who she was, where she had been, where she met her killer, how he subdued her, and where and when he killed her. Too many unknowns and the only fact that I was certain about was that another woman was dead.

I leaned back in my chair and called out to one of the older detectives on the squad, who was reading an early edition of the *Evening Standard*, with coverage of the Burning Man's latest exploits on pages 1, 3, 4, 5, 19 and across the centre pages. LONDON KILLER STRIKES AGAIN. And on page 3, POLICE BAFFLED. Baffled was right.

"Sam, any news on the DNA for the latest victim?"

"Nothing yet," he replied without looking up.

"You couldn't ring up and check, could you?"

That got me a stare over the top of his reading glasses. "Impatient, are we?"

"A bit," I admitted. "But if we find out who she is, we can go and see where she lived. Get the background."

"Sounds exciting."

"Yeah, isn't it?" I said cheerfully, affecting to take what he'd said at face value. Nothing excited Sam Prosser, but he had the magic touch with the lab; they couldn't resist him. They found it all too easy to be unhelpful when I rang them myself. I had a lot to learn.

"Hello, darling, who's that? Anneka? It's Sam, Sam Prosser here, from Operation Mandrake." Sam's voice was always gravelly, but he'd taken it down another notch so he sounded like an East London version of Barry White. It was beyond parody. "Not bad, thanks. Busy day today, though. Yeah, for you and all? Thought so." He chuckled. I could almost hear Anneka purring on the other end of the phone.

"Why I'm ringing up, darling, is to know if you got any news on the DNA of the latest victim — the one from Stadhampton Grove. Just come in, has it? You couldn't be a love and let me know who she is, could you?"

He was scribbling something on the edge of his paper, along the margin. I leaned over, trying to read what he was writing.

"Yeah . . . yeah . . . and what did that come back to on PNC? Oh, really? That sort of girl, was she? Not a surprise exactly, no." Sam looked at me and mouthed, "Drugs." I nodded.

"Anneka, my sweet, I owe you a drink . . . yeah, another one. One of these days, you and me, a big night out, I promise." More chuckling. "All right. Thanks again, sweetheart."

The phone went down and Sam turned to me, scratching his head absent-mindedly. "It's my mission in life never to meet her. Nothing could live up to the image I have in my mind. I don't want to disappoint myself."

"Afraid she's not a blonde and busty Swedish beauty?"

"It's more that I'm afraid she might actually be a stunner. You never know, she might not fancy the idea of going out with a fat, balding old fart to get bladdered in the nearest pub."

"What did you find out?" I nodded at the newspaper.

"Almost forgot . . . We've got a name and address. She was done for drugs six months ago — passenger in a car that was stopped by traffic cops in the West End, apparently. She had half a gram of cocaine on her, personal use only. They fined her and her DNA was put on the database, lucky for us." He squinted, trying to read his writing. "Rebecca Haworth."

"Hayworth? As in Rita?" I was writing it down.

"H-a-w-o-r-t-h. The address is a flat by Tower Bridge — one of those new-build ones about the size of a rabbit hutch." He got to his feet and hauled his trousers up to their usual half-mast position under his substantial belly. "It might not be current. Want to go and see?"

"Absolutely," I said, jumping up and grabbing my bag, all fatigue forgotten. "I'll drive."

"You'll drive and you'll buy me a pint when we're done." I rolled my eyes. "Fair's fair. I was perfectly happy just sitting here, not rushing around the place. You've got to look after your uncle Sammy. Running me ragged, I don't know. I'm not a young lad. I have to pace myself."

Knowing that he was perfectly capable of keeping that up until we got to Tower Bridge, I sighed and followed him out of the incident room. I just hoped it wasn't going to be another dead end.

The address Sam had was, as he'd said, a block of flats in the new yuppie ghetto to the south of Tower Bridge. Developers had taken over the area in the nineties and transformed it from a scraggly collection of old warehouses and derelict buildings into a highly desirable address for well-heeled types who wanted to walk to work across the river in the City. The streets were narrow, the apartment buildings six or more storeys high, and I felt like a rat in a maze as we nosed through the lanes, searching for Rebecca Haworth's building. I pulled in on one side of the street to let a stream of high-performance cars go by in the other direction, tapping my fingers against the steering wheel impatiently.

"Wouldn't you think they'd still be at work?"

"Hmm? Oh, them. Not on a Friday, my dear. Poets Day, innit? Shame it doesn't apply to the police."

Piss Off Early, Tomorrow's Saturday. I smiled ruefully, thinking of my abandoned plans for the evening and the awkward phone call I'd had with Ian, who had refused to see why I couldn't skip out on the investigation when my early-morning phone call had turned out to be a false alarm. The fact that a new body had turned up didn't seem to bother him. Camilla had

70

bought quail specially and if she couldn't find someone to make up the numbers, it would go to waste. I, who did not care for quail, couldn't bring myself to be too bothered. I would make it up to Camilla another time. The party would go just as well without me — in fact, maybe better. The low-paid public-sector employee was an interesting novelty, but novelties wear off, and I was acutely conscious I couldn't join in with tales of handbag shopping in Harvey Nicks or mini-breaks in five-star spa hotels in Dubai. I made them feel self-conscious and they made me feel impoverished. Not a recipe for social harmony.

"That's it," Sam said, pointing to the left. "The Blue Building. Pull in there."

There was a loading bay conveniently located in front of the apartment building and I swerved into it, not particularly concerned about straightening up. Sam put the "Police on Duty" notice on the dashboard and shook his head.

"Did you actually pass your Grade five test? Or did they let you get through under the quota system?"

"Fine," I said crisply, slamming the door and locking it. "Next time, you can walk if you don't like the way I drive."

Sam clutched his chest and staggered a couple of paces. "Walk? Me? You must be joking."

"You could do with a bit of exercise."

"I get plenty. Watch this." He sprinted up the three steps that led to the main doors into the Blue Building, which seemed to owe its name to the tiles around the entrance and in the hall. I followed Sam at a more sedate pace, looking around me, checking out the expensive furnishings, the plush carpet and the security guard who looked up from behind his desk. None of that came cheap. Which fitted with the expensive dress, the shoes, the cocaine. Rebecca Haworth had been doing nicely for herself, by all appearances, when her life was brought to an end.

Sam had made it as far as the security guard's desk and was now leaning over it, talking to him earnestly. By the time I got there he'd found out that Miss Haworth did indeed live there though Aaron hadn't seen her that day. He'd been on duty since noon, he explained.

"Then you wouldn't have seen her, my friend. She was already dead."

"Sam!" I glared at him reproachfully. It was no way to break the news. Aaron looked shocked and began stammering about what a lovely lady Miss Haworth had been, and always so friendly, and how she always asked about his family and his trips home to Ghana.

Finally he wound down. "What happened to her, please?"

Instead of answering directly, Sam tapped the *Evening Standard* in front of Aaron. It was folded to the Sudoku puzzle, which was almost complete. "Notice the front page, did you?"

"Not that — not the woman who was found early this morning? Oh my God." He leaned back in his chair, his mouth open, taking little short breaths. I was worried for a second that he was going to faint, and cut in quickly.

72

"Aaron, can we go up to Miss Haworth's apartment? Could you let us have a key?"

He did better than that. He gave me the passkey that opened every door in the building, and directions to the apartment, which was on the third floor.

"I would come with you, but I can't leave my desk," he said dolefully, clearly tempted to abandon the rulebook just for once so he could follow us.

"Don't worry," I said quickly. "We'll find it." Sam had already called the lift and I scooted across the lobby to join him in it before the security guard could change his mind. The doors slid closed and I found myself looking at my own reflection in the mirrored walls. There was no escaping it; my wrinkled clothes and wayward hair were reflected in every direction I turned. Sam, who was doing his customary impersonation of a sack of potatoes in the short-sleeved polyester shirt and brown anorak that was his all-weather outfit, didn't seem to care. I settled for staring at my feet, the only place I could guarantee to avoid meeting my own gaze. There was no way I could ever consider living in the Blue Building, even if I could afford it. I couldn't stand to see myself in such pitiless detail at least twice a day. If I was going to look like a mess, I'd look like a mess, but I'd rather not know about it.

On the third floor, we found Rebecca Haworth's apartment at the end of a corridor, the door as blandly uninformative as the rest of the ones we'd passed on the way. I hesitated, unsure whether to knock, but the security guard had told us she lived alone, and I did know for certain that she wasn't at home. I slid the key

73

into the lock and turned it, and the door swung open on to a tiny hall. Sam reached out and grabbed my arm, motioning to me to stop as I made to step inside. He jerked his head, as if to say, *listen* . . .

What I heard first was a washing machine churning. Then, underneath that, humming. A woman's voice, light and pleasant, humming a tune that I faintly recognised. Heels clicked on a wooden floor and before Sam or I could say anything, the door on the other side of the hallway opened. Framed in it was a woman in a business suit that had cost a hell of a lot more than mine. She was holding a duster in one hand, and her mouth had fallen open. The humming, I noticed, had stopped. It didn't take a genius to work out that the two things might be connected.

"Who are you?"

We'd spoken at the same time and used the same words. Her voice was higher than mine though her tone was equally sharp.

"Police," Sam said smoothly. "Detectives." He held out his warrant card for her to inspect, and she was the one person in a thousand who actually took it and looked at it. Then she turned to me and waited, her hand out, for mine.

"And you are?" I asked pointedly, passing it to her.

She took her time with my warrant card, reading the information before she answered, and that was unusual too. "Louise North. I'm a solicitor at Preyhard Gunther. I've got my driver's licence in my handbag if you want ID."

74

"We'll take your word for it for now," Sam said. "We were looking for — that is — this is Rebecca Haworth's apartment, isn't it?" He sounded dubious and I could tell he had reached the same conclusion as me: Aaron had given us the wrong number and we'd got the wrong door. But Louise nodded.

"Yes, it is. She's not here at the moment, though. Can I . . . take a message for her?"

"How do you know Rebecca? Are you her flatmate?"

She turned to look at me when I spoke and I noticed that her eyes were pale blue, and very sharp. "I'm her best friend. I just came around to see if she was OK."

"What made you think she might not be?"

She shrugged. "I just hadn't heard from her for a while. I've got a key — I used to feed her goldfish for her when she was away."

"But you don't any more?"

"It died." She stared at me. "Look, what is this about? I don't know when Rebecca will be back, I'm afraid, so there's no point in waiting. But if you want to leave your card for her —"

I pointed past her. "Is that the living room? Do you want to come and sit down, Louise?"

She wasn't stupid. She must have known from that moment that what I had to say about her friend wasn't good news. But she led us into the living room and sat down on an upright chair that was pulled out from the tiny table that stood against the wall. That left a squashy sofa — the only other furniture in the room apart from the flat-screen TV — for me and Sam to occupy. Generously proportioned the room wasn't, as

Sam had predicted. But as rabbit hutches went, it was all right.

This time, Sam let me do the talking, and I broke the news to Louise as gently as I could. As with Aaron, it was the fact that it appeared Rebecca had been the victim of the Burning Man that really shocked her, not the bare fact that the girl was dead; it was almost as if Louise had been expecting bad news of her friend, and I probed a little.

"You said you hadn't heard from Rebecca in a while — was that unusual?"

"Fairly. We've been friends since we were eighteen. We met at university." Her voice was lifeless and her eyes were fixed. She was clearly in shock.

I jumped up. "I'll get you a glass of water." I couldn't get into too much trouble with the SOCOs for turning on the tap, I calculated. Providing I was careful with what I touched, I should be able to get away with it. But when I opened the door on the other side of the living room to find a tiny galley kitchen, the washing machine I'd heard earlier was still spinning and the dishwasher hummed in the corner. Rebecca couldn't have been the one who put them on, I realised belatedly. I stared at them for a moment, watching evidence literally disappear down the drain, then went back into the living room at top speed.

"Louise, did you put the dishwasher on? And the washing machine?"

She blinked up at me. "The flat was in a bit of a state when I arrived. Rebecca wasn't massively keen on cleaning or keeping things neat. I was just tidying up.

Force of habit, I'm afraid. Rebecca and I used to live together and I've just got used to tidying up after her."

And in the process, she had destroyed any evidence of what Rebecca Haworth had been doing — and who she'd been with — before she died. I could tell the frustration was written on my face, but I couldn't do anything to hide it.

We were too late. Again.

Today was turning out to be a really bad day.

LOUISE

Dead. The word was meaningless when you applied it to Rebecca. It was impossible that she was gone.

I sat on a hard chair, feeling the seat digging in to the back of my thighs, and watched the tall detective roam around the small spaces of Rebecca's flat as if she needed to do something with her surplus energy. The fat older one sat, unblinking, a stony-faced Buddha on the sofa. If I stayed very still, if I listened very hard to what the woman was saying, I would be all right.

They thought she had been a victim of the serial killer who had been targeting lone women in South London. Or at least, the detective said, her eyes a strangely luminous grey that seemed to scan me in a very disconcerting way, it *appeared* she had been a victim of the serial killer. They couldn't be sure yet. They'd have to check.

"How . . . do you check?" I asked through stiff lips.

There would be a post-mortem. Forensic examination of the body, once it had been positively identified by a family member.

Rebecca. A body.

This was real. This was happening now. To me. I was the best friend of the victim. Her body was found this morning. On fire. *Smoke blackening skin, hair shrivelling, flames rising, her face, don't think about it, don't think . . .* I would recognise the Burning Man's signature, the detective said in her musical voice, dark shadows under the light eyes, a thin eager face. She wore heels even though she was tall, I noted, and felt a distracting gleam of respect for any woman who had enough self-confidence to do that.

My mind had drifted away from what she was saying. I needed to listen.

". . . after the post-mortem examination it might take a while for the body to be released to the family, which can be difficult. Do you know the family?"

"Yes," I said. "It's just her parents. She was an only child."

Her hand finding mine on a dark night as we ran across a cobbled square together past the high amber-lit windows of a reading room, heads bent against a cold wind, wine sharp on her breath, laughter welling up from deep within her at something she had done that she shouldn't have, something I couldn't believe she had risked and now couldn't remember. *You're the sister I should have had, Lou.*

"You said you hadn't heard from Rebecca in a while — was that unusual?"

My voice sounded strange in my ears as I replied. "Fairly. We've been friends since we were eighteen. We met at university."

It didn't begin to convey the truth about Rebecca and me. It didn't begin to suggest how close we had been. I had known her face better than my own. I would have recognised her footsteps with my eyes closed. I was who I had become because of her.

I had loved her, like so many others, but the difference was that I had known she loved me too.

I had trusted her with my life.

And she was dead.

The detective was looking at me with concern. "I'll get you a glass of water."

I watched her open the kitchen door with the fatalistic realisation that I was about to be in serious trouble. In my mind I ranged over the rest of the flat, thinking of the things I had moved, the surfaces I had scrubbed, the evidence I had doubtless obliterated. I had been everywhere, I thought. I had gone through everything. I knew that there was nothing for the police to find. The tall detective would be disappointed. She would want to know why I had been so thorough, and there was only one answer, even if I didn't think she would understand.

I had done it for Rebecca. My Rebecca.

Everything was always for her.

CHAPTER
THREE

MAEVE

The one advantage of Louise having tidied up was that the kitchen was hopelessly compromised from the point of view of forensic investigation, so I could make us all a cup of tea. I found a lone pint of milk in the fridge, still in date. The glass shelves of the fridge were otherwise practically empty — jars of mustard and a bottle of ketchup, a beribboned box of chocolates with an expiry date from February that had clearly been there, untouched, since the previous Christmas, and a lot of white wine. One shelf of the fridge was taken up with jars of eye cream, expensive moisturiser and bottles of nail varnish.

There was a box of cereal on the counter and I gave it an experimental rattle: two-thirds empty. So Rebecca lived on cereal when she needed to eat something, otherwise it was a liquid diet. The balanced nutritional intake of a single girl about town. She had worked in PR, Louise had told us, and did a lot of client entertaining so she was often out in the evenings. No point in buying food if it was just going to go off. When I had lived alone, I hadn't bothered with shopping much. Now Ian insisted on a weekly trawl around the supermarket, dodging hyperactive toddlers and slow-moving, trolley-pushing old women in pursuit of his favourite pasta sauce, his choice bottles of wine on special offer, his over-priced, over-perfect vegetables that were entirely tasteless. *I have more in common with the victim than I have with my own boyfriend*, I found myself thinking, and had to force myself to concentrate on checking out the rest of the kitchen, opening all of the cupboards and looking in the drawers.

Everything was impeccably organised. Wine glasses lined up on the shelves like rows of soldiers, and were arranged by size too. The cutlery was carefully separated into categories, gleaming in drawers. A clean tea towel hung by the cooker; the old one was presumably whirling in the machine. Again, I couldn't tell what was Rebecca's own inclination and what Louise had done since she'd been in the flat.

I poured boiling water onto teabags and thought about Rebecca's friend. She was an odd one, Louise, but then grief did affect people in odd ways. Band-box neat, unrumpled after what she had said was a lot of tidying up, she didn't have a hair out of place. Her composure had been so unshakeable that I was shocked when I came back in holding a tray of mugs, milk and sugar, to find her with her head in her hands, her shoulders shaking. Sam looked up at me helplessly and shrugged when I mouthed, "What did you do?"

"Are you OK, Louise?" I asked gently, setting a mug down on the table near her.

"Yes," came from behind her hands. "I just — just give me a minute."

I sat down and handed Sam a mug, then the sugar bowl, and watched disapprovingly as he did his best to empty one into the other.

"We were just talking about the last time she saw the victim," he whispered hoarsely. "They went out for a meal a few weeks ago. Hadn't heard from her since, so she got worried."

Murmuring something, Louise stood and walked out of the room; I cocked my head and heard a door close, followed by water running into a sink.

"Uptight, isn't she?" Sam jerked his thumb in the direction of the door.

"Do you blame her? She's just found out her best friend was murdered."

"I'm not talking about that. Who lets themselves into someone else's flat — someone they haven't seen for over a month — and tidies up? I wouldn't have the nerve, would you?"

"No, and I wouldn't want to do all that cleaning either, but I'm not Louise North. She said it was a habit. Maybe she did that sort of thing for Rebecca a lot."

Restless, I stood up and prowled around the room. It didn't take long. The room was overwhelmingly bland, the wall painted the shade of inoffensive magnolia that Ian called Rental Flat Cream. There was nothing on the small table at the wall, where Louise had sat on one of two upright chairs — socialising in this flat would be limited, but then based on the contents of her fridge I didn't think Rebecca Haworth had been the sort to throw lavish dinner parties. Beside the sofa stood a small table with a lamp on it along with remote controls for the TV, DVD player and sound system. There was nothing personal — not even a magazine. No clues there to the dead woman's tastes. The TV was large and stood opposite the sofa, its back to the balcony doors that led out onto a postage stamp of outside space where no effort had been made to cultivate window boxes or add decoration. I wandered over to stand at the door and stared out at the flats opposite where there were pots and trellises on the majority of the balconies, silhouetted against the lights from inside the flats. I couldn't see the point, personally. I wouldn't have bothered to plant anything either. Not when the balcony was too small to actually sit on it. Across the narrow street the neighbouring block was like a glassed-in hive; the occupants' lives were on display. I watched a couple kissing with what seemed to me to be excessive enthusiasm, a man lacing up running shoes, a sturdy woman eating crisps on her sofa while her TV flickered in the corner.

"Proper *Rear Window* stuff, isn't it?" Sam hadn't bothered to get up, but he was stretching his neck to see what I was looking at.

"Mmm. If I lived here, I wouldn't bother having a television. The view is far more entertaining."

"For you, maybe. But I bet you were born nosy, Maeve."

I flashed a smile at him. "How'd you guess?"

"Explains your choice of job, for starters." Sam stretched, reaching over his head without being remotely self-conscious about the sweat patches on his shirt, the wavering outlines clearly delineated like desert saltpans.

"And what's your excuse?"

"I didn't know any better," he said lugubriously. "Innocent, that's what I was. And now look at me."

"Yeah, innocent isn't the first word that comes to mind."

I turned away from the view of other people's lives and focused on the only item of furniture that was of interest to me. There was a narrow bookcase in the corner with a miscellaneous collection of novels on it and three framed photographs, which I looked at with some attention. A fairhaired woman appeared in all of them and I guessed that was Rebecca Haworth, though the body I'd seen that morning was unrecognisable, the face swollen and discoloured. In life, she had had regular features and a wide smile that showed off impeccable white teeth. Her hair had gone through various shades of blonde over the years, getting progressively lighter. One picture showed her with her arms around an older couple; parents, I assumed. The older woman was expensively blonde too and well groomed, and her daughter could have looked at her and had a rough idea of how she would look in her fifties. Rebecca had had her father's eyes, though — an unusually dark brown, almost black. It was an arresting combination with her fair hair. In another picture she was wearing black and white, an academic gown sliding off one shoulder, her head thrown back as she swigged champagne from the bottle. The end of exams, maybe, I thought, turning my attention to the other girl in the picture, my interest sharpening as I recognised Louise North. At university, she had been even more of a mouse, with long straight hair and drab clothes. Unlike her friend, she wasn't wearing make-up or academic dress, and was smiling awkwardly as she looked away from the camera towards Rebecca. The victim was the extrovert, Louise the foil for her glamorous friend. I had never liked being second best in a friendship, myself.

A voice came from behind me. "That was taken in our first year. I framed the picture that was taken of us about two seconds later. Rebecca had just finished Mods. I'd done mine the previous term."

"Mods?" I queried, turning to find Louise standing in the centre of the room, composure restored.

"Honour Moderations, to give them their full title. First-year exams. Everything has a stupid name at Oxford."

The last word fell into the room with a thud; *oh yeah*, I thought, *and I'm supposed to be impressed that you went to Oxford. Big deal.*

She had the grace to look embarrassed. "Don't get the wrong idea. I went to a state school."

But I couldn't help noticing that she'd lost whatever accent she'd once had along with the long mousey hair that was now shot through with blonde highlights and cut in sleek layers.

86

"What was that like, then? Going to Oxford?" Sam at his most avuncular.

"It changed my life."

I bet, I thought, looking at her shoes that had probably cost her more than I earned in a week. She was a long way from state school, and not looking back either.

"How did you meet Rebecca?"

She turned to face me, her chin up, as if she was braced for this question. "We met on the first day of the first year. We shared a set — rooms with a shared living space and separate bedrooms," she clarified, seeing me look quizzical. "I didn't think we were going to get on — I assumed she'd have better things to do than socialise with me. But she just scooped me up and made me part of her world." Louise still sounded surprised. "I don't think I'd be the person I am now if I hadn't ended up sharing rooms with her. I knew from very early on that it was going to be a friendship for life."

Well, she was right about that. It was just that life for one of them hadn't lasted quite as long as it might have done. I saw a shadow fall over her face as she had the same thought, and I cut in quickly.

"Louise, who's this?" I pointed at the last framed photograph — Rebecca and a man on a beach with their faces pressed close together, the wind whipping in their hair. He had been holding the camera at arm's length and the two of them looked up at the lens with shining eyes, laughing.

Louise leaned to see the picture, then straightened, her lips pulled into a narrow line. "That's Gil. Gil Maddick. He was Rebecca's boyfriend for two — no, two and a half years."

"They split up?"

She pulled a face. "Eventually. It was doomed, though, right from the start. He was . . . possessive. There wasn't room for anyone else in Rebecca's life, as far as he was concerned."

"Shut you out, did he?" Sam suggested.

"Well, he tried."

"When did they break up?"

She shrugged. "Six months ago, maybe? A bit less? I don't really know; you'll have to ask him. We didn't get on, so Rebecca didn't bother talking to me about him much."

"What did you talk about?" Sam asked.

"Everything else. She was like a sister. We were never stuck for conversation."

Like a sister, or something more? Louise had been jealous of Rebecca's relationship. I wondered if she'd been suppressing an underlying attraction to her friend — or whether she'd voiced it and found she was unrequited.

"So what happened?"

"What do you mean?"

"You said you hadn't heard from her for a while. Why was that?"

"I don't know. I tried to get in touch, but I couldn't get hold of her. I assumed she was busy." The solicitor's voice was still pleasant, but there was an edge to it that

I registered. She didn't like that her picture of happy, close friendship was marred by the facts. What she had told us was that Rebecca had cut her out of her life, deliberately or otherwise. She didn't seem to know what had been going on with her any more than I did, and with that in mind, I turned to discuss something she definitely did know about.

"When you got here, what did you find?"

"Nothing," Louise said, with a slight hesitation, as if it was a question she didn't know how to answer.

"I mean, how was the flat left? I want you to talk me through what you tidied." I gestured around me. "If you hadn't cleared up, we'd have had some idea of what happened before Rebecca left it for the last time. As it is, you're the only one who has that information. If you can, I'd like you to go through it for me and tell me what's changed."

"Oh, right." Briefly, she went through what she had done, showing me the bedroom, big enough for a double bed and a wardrobe and not much else, and the bathroom, a tiny marble-lined cube crowded with cosmetics that jostled for space on every surface. I followed her, increasingly despondent about our chances of finding any useful evidence. Bedsheets washed, floors vacuumed, surfaces dusted, bathroom and kitchen doused in bleach. Everywhere we might have hoped to find something of interest, Louise had got there first.

"Bit of a mess, was it?"

"That wasn't unusual. Generally Rebecca lived in a state of chaos."

"It's hard to keep things in order if you're not that way inclined naturally," I said, with some feeling. I turned around in the small hallway and, finding myself nose-to-nose with Sam, rotated again to face Louise. "This isn't the biggest flat in the world. I can see how it might get chaotic pretty easily. Did Rebecca like it?"

"I never asked. She lived here for over a year, though. So it can't have been that unpleasant."

"Did she live here on her own?"

"Officially." Louise came as close to wriggling as I had seen her so far. "Um — she did have the odd person who stayed over. And some of them stayed for longer than a night or two. But basically, she was on her own."

"Meet any of them?"

Louise shook her head. "She hadn't found the one. There was no one she wanted me to meet. Especially since I didn't exactly hit it off with Gil."

"So you don't have any names or contact details for any of them."

"No. But you'll be going through her email account and her phone, won't you? So you should be able to track them down that way. There's no privacy for the victim in a murder investigation, I'm given to understand."

"Not much, no." I would be turning Rebecca Haworth's life upside down and shaking it to see what fell out. At the thought of it, I folded my arms and leaned against the wall, suddenly fatigued beyond endurance. *Concentrate, Maeve.* With an effort I said,

90

"Is there anything else you think we should know, Louise? Anything that was worrying you?"

I was expecting her to say no, but instead she bit her lip. "Well . . . there was just one thing. But it's probably nothing."

"Go on," I encouraged her.

"I just — well, I thought that maybe there'd been someone here yesterday. Someone who'd had a drink with Rebecca. There were two wine glasses in the sitting room, and there was still some wine in the bottom of them that hadn't dried out completely. She didn't drink alone, Detective — only when she was with someone. And there was lip gloss on one, I noticed, but not on the other."

I raised an eyebrow. "Want a job?"

"I just noticed it," she snapped, colour rising in her cheeks. "I was trying to work out who might have been here."

"Why?"

It was an obvious question, but it seemed to make Louise more edgy. She looked away from me and swallowed before managing, "Just — because."

"Because what, exactly?"

"Well, if you must know, because I was wondering if she'd had Gil over again." The words came tumbling out, as if she'd been holding them back. "The last time I saw her, she said she was thinking of getting in touch with him again. I told her I thought it was a bad idea, and we almost had a row about it."

"Almost?"

"I never argued with Rebecca. Not properly. There was nothing she couldn't say to me, or me to her."

Right, I thought. *I'm sure.* What I actually said was, "Fair enough. But do you think she might not have said anything to you if she did contact him?"

"Maybe not," Louise admitted.

"OK. Well, it sounds as if it would be worth our while to talk to him. Does he live around here?"

"No. He has a place in Shoreditch or Hoxton or somewhere like that. Somewhere arty. I've never been." From the tone of her voice, she wouldn't be rushing there any time soon, either.

"Do you know how we might get in touch with him? Where does he work?"

"He doesn't." She met my eyes and smiled unexpectedly, if briefly. "Sorry. He alleges that he's a theatre director, but he never seems to do any actual directing. He was born wealthy so he doesn't need to work. He doesn't have an office, but I have his mobile number." She strode back into the living room, picked up her bag — Prada, and this season too — and took out her phone, scrolling through the contacts until she found his name.

Sam wrote down the number she dictated, then looked up at her limpidly. "So you didn't like him and you didn't get on, but you have his phone number?"

"Rebecca insisted," she said, her mouth thinning again. "She was the sort of girl who lost phones — she left her handbag in cabs a few times. She once dropped one down the loo. She wanted me to have Gil's number as a backup in case I couldn't get hold of her."

"And did you use it when you couldn't get in touch with her recently?"

"Their relationship was over." Again, there was a hint of satisfaction in her voice. "But I'm sure you'll enjoy meeting him. He's quite a charmer."

"You didn't fall for it," Sam pointed out.

"He didn't bother wasting any charm on me." She checked her watch. "I should go. Are we done here?"

I agreed that we were, for the time being. "We might have more questions for you later, though. We'll need your details too."

She took two business cards and a Mont Blanc pen out of her bag, then wrote quickly and neatly on the back of the cards, flapping them twice to dry the ink before laying them on the table. "Home address and telephone number. But you're more likely to get me at the office. I've put my mobile on there too."

"Even at weekends?" Sam asked.

"It's a good time to get things done." She looked defiant for a moment, reading the scepticism in his face and bristling at it.

"How does your boyfriend feel about that?"

"If I had one, he would have to get used to it. But as I don't, I'm free to come and go as I like."

"Lucky you," Sam said, grinning. She looked as if she was going to say something else in return, but settled for nodding coolly to both of us, then left without offering to shake hands.

"Not good enough to touch the hem of her garment," Sam observed once the front door had shut behind her.

"Oh, get over yourself." I frowned at him. "What would it matter if she had a boyfriend anyway? Why shouldn't she work all the hours God sends if she likes it?"

One eyebrow slid up Sam's wrinkled forehead. "Found yourself identifying with her, did you? Career women together?"

I wouldn't give him the satisfaction of agreeing with him though he could probably tell that he'd hit a nerve. I pushed Ian to the back of my mind as Sam stumped across to look at the pictures on the bookcase.

"Think there was anything dykey going on between our victim and her little friend?"

"You'd love that, wouldn't you?" I snapped, but then I relented. "I thought that too. But as it happens, I don't think so. I didn't get that impression. Just friends, I'd have said."

"Shame," Sam said easily, his hands jammed in his pockets as he rocked back and forth on the balls of his feet. "So what now?"

"I'll give forensics a call," I decided, taking out my phone. "There might be something of interest — and if there is, I'd rather not be responsible for screwing it up. So could you stop touching things, please and wait until we get the all-clear from the lads?"

"There's no evidence that anything happened here."

"No, there's no evidence that we can see that anything happened here. When they've confirmed it, I'll believe it."

"All right, missy. Make your call. And then you'd better phone the boss. He'll probably want a look around too, wouldn't you say?"

"More than likely," I said sedately, my voice not betraying the sudden increase in my heart rate though my hands shook a little. The thought of phoning Godley always made me nervous — but excited, too. And at least this time, the news I had to share with him was good.

"And the next time you decide to go off and investigate a victim's home without telling anyone where you're going or what you're doing, maybe you might think about letting your supervisors know what you're up to."

I didn't think I'd ever seen Superintendent Godley look so thoroughly angry, and in the course of this investigation I'd seen him in some fairly dark moods.

"I don't know which of you to blame. I'm surprised at both of you. DC Prosser, you should know better than to go off on a solo run like that, with your experience. And DC Kerrigan, I thought you were brighter than that."

I managed not to wince, just. His words stung, as they were meant to. I didn't dare look over at Sam, though I would have given much to see the expression on his face.

"The first thing you should have done when the ID came through was call me. What did you think you were going to achieve by coming here on your own?"

"I just thought we'd get a head start," I mumbled, staring at the knot in his tie, afraid to meet his eyes or to look away from him. Behind him stood DI Judd with a little triangular smile on his weaselly face. Behind that was a SOCO dusting surfaces with a fat brush and black powder, searching for prints. A mask hid the smirk that I knew would be there. Everyone loved it when someone else was in trouble.

"Did you. Well, that's all right then. What am I complaining about?" His voice was heavily sarcastic. "You fucked up, Maeve."

"If we hadn't got here when we did, we wouldn't have known that her friend had tidied up," I pointed out, unable to stop myself even though I knew it was stupid to argue. "We'd just have found the place all neat and tidy and never known what the real story was."

"And what is the real story?"

I talked fast, seeing a chance to redeem myself. "No sign of a struggle, but according to Louise — her friend — the place was in a chaotic state." I ran through what she had described to me. "She did think that Rebecca had been here recently. The interesting thing was that she also thought someone had been in the flat with her, more than likely last night." I explained about the wine glasses, hoping Godley would be impressed.

He frowned. "Doesn't mean it has anything to do with what happened to her, does it? As far as we know, our killer doesn't have any contact with the victims beforehand."

"Right. But maybe Rebecca went out with her visitor after they'd had a drink. Maybe they went out for a meal or clubbing or something — and on the way home, in the early hours of this morning, she ran across the murderer. Finding out who was here with her is pretty important if we're going to reconstruct her final hours."

"What an original idea," Judd said sarcastically. "Thank God we've got you on the team, DC Kerrigan."

A frown flickered on the superintendent's face for a second and I guessed he was irritated by the interruption. I managed not to look pleased. *Who's in trouble now?*

"So how are we going to track down the mystery guest?" Godley said eventually.

"According to Louise, it might have been Rebecca's ex, Gil Maddick. I can follow that up if you like."

"I do like." Godley sighed. "If it isn't him, we're stuffed, aren't we? I presume we won't get much from the forensics?"

"Louise was pretty thorough." I ticked it off on my fingers. "She changed the bedclothes and washed the sheets. She dusted and vacuumed the entire flat. She cleaned the bathroom and the kitchen, and bleached all the surfaces. She put away Rebecca's clothes and washed up all the dirty dishes."

"It's almost as if she knew we were coming," Sam chipped in mordantly. "Couldn't have done a better job if she'd been paid to do it."

"What was she, the victim's slave?" Godley was back to sounding irritated.

"She was used to looking after her. That's how their friendship worked, she said."

"So what did Louise get out of it?"

I shrugged. "Enough that she felt it was worth her while to spend a couple of hours here tidying up. Like I said, I don't think it was unusual for her to get stuck into Rebecca's domestic chores. I don't get the impression that Rebecca was that focused on the more mundane things in life. From what Louise said, she was more of a party girl."

"We'll need to find out what the victim's family and friends made of Louise. Make sure she is who she says she is." Godley was frowning again. "See if you can get hold of the ex-boyfriend, but in the meantime, we need to think about how else we might prove who was here in case that's a dead end."

"I'll check with the porter to see if there's any CCTV in the building," Sam volunteered. "Whoever was on duty last night might remember Rebecca leaving, too. She was the sort of girl you'd notice, wasn't she?"

I thought of the park, the body lying at my feet in the charred grass. Someone had noticed her, all right, in her heels and her tightly fitted dress. Someone had noticed, and hated, and wanted to destroy her.

"Good," Godley said, and Sam shot out without waiting for anything else. "Maeve, I want you to be the one who talks to Rebecca's family, her colleagues and other friends as well as the ex-boyfriend — see if you can find out what was going on in her life. Don't get started until we've got in touch with her next of kin to let them know what's happened. I don't want you getting ahead of us again."

I tried not to look disappointed. On an investigation like this, background information on the victim wasn't usually that important. It was busy work, something that needed to be done but that wasn't remotely likely to find our killer. Plodding research with formulaic questions, file-card facts no one would ever need to make a case.

"Sure. No problem. Er — any preference for where to start?"

"Take them in whatever order you like. Do me a report once you're done and put the data on HOLMES. Then let Tom know you're finished and he'll assign you something else."

Behind his back, DI Judd smiled unpleasantly. Whatever he assigned me would be the equivalent of latrine duty. That was the price I'd paid for getting to be the bearer of bad tidings twice in twenty-four hours. Godley could be superstitious. I was a leaning ladder, a crack in the pavement, a black cat in his path. Unless I could come up with something good, I was done.

On the way out to the car, I couldn't help looking for cameras in the halls and corridors. Not a one. Sam had bellied up to the front desk and was leaning over it, talking football with the security guard. I pointed towards the door as I passed the front desk. *I'm out of here. Coming?*

"Five minutes," he said, spreading his hand wide to hold up five chubby fingers. He looked as innocent, bald and plump as a toddler. If toddlers routinely sweated through their clothes. And had nose hair.

"Five minutes," I repeated. "Then I'm gone."

I got a swift grin in response. He knew I'd wait ten. He also knew I'd leave after ten minutes exactly, if he hadn't emerged by then. Sam could find his own way back to the incident room, or home, or to the nearest pub. I would owe him the pint I'd promised him. I was good for it.

The short walk to the car was enough to chill me to the bone. When I sat in the driver's seat, I spent a couple of minutes rubbing my hands together, trying to get the blood moving in them. I didn't think I would ever be warm again. The wind was coming straight off the river, cutting through the narrow streets with knife-like sharpness. I guessed the river was one of the things that had brought Rebecca to the area, though she hadn't managed to get herself a view of the Thames. She'd looked at people. And maybe, I thought with quickening interest as I scanned the apartment building opposite, they had looked at her. Looked at her and looked at her visitor. It was worth knocking on some doors, surely.

But not myself. I had my orders. There was absolutely no merit in setting off on my own initiative again, not with the superintendent's epic bollocking still ringing in my ears. Instead, I dug out my phone and rang him, explaining what I had noticed as concisely as I could, and suggesting that it might be worthwhile, if he thought it would be useful, to check it out.

"Not a bad idea. Good work, Maeve." Civility restored. I grinned as I disconnected. I wasn't home free with Godley, but I was in a far better position than

I had been before I called. I might even risk approaching the boss directly once I'd finished my trawl through Rebecca Haworth's life. DI Judd would never forgive me for bypassing him, but then DI Judd was never likely to clamour for membership of my fan club. Why put myself in the way of shovelling shit for him if I didn't absolutely have to?

No reason at all, Maeve.

I looked at the clock on the dashboard. Sam had four more minutes. Then I'd hit the road. Try to track down Gil Maddick. Find out if he had been with Rebecca. Find out what he thought of the lovely Louise. She had been right: there would be no privacy for Rebecca, but what she hadn't realised was that she would be scrutinised too. Rebecca's murder was a heavy stone dropped in the pool of her family and friends' lives. None of them would be unaffected by the ripples that spread out from it. And nothing would ever be the same again.

LOUISE

I went home once I was sure the police were finished with me for the time being, and when I walked in through the front door of my little house in Fulham, I couldn't remember a step of the journey back. The house was cold, the central heating off, but instead of going to the kitchen to poke the boiler into life I pushed open the sitting-room door and sat on the sofa, staring into space. After a few minutes, I roused myself to switch on the lamp beside me and slipped off my shoes. The objects in the room, dimly illuminated by the orange streetlight that shone through the window, now leapt into detail. The grey sofa I was sitting on, with its brown cushions. The coffee table, plain and wooden, completely empty. A television I never switched on. An armchair, rarely if ever used by any guest. No ornaments. It was a bland room, a blank waiting for a personality to be stamped on it.

Except for one thing. The picture above the mantelpiece. It was a glorious abstract, a whirl of blues and greys and white in choppy strokes that made me think of rushing water. It was an original, bought from the artist for an eye-watering amount of money, worth every penny and more. I had looked at it and loved it the first moment I saw it, at an art fair in Brick Lane, but I hadn't paid for it. I wouldn't have dared. Besides, I could never have convinced myself it wasn't a waste of money to spend thousands on a painting when posters were cheap.

Rebecca, who had dragged me to the art fair in the first place, had seen things differently.

"You'll love it when it's up on the wall. You'll have it for ever," she had predicted. "Let me get it for you, as a house-warming present."

I had demurred. Even for Rebecca, it was an extravagant gift. I had pulled her away and distracted her with some wrought-iron sculpture that neither of us liked.

And yet I hadn't been surprised when the parcel was delivered the following Saturday morning, an unframed canvas wrapped in layer upon layer of brown paper and bubble wrap, with a note from the artist that it was called *Untitled: Blue XIX* and he hoped I enjoyed owning it.

I had done more than that. I had fallen in love with it. But, in a strange way, I had never felt it was really mine. In my mind, it was always Rebecca's, an extension of her personality in canvas and oil. The sense of fast movement that it gave me; the sense, above all, of joy. That was her, not me.

I opened my bag and unzipped the inside pocket, slowly setting out on the table in front of me a number of objects.

A gold bangle, narrow and delicate.

A Chanel lipstick, rose pink.

A flat make-up mirror in a hard gunmetal-grey case.

A pen, sleek and black, with GKM engraved on one side.

A bottle of perfume, two-thirds full.

A bright pink diary.

A few old-fashioned double-edged razor blades in an envelope.

A twist of paper that contained a small amount of white powder.

Moving slowly, as if in a dream, I slipped the bangle on to my own arm where it hung, as weightless as a hair. I stretched out my hand, watching the bangle slip down to rest on my wrist, as I had seen it slide down Rebecca's arm. I picked up the perfume bottle and sprayed a little into the air, scenting it with a fresh floral that made me think of blonde hair blowing in the breeze, of a smile that lit up the room, of summer in the heart of winter. I took the lipstick and the mirror and painted my mouth, shading in the curve of my lower lip, peering to see through the scratched and dusty surface of the glass. Soft pink. My skin pale. My eyes dark, pupils dilated, surprised to meet their own gaze. I snapped the mirror shut.

The police would have told Rebecca's parents by now. They would know what had happened, but not how, or why. They wouldn't be able to believe that she was gone any more than I could. I could imagine their grief, though, and even though I felt as if I couldn't speak to them, I knew I should. I went to sit on the bottom step of the stairs, knees together, toes gripping the carpet. My hands didn't shake, even when I dialled the number I knew better than my own. The gold bangle spun and quivered on my arm and the deep voice of Rebecca's father spoke in my ear: *Hello*, he said, *Hello*, and I couldn't speak, couldn't breathe through the crushing pain in my chest that was the weight of sorrow, but slowly, clumsily, I found the words at last.

CHAPTER
FOUR

MAEVE

Sam had thirty seconds left on the clock when he stumped down the steps of the Blue Building, pointedly looking at his watch.

"Told you I'd make it."

"Just about. If I'd had to wait here any longer the tyres would have perished."

"Patience, my dear. Aaron was telling me all about our victim, along with a few other interesting tidbits. There are things you can't rush, as you should know, being a woman."

"Don't let that be innuendo. Please don't let that be innuendo. Sexism I can take, but smut really will make me puke. Now, can we go?" I was already starting the car.

"Not yet." Sam was fussing, checking that he had his notebook, his pen, his phone, his folded newspaper and all the other bits and pieces that he considered it essential to carry around with him, today collected in a plastic bag of surpassing grubbiness. I sat with the engine running and my hands tight on the steering wheel, fuming, and when Godley came out of the Blue Building and stood on the steps, talking to DI Judd, I shrank down as far as I could and hoped like hell he wouldn't notice us there. We'd been given our marching orders; we should have marched.

Charlie Godley didn't get to be a superintendent by missing much, though. Scanning the street with a practised gaze, he spotted me immediately and strode across to the car, his overcoat flapping in the wind as if invisible hands were tugging it. He leaned down to the window I fumbled to open.

"Still here? Just as well; it saves me a phone call. If you want to come along, I'm going to the morgue. Glen's doing the PM for me as soon as he can fit it in."

"M-me?" I stammered, thinking that I'd done better than I'd thought with my suggestion of talking to the neighbours. "I'd love to. I mean . . ."

I'd love to. It sounded all wrong when you knew I was talking about seeing a young woman's body cut up.

"Makes sense that if you're going to be dealing with her family and friends, you should get to know her inside and out."

"Was that a joke, sir?" I risked.

"Certainly not." He grinned. I was definitely back in favour for the time being. "Sam, I take it you don't want to come."

"I've seen more than my fair share and I've no interest in seeing any more, thank you very much." Sam looked at me piteously. "You wouldn't be able to drop me back to the nick, would you? It's just that my knees don't like the Underground. All those steps."

"Not if it's going to make me late," I gritted through clenched teeth that he could take for a smile if he wanted to.

"You've got time," Godley said tolerantly. "Glen's starting at six. You know where you're going, don't you?"

I did; Dr Hanshaw worked out of one of the big hospitals in central London and I knew where the mortuary was. The basement. It suited him and his work. I would be there on time if I had to throw Sam from the moving car to do it. Godley was opening a door for me again and I would take advantage of the opportunity or die trying.

In fact, with the exception of Rebecca Haworth herself, no one had to die and I made it to the mortuary with time to spare, having driven Sam right to the door of the police station. The last I saw of him was a stout figure shuffling happily inside, trousers sagging as usual. His brown anorak was wadded up under one arm, kept in reserve in case the weather got "really cold". I had the fan heater in the car blowing at maximum strength and I was still freezing in my giant coat, my fingernails blue-tinged and my feet like ice. I couldn't imagine what Sam's version of "really cold" would be. All I knew was that I didn't want to be around for it.

It was five minutes to six when I arrived and found Godley in the reception area of the morgue. He was sitting on a low chair with his arms folded and his eyes closed. I walked forward on my toes, trying to keep my shoes from making too much noise on the tiled floor so as not to disturb him. Without opening his eyes, he said, "Good timing, Maeve."

My shoulders slumped. "How did you know I was here?"

"It's my job to be omniscient."

I wondered if the superintendent knew that his nickname among the younger members of the squad was "God", then grinned to myself; if he really knew everything, he'd certainly have heard that.

"Glad I was able to be here." I sounded enthusiastic, but the mortuary smell of disinfectant overlaying something unspeakably rank was making me feel queasy already. On the way back to the station, Sam had been ghoulishly delighted to tell me about post-mortems he had attended, complete with detailed descriptions of maggots seething out of chest cavities and bodies literally falling apart with decay. I had seen Rebecca Haworth's body already that day and not felt ill, but I had never seen a human corpse dissected and I was beginning to regret my puppyish keenness to attend. The old rule about going to a post-mortem as part of police training was no longer enforced and I had never felt inclined to seek one out before.

"Glen's running a bit late." He stretched his arms over his head and yawned. "Sorry. Not enough sleep."

"Tell me about it," I said with feeling, then bit my lip. As a very junior member of the team, I wasn't really in the same position as the superintendent. He had the weight of expectation on his shoulders as well as overall responsibility for the investigation. I couldn't imagine how he was coping with the strain.

"I bet you've been to hundreds of these," I said quickly.

"A few. Is this your first?"

I nodded.

"Don't worry. It won't take long. And it's interesting; you'll forget what you're looking at once Glen starts to explain what he's finding." The superintendent raised his eyebrows. "You're not squeamish, are you?"

"No, sir," I lied. I had already decided that I was never going to be able to barbecue steak again after working on this case. In fact, the thought of cooking meat of any kind made my stomach turn over. Vegetarianism was looking ever more appealing.

"'*Hic locus est ubi mors gaudet succurrere vitae*'," he read from a framed poster on the wall behind me. "This is the place where death rejoices to help those who live. It's written somewhere in every morgue I've ever been in. Nice way of looking at it, isn't it?"

"Mmm." I twisted around to read the poster again, thinking about it. "This is where they tell us what happened to them, isn't it? This is where they bear witness."

"With Glen's help." He looked past me, then stood. "Ah, the man himself."

Dr Hanshaw had appeared in a doorway by the reception desk. "Sorry for the delay. We're ready now."

I followed Godley on legs as wobbly as a newborn foal's, suddenly wishing I was somewhere else. But if I was going to make a career of investigating murder, I had to steel myself. There would be worse things to see before I was finished with death. With that cheering thought, and a couple of deep breaths, I went through the double doors to the autopsy room where Rebecca

110

Haworth's remains were laid out on a high table, naked, ready for inspection. The beautiful Ali was nowhere to be seen; she didn't spend a lot of time in the mortuary, as I understood it. Hanshaw dictated his findings and she typed the reports. It wasn't, I knew, because she was squeamish — far from it; no one had ever seen her turn a hair at the most gruesome crime scene. But the pathologist didn't like too much of a crowd around him when he was working. Godley didn't count, because they were old friends, and I was there as Godley's shadow, rather than in my own right, so he probably wouldn't notice me. The only other person in the room was a pretty young man in surgical scrubs whom Hanshaw introduced as his technical assistant, Steven. As if to compensate for the surroundings, he was a ball of energy, with heavily streaked hair and three piercings in his left ear. He bounded around humming under his breath as he made the final preparations, as if there wasn't a dead girl on a table in the middle of the room, as if it was just another day at work. Which it was, for him. And it should be routine for me, too, I told myself, squaring my shoulders and bracing myself for what was about to happen.

"We've photographed her already and taken some samples for analysis." Dr Hanshaw was addressing me, his tone brusque but not unfriendly, and I guessed that Godley had asked him to explain the process to me as he went along. "We did find something odd when we undressed her. Her underwear was rolled over at the waist — the elastic tucked inside like this — and lower on the right side than the left." He demonstrated,

111

folding the waistband of his scrubs so the elastic was turned towards his body. "That suggested to me that she was dressed by someone else rather than dressing herself. It's awkward and she wouldn't have been comfortable to be walking around like that. I don't think she was conscious when she was dressed either."

Godley frowned. "Sexual assault?"

"I haven't found any sign of it." He shrugged. "I'm not sure what to make of it, but it doesn't fit in with the other Operation Mandrake cases. With the last four there was no sign of the clothing being disturbed, beyond what you might expect if someone was dragged across the ground — everything skewed a few inches out of place and so forth. But her dress was pulled down neatly. It was just the underwear that wasn't correctly positioned."

"What else?"

"Points of interest. She has an old injury, a fractured cheekbone. Healed, so certainly not recent. I've requested her medical records from her GP; you might be able to get the full story from her family. And there was this." Dr Hanshaw lifted Rebecca's right hand, turning it so we could see the backs of her fingers. He had cleaned a patch of skin that had escaped the worst of the fire damage. "Do you see these marks on the first and second fingers, just before the knuckles? I know it's hard to see with the burns, but there are marks that show up under UV light. They're scar tissue. My best guess is that they were caused by repeated instances of her teeth rubbing against her skin when she stuck her fingers down her throat."

"Why would she do that?" Godley asked.

"She was making herself throw up to stay thin," I supplied without thinking. I had gone to an all-girls school; if there was one thing I knew about, it was eating disorders.

The pathologist nodded. "Quite right. Bulimia nervosa. There's considerable acid damage to the enamel of her teeth too. I would guess that this was a long-standing condition. She was significantly underweight — forty-seven kilos."

"What's that in real money?" the superintendent demanded.

"A hundred and four pounds; seven stone six. She was five foot seven or thereabouts; her BMI was just over sixteen. BMI is body mass index," Dr Hanshaw explained rapidly, perhaps for my benefit. "A healthy BMI would have been somewhere between eighteen and twenty-five. The eating disorder complicates things for us a bit in terms of establishing when she died. There may not have been much left of her last meal. Not that I ever recommend stomach contents as a guide to when a person died. Fear puts the brakes on the digestive system. Anger speeds it up. Serious injury can stop it altogether. My preferred method would be body temperature, but with these burning cases, I obviously can't use that."

"But you've been able to make an estimate." It wasn't a question. Godley knew that the pathologist would have a fairly shrewd idea, no matter how much he protested that calculating it accurately was impossible.

113

He grunted. "Hard to say. I can't rely on rigor mortis either because of the burning; it contracts the muscle fibres. I might only be able to tell you if she was dead or alive when the fire was started. We'll see more when I open her up, but I didn't observe any soot in the airways. Now, the fire damage. Consistent with the other victims of your serial killer. Her palms and fingers were soaked in petrol, but not her face. She has full thickness burns to her forearms and thighs and her abdomen; partial thickness burns to her neck and chest. I'd estimate she has burn damage on just over fifty per cent of her body." He looked at me again. "Do you know how it's calculated? No? This area" — he held up his hand and circled the palm — "counts as about one per cent of your total body area, so that's how we measure irregular areas of burning. In a case like this, where the damage is extensive, we use the rule of nines. We allow nine per cent for each arm and the head. Eighteen per cent for each leg. Eighteen per cent for the front of the torso. Eighteen per cent for the back. And we allow the last per cent for the genitals."

I realised as the pathologist went on speaking that Godley had been right: I was interested. So interested that I had almost forgotten that the shape in front of us had once been a person, an individual with hopes and dreams and feelings. Now she was a problem to be solved, a mystery to be explored. But that didn't mean I could suppress a shudder as Dr Hanshaw picked up a scalpel and began to cut into the body, laying open the torso in a Y-shape that ran from each shoulder down to the pubic bone.

He went through the organs quickly, weighing them, taking samples, dissecting them, showing us what he'd found. Everything was normal; she was healthy enough, in spite of her lifestyle. She had had years yet before it caught up with her. The colours of her organs were unexpectedly bright, the shapes familiar from butchers' slabs, and I found myself reminded of nothing so much as the crime-scene photographs of Jack the Ripper's last victim, Mary Jane Kelly, dismembered, displayed, a heap of shadowy viscera on a table behind her. The repellent images collided in my mind with what I was watching and made my head spin. I put out my hand for balance and encountered the superintendent's sleeve. He looked around at me quickly.

"Feeling OK? Do you want to take a break? Get some air?"

I shook my head and managed a smile; I didn't quite dare to speak.

"I've taken blood samples," Hanshaw announced, "so we can get that tested along with the hair and find out what she'd been taking."

"We know she had a history of taking cocaine," Godley said.

"I could have told you that from the state of her nose. Significant damage to the septum. I took samples from her eye as well; the vitreous humour is a good place to get a chemical profile when a body has been exposed to heat. I'll take some urine for analysis, and preserve the stomach contents, such as they are, for toxicology."

The thought of a needle plunging into the victim's eye nearly did for me. And when Hanshaw picked up a scalpel and slit her head from ear to ear, peeling the skin down over her face to expose her skull, I had had enough. Mumbling an excuse, I walked with purpose to the door and slipped through it, not caring what anyone thought of me. I could not stay in that room for one moment longer. I would read the pathologist's report, but I didn't need to see any more.

In the reception area I stood by the water cooler and drank cup after cup until my stomach settled a little bit and I felt more like myself. I had to wait for Godley to come out so I could apologise to him. I felt as if I had let him down in front of Dr Hanshaw. Not tough enough, as usual. Not hard enough to be a murder detective. The gibes from the uniforms early in the day came back to me and I swore under my breath, hating the doubts I couldn't manage to dispel. Men didn't question themselves so much. Men didn't worry all the time about how they were perceived. Men did their jobs and went home, untroubled by what they'd seen — or if they were troubled, they didn't show it. And I had practically fainted. There were plenty of senior officers who were female, but I was the only one flying the flag for feminism in Godley's team, and a pretty small, ragged flag it was too.

To give him his due, Godley didn't say anything particularly reproachful when he finally came out with Dr Hanshaw.

"Feeling all right?"

"Much better." I looked at the pathologist. "I'm sorry. It was really interesting."

"Next time you should stay for the big finish. You missed the best bit. There's nothing like seeing the brain for the first time when the top of the skull is taken off."

Never, never, not in a million years. I smiled politely. "What did you find?"

"Three blows to the back of the skull with a blunt object. From the angle, you are looking for someone right-handed. The first blow when the victim was either sitting or kneeling, the other two were struck when she was lying down. I can't tell you which one killed her, but it would have been quick. She was dead before the fire was lit."

"That's something, I suppose."

"The question is whether we're looking for one killer or two," Godley said, sounding grim, and I looked up at him quickly.

"A copycat do you mean, sir?"

"I think we have to keep an open mind. Keep it within the squad, anyway, so I can keep an eye on it, but I want you to concentrate on Rebecca Haworth, Maeve. That way, if it does turn out to be the same killer, we'll know about it first. I don't want to make the press suspicious that there are two killers — they might be if I handed it over to another SIO. We don't want them to cause a panic. One serial killer is bad enough; two is unthinkable. I don't want that getting out, not least because Rebecca's murderer, if he isn't our serial killer, needs to think that we've been completely fooled. Lull him into a false sense of security and watch him make mistakes."

I could see the sense in what he was saying. The next part, however, left me cold.

"I'm going to put Tom in charge of this investigation and I want you to work on it full-time. Report to him; he'll keep me up to speed. He can pull a couple of people from the squad to give you a hand. We'll see where you are in a week's time."

I should have been pleased to be singled out for attention, to have an opportunity to shine, but I couldn't help feeling that it was a bit unfair that the price I had to pay was working for Inspector Judd. I didn't want to be left out either.

"Can I still work on the rest of Operation Mandrake? If I have time, I mean?"

He looked amused. "If you have time, of course. But Rebecca Haworth should be your first priority."

"I'll copy you in on the report," Hanshaw said, dismissing me. "Charlie, are you free for a quick half?"

The superintendent looked at his watch. "Not really, but why not."

I watched them leave together, the pathologist talking animatedly as Godley bent his silver head to listen. They made an odd couple, the one so polite, the other so brusque and awkward. What they shared was an obsession with doing a good job. And that was what I cared about too. So instead of feeling sidelined, I should get on with it.

Because if we found enough evidence to tie Rebecca's death to the Burning Man, I could get back to where I belonged.

118

★ ★ ★

In fact, I didn't make any more progress that day; I drove home after the post-mortem and went to bed. Blame it on lack of sleep, blame it on the chilling weather, blame it on the fact that I would otherwise have had to go to Camilla's dinner party with Ian, but I had the shivers and felt like death, and all I wanted was to sink into oblivion for a minimum of twelve hours. I took some flu medicine, carefully selecting the kind with a drowsiness warning on the box, and tipped myself into bed with my mobile phone under my pillow. I woke up briefly when Ian came home. He stood in the doorway for a long moment, silhouetted against the light. I didn't speak, but neither did he, and I didn't know whether to be glad or sorry when his footsteps receded in the direction of the guest room. It was what I had wanted, but somehow not that either. What I really wanted was for things to be wonderful between us. What I wanted was the relationship we had once had. I didn't want to give up on Ian. I had liked him, a lot. I still did. But he couldn't understand why my job was so important to me, and I couldn't understand why he needed to compete with it.

I slipped out of the flat early the following morning and went to work, even though it was Saturday. I found myself thinking of Louise North as I pushed open the door of the incident room and headed to my desk. Maybe she was at work too. There was nothing weird about it, whatever Sam thought. I was getting things done — and dodging my personal issues at the same time, admittedly. But that wasn't urgent, and getting

119

my career on track was. I devoted myself to ransacking Rebecca Haworth's personal life instead of my own and was moderately successful at tuning out the little commentary playing in the back of my mind that insisted I was making a mistake. It spoke with my mother's voice, so I was experienced at ignoring it.

The search team had done their work at Rebecca's flat and someone had collected a box of personal papers that was waiting on my desk. There wasn't much — bank statements, frightening credit-card statements, unpaid utility bills that had got as far as final demands. Obviously she was careless about her finances as well as housework. I set aside the phone bills for her landline and mobile with a view to going through them at my leisure. A folder marked WORK contained a company handbook for a PR agency named Ventnor Chase, a contract, and some information about Rebecca's package of benefits — salary, company pension, and health and life insurance. I skimmed it, my lips pursed in a soundless whistle. She had been well paid for what she did. No wonder she could afford her expensive flat and her drug addiction.

I flipped through the remaining pages in the file, then stopped. At the very back of the folder, I found a severance letter and a P45. Her employment at Ventnor Chase had come to an end in August, but they had paid her off with a small lump sum and continued her benefits until the end of the year or until she found another job, whichever came sooner. She had signed a confidentiality agreement, promising not to talk about the company or why she had left it. I sat and frowned at it, trying to remember if Louise had said anything about where she worked. Did she have another job? Or was she out of work? That might explain the unpaid bills. On the other hand — I checked the most recent bank statement — she had a couple of thousand pounds in her current account. And people did live with massive credit-card debt hanging over them. I had been brought up to pay off my card every month; I came out in a cold sweat at the thought of having to pay interest on the balance. But I was in the minority. Like everything else in Rebecca Haworth's life, her financial status was turning out to be more complicated than it first appeared. I piled everything back into the box with a sinking feeling, and went off to talk to someone who might be able to tell me what was really going on.

Gil Maddick lived in the East End near Columbia Road flower market, and sounded extremely wary about letting me into his flat when I phoned him.

"Can't we meet somewhere else? I'd prefer to talk to you in a café, or something."

"I'd rather have our conversation in private, Mr Maddick." I was fed up with people acting as if I had scabies just because I happened to be a police officer. It was almost a point of honour to get inside his front door. He backed down with bad grace when it became clear to him that I was implacable, much to my delight, though I managed to keep a lid on it. Undisguised triumph would not have been professional.

I arrived at his flat on time and with every intention of being civil, but something about Gil Maddick raised my hackles from the start. He lived in a small street of early Victorian houses with shops on the ground floor — art, clothes, handbags, hats, all exquisite and all far outside my price range. His flat was above a tiny dress shop with one perfect white dress in the bow-fronted window. It was as flawless and crisply curved as a tulip, and I longed for it, pointlessly, as I had no reason to buy it even if I could have justified the extortionate cost. The door to his flat was painted navy blue with polished brass fittings and I gave it a crisp rap with the owl-shaped knocker, enjoying its cool weight in my hand.

The door was opened by a tall, spare, dark-haired man whom I recognised from the picture I'd seen in Rebecca's apartment. He stared at me expressionlessly and turned away, leaving me to come in and shut the door before following him up a narrow flight of stairs. On the first floor there was a sitting room with a minute kitchen behind it. Another set of stairs climbed to a second floor where I assumed he had a bathroom and bedroom. Every inch of wall that I could see was covered in bookshelves. The doors and window frames were black, the floor boards painted grey. He had two chairs, a desk and a music system in his sitting room, and nothing else, but the chairs were leather and chrome and I recognised them as design classics of the kind Ian liked. No expense spared. No excuses made. It was the home of a man who knew what he liked and rejected what he didn't — uncompromising. And mildly uncomfortable if, like me, you were not welcome there.

122

I sat down without waiting to be asked in one of the chairs and cleared my throat. "I explained to you on the phone why I'm here."

"That's not strictly true. You told me you wanted to talk to me about Rebecca. You didn't say why." He went over to the window and leaned against the frame, staring down into the street. It was a graceful position but not posed, and the cool winter daylight fell on his face so I could see it clearly. He was handsome — very — with a straight nose, a determined jaw and expressive black brows over blue eyes. Everything about his demeanour conveyed extreme reluctance to engage with me and I started to wonder how long it would be before he threw me out.

"You knew she was dead when I phoned you." I had been expecting to break the news, but he had interrupted my carefully prepared explanation before I got very far.

"I'd been told. One of her friends called me. She thought I would want to know. I can't think why." He spoke rapidly and the light caught a muscle that was flickering in his jaw. *Tense, are we?*

"Which friend?" I asked. "Louise North?"

"Louise?" He shook his head, looking amused. "No. Louise would never call me. It was Tilly Shaw. She was Rebecca's best friend."

"I thought that was Louise." I was writing down Tilly Shaw's name nonetheless.

"So did she." He shrugged. "Tilly was more like Rebecca. I could never really understand why Bex and Louise were still friends. They didn't have much in

123

common any more. Louise was a bit needy, always trying to get Rebecca's attention. Tilly's more her own person. The two of them didn't like one another. All very petty."

"So which of them was really her closest friend?"

"Both, I suppose. Neither." He yawned. "It was boring. I tried not to get involved."

"Louise said that you and she didn't get on very well. She said you tried to shut her out of her friendship with Rebecca." I was trying to provoke a reaction.

"Did she?" He sounded interested. "Why did she say that, I wonder?"

"Have you been in touch with Rebecca recently? Did you see her before she died?" *Cards on the table.*

"The last time I saw her was in July. Technically, before she died, but I don't imagine that's what you were implying."

"So you weren't with her on Thursday night."

"No." He was looking at me now and his eyes were icy. "Is that what Louise told you?"

"She suggested it. She wasn't sure."

"She was wrong."

"Where were you on Thursday night?"

"Are you really asking me for an alibi?" He sounded incredulous. "Why would I want to kill my ex-girlfriend?"

"You haven't answered me." I gave him back the expressionless stare he'd greeted me with.

"I was here. Alone."

"All night?"

"Yes."

"Can anyone confirm that?"

"I really doubt it. I didn't go to the trouble of ensuring that someone knew my whereabouts because I didn't know I was going to need an alibi. If I had been involved in killing Bex, I would probably have thought of that and I might have a story for you." His tone was pure acid.

"What happened with you and Rebecca?"

"I don't see what business it is of yours."

"Everything is my business. I'm a police officer. Rebecca was murdered. It's my job to find out as much as I can about her."

"It's not relevant."

"It's up to me to decide that, I'm afraid."

"You want all the messy details, do you? Well, I'm sorry to disappoint you, but there aren't any. Nothing happened. Nothing except that she and I wanted different things and it became apparent that staying together was going to make neither of us happy. We had no option but to go our separate ways."

"Whose decision was that?"

He looked back towards the street, and when he spoke, he sounded remote. "Mine, I suppose. She agreed with me."

She had had her pride, I guessed. But she had made it easy for him. And from what Louise had said, she hadn't been able to forget him.

"You said you wanted different things. What did she want?"

He shook his head. "It's too late for relationship counselling."

"That's not why I'm asking." I leaned forward, a supplicant rather than an interrogator. "I need to build up a picture of what she was like. I need you to tell me about her because that's the only way I can understand her."

He didn't speak for a moment, considering it. "I don't know if I can help you."

"You knew her better than most people. You were together for a long time."

"Just over two years. Not that long."

I didn't answer, letting the silence stretch out so he felt compelled to fill it.

"You aren't giving up, are you? You're tougher than you look." He walked over and sat down in the other chair, looking at me with amusement in his eyes. I realised that the half-smile on his face was intended to be charming and couldn't bring myself to respond in kind. Maddick was the sort of man who liked to feel he was irresistible to women, and I fell into the right age-bracket and gender. The flirting was practised and automatic, and wasted on me. I liked funny and passionate, not arrogant and egotistical, no matter how attractive the packaging.

"She wanted what everyone wants. The happy ending. Marriage, kids, they all lived happily ever after." He looked down for a second, suddenly serious. "She didn't get any of it in the end. Poor bitch."

"It's what everyone wants ... but not what you wanted."

He shrugged. "Maybe one day. But not now. And not with her."

126

"Why not?"

"Bex just wasn't the sort of person I wanted to spend the rest of my life with. She was for a good time, not a long time, if you know what I mean." He raised his eyebrows, inviting a laugh which didn't come. "She was fun, but she gave you back what you wanted to see. I never had a single argument with her. Not one. That's not normal. I used to try, sometimes. I'd push and push, and all she ever did was cry and apologise to me for something she hadn't even done."

"That sounds like a great relationship," I observed, forgetting for a moment my role as the impartial representative of the Metropolitan Police.

He looked irritated. "You're missing the point. She was simple. Straightforward. She wanted to be liked — loved, actually. She gave affection unquestioningly and unstintingly, like a dog. I couldn't respect her because she didn't respect herself."

And you manipulated her so you could feel big about yourself. I was not warming to Gil Maddick. "How did she fracture her cheek?"

"Oh God, that. She fell over." He thought for a second. "It was about a year ago. She was pissed after her Christmas party. She was going up the stairs here and tripped — smashed her face into the floor because she didn't put out her hands in time. She was miserable for a few days. Beautiful black eye, too."

"Did you see it happen?"

"Heard it. I was upstairs, in bed."

How convenient. I changed tack. "Did you know about her eating disorder?"

He stared at me. "No. She didn't have one. Didn't need one. She was a gannet — couldn't eat enough, never put on a pound."

"Because she threw up most of what she ate. She was bulimic." He shook his head. I moved on. "Did you know about her drug addiction?"

"Drugs?" He started to laugh. "What the fuck are you talking about? Sorry to swear, but this is ridiculous. *What* drugs?"

"Cocaine."

"She wouldn't even drink coffee when we were together. She said it made her too jittery."

"Maybe she didn't want you to know about it."

"Maybe not." He was still staring at me. "What else are you going to tell me about her?"

"Do you know where she worked?"

"Ventnor Chase. It's a PR agency."

"She hasn't worked there since August. You really weren't in touch with her, were you?"

"We were supposed to go for a drink last month. I cancelled. Couldn't face it in the end." He was staring into the distance. "You think you know someone."

"Apparently she wasn't as simple and straightforward as all that." I flicked back in my notebook. "Can you give me a contact number for Tilly Shaw?"

He took out his mobile phone and scrolled through the address book, handing me the phone so I could write down her number. "I never meant to lose touch with Bex. We ended things amicably — I thought we would stay closer than we did. She was all right."

"She obviously thought a lot of you." I stood up, looking down at him. "She made you the beneficiary of her life-insurance policy. Luckily for you, the policy runs until the end of the year. You're in line for quite a pay-out, Mr Maddick."

"I — I had no idea."

"Before you can claim it, you'll have to prove you weren't involved in her murder. Good luck with that." I walked towards the door. "I'll see myself out."

I left him sitting in his over-designed chrome and leather chair, staring into space. As I walked down the street, I tried to analyse why I had disliked him so much. Something about him was unsettling. Something made me edgy. I thought he was a smug, manipulative creep, for all his good looks. But being a creep wasn't an arrestable offence.

On the bright side, it was a life sentence.

LOUISE

It seemed to me as if I didn't sleep at all on Friday night, but I must have drifted off at some point because I woke up stiff and cold in the morning with the duvet sagging on the floor and what felt like grit behind my eyelids. It was still early, still dark outside and quiet, with the hush that only fell at weekends, when all my early-rising, over-achieving neighbours gave in to exhaustion. No one was stirring yet. I looked out of my bedroom window at the bare, frosty gardens on either side of my own, and across to the backs of the houses in the next street. There were no lights on in any of the rooms and no signs of life, just blank windows that stared blindly back at me.

I couldn't go back to sleep; I couldn't switch off. I felt more alive than usual, more aware of my physical self and its surroundings. I was exceedingly conscious of the dense pile of the carpet under my feet, the soft felted flannel of my ancient pyjamas on my skin, the chill from the air leaking into my bedroom through the old sash window. My hair curled against my neck, feeling like a soft fingertip stroking the skin, and I shook it away with a quick movement and a shiver. The shiver, I told myself, was because the house was freezing and I shuffled downstairs in a thick towelling dressing gown to make a cup of tea, taking it back to bed. I left the bedside lamp off and sat upright against the pillows watching for the dawn, the mug clasped in both hands, sipping the steaming liquid and planning. I made a list for myself of tasks for the day, the week, the remainder of the month. Nothing was to do with work; everything was to do with me, with how I was and what I could be. Rebecca had coaxed me for so long to change myself. The irony wasn't lost on me that now, when her voice had fallen silent for ever, I was finally starting to do what she'd suggested.

By the time I left the house some two hours later, I had been through every room, collecting and bagging up clothes, shoes and bed linen that needed to be thrown away. It was all destined for the dump, not good enough even for a charity shop. I threw out a few of the more unflattering items in my wardrobe, things I had meant to get rid of for a long time — sagging suits I had had since I was a trainee, old jeans with tar on the cuffs, a pair of trainers that had seen better days. I hesitated over a jumper with a hole in the sleeve that I had found when I was a student, thrown over the back of a chair in the Law Bodleian. It had had the exciting strangeness that someone else's clothes always seemed to possess for me, as if by wearing it I borrowed something from a different personality, tried on a different life. I couldn't bring myself to get rid of it now, and in fact I found myself putting it on before I left the house.

I was glad of it; the morning air was cold as I walked quickly to the Underground station along silent streets. I liked travelling on a Saturday, especially early. The trains were empty and on time, the other passengers more relaxed and considerate than during the week. You had space to think. But then, I had been doing too much thinking lately. I sat and looked at my reflection in the window of the train, distorted and doubled by the thick glass. Both versions of me looked pale, washed out in the fluorescent lights of the carriage, and from lack of sleep. It was a relief when the train stopped at Earls Court and a man sat opposite me, blocking my view. When I changed trains at Victoria, I didn't bother to sit down, just stood holding on to a pole, staring at the floor. I counted under my breath, clearing my mind of anything but the numbers: how long it took the train to go between stations, how long it stopped, how many people got off, how many got on. Numbers were straightforward. They quietened my mind.

I started at Oxford Circus and worked my way along the street. I was looking for a dress, but not just any dress. It had to be dark, as plain as I could find, but not drab. The Haworths, they had told me, were thinking of having a memorial service for Rebecca. They'd been told they might have to wait some time before her body would be released but they needed the consolation of some kind of ceremony to mark her passing. I would be invited, they said. The service was a bad idea and it was too soon, the grief too raw for public display. I would have to be there, nonetheless, to support the Haworths. It was what they would expect and I couldn't let them down. And I might as well look as good as I could; it was a way of remembering Rebecca. I hadn't lost sight of the fact that Rebecca's friends would be there too — the ones who remembered me as a quiet mouse happy in her shadow, if they remembered me at all. I wasn't that person any more. I wanted them to look at me, not past me. I wanted them to see me for what I was.

I found it in Selfridges, a midnight-blue dress in fine wool with bracelet-length sleeves. It had a straight skirt, a tiny waist and a low round neckline. The saleswoman was delighted, all the more since I took her suggestion of a new coat to go with it and bought a blindingly expensive one that fitted like it had been made for me and flared into a soft bell-like skirt. I bought shoes to go with it, and a wide grey cashmere scarf. I handed over my credit card without the least hint of guilt. It was all *right* — right for the occasion, right for me.

I found myself struggling to manage all of my bags as the street became busier towards lunchtime. I was suddenly exhausted, thirsty and conscious of the fact that I hadn't had any breakfast. It was unthinkable to attempt another tube journey with all of my shopping. A black cab rolled towards me with its orange light on and without thinking I put out my hand to hail it. The driver pulled in to the kerb a couple of yards ahead of me and I hurried over, only to fall back, catching my breath as another woman got there first. Long blonde hair piled up messily, slim legs in black tights and high-heeled ankle boots, an elegance of movement that was totally unstudied, narrow hands, a red coat, a sweet curve of cheek as she laughed, a neat, flat ear decorated with a small diamond hoop earring — it was Rebecca who got to the door before me, Rebecca who leaned in to talk to the driver, Rebecca who stepped into the back of the cab and sat back, waiting to be taken where she had asked to go. It was her — and then it wasn't. A stranger looked out of the cab window at me, a woman much plainer than my friend, with a gap between her front teeth and over-plucked eyebrows. The shape of her face was wrong, the hair was too brassy, the coat cheap and gaudy with gold buttons. The resemblance was fleeting and once I had seen her properly, I couldn't see Rebecca in her at all, but as the taxi drove away I still stared after it. I suppose she must have thought I was angry that she had stolen my cab, but I didn't care about that, not really. There would be another one soon, and indeed there was, and this time I got into it before anyone else could get there first. I sat in the back and watched the shoppers jostling on the pavement, looking without meaning to for fair hair, for a quick turn of a head, a flash of a smile.

Looking for something that was gone for ever.

I came home to my small, cold house and ate, standing up by the fridge: an overripe pear that dripped juice down my wrists, a curl of salty ham, a fig yoghurt. It was an unorthodox lunch but I was too hungry to cook and too impatient to go out for food. My muscles ached from the physical effort of shopping and I found myself laughing at how weak I was, how tired, after a morning of self-indulgence. I hung up the new clothes, taking off the labels that told the story of how much I had spent. Then I ran a bath and soaked in it for a ridiculously long time, adding more hot water when it threatened to cool down, drifting, holding up my hands and looking at them as if I'd never seen them before.

When I finally gave in and got out of the bath, I put on a plain black jumper and skinny grey jeans, tying my hair back out of the way. In the kitchen, I marshalled my supplies of cleaning products, preparing to clean the entire house. I would start with the bathroom, I decided, and headed into the hall with an armful of cleaners and bleach. Housework was therapeutic, and restful, and totally necessary, I thought, pulling a tangled cobweb off the stairs with a shudder. I passed the phone in the hall and, as an afterthought, backtracked to check for messages, frowning to hear that there was one, picking up a pen to write down anything important. There was a tiny pause before it started. The voice that spoke into my ear was low, heavily ironic, instantly recognisable, and I dropped the things I had been carrying so I could hold on to the receiver with both hands. My heart was thumping. I didn't know he had my home number. I didn't know he knew where to find me. I had heard a lot about Gil from Rebecca. I knew he was demanding, manipulative, possessive. I also knew he was exciting, charismatic, unforgettable. I had mentioned his name to the police because if they wanted to know about Rebecca they had to know about Gil.

"Louise. It's Gil. I would apologise for phoning you out of the blue, but I understand you've been talking to the police about me, so I suppose I'm on your mind.

We should talk, I think. About Rebecca." There was a pause, so long that I thought he had finished, before he said, "There's plenty to say." Another pause, a briefer one. "I've missed you, Louise. I'm glad to know you'd been thinking about me. I certainly hadn't forgotten you. Call me back when you get this message."

Listening to his voice, I could picture his face precisely, the simmering anger overlaid with a veneer of cynicism and wry amusement. I listened to it again, dwelling on the way he said my name, drawing the second syllable out teasingly. I played it again. I deleted the message before I could play it a fourth time, and hung up the phone, dropping the receiver with unnecessary force. I looked up to see my face reflected in the hall mirror, the eyes wide, looking too big, my cheeks and slightly parted lips colourless. The dark material of my jumper disappeared into the background, making my head float as if it had been cut off. I felt exposed. He had always ignored me before. All his attention was always on Rebecca, as if no one else even existed.

I would not call him. Not then. Not ever. I would go on with my plans for the day.

But as I went up the stairs to scrub the bathroom as I had intended, I couldn't hide from myself that I was afraid.

CHAPTER
FIVE

MAEVE

After I had finished with Rebecca's ex-boyfriend, I made my way back to the incident room. I was looking forward to spending the rest of Saturday at my desk, considering the four blue lever-arch files on my desk fat with notes on the Burning Man murders — witness statements, forensics analysis, the pathologist's reports on the autopsies, crimescene photographs. The sad thing was I wouldn't have wanted to be anywhere else, even if I hadn't had a message on my phone from Ian to tell me that he was going to the cinema with some friends. I was, apparently, welcome to join them, but since it was an ultra-violent horror film, it was an easy decision for me. I got to see plenty of real horror at work; I couldn't sit through a fake version of it in the name of entertainment. Besides, the friends he was with were not my favourites. Like Ian, they worked in the City; like Ian, they were comfortable with flashing their cash. But they brought out the braying idiot in my boyfriend and I couldn't stand to be around him when he was like that.

Better to stay at work and spend my time going through the files once more, to see if there was anything that I and everyone else had missed. Somewhere in all those words and images, there had to be some answers.

When I got there, the room was emptying out, some officers heading off duty, others going out to do more house-to-house enquiries where the residents hadn't been available before, or to man checkpoints in the Burning Man's area of operations so they could speak to motorists driving through it. They had ANPR units set up — automatic number-plate recognition — to help with identifying cars that might be of interest, and if nothing else, they tended to pick up a fair few drivers who didn't have insurance or full licences. We were spreading the net widely but that made it all the harder to pick out our particular fish from the catch.

Superintendent Godley was in his glass-fronted office, the door closed. He was on the phone. He leaned his forehead on one hand, shading his eyes, as if he needed to concentrate on a difficult conversation. He looked exhausted. As I watched, he hung up, then sat for a second without moving.

DI Judd interrupted him, knocking on the door and poking his head in without waiting. They had a brief conversation that ended with the two men turning to look at me. I ducked my head behind my computer screen, hoping that they hadn't seen me staring at them. I was aware of Godley crossing the room in my direction, the inspector a couple of paces behind him.

"Maeve, I was just talking to Tom about the Haworth investigation, letting him know how we're going to take the investigation forward."

"Oh, right," I said, trying to work out why Judd looked so irritated. He ignored me and spoke to Godley in a low voice.

"Just don't put a note in your policy log, Charlie. It'll be disclosable to the defence if we ever catch this guy. They'll know we weren't sure about putting this murder down to him and that won't help us in court."

Godley's face was shuttered, remote. "I've made my decision and I'm going to stick to it. I'll answer for it in the box if I have to."

"You don't honestly think there are two of them out there, do you?"

Godley looked at me. "Tell him about the differences we've observed, Maeve. It's a reasonable suggestion."

Judd pulled a face and turned to me. "Was this your idea?"

"No, but —"

Judd didn't wait to hear what I had to say. "We'll be making a big mistake if we're anything less than definite about this case. If we lose this one in court because the jury don't understand how you've decided to run it —"

"It'll be up to me to take responsibility," Godley finished for him. "And I will. It's my name on the line, Tom, not yours."

"That's not what worries me."

"I know you are worried about making a strong case, but need I point out that we have to catch him first? I get a bad feeling about the latest murder; I want it investigated as if it was a new crime, not part of the series, until we're sure it fits in. End of conversation."

139

Judd and I watched as Godley strode away, head down. I had never heard him speak to the inspector that way before. Neither, it seemed, had Judd. He turned back to me.

"Follow whatever wild-goose chase the boss is on and then get back to work on this enquiry. But don't bother me with the details. If you find anything that proves this murder is part of the series — or proves that it isn't — let me know about it. Otherwise, I really don't care to hear about it."

"Fine," I said, smarting a little from his tone. "I'll just get on with it."

"You do that." He stared at me for a second. "Don't think this is a sign that the boss likes you, Kerrigan. It's the sort of job you'd give to someone you didn't want fucking up elsewhere. He's got you out of the way."

What he said was uncomfortably close to what I had thought myself, but I managed not to react. If my face was hot as he walked away, picking up his coat as he went, it wasn't surprising — the incident room was always boiling, the radiators on twenty-four hours a day. It was unpleasant even for me, and I could generally stand any amount of heat. The air was stagnant and we relied on a few ancient, highly prized fans to push it around. This late in the day, one or two were unattended. I went on the hunt, picking my way around the desks with care, because the hazards underfoot included loose sheets of paper, empty water bottles and discarded sandwich wrappers. In spite of the grand title, the incident room was an absolutely bland office space. It might as well have been a call centre, and not a very good one at that; the place was a tip. Stained mugs stood at practically every workstation. Someone had ripped open a packet of digestive biscuits beside the photocopier. I could tell this because at least two seemed to have disintegrated on contact with the air. Passing foot traffic had worked the fine beige crumbs into the fibres of the nylon carpet tiles and even though I wasn't the tidiest person in the world I yearned for a vacuum cleaner. If there had been one standing beside the mess, already plugged in and waiting to go, I wouldn't have touched it in front of any of the other officers, though. I wasn't stupid. I didn't wash up or make tea; I never tidied. Show the slightest hint of weakness and I'd be looking after all domestic duties for the entire squad in a heartbeat.

I returned to my desk triumphant, carrying a nine-inch non-rotating number that wheezed asthmatically and didn't seem to do much more than ruffle the pages on my desk. They flapped like wounded birds. Cooling of the atmosphere was not particularly noticeable, but I didn't care; I had stolen it from Peter Belcott's desk and I would have cherished it for that reason alone. A cold Diet Coke from the vending machine took care of my caffeine craving and also made a handy paperweight. I knotted my hair up at the nape of my neck, stuck a pencil through it to hold the makeshift bun in place, jammed my hands against my ears to block out any distractions, then got down to some serious reading.

I hadn't been concentrating for long when the fan clicked off. I looked up, outraged.

"Turn that back on."

Rob was standing beside my desk, his finger over the off-switch, shaking his head. "What do you think you're doing? Isn't it time you went home?"

I shrugged. "Maybe. But I'd rather look through the files again."

"You know how to live, don't you?" He picked up a booklet of photographs from the third crime scene and flipped through it idly, and I couldn't help but look as well at what was left of Charity Beddoes, twenty-three, the tall, beautiful post-graduate student at LSE, who owed her height and blue eyes to her English father and her hair and skin colour to her Nigerian mother. There was a narrative to the procession of images. The path that led into the copse where her body had burned. Charred bark and branches. A close-up of what might have been the edge of a footprint. Blackened skin. A twisted torso patched with the remains of her clothing. One leg, weirdly, that wasn't damaged by the fire, brown and perfect from the middle of the thigh down to the foot, a long graze on the calf where she'd been dragged along the ground. It had happened, I knew without referring to the pathologist's report, around the time of her death, though he couldn't say for certain whether she'd been alive to feel it. But she must have felt something. Fourteen separate injuries to her skull and face — fourteen blows with an instrument similar to a claw hammer, according to the pathologist. Defence injuries to her hands and forearms where she'd tried to shield herself, though her hands were bound in front of her so she couldn't fight back. Broken

142

teeth. Broken bones. Nothing for her family to recognise, if they had wanted to see the body, and I hoped like hell they hadn't. It would be no way to remember someone you loved.

Rob cursed softly and threw the booklet onto the desk in front of me.

"Let's get out of here, Goody-two-shoes. You need a rest and something to eat. You look like shit."

"I only keep you around for the morale boost, you realise."

"I live to serve." He grabbed the back of my chair and spun it around so I was facing the door. "Come on. Up. Let's go for a drink and a curry."

I stayed where I was. "I'm not going anywhere. I promised myself I'd read through the notes on the cases while I had the time to do it."

"Oh, Jesus." He ran his hand through his hair. "All right. I give in. I'll let you do your reading. But I'm not letting you stay here. It's too depressing. I'm taking these files away and you're going home. I'll come over with them later on and we can go through them together."

"Don't boss me. I'll go home when I'm ready and — Rob!"

He'd scooped up the four folders and was heading for the door. "You'd better text me your address. Do you prefer Indian or Thai food?"

"Rob, come on. Don't be ridiculous."

"You're right. It's got to be pizza. Everyone loves pizza." The last sentence was delivered over his shoulder as he disappeared through the swing doors out of the incident room, leaving me sitting on my chair, opening and closing my mouth futilely. I had been outmanoeuvred. Hijacked. And I knew Rob well enough to know that if I wanted to see my files again, I'd need to go along with what he'd suggested. To be honest, I didn't mind too much. It didn't sound like a bad idea.

Not then, anyway.

The phone was ringing when I opened the front door but I couldn't make myself run for it. I trudged up the stairs carrying my jacket and my shoes, which I had taken off as soon as I got inside. My bones were aching; I felt a hundred years old. As I reached the top of the stairs, the answering machine kicked in and I listened for a second to my mother's voice, trying to gauge whether her hollow tone meant that there was something genuinely wrong or if it was her usual guilt trip.

"Maeve. I was hoping to speak to you, actually. I wanted to have a word. But you're not there." Long pause. "Maybe you'd call me when you get the chance." Another pause. "It's nothing important. We just haven't spoken for a while and your father was worried."

I snorted. Dad would not have been worried in the least.

"I was speaking with —" *Bee-eep*.

I threw my jacket and shoes down on the sofa in the living room, then lifted the shoes off it again and pawed guiltily at the dust marks they had left on the purple

144

suede. Who had a purple suede sofa, anyway? It was about eight feet long and vilely uncomfortable, but had been extremely expensive, Ian had told me, round about the time I put a mug of tea down on one arm and left a ring on it. I would have preferred something comfortable and saggy, something you could lie on while watching TV and eating chocolate. Something you could actually use.

The phone rang again.

"Maeve? It's your mother. Your machine cut me off." Aggrieved to the power of ten. *Maybe if you didn't leave ten-minute messages, you'd get to the end of what you wanted to say before the machine ran out of patience.* "I was saying, I was speaking with your auntie Maureen. Denise is pregnant, due in May. Of course, she said she was delighted about it — what else could she say? No word of whether Denise and Cormac will be getting married. I thought you should know, though. Ah, it's a blessing really. Maureen will love being a grandmother. She was asking for you, but I told her there was no sign of anything like that on the horizon. With your job I don't know how you'd fit in a baby anyway. As I told Maureen, I never seem to be able to get hold of —" The machine beeped again, and blessed silence fell. I rolled my eyes and wandered back out of the living room as the phone started to ring again. There was no way I was going to answer it. Much better to leave her to ramble on.

I would call her, I promised myself, tomorrow, though I hoped she wasn't going to have another go at me about being a policewoman. I'd been in the job for five years and she still wasn't used to the idea, not least because I had a slew of cousins back in Ireland who had very little time for the British authorities. I didn't think any of them were actually in the IRA but they were committed nationalists, the kind of people who knew all the words to "A Nation Once Again" and could list the signatories of the 1916 Proclamation in order off the tops of their heads. Mum had kept my choice of career quiet for as long as she could, hoping I'd change my mind, and she still tended to avoid talking about it within the extended family. I had schooled myself not to mind, but it still got to me occasionally. There's nothing like making your parents proud.

In the kitchen I went straight to the kettle and made myself a mug of tea, downing half of it before I noticed the note stuck to the fridge door, in Ian's tight, hard-to-decipher writing. *Your mother rang. Call her.* The second sentence was underlined. Poor Ian. She didn't like him much — didn't like the fact that we were living together, or that he wasn't a Catholic. It made it worse that he wasn't committed to any religion, in fact — she could have come to terms with a Prod. But the godless and my mother would never see eye-to-eye. I wondered briefly what they had found to say to one another. One of Mum's major gripes was that Ian never said anything to her when he answered the phone; he would practically throw it at me when he heard her voice on the other end. The soft Donegal accent that she hadn't lost in thirty years of living in England sometimes disguised the spikiness, but you always had to watch out for it. She could skewer you with a well-turned phrase. I shuddered. No, I definitely wasn't strong enough for her tonight.

I had a shower, hoping it would revive me. I must have taken longer about it than I'd thought because the doorbell rang before I could get dressed. I wrapped a towel around me and padded down the stairs to answer it, wishing that the towel was a little bit longer.

It was fair to say that Rob didn't mind. He pursed his lips in a soundless whistle when I opened the door to find him balancing two pizza boxes on one hand. He had the folders under one arm, and a bag containing two six-packs of beer in the other hand. It was strange to see him out of context, and I found myself staring at him as if I didn't know him for a second, at the wide shoulders and the clear blue eyes that were scanning me from head to toe.

As soon as he spoke, the spell was broken. "Nice outfit. That is not going to help me to concentrate on the case, though."

"Drop dead." The pizza boxes were in serious danger so I rescued them and led the way back up the stairs, hoping that the view he was getting wasn't too revealing.

"Huh." He stopped at the door to the sitting room and looked in with frank interest. "I wouldn't have thought of you as the interior-design type, Maeve."

It was the sort of room that Ian's friends adored — big, full of statement furniture and what Ian's interior designer called found objects on the walls, which to my mother (and to a lesser extent, me) looked like junk. I looked around, trying to see how it looked to Rob. Pretentious, probably. The purple suede sofa looked especially gaudy.

"Nothing to do with me. It's all Ian's."

"Oh yeah?"

"Mmm. He got some designer to choose all the furniture and decorate it. You're supposed to think wow."

"Wow," Rob deadpanned, sounding anything but impressed. "What belongs to you in here?"

Just for a moment, I couldn't see anything. "This and that," I said lightly, though, because I didn't want to examine the ramifications of not actually having any possessions in the main room of the flat where I lived.

"What about that?" He pointed up at an African mask that hung on one wall. It was about eighteen inches long and brutally ugly.

"It cost a fortune. The designer found it in a flea market in Paris."

"I think it's looking at me."

I was getting bored and my towel was slipping. "Do you want to sit down or what? I've got to get dressed."

He shoved his hands in his pockets. "I'm sort of scared to. What if I drop my pizza or knock over my beer?"

"Then Ian will kill you and there's nothing I can do to protect you."

"Where is Ian anyway?" He looked around as if he expected him to materialise from behind the curtains.

"Out. Cinema. Not due back for ages yet." I blushed as I said it, realising that it sounded as if I was calculating the time I would have alone with him. And my towel had slipped again. I hauled it back into place firmly. "Look, put down the files. We'll eat in the kitchen first."

"Good idea." Rob propped them up against the doorframe and followed me to the kitchen. I put the beer on an empty shelf in the fridge.

"See if you can detect plates and napkins while I'm getting dressed."

"Will do." He was prowling around the room, looking at everything, probably missing nothing. Feeling exposed in a way that had nothing to do with being almost naked, I hurried off to get dressed, putting on jeans and a T-shirt in record time.

He was still standing when I came back, but he had opened one of the boxes and was chewing as he looked around. He surveyed me briefly. "I preferred the other look, but that'll do."

"Glad to hear it. Can you sit down at the table? You're dropping crumbs."

"Mmph." He headed to the fridge and pulled out two beers instead, handing me one of them. "Did you call your mum?"

"What? Oh. No." I reached over and ripped the note off the door, balling it up. "It wasn't important."

"Bad daughter." He wandered around the room. "What's with the mugs? Does this place double as a kindergarten?"

I didn't bother to look; I knew what he meant. One wall of the kitchen was covered in shelves where twenty-six brightly coloured mugs were arranged, each decorated with a letter of the alphabet. The kitchen units were bright red. The walls were cream. The effect was, Ian's friends thought, stunning, but then they didn't mind sitting on the vilely uncomfortable wire chairs that were "genuine mid-century antiques" around the 1950s diner table that took up the middle of the room. If you weren't into that sort of thing, it was all a bit bright. I would have preferred something cosier myself. But, as Ian had informed me on more than one occasion, I didn't know anything about style.

"Do you ever use the mugs to leave each other messages?"

"Not really." I didn't dare to disturb them. And I didn't think Ian would find it funny if I did. Not that I was going to say that to Rob. "It's hard to think of sentences where you can only use each letter once."

"Right." He didn't sound convinced, and I had an uncomfortable feeling that he knew what I had been thinking. I busied myself with hunting through drawers for a bottle opener. I was sure we had one somewhere, but looking at the tangle of whisks, ladles, peelers and other odd bits of kitchen cutlery that had knotted themselves together, I gave up.

"Have you got a bottle opener?"

"On my key ring."

"Why doesn't that surprise me?"

"Because I'm always prepared." He came over and took the beer out of my hand to open it for me.

"Because you wouldn't let anything stand between you and a nice cold beer."

"That too." He pulled out one of the chairs with a flourish. "Take a seat, madam, and dig in before I eat the lot."

I hadn't realised how hungry I was until I started eating, but after the first couple of mouthfuls my appetite kicked in. Forgetting about the murders — forgetting about Rob, even — I devoted myself to my pizza wholeheartedly. All that I managed to say was an occasional muffled, "Oh God. This is so good." I ran out of steam halfway through the last slice, putting it back into the box with a sigh.

"I ate too much but it was worth it."

"It's put a bit of colour in your cheeks, anyway." He had finished before me and was watching me across the table, turning his empty beer-bottle around and around in quarter-turns.

"Right. I suppose we'd better get on with it," I said abruptly, feeling unsettled all of a sudden. *Back to business*.

He stood up and stretched. "Don't sound so unenthusiastic. You're the one who insisted on taking work home with you."

"Yes, but I can't remember why."

"Because you want to be the best detective in the whole wide world," Rob singsonged. I ignored him and headed to the fridge for fresh beers, leaving the pizza boxes where they were. A little mess wouldn't kill anyone. And I would probably have time to tidy it up before Ian got back.

In the sitting room, we sat side by side on the sofa and I opened the files, fanning them out on the coffee table like a deck of cards, open on the first page where there was a photograph of each of the women who had died. Four queens and it was still a losing hand. Five, if you included Rebecca Haworth. She didn't have a file yet but the details were fresh enough in my mind to recall the little we knew. I looked at the victims' faces and swallowed, trying to quell the panic that was rising in me. He was out there, feeding off the memories of killing young women, building up to his next attack. We would never catch him unless we got lucky or he got careless, and so far neither seemed likely to happen. And every second brought another death closer. We had no more time to waste.

"We don't know the first thing about our murderer, so we need to start with the victims," I said, trying to sound positive. "What have they got in common, aside from the obvious?"

"Take them in order." Rob started off, checking the file now and then to be sure of the details. "Victim one is Nicola Fielding, twenty-seven, killed in the early hours of the eighteenth of September, a Friday. Her body was found in the south-west corner of Larkhall Park, less than half a mile from where she was living in Clapham. Blue eyes, long brown hair, dressed to kill, or be killed, in heels and a very short skirt. But Nicola was a good girl; she was out on her best friend's hen night at a nightclub in Clerkenwell. It was unusual for her to be out late. She was originally from Sunderland. For the last year or so she had been working as a nanny for a couple named . . ."

"Cope," I supplied. "Daniel and Sandra. She looked after their two children aged three and five."

"And the Copes were devastated, not unreasonably. We had a look at Mr Cope but he's in the clear."

I took over. "We know that Nicola didn't catch the last tube, which she'd planned to do. She got the night bus instead and got off on the Wandsworth Road at two thirteen a.m. It was a ten-minute walk from there to the Copes' house, where she lived in a self-contained apartment in the basement — one of the perks of the job.

"All that we know about what happened next is that at some point between the bus stop and the Copes' house, she encountered our murderer. Approximately forty-three minutes after she got off the bus, a passing motorist spotted a fire burning in Larkhall Park and phoned the fire brigade. The responding unit discovered Nicola's body. She had been incapacitated with a stun gun and beaten to death with a blunt instrument, which the pathologist suggested was most likely to be a hammer."

"Available from all good DIY and hardware stores, and essentially untraceable." Rob leafed through the file until he found a map of the area. "The park isn't on the most direct route from the bus stop to her home. But we don't know if she walked there or if she was driven."

"It's a CCTV black spot," I said, thinking without enthusiasm of the hours I had spent scrolling through footage we'd pulled in from local businesses. I had watched it until my eyes crossed, until I saw fuzzy black-and-white images of cars in my sleep. I could remember some of it literally frame by frame. "I didn't pick her up on any of the cameras. And we've managed to trace the majority of the cars that were seen in the area. They've also been cross-referenced against the footage from the other crime scenes without finding any matches."

"Don't get ahead of yourself." Rob tapped my knee. "We're concentrating on Nicola first."

The place where he'd touched me tingled. Without thinking about it, I covered it with my hand. When I looked up, Rob was frowning. Quickly, I went on.

"This report from the psychologist suggests that the murderer might be on foot because the bodies are discovered so close to where the victims were last seen in very public places; highly risky for our killer. So either our murderer is impulsive and unwilling to remove them to a quieter location, or he gets a kick out of the risk involved in murdering them in the open, or he has no means of transport. Whether he was on foot or in a car, our best guess is that she didn't know him — we've traced and spoken to practically everyone she'd known since she was at school, and no one rang any alarm bells." The file was fat with interviews with her friends, relatives, chance acquaintances, other passengers who had been on that night bus and had come forward. No one had seen anything. No one had heard anything. No one had noticed anything out of the ordinary. "Somehow, he persuaded her to trust him."

"She was a nice girl, by all accounts. Gentle."

"The ideal victim. No sign of a sexual assault but he did take a trophy — a heart-shaped locket. She always

154

wore it and we know from the photos of the hen night that she had it around her neck that evening. It hasn't been found." I flipped through the pictures from the crime scene. Establishing shots. Close-ups. A jigsaw puzzle of body parts, each injury carefully catalogued, measured, captured in colour for posterity. Something that had been a girl named Nicola, once. Before Nicola became prey.

Rob's voice called me back to the conversation. "The accelerant used was common-or-garden petrol. Analysis of the chemical profile came back to BP. There's about a million BP petrol stations in the greater London area, so that didn't help much."

"Seventy-five, actually. And the nearest ones are here." I flattened out the map and pointed. "Kennington, Camberwell, Peckham Rye, Clapham Common. Further out, you've got Tooting, Balham, Wandsworth, Wimbledon Chase. And there's nothing to say he bought the petrol in that area. It wouldn't have been an exceptional amount, either. Not more than a can."

"No one is going to remember selling that," Rob agreed. "Besides, we don't know what we're looking for. There was no sign of a container at any of the crime scenes."

"Except the one this morning. They found a red can hidden in a front garden nearby."

"But we're not sure it connects."

"We are not."

I leaned back and tilted my beer to my mouth. Rob was watching me. "What are you thinking?"

"If I was walking home on my own in the middle of the night, there's no way I'd stop to chat. How is he getting them to trust him?"

"If we knew that, we wouldn't be having this conversation because we'd have found him by now," Rob said flatly. "He's got to have some trick. Like Ted Bundy had the fake broken arm — you know, 'Can you help me with my luggage?' And then next thing you know, lights out."

"Nicola was a nanny. Victoria Müller, victim number three, was a care assistant. Both of them were used to helping people. Maybe he's making himself look vulnerable."

"Could be. See any cripples on the CCTV?"

I shook my head. "There were very few pedestrians at all. We traced a lot of them. The *Crimewatch* appeal was good from that point of view."

"Yeah, but that was the only way it was useful."

It was after the third murder that Godley had gone on television to plead for the public's help. We had got literally hundreds of phone calls but if there had been anything truly useful, we'd missed it in the welter of cranks and oddballs that a TV appeal always seemed to attract.

I flipped Nicola's file closed and slid Alice Fallon's out from under it. "Our youngest victim. Alice Emma Fallon, nineteen years old, murdered on Saturday the tenth of October. Her body was left in a recreation ground in Vauxhall, not far from the New Covent Garden market."

The pictures showed swings in the background, a slide, brightly coloured play equipment. The foreground was a hideous contrast. Her body was found by a white-painted wall at the back of the recreation ground and the flames had scorched a semi-circle on it that was a testament to the ferocity of the fire. Alice, who in life had been sweet-faced and plump, with straight light-brown hair that she wore long and parted in the middle, was not the Alice in the pictures from the crime scene.

"Similar injuries to Nicola; similar MO. He used a stun gun on her. She was missing an earring, a peacock-feather mounted in silver with a turquoise bead. Very distinctive. Bought on a family holiday in Colorado, so while it isn't quite one-of-a-kind, I think we could be fairly sure that it was the only one knocking around South London in October."

"Alice was a student and lived in Battersea. She was killed between eleven o'clock and midnight. She had been walking back from a night out with friends in Vauxhall and she never made it home."

"And that was all she had in common with Nicola. Apart from long hair. And being dead."

"Thanks for clearing that up," Rob said ironically.

"Pleasure." I flipped open the third one. "Next up: Miss Müller. Aged twenty-six, single at the time of her death, originally from Düsseldorf but had lived in the UK for five years. She was renting a flat in Camberwell. On the night of the thirtieth of October, Victoria was working a late shift at a nursing home in Wandsworth. She finished work at four in the morning and accepted a lift home from a colleague who lived in Hackney — Mrs Alma Nollis, forty-three. Rather than driving her right to her door, Mrs Nollis stopped at the traffic lights at Stockwell tube station and let her out. Victoria should have walked about a mile to her flat, but she ended up in a small, very overgrown park in front of a condemned apartment block — no residents to notice anything out of the ordinary, and no one else saw anything, naturally. Her body was found at twenty past six by a jogger who almost ran through the crime scene before he noticed what was in his path."

The jogger had been sick when he realised what he was looking at. When DI Judd had played the 999 call in our briefing there had been loud amusement as he gulped and retched on the phone. I did not feel like laughing, looking at the pictures in the file and the pathologist's report, where an outline of Victoria's body was dotted with marks indicating injuries. The care worker had been savagely beaten before she died, with multiple fractures to her eye sockets and her nose. He had broken her jaw in five places. He had knocked out several teeth. He had fractured her skull, her left arm, her ribs and her collarbone. He had kicked her repeatedly, the pathologist believed, given the injuries she had sustained. He had stamped on her right hand. He had used his fists and his feet as well as the hammer. He had taken two silver rings off her left hand; they were unique because she had made them herself, a little fact that made me sad every time I thought of it. He was learning to take his time, Godley's tame criminal psychologist had said. He was

158

gaining in confidence. He had wanted to linger over the killing. He had wanted to enjoy hurting her. He had wanted to obliterate her features and punish her for existing.

Victoria Müller had been a slight girl, only five foot one, and delicate. She had weighed just over six stone. She had struggled with a stammer, her parents had told the family liaison officer; she had not been confident with men, or with her manager at the care home who had refused to allow her to work day shifts even though she didn't own a car and found it hard to get home in the middle of the night. She had been bullied in school. She had liked black-and-white films and Hello Kitty knickknacks. She drank white wine, when she drank, but she hadn't been out much since moving to Camberwell a year ago. She had had wide-spaced eyes and a turned-up nose, elfin rather than pretty but essentially attractive. She had been shy. She had been gentle. She had put up a fight that night, if the story told by her injuries was to be believed. And she had died where he burned her, in a thicket of trees in a small park, not far from the road but hidden from view.

"He found a better place this time," I commented. "He could take longer over it. Maybe spend some time watching the body burn."

"Sick fuck."

Rob was shaking his head. I wondered if, like me, he had thought about Victoria's last moments. Her fear. Her pain. Her total helplessness in the face of an assault so violent that I literally couldn't imagine what would make one human being want to do such damage to another.

The food seemed to have turned to lead in my stomach, a dull dragging weight that made me suddenly nauseous. I put my drink down and leaned forward, affecting to look more closely at the files.

"Are you OK?"

I dredged up a smile. "Sure. Never better. Why?"

"You've gone very pale."

"That's my Irish heritage. I don't tan easily."

Rob made a sceptical noise deep in his throat, but to my enormous relief he didn't push me further. I didn't want to admit how much these murders upset me — I didn't want to admit it to him nor to myself. But there was something pathetic about Victoria Müller that got me every time. She had deserved more from life than she'd got.

"As far as we know, she had nothing in common with Nicola Fielding or Alice Fallon; no friends, no acquaintances, no colleagues . . ."

"They never lived in the same areas at the same time. They didn't share any interests."

"And nor did victim number four. All of which tends to suggest that they were selected by chance," I finished. "They crossed the path of our killer and ended up dead."

"Before we go on to unlucky number four, do you want another beer?"

"Why not," I said, and Rob headed into the kitchen, returning in a very short space of time with two bottles that were frosted with condensation.

160

"Victim four was Charity Beddoes, the LSE student — mixed race, very pretty, very clever by all accounts, lived in Brixton. She died on the twentieth of November, at some point between ten past two, when she left her boyfriend at a house party in Kennington after an argument, and five, when her body was found by a taxi driver who was passing Mostyn Gardens. He thought at first that someone was burning rubbish. Then he put two and two together and called us."

Rob was reading the boyfriend's statement. "She was pissed, according to this. And royally pissed off with him. He'd been upstairs with another girl and Charity 'jumped to conclusions'. I don't blame her. Still, that is bad luck, isn't it? Not only are you brutally murdered, but you find out your boyfriend is cheating on you beforehand."

I was about to reply but someone else got there first.

"Who said anything about cheating?"

Ian was standing in the doorway, staring at the two of us with what seemed to me to be a hostile expression.

"You're home," I said unnecessarily. "I wasn't expecting you yet. How was the film?"

"Fine."

I waited, but Ian didn't offer any more details. His mouth looked tight; always a danger sign. "Er . . . sorry I didn't make it to the cinema. You know it's not my kind of thing, though."

He was staring at the photos on the coffee table with disgust. Rob quietly closed the folders and stacked them at one end of the table, and Ian switched his attention to him without noticeably altering his expression. "Hi."

"Rob came over to talk about the case. You remember Rob, don't you?" They had met at the team barbecue last summer. It had not been a conspicuously successful meeting, I recalled a little too late.

Ian looked at him without enthusiasm. "All right?"

"Yeah. You?"

"Yeah."

Silence. I filled it with, "So, how were Julian and Hugo?"

"Fine." He unbent slightly. "Hugo's just got back from the Maldives."

"The Maldives," Rob repeated. "Lovely."

You would have had to know Rob very well indeed to spot that he was taking the piss. I managed not to react. Fortunately, Ian didn't notice, or if he did, he didn't react to it.

"It sounded like a good holiday." He looked at me. "I left early because I wanted to make sure you were OK."

"Thank you. That was so sweet of you. You really didn't have to."

"Yes, I realise now I needn't have bothered. You should have told me you were having a quiet night in."

"We were working."

Instead of replying, he raised an eyebrow, staring pointedly at the empty beer bottles on the table in front of me. Just like that, I was angry — furious, in fact. "Do you really want to do this now? In front of my colleague?"

162

Rob got to his feet and stretched. "I think that's my cue to leave," he said to no one in particular. "I'll see myself out. See you on Monday, Kerrigan."

"Take the rest of the beer with you. It seems a shame to waste it on us." Rob nodded to me, and edged past Ian, who stepped out of his way but didn't take his eyes off my face. I listened to Rob's footsteps in the kitchen, then on the stairs, and after a moment heard a faint thud that was the front door slamming.

"Nice, Ian. Thanks a lot."

He tilted his head to one side. "Sorry. You should have told me you wanted the flat to yourself. Did I come back at a bad time?"

"For God's sake, does it look as if we were having fun?"

"I'd say you were having a certain amount of fun, yes. Get down off the cross, Maeve. I know you'd rather be working than doing pretty much anything else. Don't tell me you were sorry that you couldn't go out with me and the boys."

"Not particularly," I allowed. "But that's just because I don't have a lot in common with them."

"Sometimes," Ian said levelly, "I wonder what you have in common with me."

If I had said anything at all in return, it might not have been so bad, but the words fell into the space between us and I couldn't think what to reply. Nor did I know what to say when we went into the kitchen and found that the middle shelf of mugs had been rearranged so that it spelled out, unforgivably, a word

163

that I had often heard Rob use. There was nothing I could say.

Not when that particular word seemed to say it all.

LOUISE

I was halfway up a ladder stripping wallpaper when my mobile rang. I might not have bothered to answer it if I hadn't been glad of a rest — my arms were aching — and I hopped off the ladder to see who was calling, raising my eyebrows when I saw the name on the screen.

"Hi, Tilly."

"Oh, Louise. Sorry to bother you on a Sunday morning. I hope I didn't get you out of bed. I don't like ringing people too early at the weekend, but given the circumstances I thought I'd better." Her voice was breathy and she gabbled, the words tumbling over one another so I had to listen closely to work out what she was saying. "Isn't it awful about Rebecca? I just can't believe it."

I mumbled something about how I couldn't take it in either.

"I've just been talking to Gerald and Avril about this service for Rebecca."

Gerald and Avril, also known as Mr and Mrs Haworth, Rebecca's parents. I felt unreasonably irritated. Tilly had gone to school with Rebecca; her mother had been best friends with Rebecca's. That didn't mean that she was somehow a better or closer friend to Rebecca, but she acted as if it did.

"They hadn't made definite plans yet. I spoke to them about it on Friday." I couldn't resist telling her when we had talked, from a childish desire to let her know I'd spoken to them before she had. She breezed on, unmoved.

"Oh no. I've been working on it for them. I really love the idea of getting together with everyone who loved Rebecca so they can remember her and celebrate her life and whatever. It's on Wednesday."

"Isn't that a bit soon?"

"It gives everyone something to distract them. I'm picking the music. Gavin is finding nice readings for people to do." Gavin was her boyfriend, a recent acquisition, and I couldn't quite see what business it was of his; he had barely known Rebecca.

"I don't think I'd be able to do a reading." I was hoping to forestall the request.

"Oh, I wasn't going to ask you anyway. I've already got all the readers lined up. I just wanted to let you know it was happening. It's at the Haworths' parish church — have you ever been to their house?"

"Many times," I said through gritted teeth.

"Well, it's the one at the top of the lane when you turn off the main road. You can't miss it."

"Yes. I've been to the church before too."

"Oh good. It's supposed to start at twelve noon, and then everyone's to come back to the house for something to eat." I could hear her flipping pages. "I've got a list of Rebecca's friends from when I organised her twenty-fifth birthday party, but if there's anyone you can think of who should be included — people from university, I suppose — can you let me know who and how to get in touch with them?"

I said I would have a think and get back to her, not meaning it. "Who else will be there?"

"Everyone who was important to her."

I hesitated for a second, then plunged. "Even Gil?"

"Of course. He was the first person I called." She sounded surprised that I even asked. Of course she had invited him. I swallowed, trying not to overreact. There was no reason to be frightened of seeing him. The dry mouth was unnecessary.

I said goodbye to Tilly and went back to stripping the muddy orange paper that must have been on the walls of the spare bedroom since the eighties. I had plans for the room that included billowing curtains, white-painted floorboards with a sheepskin rug in place of the brown carpet that I had just ripped out in a fog of dust, new pillows and a new mattress for the bed, and pale pink wallpaper with a delicate pattern that would make anyone waking up there feel as if they had slept in a cloud. It was hard work, but satisfying, and I had found myself singing under my breath earlier in the day, but after Tilly's phone call I didn't have the heart for that. I finished the wall, because I'd promised myself I would, and gave up for the day.

I couldn't stop myself from thinking about the memorial service; I kept coming back to it, no matter how I tried to distract myself. The people who would be there, people I hadn't spoken to for years. How Tilly had cut me out of the service — how even though I had intended to take a back seat, it rankled. How it would be Rebecca's last party, if you didn't count her funeral, but I thought that would be a quieter affair. The Haworths would want to keep it to themselves. And those who had loved her, of course, like me.

The thought led me back to the same place I always ended up. Gil had loved her. Gil would be there. I would see Gil. He would see me. And the thinking part of my brain was sure I didn't want to see him. I had told the police that we didn't get on, but that wasn't true. I had loathed him, but I suspected he hadn't cared enough about me to feel anything. And I had loathed him all the more because I couldn't help but find him intriguing. He had enslaved Rebecca; she had an absolute blind spot where Gil was concerned. I had deplored it, and had told her so, urging her to get rid of him, but I had never been surprised she didn't follow my advice. I knew he was trouble, but I still wasn't sure I would have been able to tear myself away from him, if it had been me.

Then again, I hadn't needed to worry about that. With Rebecca around, it would never have been me.

CHAPTER
SIX

MAEVE

"I just can't believe it. Of all the people. I just — I can't — I'm sorry . . ."

From all the gulping and handwaving I could tell that Jess Barker was about to break down again. I leaned forward to prod a box of tissues in her direction with the end of my pen and suppressed a sigh. It wasn't that I was unsympathetic — far from it, her grief was obviously genuine. But all I had heard so far was that Rebecca had been "A brilliant colleague. Just brilliant. She made everyone happy when she was in the office, you know?" I did know. I had heard it from all of Rebecca's colleagues at Ventnor Chase, the PR company that had been her place of work for four years, which occupied the shell of a Georgian townhouse in Mayfair. And none of them had been able to tell me why she'd left the expensively furnished office four months earlier and never come back. I had heard stories about her wanting to start up her own company, vague mutterings about a desire to go travelling, or a new job lined up in New York. No one had known the specifics. Anton Ventnor was the only one who might have known what had really happened,

169

and he was unavailable, his secretary informed me. Out of the country. Geneva, she thought, but he was scheduled to head for Vilnius the following day. No, she didn't know when he would be back. Yes, she would ask him to get in touch.

"No one is out of reach these days," I had pointed out to her. "You can get through to him in five seconds if you feel like it. I bet he has a BlackBerry. Or an iPhone. Something that works internationally."

Mr Ventnor, it seemed, did not. Mr Ventnor liked to concentrate on whatever he was doing. Mr Ventnor was frequently absent from the office, and when he was, he phoned in once a day for a ten-minute update on what was going on. She would mention my request for an interview when he called in the following day. I would have to be patient and wait for him to get in touch with me.

I did not feel like being patient, obviously. I had requisitioned the personnel files and found them blandly uninformative about why Rebecca had suddenly left a job that, by all accounts, she had loved — a job that she had been born to do, according to more than one colleague. And no one would tell me what had prompted it. My last chance was sitting opposite me, her mascara dissolving beneath wet blue eyes.

"Do you think you might be ready to carry on?"

Jess, who had been Rebecca's assistant, whom I had saved for last anticipating that she would tell me the real story, blew her nose loudly. She looked at me

170

beseechingly over the tissue. "Yes, of course. I'm so sorry."

"Not to worry. Take your time. I understand that it's difficult. Did you work with her for a long time?"

She nodded. "Almost a year."

I estimated that Jess was about twenty-two; a year to her probably seemed like a long time.

"Would you say that you knew her well?"

"Absolutely. She used to talk to me about everything. She was completely open — just wanted to share things with me. I used to make her a cup of tea when she got into the office every morning and she'd get me to sit down and chat about what I'd done the night before and what she'd done and what sort of journey we'd had going home or coming in and what we were wearing — you know. Just chat."

It sounded like hell to me, but then I wasn't designed to work in an office like that.

"So presumably you would know why she decided to leave Ventnor Chase." I almost held my breath as I waited for her reply. *Oh, come on. Someone must know* something.

The light coming through the window behind her made a halo of her hair, fair corkscrew curls that stood out from her head, and of course she was ethereally pretty in spite of the runny nose and red eyes. But for me, the thing that made her truly angelic was the fact that she took roughly two seconds to overcome any reticence her employer might have expected. She sat up and started to fiddle with the tissue, tears forgotten, intent on sharing what was obviously going to be prime gossip.

"Well, I probably shouldn't say this, but things had got a little bit — you know. Strange."

"How do you mean?"

"I think Rebecca was on drugs." She mouthed the last two words rather than saying them out loud.

"What makes you think that?"

"She started to miss work. She didn't turn up to events that she was supposed to be running — she didn't even phone to say she wasn't going to make it. I had to make excuses for her, but I couldn't pretend she'd been to things when she hadn't. When Mr Ventnor found out, he went mad."

"And Mr Chase? What did he think?"

"There is no Mr Chase," Jess said with a dimple. "Mr Ventnor thought it sounded better to have two names."

Which explained why Ventnor's sour-faced stuck-up PA hadn't been able to give me a number for Mr Chase. It did not explain why she hadn't told me that he only existed on the office stationery. I added another black mark beside her name on my hit list.

"So Rebecca had become unreliable. When did that start?"

"About six months ago. But it was getting worse. And she was never in the office — she'd miss three days in a row and then come in as if nothing had happened. And she'd lost loads of weight; she was starting to get wrinkles around her eyes — you know, here," Jess said, helpfully indicating the area she meant on her own very smooth, very perfect face. "I was really worried about her, actually, because she was starting to look gaunt and it made me realise that you really do have to chose between your figure and your face when you get to that age."

"She was twenty-eight," I found myself saying in an injured tone. My age, as it happened.

"Well, exactly." There was a pause as Jess blinked at me. So twenty-eight was over the hill. I was beginning to feel self-conscious. Fortunately, Rebecca's assistant didn't need any prompting now that she had got started.

"It was little things, you know? Like she hadn't had her roots done for a while. And she came in one day with a ladder in her tights and hadn't even noticed."

"That's hardly conclusive," I objected. "Anyone could ladder their tights and not notice. And if she was busy — setting up her own company, maybe — she might not have had time to get her hair done."

Jess was shaking her head. "No way. Rebecca was always perfect. 'Appearance matters.' That's what she always said to me. I used to schedule all of her appointments for treatments. She had a massage every week, and a facial every fortnight. She had a mani-pedi on Tuesdays at lunchtime. She got her hair cut every six weeks and coloured every month. But in the end she just stopped turning up for the appointments. It used to be that she always had a spare outfit in case she spilt anything on what she was wearing — she couldn't stand to look messy. She was the same about her office.

She could find her way around her desk in the dark, she always said, because she had a place for everything."

I made a note of that, amused that Rebecca had been able to keep things tidy at work when according to Louise her flat had been the opposite of neat. But people were often very different at work.

Jess went on. "She always looked pulled together, as if she had everything under control, you know? Which was ironic, because she was totally bulimic."

"How do you know that?"

"She completely kept it a secret. No one would have known except me, and that was only because my desk is beside the toilet and I could hear her in there — I know, best desk in the office, lucky me. I used to get her lunch and whatever it was, I'd just be thinking, we'll be seeing *that* again before too long. I mean, she was human. She wanted to look a certain way and I guess it was the easiest way to do it. And she was managing to keep it together." She stopped and ran both hands through her hair, shaking it out, before she continued. "It was only a few months ago that things just started to slip. She wasn't herself. And she wasn't trying to set up her own business; that's horseshit."

I must have looked surprised because Jess blushed and covered her mouth.

"Sorry. I shouldn't swear. But it is. There was no way she would have wanted to leave. She loved it here, and she got on really well with Mr Ventnor. She used to go into his office and sit on his desk and just talk to him. No one else ever did that. It was like she wasn't remotely intimidated by him."

"Should she have been?"

"Yeah," Jess said, round-eyed. "He's fucking scary. Sorry. I mean —"

"It's OK," I said quickly. "Go on. She loved her job and she wasn't planning to leave, but things were getting a bit out of control. That still doesn't mean she was on drugs. She might have been stressed. Or depressed."

"Oh, she was probably stressed, but that was because she was overdrawn," Jess said with a matter-of-fact flip of her hand. "She was totally broke, she told me. And it was definitely drugs. One time, I went into her office to see if she was OK before I left for the day, and she had a mirror on her desk with white powder on it and I was like, hello, obviously coke, but I didn't *say* anything and she didn't either. She just put a file down on top of the mirror and pretended she was reading it. She didn't have to hide it. I wouldn't have minded." She must have noticed the look I was giving her. "Oh, I wouldn't have tried it myself. I know it's illegal. It's just — well, it wasn't that much of a shock, that's all. I'd thought she was probably doing something like that."

"Do you think Mr Ventnor found out about the drugs?"

She shrugged. "Maybe. But I think it was more that he was concerned about the company's reputation. Reputation is all we've got. That's what Rebecca used to say — you know, before. She had started to be unreliable, and the clients were noticing, and it was like, why keep her around if she's not able to do the job, you know? Better to let her go and find someone to

175

take her place, even though she was just amazing at what she did and if you ask me they never found the right person to take over from her — I mean, they shared out her clients and they hired someone to replace her, but she's not even close to being like Rebecca was."

"Is that your ambition? To be like Rebecca?"

"Not now, obviously. But before, yeah. Why not?"

Because being perfect ate her up and spat her out. Because she'd lost her job when her drug addiction had taken over her life. Because her fridge had been almost empty and her life had been chaotic. And all that was before she had died an appalling death. I settled for saying, "I can think of better role models."

"Well, I can't. She was brilliant. She was a fantastic boss and like I said, she was great at her job."

"Was she sorry to leave?"

"Gutted."

"Bitter?"

"Not at all. That wouldn't have been like her. The closest she came to being bitter was when she came into the office with a friend the weekend after she got fired and tidied out her desk. I'd offered to help, but Rebecca wouldn't let me. They had a laugh, she said. They even had a Chinese takeaway — Rebecca left me a note apologising for the mess, because the cartons were still stacked in her office when I came into work on the Monday. And she paid for it on her company credit card. She said Mr Ventnor owed her a good meal."

"Who was the friend?" I asked. "Did she say?"

"I'm trying to remember." She bit her lip, staring at the ceiling as if inspiration might come from above. "It's gone. No one I'd ever met."

"Do you know if she was in a relationship? I mean, was there anyone special in her life?"

"Oh my God, so-o-o many men. She was always getting flowers delivered to the office and guys would call all the time asking to speak to her. She could have been out on a date every night of the week, but she wasn't interested in most of them. Sometimes she met up with them anyway, just for the sake of a night out. She said it was a good way to try out bars and restaurants. And she always had the escape route planned. She'd go to the loo, then text me and get me to phone her up as if there was some emergency at work so she could leave. There was one time that her phone couldn't get a signal in the bar because it was in a basement — she said she'd have chewed her own leg off to get away from her date, so she was properly pissed off. After that, she got in the habit of telling me where she was going and who she was meeting. If I didn't hear from her by nine o'clock, I was supposed to ring the place anyway, just in case. She said she could tell in the first minute if she was wasting her time or not — like, first impressions were so important to her. And even though she went out with some really sweet guys, she never met anyone that she wanted to date properly. But I got the feeling that was because she'd already met The One, but it hadn't worked out which was totally tragic. She had this boyfriend for ages, and when they broke up . . ." Jess bit her bottom lip and rolled her eyes, managing to convey a whole sorry break-up saga with one facial expression.

"Do you recall the boyfriend's name?"

"Something beginning with G. Gordon. Guy. No. That wasn't it. Guh-guh-guh . . ." she snapped her fingers. "Gil. I can't remember his second name, I'm afraid, but I've probably got it written down somewhere. I don't know why they split up; she said he'd basically turned evil on her."

"How do you mean, evil?"

She shrugged one shoulder. "She never really said. But she warned me about men, and trusting them. She was really bitter after they broke up, I thought. She found it hard to let anyone else in. And if you ask me, that break-up was when things started to go off the rails for her."

His charm had been lost on me, but I could see how a man like that might make quite an impression. With a sigh, I turned over a new page in my notebook. "Do you have any idea who Rebecca dated after she and Gil broke up — and the ones she turned down?"

"I can try and remember," she said dubiously. "I mean, it's not as if I kept a proper record of her private life. Just work." She patted the brightly coloured spiral-bound pad that lay on the table in front of her, a sparkly pen clipped to the cover. "I write everything down. Everything. But I don't delete emails — our email system archives everything — it would still have lots of her emails to me and . . ." She looked a tad embarrassed. "There's probably a fair few emails from men too. She used to forward them to me if they made her laugh — like if one of the guys was particularly pathetic about begging her to see him, or cross about being dumped. I can let you have copies of any that I find."

I smiled. "Lucky for me that you're so organised."

"That was another thing Rebecca taught me. Because you think you'll remember stuff, but you don't. So always write things down. Save everything. And always keep a record so you know what you did and when. It makes everything easier in the long run, Rebecca says." Jess stopped short and put her hand over her mouth, before correcting herself. "Said. Rebecca said. She always carried a diary and wrote notes in the back. I used to tease her about it, actually, because I mean who has a paper diary these days? But she said it was better than having an iPhone or whatever because she couldn't wipe the whole thing by pressing one button, or knacker the memory by spilling a drink on it. Been there, done that, she said. Pen and paper all the way. And she was right, you know. So I started to do the same."

I bit the end of my pen, trying to remember if I'd seen a diary in Rebecca's flat. "Did she always have it with her?"

"Pretty much. She called it her second brain. It's a Smythson. The cover was pink leather. Bright pink. Like a Barbie diary."

I had to assume I would have noticed that if it had been there. I scrawled a query in my own notebook to check it out. When I looked up, Jess's eyes had filled again.

"Sorry. It's just — it brings it all back, you know? I can't believe I'm never going to see her again."

I had done sympathy and the clock was ticking. I cleared my throat. "Any chance of getting that list together now? I can wait."

"Sure. I've got records of her voicemail messages since she left too, if you'd like them. Mr Ventnor wanted me to keep checking it to make sure we didn't miss out on any of her clients. People still call for her, you know."

"That would be brilliant."

She got up, sniffing, and made for the door. With one hand on it, she hesitated. "Please — I don't want you to think less of Rebecca because of what I've told you. She was an amazing person. She didn't deserve what happened to her."

"That's sort of the point of my job," I said gently. "No matter who they are or what they've done, they never deserve it."

"Never?"

I shook my head.

"OK. I'll be five minutes." She disappeared, then popped her head back in. "Make that ten. There were a lot of guys."

I took a good lungful of frigid, petrol-scented air when I made my escape from Ventnor Chase. Rank though it was, it tasted like freedom. I was waiting for a lift, but as far as I was concerned it was a million times better to wait outside than in the soulless reception where a flat-screen TV tuned to Sky News hung behind the receptionist's desk, providing me with an unsolicited update every fifteen minutes on the lack of progress in the hunt for London's current serial killer. I had become extremely tired of the offices while I'd been waiting for Jess to come back. The quiet tastefulness of beige carpet and mushroom-coloured chairs grated on me. It was too perfect, too manicured. Too good to be true, just like Rebecca. The more I found out about her — about the secrets she'd been keeping, and the life she'd been busily dismantling — the more I felt that Rebecca had been a disaster waiting to happen.

While I leaned against some railings, I went through my notes and found Louise North's business card. I dialled the number for her direct line and got voicemail, then tried the mobile number on the back. It was neatly written in black ink, definite and precise like the woman herself. She answered on the second ring. She sounded completely unsurprised; it was as if she had been expecting me to call.

"What have you found out?"

In spite of myself, I bristled; I had not rung to report on what I had achieved (or failed to achieve, I had to admit) in the days since I'd last spoken to her. I did not, I assured myself, have to justify myself to Louise North. So it was doubly annoying to hear the apology in my voice when I spoke.

"We're still following up some leads, Louise. Making some progress. But nothing substantive yet."

"That's disappointing. How can I help?"

"Did you know that your friend had a drugs habit?"

Silence at the other end of the line. I waited, counting off the seconds in my head. Three . . . four . . . five . . . There are comparatively few people who can stand to allow a silence to develop for longer than a couple of seconds on the phone, but it was a full seven seconds before she spoke again.

"I had some idea, yes. Is that relevant to how she died?"

"We'll see," I said, not really knowing myself. "Er — how did you form that idea, may I ask?"

"Various things."

More silence. I pulled a face; she was the wrong kind of person to talk to on the phone. I should have gone to see her. She had less room to manoeuvre when she was sitting in front of me. "Do you mind telling me what those things were?"

"She had become erratic. She was always a bit unreliable, but she was getting to be completely impossible. She made arrangements to see me and then didn't turn up. She was hard to get hold of. I mean, that's why I went around on Friday. To see her. Because it had become so difficult."

"When you were tidying," I said, knowing what the answer would be, "did you find anything that might have proved it? Drugs? Or drugs paraphernalia?"

"Yes."

"Which?"

"Both," Louise said tightly. "In the bathroom, by the sink. White powder, which I assumed was cocaine. I flushed it down the loo. And there was a mirror with a

182

razor blade on it. I got rid of that too. I had it in my handbag when I left the flat."

"And you didn't think to mention anything about this when I asked."

"It wasn't relevant."

"Isn't that for us to decide?" I could feel a headache starting, a throb behind my left eye, and I pressed the heel of my hand against it.

"I suppose so." There was another pause. Then, "I'm sorry. I made a mistake. I was trying to protect Rebecca, and her parents. I had been hoping to talk to her about it — get her to get help. But I never got the chance."

"Once you knew she was dead, you might have thought better of hiding it. I gave you every opportunity to come clean when we were looking around the flat the other day."

"I was in shock."

"Clearly. It just makes me wonder what else you found that you didn't think of sharing with the police."

"There wasn't anything else."

"I'd like to be able to believe that," I said, sounding as cross as I felt. "But I can't exactly take what you say at face value any more."

"I've apologised, DC Kerrigan. What more do you want?"

"I want to know what happened to Rebecca's diary. Did you think that was worth spiriting away too?"

"What diary?" She sounded wary.

"The one that she always carried, according to her assistant. A pink one. We didn't find it in the flat."

"Neither did I."

"Are you sure about that?"

"Positive."

"The diary would tell us what she was doing right up to her death, wouldn't it? She wrote down everything in it, I believe. Maybe things that you think we shouldn't know."

"I didn't see it."

I wouldn't have described Louise North as flustered, but there was definitely tension in her voice. I wondered if she ground her teeth in her sleep. All of that stress had to come out somehow.

"Right. Well, I would appreciate it if you would share information with me instead of trying to hide Rebecca's secrets out of misguided loyalty."

"Point taken." The veneer of calm had cracked; she sounded properly pissed off and I suppressed a grin. A beat, and then she spoke again, this time with a more measured tone. "If I think of anything, you'll be the first to hear about it."

I thanked her cordially enough and rang off, then swore. I'd meant to ask her if she'd been the one who helped clear out Rebecca's office, just so I knew. It didn't matter enough to call her back, but I made a note to ask her about it the next time I spoke to her.

A silver Ford Focus had pulled in next to me, and the driver was revving the engine in a very irritating manner. I bent down to look in through the passenger window, which was open.

"Looking for business, love?" said the man in the driver's seat.

"Sorry, I don't do Mancunians."

Rob snorted. "That's about all you don't do, if half of what I've heard is true."

"Probably only a quarter of it is worth believing," I said primly as I folded myself into the car. "And even then some of that is wishful thinking."

"Oh, but it's fun to think about, isn't it?"

"It's more fun to do it, to be honest, but you'll have to settle for thinking, my friend." After five years in the job, I had enough material for twenty sexual harassment cases if I had wanted to take them, but the constant innuendo never really bothered me. For one thing, I had never actually slept with anyone in the Met, so any speculation was just that. For another, it made me laugh. And when laughs were otherwise thin on the ground — like now — any excuse would do.

But there was one thing I wasn't laughing about. I turned to glare at Rob. "Gobshite? Was that the best you could do?"

He looked wounded. "What do you mean?"

"The mugs, Rob. Don't play the innocent with me. You wrote 'gobshite' in mugs in my kitchen."

"It's Ian's kitchen really, isn't it? I hope he didn't think I meant that *he's* a gobshite."

"What else was he supposed to think?"

Rob shrugged. "That I wanted to write the longest swearword I could think of that didn't use any letters twice. It was either that or knobhead."

"You *twat* . . ."

"Four letters and too many Ts. Try again."

"I'd rather not." I bit my lip, trying to keep a straight face and failing. "For God's sake, Rob, he was pissed off already."

"I'm sure you made him feel better." Abruptly, he changed the subject. "How did you get on at Rebecca's office?"

I filled him in on what I'd learned at Ventnor Chase and he looked thoughtful. "Not the most stable person, was she? Drugs, an eating disorder, unemployed at the time of her death . . . It was all going a bit wrong."

"You can say that again. Perfect on the outside, rotten on the inside. Troubled was not the word."

"So, DC Clever Clogs, do you want to hear the results of the house to house?"

"More than anything." I felt excitement squeeze my stomach.

"No one saw anything."

"Seriously?"

"Very much so. Lots of them recognised her, lots of them remembered seeing different men there with her from time to time, but none of them remembered what happened on Thursday night, if anything did. Do you know what bothered me the most?"

"Obviously not," I said patiently. "But I suspect you're going to tell me."

"None of them cared. When we told them she was dead, none of them actually cared. One of them asked what the square footage of her flat was. Fucking animals. I hate London."

"So why live here?"

He shrugged. "If you want exciting crimes, go where the exciting criminals are, and that means London. But that doesn't mean it's a good place to live."

"Or die," I said soberly.

"So have you worked out who killed Rebecca yet, if not the Burning Man?"

"I've got an idea."

"Already?" He raised his eyebrows. "Not her boyfriend."

I looked at him, deflated. "How did you know?"

"It's always the boyfriend. Too obvious."

"Murderers *are* obvious," I insisted. "It all fits. Can you think of a better way of getting rid of someone than to make it look as if a serial killer has targeted them? Get the police looking the wrong way, sit back and act as if you're in mourning. Wait for the dust to settle and go on with your life. It's perfect. Rebecca's assistant said that Gil was the love of her life. She thought it was a real turning point for Rebecca when they broke up, and not the good kind of turning point. I think she was obsessed with him. I think she'd have done anything for him, including going to the dodgiest bit of Kennington in the dead of night to meet him. I think she trusted him and the feeling I get is that maybe she shouldn't have."

Rob looked at me with a frankly sceptical expression. "You've met him, haven't you? What did he say to make you so suspicious of him?"

"Honestly, I don't know." A chill raced over my skin and I shuddered. "He gives me the creeps."

"OK. I'm sure that will be enough for the CPS."

187

"Obviously it isn't," I snapped. "But I'm working on it."

"Course you are. Let's go and talk to this friend of hers, then. What's her name?"

"Tilly Shaw. Short for Matilda, presumably."

Rob pulled out into the traffic at speed. He always drove as if he was just behind the lead car on the last lap of the Grand Prix and I braced a hand on the dashboard to steady myself. A horn blared and I flinched, looking over my shoulder to see a black cab filling the back windscreen, altogether too close for comfort.

"Jesus. I'd like to get there in one piece if that's OK with you."

"Fine by me." He accelerated to get through the lights before they changed to red and didn't quite manage it. "Just sit back, relax and enjoy the ride."

"Two of those things are completely impossible with you behind the wheel, and I'm already sitting as far back as I can," I pointed out.

"Anyone who drives like you can't really complain."

"I drive perfectly well," I said with dignity. "It's just parking I can't do."

"Oh, nothing important then."

"No one ever died because they couldn't parallel park."

"Well, we're not dead yet."

"Yet is right. Just stop talking to me, OK? Just . . . concentrate."

"I can drive and talk."

I shook my head, pressing my lips together, and refused to speak again until we arrived at Tilly Shaw's address. She lived in Belsize Park, in a small one-bedroom flat carved out of a larger Victorian house, and standing in the communal hallway with a bitter draught whistling around my feet I feared the worst, but her door opened with a blast of heat. Tilly was small and ravishingly pretty, with dyed red hair cut in a deep fringe. She was wrapped in layer upon layer of knitted material, not all of which was immediately identifiable as a specific garment.

"I've got all the radiators on because it's so unbelievably cold in this house, especially with this weather, I mean, my God, I've forgotten what it's like to be warm, but if it's too hot, let me know, or if you want a hot drink or anything, just say, because I can easily make some tea. I mean, I would like some tea myself, so it's no trouble to make you some."

She gabbled on and on and I shrugged at Rob as she led the way into her flat, which was tropical. Rob immediately ripped off his coat and suit jacket and had one hand on his tie knot when he noticed me glaring at him.

"I'll have a glass of water, thanks," he said to Tilly, who darted off to the kitchen at top speed. I took the opportunity to look around the room, which was crammed with old, dark furniture that was too big for it — a triangular cupboard looming in one corner, a square tapestry-covered ottoman that barely left any room to move around it, an elderly Knole sofa and two fat, sagging armchairs. The rest of the place was decorated in a style that I recognised from those friends of mine who had spent a lot of time travelling, picking up bits and pieces magpie-style to remind themselves of where they'd been — batik fabrics, embroidered panels, odd bits of pottery and glass. It made for a weird combination.

"My parents gave me most of this stuff when I moved to London." She had come back with Rob's water and was watching me when I turned around. "It was all stuff they didn't want at home. I think they thought I might have a bigger flat than this."

"It's nice."

"It's not," she countered. "But at least the furniture was free."

"Makes up for a lot, doesn't it?" Rob said with a grin that got him a swift, winning smile in return. Then her face became serious.

"You wanted to talk to me about Rebecca. How can I help?"

I went into my little spiel about wanting to build up a picture of Rebecca so that I could understand her better and Tilly nodded.

"It's like acting. You have to understand the character before you can know how she would behave."

"Are you an actress?" Rob asked, ignoring the fact that I was glowering at him for drawing the conversation off course.

"I have been. And a waitress. And a receptionist. And a temp. A dog walker. A pastry chef. A shop assistant." She beamed. "More things than you can imagine, basically. I still haven't worked out what to do with my life." Again, the smile ebbed away and she looked pensive. "I thought I had plenty of time. This thing with Rebecca — being murdered — I mean, it's just so weird. So completely wrong. But then, she always said it would happen, so I shouldn't be surprised."

I sat up, electrified, and Rob leaned forward. "What did you say?

"She always said she would die young," Tilly said matter-of-factly. "Something really awful happened and she said she was responsible. I don't know what it was — she never told me and I wasn't in touch with her at the time it happened anyway. I was living in Prague when she was at university, and it was around then, I think. I was studying sculpture," she explained, seeing Rob looking quizzical. "It didn't work out."

I tried to drag her back to the subject I was really interested in. "So something happened. Why would that mean she was going to die young?"

"The only time we talked about it, she said . . ." Tilly screwed up her face, remembering. "She said she owed her life for someone else's and that she'd have to pay sometime."

"And didn't that strike you as odd?" I demanded.

"Not really. She could be quite intense. But she really believed it. And now I realise of course that she must have had a premonition," she said calmly.

"Do you believe in that sort of thing?" I had the faintest inkling that Rob's interest in Tilly was waning.

"Sure. Why not? Past lives, second sight, destiny, fate — all that stuff." She must have seen us both looking sceptical. "OK, but who was right this time? I mean,

Rebecca did die like she'd said she would. It was her destiny, and you can't fight your destiny."

"When did she tell you about her — um — destiny?" I was afraid to catch Rob's eye.

"About two years ago. New Year's Eve. A girl I knew had a party and we got totally shitfaced on gin cocktails and ended up sitting side by side in the bath with our legs over the side, crying our hearts out over nothing, while some guy was sick in the sink. I possibly wouldn't have remembered it but she said it again in the morning when we were trying to get over our hangovers by eating a cooked breakfast in the greasy spoon down the road. God, that was a mistake. The day went horribly wrong from then on." She shuddered.

"Speaking of things going wrong, what can you tell me about Gil Maddick?"

"Gorgeous Gil. What do you want to know?"

"What happened with him and Rebecca?"

"The usual story. They were a great couple, really happy together, and then one day, they weren't. He wanted out and she had to let him go."

"I've heard he was possessive — that he shut people out of Rebecca's life."

"Where did you hear that?"

I didn't answer, waiting for her to respond to my question first. She sighed.

"He wasn't possessive, exactly, but there wasn't a lot of room for anyone else in the room when they were together. He did kind of absorb her light, if you know what I mean. He was always what she focused on, when he was there. And if you were hanging around with

192

them, pretty soon you felt as if you were in the way. Not because of anything they said, but just the way they looked at one another. I always thought it was a sign of how much they loved each other. It just goes to show, you can't always tell which relationships are really going to last."

"Did you ever get the impression that the relationship was abusive?" I asked baldly, and she looked affronted.

"No way. Never. Not in a million years."

"Are you sure?"

"Positive. She'd have told me." She sounded certain and Rob shifted in his seat in a way that I interpreted to mean *move on*.

"Did you know Rebecca had left Ventnor Chase?"

She looked troubled. "Yes, but I wasn't supposed to. I only found out by chance. I was at a job interview two months ago, just down the road from Rebecca's office, and it finished around lunchtime. I thought I'd pop in — see if she wanted to grab lunch somewhere. I really wanted to see her, just to catch up. And the receptionist told me she'd left. I couldn't believe it."

"Did you talk to her about it?"

A nod. "I mean, I tried. I rang her as soon as I walked out of there. But she wouldn't tell me what had happened, really — she just kept saying it didn't matter, and she was fine, and it wasn't a big deal." She looked at me earnestly. "It really bothered me. Because I'm always unemployed. I just can't seem to find a job that I want to do for longer than a month or two, even if I think it's interesting at the start. Rebecca wasn't like that. She'd found her niche. She really, really loved her job. I don't think she could have been OK about not working there when she didn't say anything about it, do you?"

"Someone helped her to clear out her things. Do you know who?"

Tilly's lips tightened. "I bet I can guess. Rebecca's slave."

"By which you mean . . ." I was fairly sure I knew what name she was going to say.

"Louise North. Now there's someone you should talk to about being jealous. Talk about obsessed."

"What do you mean?" I was interested in Tilly's views on Louise.

"She's not my favourite person. Rebecca was far too loyal to her. She wouldn't listen to any criticism of her, so I never bothered saying anything to her about it, but I just couldn't get on with Louise."

"Why not?" I was interested.

"You know how in a group of people there can be three or four conversations going on at once? Well, Louise would always listen to Rebecca's. Even if you were supposed to be talking to her, she would just ignore you and concentrate on what Rebecca was saying. It was rude." Tilly blushed. "You probably think that sounds stupid. It's just an example. Mainly, I didn't get on with Louise because she made it clear that she wanted to get rid of me. She's one of those people — you know, you can't be friends with anyone but me. She wanted to keep Rebecca to herself. It would have driven me mad, but Rebecca never minded. She just used to say that they had more in common than you'd think, and then she'd change the subject."

I felt a little bit sorry for Rebecca. It must have been hard work trying to keep the peace between her two competing friends. I couldn't think of two more different people than Tilly and Louise and I wouldn't have wanted to argue with either of them, or be around when they were fighting among themselves.

Tilly didn't have much more to say that was of any interest, and as we drove away I sighed deeply.

"Didn't find out as much as you'd hoped?" Rob asked.

"Actually, I found out a little bit more than I wanted to. Why couldn't she just make my life simple and tell me that Gil Maddick was a violent thug who'd threatened Rebecca's life when they split up? Mind you, it does sound to me like he was the controlling type."

"What do you think of Rebecca's premonition?"

"I think that if she could really see into the future, she should have done a better job of not being murdered."

"But it was her destiny. You can't fight your destiny," Rob quoted.

"Oh yeah. And what's your destiny?"

"A pint, a pie and an early night." He shrugged. "Well, you've got to aim high, haven't you?"

"Live the dream, Rob. Live the dream."

LOUISE

I stayed in a B&B in Salisbury the night before Rebecca's memorial service so I could visit the Haworths on my own, without the distraction of other people around. If speaking to them on the phone was hard, the thought of seeing them was much worse. I spent the train journey staring out of the window, too tense to read or work. I had taken a few days off on compassionate leave, and I was glad of the time to myself; I would have been useless in the office in any case. When I got off the train I made myself go straight to the Haworths' house, knowing that if I put it off I would find an excuse not to go.

Gerald saw the taxi pulling into the drive and came out before I had got out of the car, his wallet in his hand.

"I can pay for my own taxi," I said, pawing through my handbag in search of cash, but he had already done it. He brushed off my thanks.

"Don't worry. My pleasure. I'd have picked you up if you'd told me you were coming by train. Is there something wrong with your car?"

"Something pretty fundamental. I've scrapped it. I decided I needed a new one."

"About time too. The Peugeot was a breakdown waiting to happen." He drew me into his arms for a quick hug. "Thank you for coming to see us, Louise. Avril and I appreciate it."

"How are you?" I scanned his face. "You look tired."

"I was just going to say the same to you." His arm was heavy on my shoulders as he wheeled around and guided me into the house, to the big warm kitchen where Avril was sitting in a wicker chair near the Aga, her hands in her lap, gazing into space. She looked up when I said her name and her face lit up.

"Oh, Louise! You're here already. How are you?"

"Fine," I said automatically, although I wasn't and she could see that I wasn't. It was acutely painful to be in those familiar surroundings without Rebecca, to know that she wasn't going to breeze through the door and sit down at the table. I had eaten countless meals there with her over the years, talked, laughed, drunk tea and baked cakes. Her shadow was everywhere around me and I couldn't believe that I wouldn't see her there ever again. It was awful for me; it must have been unbearable for her parents. This was the house where Rebecca had grown up, where she had taken her first steps, said her first words, learned about the world. This was the place where she became the person I'd met as a teenager, and these were the people who had loved and encouraged her every inch of the way. She had grown up surrounded by love, but in the end, love hadn't been enough to keep her from harm, and the knowledge of what the Haworths were experiencing brought tears to my eyes.

197

"Don't." Avril stood up and came over to me to hug me. "If you start crying, I'll start, and I don't think I'll be able to stop."

I swallowed and nodded, trying to smile. Without really thinking first, I found myself saying, "I wanted you to know, I always wished you were my parents. I know no one could ever replace Rebecca, but if you could think of me as another daughter, I'd be so happy . . ."

I trailed off, seeing the shock on Avril's face before it was replaced with a polite smile. I had chosen the wrong time and used the wrong words. Avril was far too kind to say it, but I knew rejection when I saw it.

"Before we forget," Gerald said from behind me, where he was putting loose tea into the teapot, "we wanted you to choose something of Rebecca's. I don't think she'd made a will, but I'm sure she'd have wanted you to take something that's special to you as a keepsake. We thought you could choose first, before anyone else, since you're here tonight."

"I don't need anything —" I began, but he held up a hand to forestall me.

"Just run up to her room and make your choice. We've left out everything on her bed. It doesn't matter to us what you take. Anything you like."

"Really, we mean it," Avril said, smiling again — but it was a real smile this time. "We don't want to throw them away, but we don't have any use for them ourselves. And we have plenty of things around us that remind us of her."

It was easier to go along with it than to argue with them, though I wanted less than anything to go into Rebecca's room. I felt as if I was wading through knee-high water as I left the room and dragged myself up the stairs. I stood on the landing for a moment with my eyes closed but in the end I pushed open the familiar door, painted somewhat inexpertly with pink roses by the fourteen-year-old Tilly, and stood in the doorway. Someone — Avril? — had spread a linen sheet over the bed, and on the sheet there were little piles of clothes, jewellery, knickknacks of various kinds. The rest of the room was the same as ever. Pale blue curtains at the high windows, walls papered in a pretty floral print, a thick-piled grey carpet on the floor with a stain by the dressing table where a bottle of nail varnish had spilt, once upon a time. A tall Georgian chest of drawers against one wall, the top covered with the silver-lidded cut-glass perfume bottles that Rebecca had loved to collect. An armchair in the corner with her beloved toy rabbit on it. He had been too precious to take to university, or to London, she had once explained to me. He lived in her room, where it was safe.

I made myself go over to the bed, passing a wall of cream-framed photographs without looking at them, knowing that I would see myself, among others, and Rebecca, Rebecca, Rebecca . . . I looked down at the collection of things on the sheet, stirring a tangle of necklaces and bracelets with one tentative finger, picking up and putting down a small china vase that had stood on the dressing table. She had cut flowers from the garden for it, I remembered — whatever was in season. Holly at Christmas, for want of anything else, and the heavy green smell of it had scented the whole room.

I took her college sweatshirt. No one else was likely to want it. No one else would remember her lying on the floor wearing it over her pyjamas, eating dry cereal from the box and trying to memorise Tudor religious martyrs before Mods. It had faded on the cuffs from much washing, the material soft and slightly limp. I hugged it to myself for a moment, then looked at what was left on the bed. The Haworths had said to take something special. In among the jewellery, there was a pair of earrings that I had always loved, square peridots, the acid green of sour wine gums, that hung from fine gold loops. I picked them out of the pile and slipped them into the pocket of my jeans, just as I heard footsteps approaching the doorway.

"Did you find something, Louise?" I showed Avril the sweatshirt with a smile and she nodded. "Perfect. It goes all the way back to when you first met, doesn't it? We bought it for her on her first day at Latimer College, in Shepherd and Woodward on the High."

"I remember," I said softly.

"That's just what I would have wanted you to pick." She patted my arm. "Come downstairs and have some tea. Are you sure you won't stay here tonight? We'd be happy to have you."

I explained again that I had booked a room elsewhere and followed her down the stairs, carrying the sweatshirt like the sacred relic it was, with the earrings tucked away at the bottom of my pocket, a secret between Rebecca and me.

CHAPTER
SEVEN

MAEVE

Rebecca's parents didn't invite the police to her memorial service, but they had been kind enough to allow me to come anyway. I lurked at the back of the pocket-sized parish church in my least scruffy suit, then followed the mourners back up the lane to the Haworths' substantial house on the outskirts of Salisbury. I had left London on an iron-grey December day and gone to Wiltshire to eavesdrop at the service with the barest approval from DI Judd, who had sneered that he didn't see how it would be useful but I might as well go as do anything else. Nettled, I was determined to bring back something worth knowing.

The house where Rebecca Haworth grew up was Georgian and stood foursquare in its own grounds. I had left my car at the church, at the tail end of the line of mourners' cars, most of which were far nicer than mine. As I walked up the lane towards the house, a big black Mercedes with tinted windows oozed past me and turned into the drive, gravel crunching under its wheels. The driver got out smartly and opened one of the back doors and I wasn't surprised when the passenger proved to be a small man with sandy hair so thick it looked like a wig, and a beaky nose. I had spotted him in the church, where he had been surrounded by people I recognised from my visit to Ventnor Chase. It didn't take a great deal of intuition to work out that this was the famous Anton Ventnor himself, too important to walk the few hundred yards to the house. I followed him down the side of the house towards the back garden, pausing only to examine the building and its view. Big sash windows stared blankly at a vista of fields and bare hedges that unrolled like barbed wire across the hills. I wondered if the teenage Rebecca had been very bored.

The Haworths had decided to keep their visitors out of the house, probably wisely, and had erected a marquee in the garden, complete with fan heaters. It lent the scene an oddly festive air, like a wedding, except in place of the bride and groom I found a drawn and tired couple who were going through the motions of being good hosts. Years of practice, and what I recognised as deeply felt pride, gave them composure, but Rebecca's mother looked through me rather than at me and held on to my hand for a moment too long when I introduced myself.

"Thank you so much for coming. It's so very kind of you," she said in a voice that was deeper and warmer than I had expected, and I mumbled something about wanting to represent the investigating team, though I had the impression that she wasn't actually listening.

She was brittle, close-up, with a fretwork of lines around her eyes and a quiver in her jaw that she couldn't quite control. But she was a beautiful woman nonetheless, with good bones and expensively coloured hair. Her black dress was tailored to her frame and she wore elegant heels that flattered her narrow ankles. Like the house itself, Avril Haworth was the beneficiary of years of care, money and attention, and she had not lost her polish in the days since Rebecca's death, even if the light had dimmed in her eyes.

It was her husband who gently took her hand out of mine and guided me to one side, away from her. He was tall, an imposing presence in an impeccable suit and ink-black tie.

"You'll want to have a word with us, I imagine, and I would like to talk to you about the investigation. But now isn't the right time. We have guests . . . responsibilities . . ." He gestured vaguely.

"I understand — I don't want to intrude," I said, hating that I'd pushed my way into their private world. "I can come back another time, if you'd prefer."

"That won't be necessary. You can speak to us today, once everyone has gone. They won't stay long. Avril thought that we should invite Rebecca's friends to join us here since so many of them travelled down from London for the service, and of course our friends are here too. It's very simple, though. A buffet. Just sandwiches and tea or coffee. With the weather, we thought people would need warming up." He looked around, the dark eyes that I'd noticed in his photograph scanning the gathering, missing nothing. "We decided not to serve alcohol. It's not a party, after all. And most of the guests are driving."

204

I nodded, reflecting on the unmistakable steel in his voice. Rebecca's father was not a pushover, grief-stricken though he was.

I left Gerald Haworth to his guests and slipped through to the far side of the marquee, picking up a glass of water from a bow-tied waiter on the way. I took up a position on the edge of the crowd, trying to fade into the background. There must have been sixty people there, mostly wearing sober colours and muttering quietly to one another. The noise level was not what might have been expected from such a large group, but as Gerald Haworth had said, this was not a party. I saw Anton Ventnor in the centre of the marquee, surrounded by his staff. I had imagined an imposing, powerful man from what I had heard from his employees, and was amused at my own assumptions. He spent most of the time looking around him, but he had an odd trick of holding his glass in front of his mouth on the rare occasions that he actually spoke. It was something I associated with habitual liars, and my interest sharpened. I might not have managed to speak to him so far, but Anton Ventnor was definitely still on my list. The others from Ventnor Chase were slightly too well dressed for the occasion, I thought — teetering in fashionable heels, expensively made-up, carrying the latest in designer bags. That was the pond Rebecca had been swimming in. That was how she had chosen to live her life. I could tell that status was all-important for them, and wondered if any of them had bothered to keep in touch with her after her dismissal, or if she had even wanted them to. Rebecca's background was one of effortless success and accomplishment; I wondered how she had coped with disgrace.

The older guests had to be neighbours and friends of the Haworths, but there were plenty of younger people there too, including Tilly Shaw who was everywhere at once, hugging people tenderly, passing around plates, moving chairs from one end of the marquee to the other for the sake of the frailer guests. She had straightened her hair and added a black streak to the front. It went well with her short, tight dress. Not conventional mourning wear, but then nothing about Tilly was particularly conventional. I looked for her polar opposite and found her after a few seconds — Louise North, whom I had spotted in the church, though I didn't think she'd seen me. Her head had been bent as she sat in the pew behind the Haworths, and I hadn't noticed her looking around. At one point she had leaned forward to put her hand on Avril's shoulder as Rebecca's mother shook with sobs. I guessed she must have known the Haworths for a long time. She was standing on the other side of the marquee, holding a cup of tea but not actually drinking it, listening to an elderly man in a stripy tie who was waving his hands around wildly as he talked. To give her her due, she didn't appear to flinch, even when he got pretty close with the disintegrating sandwich he was holding in his right hand. I would have laid money that he was also a spitter.

Louise wasn't wearing make-up and her cheeks were pale, her lips almost colourless, but she looked smart in a navy-blue coat that fitted her frame beautifully. Her hair was scraped back into a ponytail that was so tightly controlled not a single wisp appeared to have worked free. I put a hand up to my own head, suddenly self-conscious about the state of my hair, which had dried wild again. It was hard to look groomed when every gust of the scarifying wind carried a handful of rain. The fact that Louise North had managed it was mildly irritating.

I was just thinking about going to her rescue when someone jostled my elbow and I moved out of their way automatically, murmuring something that might have been taken as an apology. Instead of going on, however, they stood beside me, a little too close for comfort. Gil Maddick, today film-star handsome in a dark suit with an open-necked white shirt. I guessed it was about as formal as he got. He grinned down at me without the least hint of warmth.

"Fancy meeting you here. What brings you to this part of the world? You can't possibly think you're going to find the killer at Rebecca's memorial service."

"I'm representing the investigative team. May I ask why you're here? I had the impression that you didn't care too much about Rebecca or what happened to her."

"I was invited."

I raised my eyebrows. "Really? By the Haworths? Didn't they know you and Rebecca had split up?"

"Silly Tilly asked me to come along and pay my respects. She helped to organise this ridiculous shindig. A funeral with no corpse. *Hamlet* without the prince."

He spoke lightly, but again I had the impression that he was under pressure.

"You didn't have to come," I pointed out. "I'm sure no one would have noticed."

Instead of answering me, he stared over my shoulder, and I turned to see that he was looking straight at Louise North. Almost as if she'd felt his eyes on her, she looked up and met his gaze. I didn't see her blink; she might not even have breathed. She reminded me of a hare in long grass, startled to have been seen, ready to run at a moment's notice.

The look on his face when I swung back was unreadable, at least to me. It took him a second or two to remember that I was standing there, and I needn't have bothered waiting for a reply, because all I got was a muttered, "Excuse me," before he walked off towards the buffet. And when I looked back in Louise's direction, she had disappeared.

It took me quite a while to get close enough to Anton Ventnor to strike up a conversation, surrounded as he was by attentive acolytes. In the end, I stalked him until he went to the very posh Portaloos the Haworths had hired, and lay in wait outside. He did not look altogether thrilled to be accosted by me, but good manners or good training won out.

"How can I help you, Miss . . ."

"Detective Constable Maeve Kerrigan," I said firmly, enunciating each and every last syllable.

He snapped his fingers in recognition. "You wanted to talk to me."

"And you never called me back. Not to worry. Now's as good a time as any."

His eyelids flickered. "Is it? I don't think —"

"It won't take long." I grabbed his arm and steered him through a gap in the tent, towards an unoccupied corner of the garden. He came without demur, probably too startled by the physical contact to offer any resistance. Besides, he was a good five inches shorter than me, and twenty years older, and I didn't think he was in peak physical condition. I was stronger than him and he knew it. And I had counted on him not wanting to make a scene.

A small stream cut through the Haworths' garden, and they had put a wrought-iron bench beside it. Overhung with the long trailing strands of a weeping willow, it was an impossibly pretty, romantic setting in spite of the fact that the willow was bald at that time of year and the ground underneath the bench was muddy. The effect was rather spoilt in any case by the small, cross, middle-aged man in a tight-fitting suit who was sharing the bench with me, even before you noticed that his wig was making a bid for freedom down the back of his head.

"Surely this could have waited until we got back to London." He sounded irritated.

"Don't you want to get it over with now?" I took my notebook out of my bag and flipped it open. "You were Rebecca Haworth's employer for four years, is that right?"

"If you say so." He caught the glint of annoyance I couldn't quite suppress, and sighed. "Yes, then. I hired her four and a half years ago. She was a very important part of my team and I paid her very well indeed."

"What sort of a person was she?"

He stared into the distance, considering. "If you'd asked me that eight months ago, I'd have told you that she was the dream employee. Hardworking, dedicated, never put herself before the work. She was excellent with our clients. Well liked in the company."

"Did you like her?"

He turned to look at me, eyebrows raised. "Not more than I should have. We had a pleasant professional relationship, no more than that."

"Why did Rebecca leave the company?" I wanted to hear his version of events.

"She left because I asked her to go. She wouldn't have gone of her own volition, I can assure you. Unfortunately she had developed some bad habits — well, one bad habit, to be precise — and became unreliable. I couldn't let her continue to work in my company. The damage to our reputation was insupportable."

"Did you confront her about her cocaine use?"

He spread out his hands. "What could I say? I didn't want to waste my time with her. If she had genuinely cared more about her job than about the drugs, she wouldn't have let them interfere with her ability to work. She had made her choice already. I simply formalised it."

"So you didn't give her an opportunity to get clean before you sacked her."

210

"I think you'll find that she resigned." His voice was nasal and high-pitched, and at that moment utterly smug.

"I'm sure she wouldn't have had a leg to stand on at an employment tribunal. But she'd worked for you for quite a while. I understand from her colleagues that she was very upset to be leaving Ventnor Chase."

"That is an understatement." He gave a little giggle. "I might have been prepared to give her another chance if she hadn't reacted the way she did. It showed me she had lost all sense of judgement — all her self-respect. She offered me — I think the phrase is sexual favours? I had to decline, of course." He took out a purple handkerchief that matched his tie and blotted his upper lip deliberately. "I thought it was an extraordinary thing to do. I had known for some time that she was promiscuous, but I was inclined to turn a blind eye. Once she brought it into the workplace, I'm afraid I had had enough."

"She was desperate," I said quietly. *She must have been.*

"That was nothing to do with me. I couldn't employ her any longer. Not after she grovelled like that."

He stood up and wadded his handkerchief back into his pocket. "If that's all you need from me, I must go. I'd like to get back to London before the end of the working day. You can contact my PA if you have any more questions for me."

"Great," I said unenthusiastically. "Thanks."

He started to walk away, then stopped and turned back. "You know, she was a good member of my team. She'd have kept her job if she hadn't begged me to change my mind. Never beg, DC Kerrigan, no matter how tempting it may be."

I could taste my dislike for him. "I'll try to remember that."

He nodded, then strutted away, trying and failing to look like a taller man than he was. Anton Ventnor, prize git. I would have dreaded going in to an office he ran; I would have been delighted to get away from him if I'd been in Rebecca's shoes. But I wasn't Rebecca; I didn't even really know what she was like. The highly organised business-woman. The good-time girl you'd never marry. The loyal, scatty friend. The desperate employee. I had no doubt that I would get a different account of Rebecca's character from her parents, when I spoke to them. She had been whatever people wanted her to be, right up to the moment when what they wanted her to be was dead.

I couldn't face returning to the marquee immediately — I wanted to let Ventnor get a good head start so I didn't have to see him again. I wandered in the other direction instead, following the bank of the little stream, my feet slipping on the grass that was still patched with frost in places. I came to a brick wall enclosing a formal garden, its iron gate standing ajar. It was a rose garden, I discovered, and particularly bleak at that time of year when neither leaves nor flowers relieved the greyness of the scene. The bare ashy branches bristled with thorns like an illustration from an old-fashioned edition of *Sleeping Beauty*. The garden was divided into four beds with a cobbled path between each, leading to the centre where a sundial

212

stood, the spherical kind made of a collection of rings speared through with an arrow. It was a lovely thing but useless in the flat winter daylight that wasn't bright enough to cast proper shadows. Not, it had to be said, that I was very good at reading sundials at the best of times. I walked along the path to get a closer look. The sundial stood on a stone plinth. Around the base there was an inscription chiselled in narrow script and I tilted my head to one side to read it.

• DO NOT KILL TIME •

"There's more on this side."

I hadn't noticed anyone else in the garden, but when I looked up, Louise North was standing opposite me, her hands buried in the pockets of her coat. She had wrapped a soft grey scarf several times around her neck, muffling her up to the ears. Her nose and eyes were red, which could have been because of the cold or her grief, and a few strands of her hair had come loose, framing her face so that she looked softer, younger, more human, and infinitely more likable.

"Let's see." I came around to her side of the sundial and read:

• IT WILL SURELY KILL THEE •

"Very cheerful."

"I wouldn't think that Avril and Gerald imagined a day like today when they commissioned it. It's the sort of thing Avril loves. Have you been inside the house?"

213

I shook my head. "I'm talking to the Haworths later on."

"You'll see what I mean then. She never misses an opportunity to share a little wisdom, put it that way."

I looked back at the sundial and reached out to trace one of the rings with a finger. "How does this work, do you know?"

"It's called an armillary sphere. The arrow runs through it from north to south. When the sun shines on it, you're supposed to be able to tell the time from where the arrow's shadow falls on this band around the outside. If you look closely, you can see it's marked with the hours."

I looked at where she was indicating and saw faint indentations in the brass ring that proved to be, on closer inspection, roman numerals. "And can you? Tell the time, I mean."

"Sort of." She smiled. "Clocks are easier. But this is Gerald's pride and joy. This little garden is the reason he bought the house in the first place. It was the vegetable garden originally, but the minute he saw it, he knew what he wanted to do with it. He cleared the whole thing, laid out the beds and planted the roses. They're wonderful in the summer. He only likes the old-fashioned kind, damask roses, because the scent is so incredible." She pointed. "They all have names, look."

I hadn't noticed it before, but at the base of each bush there was a little plaque. I walked around, reading them. *Pompon des Princes. Comte de Chambord.*

Madame Hardy. La Ville de Bruxelles. Blanc de Vibert. Rose du Roi. Quatre Saisons.

"It's like heaven when they're all in bloom. But most of the year, they're just a hell of a lot of work for not very much reward." Her tone was indulgent rather than disapproving.

"Rebecca didn't take after her father, did she? She didn't even have a pot plant in her flat."

"She couldn't see the point. And a plant wouldn't have lasted long if she had tried to look after one." Louise shook her head. "She had enough trouble looking after herself. She never even managed to remember to collect her dry cleaning."

I was only half-listening to Louise. My attention had been caught by something else. In shaking her head, she had loosened the scarf around her neck so that the fine material — cashmere, at a guess — sagged forward, exposing her throat. On the right side of her neck I could see an oval blood bruise, shocking against her pallor, shocking also in its implications. Because her neck had been conspicuously unmarked when I'd seen her earlier in the marquee, which meant that somehow, at some point between then and now, she had been branded with what could only be a love bite.

"That looks nasty," I said mildly, pointing at it. "You might want to cover it up before the Haworths see it."

Her hand flew up instantly to hide it, and colour flooded into her cheeks. Most people would have said something to explain it away, even if it was an obvious lie. Louise North had far more self-possession than that. She settled for giving me a meaningless half-smile as she rearranged her scarf, pulling it more tightly around her neck.

"Much better."

If she heard the mockery in my voice, she didn't acknowledge it. She pulled back her sleeve and checked her watch, revealing a reddish mark that circled her narrow wrist just above the strap. She saw it at the same time as me and shook the material down again in a hurry. "I'd better get going."

"Of course," I said blandly, and moved out of her way so she could get past me. Instead, she stopped and bit her lip, uncertain for once.

"DC Kerrigan, can I ask you a favour? Could you keep me informed about how the investigation is going? It's just that — well — I'd like to know what's happening. If you're making progress, I mean. I know I'm not part of the family — not formally — but Rebecca was like a sister to me. I just can't stop thinking about what happened to her and I can't keep bothering her parents to find out if they've heard anything." Her voice cracked a little and her eyes were suddenly swimming with tears.

I told her I would, and then watched her walk out of the garden with her head bent, her arms wrapped around herself. If it was acting, it was impressive. If it was for real, it made me even more confused about Louise North than I had been already.

The marquee had emptied out by the time I went back. Only the die-hards remained, an odd collection of elderly people who had nowhere better to be and a clutch of younger types, all mid-twenties, who had a little party of their own going on in one corner. Every so often there was a burst of loud laughter from them. It jarred, considering the nature of the occasion, but I had often noticed that these gatherings brought out the heartiness in mourners. It was as if the life force needed to declare itself again, having looked death full in the face for too long.

"Rebecca's friends from university," Gerald Haworth observed, coming to stand beside me. "It's something of a reunion for them. I haven't the heart to send them home. She would have loved bringing people together." He sounded wistful, but also very tired.

"If you don't want to boot them out, I'm quite happy to direct them to the nearest pub."

He looked at me like a drowning man spotting a life jacket within arm's reach. "Would you? There's one about a mile down the road."

I got the directions from him and sauntered over to the little group, nine of them. "I think it's time you moved on and gave the Haworths a bit of peace. Would you mind taking this little shindig to the pub?"

The man that I had marked down as the troublemaker of the group, tall, broad-shouldered and barrel-chested, with the sparse fair hair and high colour of the classic upper-class Englishman, looked me up and down with frank appraisal. "And who are you, might I ask?"

I introduced myself, leading with my rank and leaving out my first name. He could bloody well DC Kerrigan me and like it, I found myself thinking.

The girl next to him grabbed his arm. "Come on, Leo. She's right. We're making too much noise."

"I don't see why we should have to move just because Plod wants us to," he objected, staring down at me belligerently with glassy eyes. I could smell alcohol on his breath from where I was standing, and acting on a hunch, I reached out and slipped my hand into his jacket pocket, coming up with a silver hip flask before he had time to react.

"Classy," I said, waggling it at him. "Needed a bit of Dutch courage? I hope you're not driving."

"He's not," one of the other men said quickly. "I'm taking him back to London and I haven't been drinking."

"No chance, Mike. You're not driving my car." Leo swayed slightly as he spoke. The girl dragged on his arm again and he shook himself free, snapping, "For God's sake, Debs."

"I'd like to see you take his keys now, please. And make sure you have insurance that covers you before you take the car on the public road. I'll be letting my colleagues in Traffic know to keep an eye out for it on the way back to London."

Mike held out his hand and after a moment Leo dug into his trouser pocket and dropped the keys into his outstretched palm.

I flicked open the hip flask and tilted it so the remaining contents spattered out onto the carpet-tiled floor of the marquee, which soaked it up quickly. "Oh dear. You seem to be out of booze. Time to go, I think."

218

The others had already started to drift away, leaving Leo staring down at me like a baffled bull, flanked by the girl and Mike, who had taken his other arm. I kept my expression completely neutral, careful not to suggest any hint of amusement at the man's expense. Nine-tenths of wielding authority was having the confidence not to make a song and dance of it, I'd always found on the street. You had to leave people a bit of self-respect, and somewhere to go. And in this case, given that the somewhere was a pub, it wasn't such a tough decision after all.

"Can I have that back?" Leo nodded at the hip flask.

"With pleasure." I handed it over and watched his friends wheel him around and point him in the direction of the exit, where Rebecca's father shook their hands.

It took another half-hour for the remaining mourners to take the hint and say their farewells, leaving only the caterers, who were collecting cups and glasses, stacking chairs and folding away their trestle tables. The empty marquee flapped and billowed in the wind, and a draught I hadn't noticed earlier whistled around my ankles. Avril Haworth sat down on one of the few chairs that remained and watched them tidying up with a glazed expression on her face, as if she wasn't really seeing them. Her husband was writing a cheque in the corner. I went across to where she was sitting and, on an impulse, bent down.

"Mrs Haworth? Can I get you anything — a glass of water, or . . ."

I trailed off as she shook her head. "So kind of you. But really, I'm all right. I just need a little rest. We haven't been sleeping well since —" She broke off and put one hand to her head. I took the other one in mine. It was bloodless and chilled.

"You're freezing. I think we should get you indoors."

"I'll take her." Gerald Haworth bent over his wife and helped her to her feet. "Come in, DC Kerrigan. I haven't forgotten that you're here to talk to us."

"If it's not a good time . . ." I began, inwardly swearing at my complete inability to be forceful. If I had to come all the way back to interview them another time, it would be my own fault.

"No, no. We'll talk to you now. We'd rather get it over with."

He spoke for both of them, I noticed with an automatic jolt of feminist outrage that I instantly suppressed because really, Avril Haworth looked in no condition to make any decisions for herself. Supported by her husband, she walked the short distance across from the marquee to the back door of the house, which he had taken the precaution of locking.

"I was warned to be careful," he said heavily, turning the key and opening it for me to go through. "Burglars target houses where there's been a bereavement, I understand."

"Some people have no conscience, Mr Haworth."

"Gerald," he corrected me. "And Avril."

"You must call me Maeve, then."

"It's a pretty name," Avril said vaguely. "The original Maeve was an Irish queen, wasn't she?"

"Apparently so." In fact, I had been named for my great-grandmother but I didn't bother to share that with them. And she had been regal enough in her own way, by all accounts.

I stepped into a small tiled room where coats hung on hooks and wellies and outdoor shoes slotted neatly into a bench. A set of shelves was filled with gardening equipment and a range of terracotta pots stood in stacks along one wall. Above them, a little stone plaque read: "To garden is to open your heart to the sky", and I recalled what Louise had said with an inward sigh. There was something fundamentally innocent about the Haworths and their perfect life, something that I didn't think would survive the experience of losing their daughter, and I wished things could be different.

The Haworths led the way through a big, warm kitchen into a sitting room. Comfortably shabby but indefinably gracious, the room was instantly welcoming as Gerald went around the room turning on lamps. His wife sat down on the edge of a sofa and I sat down opposite her, in an armchair that would be difficult to struggle out of when the time came to go. I was glad of the cushion I tucked in behind me, noticing in passing that it was embroidered with "A Happy House is a Home". *And an unhappy house is hell on earth.*

"I'm sure the last thing you want to do is to talk to me at this stage in the day," I began. "I really appreciate it."

Gerald made a sharp gesture. "Don't mention it. Anything that might help."

"I've been trying to get some idea of Rebecca's personality by talking to people who knew her well. I

221

wonder — if it wouldn't be too upsetting — if you could tell me about your relationship with her. What was she like?"

It was Avril who answered me, and if tears were standing in her eyes, her voice was steady. "She was like sunshine on a cold day. She was the light of our lives."

Her husband cleared his throat. "We were very proud of her, of course. But she really was special. Bright, funny, popular, loving — everything you could wish for in a daughter. You only have to look at the people who came here today. There were friends of hers from kindergarten and primary school, not to mention her university friends and her colleagues. She was very much loved, you see."

"It was very good of the Ventnor Chase people to come down, wasn't it?" Avril turned to her husband. "Especially when they must be so busy. I mean, they have to manage without her too. Mr Ventnor told me he didn't know how they're ever going to replace her."

So Avril, at any rate, had no idea that her daughter wasn't working there at the time of her death, and Anton Ventnor had been kind enough to let her go on thinking that. I would have felt one degree warmer towards him if I hadn't suspected that he had enjoyed the deceit.

"Did Rebecca ever talk to you about work?"

"Only to say things were going well," Gerald said. "She worked very hard. We worried about her, sometimes, because she was out all the time. Always going at a hundred miles an hour, that was our girl. But you couldn't tell her anything. She had to find her own way. We didn't expect anything of her, except that she should be happy. And I really do believe she was."

I mumbled something that might have been agreement, my tongue suddenly feeling too big for my mouth. I should have asked Anton Ventnor for tips on how to lie.

Over the next hour, I learned that Rebecca had been a precocious but polite child who had loved reading, horses and, as a teen, cross-country running. In time she had grown out of the horses but kept up the running and the reading. She had applied to Oxford to study history rather than English because she had thought a history degree was more likely to be useful. Her life was one of privilege but Rebecca had worked hard for what she got, and had been overjoyed to get into the college of her choice at Oxford.

"She met Louise there — did you get a chance to talk to her? Lovely girl. They were such close friends." Avril sounded dreamy, as if she had lost sight of the reason for our conversation in the pleasure of recollecting happier times. The table at Avril's elbow held a framed print of the same picture of Rebecca and Louise that I'd seen in Rebecca's flat.

"Did she like Oxford?" I asked, thinking of what Tilly Shaw had told me. I still hadn't managed to work out what had happened to Rebecca to make her think her life was forfeit.

The Haworths looked at me for a moment, then at one another, and there was an uneasiness in the silence that fell before Gerald spoke.

"She did. But she struggled a bit in her third year. She deferred, in fact — left Oxford three weeks before she was due to start her final exams and had to go back the following year to sit them."

"What happened?"

Avril took over. "Oh, it was tragic. One of the boys in her year died — he drowned, actually. It happened on the first of May — you know, May Day, during the celebrations that they have every year. And Rebecca couldn't get over it. She felt things very deeply, you see, and she started having nightmares about him. She couldn't study, or eat, or anything, so in the end we went up and got her. Her tutor was tremendous — he managed to get the history faculty to allow her to defer, and when she went back the following year, even though she wasn't able to have any formal tuition, he saw her a couple of times to talk over the papers she was going to be sitting. He was really so kind. Can you remember his name, darling?"

"Something Faraday. I'll look it up. I think she has one of his books in her room." Completely unconscious that he had used the present tense about his daughter, Gerald got up and left before I could tell him I would find it out from the college.

"So this boy — was he Rebecca's boyfriend?"

"Not officially, as far as I knew, but you know what they're like at that age. It was all completely innocent, from what Rebecca told us. He was a lovely boy, though — Adam, he was called. The surname was something like Rowland. No, Rowley, that was it. Adam Rowley. It was *so* sad. Really, it was the first shadow in Rebecca's life. Her grandparents had died, but when she was too little to remember them, so it was really the first bereavement she'd experienced, and it hit her terribly hard. She lost so much weight — just cried all the time. It took her months and months to get back to normal. And when she did go back to Oxford to sit her exams, of course it was terribly difficult and she did wonderfully well considering."

"How did she get on?" I asked, for the sake of being polite more than anything else.

"She got a 2.2," Avril answered bravely. "She was on for a first, they said, before she had her trouble with her nerves. But of course we were just delighted that she got her degree in the end."

I made a note of the name; I would chase it up with Thames Valley CID.

"Caspian Faraday." Gerald came back into the room, slightly out of breath, holding a hardback book.

"Oh, well done for finding it," his wife said.

"Not difficult. She'd shelved it alphabetically. You know Rebecca, everything in its place." The Haworths hadn't been to Rebecca's flat much, I surmised.

He handed the book to me. "Faraday published this a couple of years ago. We gave it to Rebecca for Christmas when it came out. I don't know if she ever had a chance to read it, though. It's about the Hundred Years War. He's made a bit of a career out of the Plantagenets. Television and so forth. This was a bestseller."

I flicked through the pages idly, stopping at the back flap where a black-and-white author photograph revealed that Caspian Faraday was not the elderly, bespectacled, tweed-jacket-wearing don I had been imagining, but a seriously attractive, chiselled man in his late thirties with cropped fair hair and piercing eyes that were translucent in the picture. They just had to be bright blue.

The Haworths seemed to be waiting for me to say something. "Very interesting."

"It is," Gerald said. "He really knows his stuff. Rebecca worshipped him."

I would need to talk to Dr Faraday. And if I was going to talk to him and the police who investigated Adam Rowley's death, I might as well make it a field trip rather than doing it all by phone. As today had reminded me, it was always good to get out of London for a few hours, good to get away from the overheated incident room and the constant jockeying for position that was a permanent feature of Godley's team.

Rebecca's parents seemed to have run out of steam all of a sudden. Gerald had sat down beside his wife again and she took his hand, then leaned against his shoulder as if she couldn't hold herself up any more.

"I should go," I said quickly. "I've taken up too much of your time."

"Rebecca was very good about staying in touch, but we didn't come up to see her in London much. You'd have to talk to her friends and her workmates to find out about how she lived once she left home," Avril said vaguely.

"I've been speaking to them already. They've been very helpful."

"All we know," Gerald said, and his eyes were full of pain, "is that she was doing very well. Very well indeed. She was happy. And she had everything to live for. So please, Maeve, do find the person who did this to her, for our sake."

It wasn't the first time a victim's family had appealed to me to deliver justice for them, but it brought a lump to my throat and I had to cough to clear it before I could respond.

"I'll do my best. You have my word."

"It would mean so much to us," he said, and I looked away as his chin quivered, knowing that he would want to seem in control.

"We wanted more children," Avril said, and her voice was heavy with grief. "But it wasn't to be. She was really our world." She sat up again, her head held high, dignity intact. "So is there anything else we can help you with? Anything else we can tell you?"

I shook my head. She had said all there was to say.

LOUISE

I realised almost as soon as I got there that going to the memorial service was a mistake. I should have said my goodbyes to the Haworths the night before and stayed away. I felt awkward when I walked into the church and saw a cluster of ex-Latimer people in one of the side aisles. I didn't know them well enough to make conversation but I couldn't ignore them completely without seeming rude. I settled on a half-wave and not-quite-a-smile. A cheery hello seemed inappropriate anyway, given the circumstances. They acknowledged it in much the same way, the girls turning around to look at me with frank interest, assessing how I had changed, what I was wearing, how much I was probably earning. I didn't waste time wondering about them in the same way, mainly because I didn't care enough to bother.

As I sat down in the second pew from the front, a skinny arm snaked around my shoulders and I almost gagged on the overwhelming vanilla scent that Tilly always wore.

"Thanks for coming. I'll talk to you later on, OK?"

She was gone before I had a chance to reply and I settled back into the pew, knowing that she wouldn't necessarily be back, which was fine by me. I had little enough to say to her at the best of times. She was in her element, meeting and greeting as if she was in charge of the ceremony.

I had been worried about breaking down in public, but in fact I didn't feel anything as tribute was paid to my best friend and her beautiful, too-short life. I felt numb. In fact, I went away somewhere inside myself and it took a tremendous effort to take note of what was going on in the church, of Avril's distress, of the somewhat incongruous readings Tilly had chosen. When it was all over, I followed the mourners back to the house without really thinking about it. It seemed easier to drift along in their wake, to pick up a cup of tea from the buffet and adopt a listening expression as people I'd never met before and would never meet again talked at me about nothing. I felt vacant. Not myself. And when I looked up to find Gil Maddick staring at me through the crowd, it was like plunging through ice into deep, cold water. Once I locked eyes with him, I couldn't break my gaze. I had looked for him in the church and not seen him; I had scanned the crowd casually on my arrival at the house and thought that he had decided not to come. I would have seen him if he had been there, I knew that much.

As he turned back to the person he was with — the police officer, I realised with a shock of recognition — I made myself move, mumbling something polite to the Haworths' ancient neighbour as I turned away from him. I slipped out through the side of the marquee and walked at speed through the garden, putting space between me and Gil. The cold air was reviving and I took deep breaths, trying to slow my pulse. There was nothing to worry about. Certainly nothing to fear. But seeing him in person had been jarring and I didn't truly relax until I had slipped through the gate at the end of the garden and reached the sanctuary of the orchard. The trees stood in tidy rows, spreading bare branches overhead, and I walked down the line of quinces. Their fruit was far too bitter to eat, the summers not long enough or warm enough for them, but Gerald delighted in the blossom in spring. They were his investment in the future, he'd told me. By the time the climate had warmed up a degree or two, they would be mature and ready to fruit in abundance. It was his particular sort of quixotic logic, and it always surprised and amused me.

I turned the corner at the bottom of the orchard, still thinking about trees, and walked straight into Gil's white-shirted chest with a gasp of surprise. He caught me, holding on to my upper arms.

"We meet at last. You didn't call me back, Louise."

"I didn't have anything to say to you." My heart was racing but I forced myself to meet his gaze as if I was completely calm.

"No? You've been saying plenty to other people, though, haven't you? I've had the police around, talking to me about poor darling Rebecca."

"They've been talking to all her friends. They talked to me too."

"I know. You're the one who pointed them in my direction, aren't you?"

230

"If you have nothing to hide, you shouldn't have been worried about it."

"Why would I have anything to hide? She was murdered by a serial killer. Nothing to do with me."

With some difficulty, I freed myself so I could reach into my pocket. "I found this."

He took the pen from me and turned it around, reading the initials.

"That's you, isn't it? GKM. Gilbert K Maddick. What does the 'K' stand for? Kenneth?"

"Kendall. Family name." He handed it back to me, outwardly unmoved. "Sorry, I've never seen that before."

"I found it in Rebecca's flat. You were there, weren't you?"

"Not recently."

"It was on the coffee table."

"Maybe she knew someone else with the same initials." He sounded bored. "I really don't know anything about it, I'm afraid. And I don't see that it's any of your business."

"I'm making it my business."

He still held me lightly, so I couldn't turn away. "Poor Louise. What are you going to do with yourself now that Bex is gone?"

"Don't take the piss," I said sharply. "She was my friend."

"I wouldn't dream of it." He looked down at me. "You look tired, Louise. But dry-eyed. No tears. Your best friend is dead and gone and you haven't cried today, have you? Not in the church, not here at her house. I've never met anyone so cold."

"I'm not cold," I said automatically, then almost laughed as I realised the irony in it; I was contradicting the words with my very manner. Someone more emotional might have been upset by what he was saying, but it didn't annoy me, so it had to be true. *Quod erat demonstrandum.*

"There's no passion in you," Gil went on. "At least, I've never seen it."

"Trust me, you never will." I twisted free of him and started to walk off, but he grabbed my wrist, pulling me back.

"Where are you going?"

"Away from you."

He stared down at me, frowning, seemingly at a loss.

"Look, what do you want from me?"

"Strangely enough, this." He bent his head and kissed me, hard, before I could move away, and for a couple of seconds I found myself responding, pressing against him. A wave of desire swept over me and I swayed, all caution swept away, my mind a blank.

But then the thoughts started to drop back into my head like stones toppling into a deep well. This was Gil. And it was wrong. More than that, it was stupid.

I pushed my hands against his chest and he let go of me.

"Well, what a surprise. She isn't cold to the touch after all."

"Why don't you piss off and leave me alone." I was struggling to maintain my composure, pretending to be unmoved, but my face was flaming.

"Would you like me to? Really?"

I couldn't answer him. What I really wanted was for him to kiss me again. I settled for asking, "Why are you doing this?"

He shrugged. "Because I want to. I have always wanted to, I think."

"Bullshit. You avoided me the whole time you were with Rebecca. You barely spoke to me."

"I was afraid she'd notice that I was more interested in you. I liked her, you know. But I was always intrigued by you, Louise. And I've never known quite what you're thinking."

"Just as well, probably."

He laughed. "Yes, you've never made any secret of not liking me. Don't worry, I don't care about that. I'll convince you."

"You won't get the chance," I assured him, edging backwards. I needed to get away from him. I needed to think.

"Won't I?" He stepped closer, following my steps like a dancer. "You don't kiss someone like that and walk away, Louise."

"Watch me."

"One for the road?" He raised his eyebrows and laughed as I shook my head. "You want to say yes, don't you?"

"If I wanted to say yes, I would say it."

"So you don't want me to kiss you again. Just so I'm clear."

"No."

"Ever?"

"Never."

"Because I was thinking . . . next time, I might kiss you here." He trailed his fingers down my arm until they reached my palm, where he folded my fingers over. "Or here." His hand moved to cup my breast and even through layers of clothes I could feel his warmth. "Or here."

I couldn't help myself; as his hands moved about my body, I melted into his arms again. It was the last time, I promised myself. He was the one who broke away, at last. With a self-satisfied smirk, he ran a finger down my neck. "Oh dear."

"What is it?"

"I've left my mark. You've got a beautiful love bite." He pulled my scarf up around my throat. "That must mean you're mine now."

"What are you, a teenager or something? You can't have done it by accident." Not only was it starting to ache, but it would take days to fade. And in the meantime, it announced to anyone who cared to notice it what I had been doing.

"Sorry," he said, not sounding it, and started to walk away. "I think we should get back, don't you? Before someone notices we're gone?"

I watched him go through the orchard, whistling as he went. He didn't look around to see if I was following. I pulled the scarf more tightly around my neck and wished I had a mirror. All he had wanted was to make me respond to him, to see if he could. I felt humiliated, as if what he had said and done had been the most crude of practical jokes. And I had fallen for it from a height.

"For the last time, though," I said aloud. "Never again."

I left the orchard by a different gate, coming back through the other side of the garden so I wouldn't run into him again. Nor did I, but I found the police detective wandering around the rose garden and stopped to chat to her. It was utterly predictable that she would notice the mark on my neck; she didn't seem to be the sort who missed much.

I phoned for a taxi as soon as I left her, heading back into the marquee to say goodbye to Rebecca's parents. I saw Avril first and went over to her, realising too late that Gerald was deep in conversation with Gil.

"I've got to go, I'm afraid, if I'm going to make my train."

"Thank you for coming, darling. It meant so much." She clung onto my arm. "Do come back and see us. Often. We'll miss you if you go away."

"I promise, I will."

"Can I give you a lift?" Gil sounded pleasant, polite, a little bit remote and I couldn't look at him as I shook my head.

"I'm getting a taxi."

"No need for that," Gerald said firmly. "Gil's car is outside. Let him drive you. He's leaving now too."

I did my very best to argue my way out of it, but the Haworths were determined, and Gil listened to my protests with a studiously neutral expression. I had to agree in the end, of course, as I couldn't tell them why I didn't want to go two yards down the road with their daughter's ex-boyfriend, let alone as far as the station.

I glared at Gil as he opened the passenger door of his low-slung vintage Jaguar, sleek in British Racing Green. He waited patiently for me to get in. "Don't think I'm pleased."

"Aren't you? It's better than a dodgy local cab that smells of pine air freshener."

"The company leaves something to be desired."

"Don't be a bitch. I'm doing you a favour."

He slammed the door on me and walked around the back of the car, taking his time, whistling as he sat into the driver's seat.

I looked across at him, at the little smile that curved the corners of his mouth, at the total confidence that emanated from him, and somehow I wasn't surprised when he drove straight past the station without stopping.

"After all, we're both going to London. Why not go together?"

There were too many reasons to list them so I stared out of the window instead, hiding a smile of my own. I rarely gambled — I liked certainty in all things — but for once I was enjoying the recklessness that came from being in this situation, the exhilaration of being in freefall and not knowing where I was going to land. I could cope with Gil, I thought. Trouble he may be, but I knew a fair bit about him. Forewarned was forearmed. If he messed with me, Gil Maddick wasn't going to know what had hit him.

At least, that was what I told myself.

CHAPTER
EIGHT

MAEVE

I arrived in Oxford two days after the memorial service with a notebook full of questions and a bad feeling in the pit of my stomach. It wasn't actually that far from London, but the train journey had taken a surprisingly long time, stopping at every hole in the hedge between Paddington and the university city. It had been a slow trip and felt slower because the heating was broken. The inside of the windows in my carriage had frosted over by the time we pulled into the station, and I was chilled to the bone.

The day was raw and dank. Fog hung in the air and I tucked my chin down into my chest, walking fast to get to where I was going without being tempted to do any sight-seeing. The city was hiding its charms effectively as my route took me through the shopping precinct that was somehow more depressing for being decked out with uninspired Christmas lights. The colleges carried on their business behind high walls that hid most of the grandeur I had been expecting. In fact, the main difference between Oxford and any other provincial city was the number of tourists mixed in with the Christmas shoppers in the crowds I had to dodge on my way down the wide, busy street named St Aldates. I was curious enough to look through the heavy, imposing archway on my left as I walked past Christ Church, or I would have looked if a bowler-hatted man with a purple-veined nose and a forbidding expression hadn't been barring the way. A sign in front of him declared the college to be closed to the public. It might as well have said "no riffraff".

I had arranged to meet DCI Reid Garland at St Aldates police station, although he had retired the previous year. On the phone, he had sounded positively cheerful at the prospect of going back to his old stamping ground, and when I asked for him at the desk, the receptionist pointed one manicured finger at the waiting area with an indulgent smile. I turned to see a heavyset man in a blazer, grey flannel trousers and a dangling tie sitting on one of the plastic seats with his hands clasped loosely between his knees. He had probably noticed me the moment I walked in, but was affecting to read the notices on the board by the front desk. The tie was a particularly offensive shade of purple and narrower than was currently fashionable; I guessed he'd had it since the eighties. He wore a Thames Valley CID enamel pin in his lapel, and the material of his blazer was shiny with wear on the shoulders and elbows.

"DCI Garland?" I ventured.

He was on his feet surprisingly quickly for such a big man, one hand extended for me to shake. "Hello, my love. Maeve, isn't it? I've arranged for us to use one of the interview rooms here — hope you don't mind, they're not the most comfortable places but they are private and I thought we wouldn't want to have anyone listening to our conversation, if what I understood from you on the phone is right."

He carried on talking as he led the way into the back office, his voice deep and accented with the local lilt, the vowels as rounded and smooth as river pebbles. He had picked up a file from the seat next to him in the reception area, and I stared at it covetously as I walked behind him.

"I was glad you called, even though it was out of the blue. I said to Mrs Garland, I always knew this case would come up again. I never liked the way it was left, you see." He held open the door for me and I found myself in a small white-painted room with all of the charm I expected of interview rooms, which was none at all. I settled at the table and flipped open my notebook, but if I had thought I was going to be interviewing DCI Garland, I was wrong. He sat down on the other side of the table with a barely suppressed grunt of effort and put the file in front of him, then leaned a meaty elbow on it.

"Now you tell me what's been going on with this serial killer. How many victims are you up to now?"

"Four," I said. "It looks like five, but we're not convinced girl number five was the same killer."

"Is that so? I was wondering what brought you to Oxford. I couldn't see how it fitted in."

"Well, maybe it doesn't," I said honestly. "But I've been looking into Rebecca's background, and I was interested in finding out more about the death of Adam Rowley."

"Any reason why in particular?"

"From what her parents said, she had a very strong reaction to his death — strikingly so, considering they weren't in a relationship. Not formally, anyway."

"Is that it?" The retired policeman had a crease between his eyes that was on the verge of deepening into a frown.

"Not quite. I spoke to a few of Rebecca's friends from college after the memorial service. They had some . . . interesting things to say."

I had doubled back to talk to the pub-goers once I'd left the Haworths. I had found a group that had shrunk to six, including Mike the designated driver who had a sparkling water in front of him, loud-mouthed Leo and Debs, who was, I had to concede, a bit of a drip, but who had been only too pleased to talk about Adam Rowley. Leo had spent a long time telling me how much he and his friends had adored Rebecca, though none of them had been able to persuade her to go out with them. I admired her taste.

"Go on," DCI Garland said.

"According to them, the rumour in college was that Rebecca knew something about what happened to Adam Rowley. He was a bit of a lad and he had a reputation as a heartbreaker — lots of girlfriends, lots of one-night stands. Rebecca had had a crush on him for years, and a couple of weeks before he died, she 'got her man', as one of their friends put it." That had been charming Leo, removing his nose from a gin-and-tonic

240

to speak. "It didn't go anywhere and she couldn't come to terms with the rejection. The gossip was that she had become obsessed with him — couldn't be in the same room with him without bursting into tears. After he died, she fell apart completely. No one actually said she was responsible for what happened to him, but there was a lot of speculation, not that I give that too much weight. All I got from her friends was hearsay. I mean, he drowned, didn't he? Wasn't it an accident?"

DCI Garland folded his massive arms across his chest. "Could have been. Wasn't. Not that I could prove it, mind you. The coroner decided to record an open verdict but he was fairly clear that it was probably an accident — the boy had been drinking and he'd taken a handful of drugs. By all accounts he was off his face that night. All I can tell you is that Adam Rowley was a shit, and if my daughter had been seeing him, I'd have been seriously tempted to kill him myself."

I raised my eyebrows. "That bad?"

"That bad." Garland opened the file and took out a glossy eight by ten photograph which he skimmed across the table. "This was Mr Rowley. Butter wouldn't melt."

It was a blown-up detail from a larger picture and the contours of his face were slightly blurred, but the poor quality couldn't disguise the fact that Adam Rowley had been a beautiful young man. His black eyebrows were straight over deep blue eyes and his hair was short, revealing nicely shaped ears. He had high cheekbones, a lazy grin that showed white, even teeth and a square jaw that saved him from looking too pretty. But what really made me jump was the striking resemblance he bore to Gil Maddick.

When I looked up, Garland was looking at me quizzically. "Problem?"

"She had a type, that's all. Go on. Tell me about Adam."

"He was twenty years old when he died. Twenty years and two months, to be exact. And I'd say he'd spent every moment of his life causing trouble. He was bright enough. He was studying maths, so he'd have to be. And he played tennis to a very high standard — if he hadn't been so busy having a social life, he could have played for the university, I was told." Garland shook his head. "He had an eye for the ladies, no question about it, but what Rebecca's friends didn't tell you was that he had a couple of nasty STDs, and he knew it, and he always refused to use a condom. He said it was the best way to make sure they never called him again when he dumped them."

I made a note to check Rebecca's medical history to see if she'd had any problems with sexually transmitted diseases, as Garland went on.

"He liked to play with people too. We found a chart in his flat when we searched it. He'd made a note of each of his . . . conquests, I suppose you'd call them, and gave them marks out of ten. Double points if they were already in a relationship and he'd persuaded them to cheat. Triple points if he could persuade them to do things that a normal person like me would consider degrading. There were pictures of some of them, taken without their knowledge I have no doubt. He treated

242

them like dirt, you see, and laughed about it with his friends, and I didn't warm to him, I have to admit."

"So what happened? How did he die?"

"Have you been to Latimer College yet? Do you know where it is?" When I shook my head, he licked his thumb and went through the file until he came to a map of the city. He turned it around and pointed. "This is the college, here, at the far end of the High, just before Magdalen Bridge. The Cherwell is the river, here." He traced a line down the side of the city. "One branch of it runs right alongside the wall of Latimer and it actually cuts through the grounds here." He tapped his pen on the page. "This is where we think Rowley went into the water. The body wasn't found for seventy-two hours. The Cherwell flows into the Thames here, not far from Latimer College, and the corpse had gone with it. It bobbed up again at Goring-on-Thames, just this side of Reading. We were lucky it came up at all. The river takes a few every year that go all the way to the sea."

"So what makes you think he went in at Latimer? Were there marks on the ground?"

"No sign of a struggle and no damage to the riverbank, but then he didn't have a mark on his body, give or take a few abrasions that most probably happened after his death. One way in and out of college and the night porter swore he hadn't seen him leave. I trusted his word. He was a good man, Greg Ponsett. Ex-Navy. If he said it, he meant it." Garland sighed. "He's dead now. Lung cancer."

"I'd like to read his statement," I said, hoping that the detective might take the hint and just give me the file.

"Nothing in it. Just like there's nothing in any of the other statements in here." He riffled the edge of the pages with his thumb. "They closed ranks as soon as the police became involved. No one was talking. All I know about Adam Rowley, I got off the record from staff and students. And it didn't matter anyway, because I couldn't prove it was murder in the first place."

"But you think he was killed."

"I'm sure of it." Garland's eyes were steady on mine. "No question."

"It could have been suicide," I suggested.

"Not him. He was in love with his life. He had everything going for him. He was doing nicely with his academic work so there were no problems there, he'd lined up a traineeship at a bank to start the following September, he'd bought himself a ticket to go around the world during the summer — he'd just applied for a load of visas the day he died — and he had no money worries. Suicide definitely didn't fit." Garland shook his head. "It was the way it happened that made me sure it was murder. He wasn't averse to taking drugs, but there was absolutely no reason why he should have been looking for sedatives on the thirtieth of April. May Day is a big deal in Oxford. The kids stay up all night so they can head down to Magdalen Bridge at dawn and party. Nightmare to police. If he was on something, it would have been coke or speed. Not diazepam."

"So what — someone drugged him without him knowing it?"

"That was my theory. Or they told him he was taking uppers. Then, when he was nicely out of it, they rolled him into the water and let the river do its work."

"Who did you have in mind, though? Not Rebecca."

"I doubt it. I met her, you know. Interviewed her. She was broken up about it, but she wasn't the sort to be capable of murder. She'd have confessed if she had done it. She was that type. Too nice for her own good. In fact, apart from his family, I'd say Miss Haworth was one of the few people who were actually sorry Adam Rowley was dead."

"So who then? You must have had some ideas."

"I did. I do. But I don't want to put them into your head." He closed the file with an air of finality and pushed the whole lot across the table to me. "I know you want to look at this yourself. I've been indulging myself, talking about the old case, but this one stuck in my mind. You go through the paperwork and come back to me. Tell me what you think."

"How long have I got?"

"That depends," Garland said seriously. "How worried are you that the person who killed Rebecca will kill again?"

I had chosen to view the retired detective's last question as rhetorical, but as I walked back up St Aldates with my head bent against the cold, and the file — which was too big to fit in my bag — clutched to my chest, I found myself wondering about the possible

245

suspects. Really, there was just the one suspect in my mind. And that person was unlikely to have been too concerned about what happened to Adam Rowley. This trip had all the makings of a classic waste of time, but I had never been able to leave a mystery alone, and like Reid Garland, I was convinced that there was more to the student's death than had been proved.

There was a coffee shop about halfway along the High Street and I took refuge with a giant mug of coffee and a bun, sitting in the steamed-up window where I could watch the passing pedestrians and count the buses that thundered up and down the curving street, looking exotically modern against the medieval backdrop. The coffee shop was packed with students, all eking out their drinks and talking at the tops of their voices. Peaceful it was not, but I was warm for the first time since I'd arrived. I had an hour or so to kill before I had to present myself at Latimer College, and it seemed like a good idea to read up on Adam Rowley's untimely death while I had the chance.

Garland had written a lengthy case summary for submission to the coroner's court, thirty pages or so of typed narrative on what had happened to the student. I skim read it, looking for any nuggets of information that the retired DCI had forgotten to share with me. Adam was from Nottingham, the younger of two sons, and his father was a doctor. He had won every possible scholarship during his privileged journey from private prep school to public school and then Oxford, where he had continued his high level of academic achievement and managed to find time to dally with more than a few of his fellow students. He had spent his last morning alive in college, in his room. First-year and third-year students were accommodated within the college itself, and he had occupied what Garland had described as a particularly nice room on the first floor of Garden Building overlooking the river. The scout, a kind of housekeeper who looked after his staircase, had spoken to him at ten to eleven, when he had been going out to a tutorial in another college. He had eaten lunch in hall on his return to college, then divided his time in the afternoon between the college library and the junior common room. At six, he had eaten dinner in hall. (Garland appended a note here to explain that dining in hall was free for scholars — Rowley had qualified by doing well in his first-year exams and took full advantage of the perks.) He had been in the college bar at eight o'clock and stayed there until it closed at half past eleven. The college bar was heavily subsidised and had been running a promotion: all spirits reduced to a pound a shot and mixers for free. It had been, Garland suggested delicately, a busy evening, and most of the students had been thoroughly drunk by the end of the night. Various all-night parties had been taking place across the university, and the sole exit from the college, the porters' lodge, had been busy. As Garland had told me, the porter on duty had affirmed that Adam Rowley hadn't left, and CCTV from the lodge appeared to confirm that. None of his friends had seen him after the bar closed. No one had known where he was planning to go. He had been invited to three different parties and it appeared that everyone had

247

assumed he had gone out. But instead, it seemed, he had gone back to his room.

At some point between midnight and 1.15 a.m., one of Rowley's neighbours on his staircase, Steven Mulligan, had heard footsteps accompanied by loud whistling, which he associated with Rowley (and had complained about in the past). He thought the student was leaving the building rather than returning, though as he had been woken up from a deep sleep, he wasn't entirely sure. And that was the last that was heard of Adam Rowley, if it had indeed been him in the corridor. No one had seen him walk down to the river. No one had seen him fall, jump or be pushed in. None of his friends had been too concerned for his whereabouts initially, assuming that he had met a girl that evening and was therefore busy elsewhere. He had had no commitments on 1 May, which was a Wednesday. No one had thought it necessary to raise the alarm until late on Saturday, and when they did become aware that Adam was missing, there was very little to suggest where he had gone. His room was as he had left it, his wallet and passport still on his desk. His mobile phone was not in his room, nor was it ever located. The phone records and cell-site analysis showed that the phone had been in the general area of Latimer College until 2 a.m. on the morning of May Day, when it had been switched off, powered down or simply ceased to work. It didn't take a genius to work out that there was a good chance that at 2 a.m. Adam Rowley's phone might have been in the Cherwell along with its owner.

The college had contacted the police once Rowley's friends had raised the alarm, but their investigation had been somewhat cursory, reading between the lines, until early morning on 6 May, when Mr Bryan Pitman, a tourist visiting Goring-on-Thames on a fishing holiday, had seen a dark shape caught in some low-hanging bushes by the river's edge and abandoned his rod to see what it was. It was good luck that the river had given Adam up at all; it was even more fortunate that he had a swipe card that gave access to the computer room and library in Latimer College in the front pocket of his sodden jeans. Thames Valley Police had wasted no time in identifying the young man. The college had wasted no time in denying all responsibility. And the post-mortem had revealed, among other things, that his last meal had consisted of toast and blackcurrant jam and had been eaten not more than two hours before he died, that he had a blood alcohol level of 240 mg per 100 ml, more than three times the legal drink-drive limit, that he had taken a significant amount of diazepam and would, the pathologist thought, have been confused at best given that combination of intoxicants, and that injuries to his face and head, including a contusion at the base of his skull, had probably occurred after his death as the dark river washed him thirty miles downstream.

I abandoned the summary in favour of the photographs, of which there were many: the close-up Garland had shown me of Adam Rowley, alive and well, and two others taken in the year before his death that confirmed the impression I had formed that he had been an exceptionally handsome young man. Then the pictures from the riverbank of a very different Adam Rowley, bloated and pale, bloodless scrapes on his forehead and jaw, his hands wrinkled and soft with the uppermost layer of skin beginning to detach. I turned the photographs face down after a quick look, conscious that the busy coffee shop was not an ideal place to examine them. There were still pages and pages left in the file and I flicked through them with a rising sense of despair; I just didn't have time to absorb all the information that DCI Garland had so lovingly preserved. Witness statements, maps, a floor plan of the Garden Building at Latimer College which Garland had marked with an X to indicate Adam Rowley's room, cell-site maps that proved the location of Adam Rowley's mobile phone during the week preceding his death, right up until the signal disappeared.

I went through the stack of statements methodically until I found Rebecca Haworth's. I read it with interest, hoping to see a glimmer of her personality, but the process of creating the witness statement had brought about a deadening effect. So much depended on the police officer who wrote up the statement; Garland's colleague had been addicted to jargon. Despite the stilted, formal language ("I reside at an address known to police . . . I have known Adam ROWLEY for approximately two and a half years . . . I last saw him on 30 April in the Latimer College Bar, at approximately 10.30 . . . This statement is true to the best of my knowledge and belief . . .") Rebecca's emotional state bled through. She had seen nothing,

250

she knew nothing of what had happened to him, but that she was mourning him there could be no doubt. She couldn't believe he was gone. As Garland had said, she seemed to be genuinely broken up about his death. She also had a firm alibi for the night in question, having been at a house party in east Oxford with about thirty other students who could vouch for having seen her there.

Two statements later, I was intrigued to see a terse one with Louise North's name on it. She had been working in the college bar on the night in question, and had served Adam Rowley a number of times during the evening, though she hadn't noticed him particularly. It had been a busy night. She had been one of five bar staff on duty, and had gone to bed after closing time. She had known Adam Rowley slightly, but had rarely spoken to him. Clipped, businesslike, unemotional. Louise hadn't changed much since college, I guessed. I would ask her about Adam when I saw her next, since she had known both him and Rebecca. I had a feeling, though, that she would not have been of interest to Adam, considering his particular tastes.

Garland had collected statements from Rowley's tutors who were united in the view that he was bright but lazy, and from his neighbours in Garden Building who had found him noisy and inconsiderate. Rowley's friends had been kinder, as might have been expected, but there were remarkably few notes of genuine emotion. I couldn't escape the feeling that Rowley had been a bully, and that even his friends had been almost relieved that he was gone.

Leaving the rest of the witness statements as a task for another day, I turned to the pathologist's report, which informed me that all fresh corpses immersed in water sink to the bottom in the same position, face down, head hanging, and that the lacerations to Adam Rowley's face were consistent with this, rather than suggestive of any antemortem violence, though he couldn't be definite about that. Rowley's lungs were over-inflated and heavy with fluid; his airways and stomach contained silt and other foreign matter from the river. Nonetheless, the pathologist noted, and I couldn't help reading it in a scolding tone of voice, the sort I had heard so often from Glen Hanshaw, that wasn't proof of drowning because "there are no autopsy findings pathognomonic of drowning. Rather, all other causes of death must be excluded." The debris from the river could have washed into his body during his long immersion in the water. It was necessary to consider that some other catastrophic event had preceded the victim entering the water. The pathologist warned that the blood-alcohol concentration could not be relied on because of the volume of water that Adam might have absorbed. He could state with a reasonable degree of certainty that the victim had been significantly intoxicated, however. On balance, therefore, the pathologist was prepared to allow that drowning was a likely cause of death. I rolled my eyes. It was a report that was typical of a practised expert witness. Here is my fence; allow me to sit on it. Reid Garland had sounded far more certain in his case summary, but I recognised the copper's overwhelming desire to make a

252

case. The coroner had noted it too, and had not been moved. An open verdict was probably fair, I thought, considering what I had read. But I could also list the unanswered questions that had stayed with the officer in the case for seven long years. Who gave him the drugs? What had brought him to the riverbank that night? Did he fall or was he pushed? Who might have wanted him dead? And why was Rebecca Haworth, among all of his friends and acquaintances, so desperately upset by his death?

There was, however, no escaping the final question. If Garland hadn't solved those mysteries in seven years, what chance did I have?

Professor Stanwell Westcott had rooms in the third quad of Latimer College, in Staircase Sixteen, or so the porter informed me to my complete bemusement when I asked how to find him at the lodge. I had ignored another neat, white-painted sign announcing that the college was closed to visitors and passed through the doorway with a distinctly through-the-looking-glass feeling as the traffic noise faded behind me. The short, barrel-bodied porter, who was at least hatless, became much more helpful when I produced my warrant card and a smile designed to take the sting out of the formality. He shot out from behind his desk and insisted on taking me all the way to Professor Westcott's door himself. I followed him through immaculately lawned courtyards that were, he explained, called quadrangles, quads for short, this one built in the early sixteenth century, that one added on ninety or so years later, the New Buildings over there a Victorian addition despite the name, the dining hall to my left up those steps, and as he carried on giving me a lightning-fast guided tour, I tuned out. I was imagining a young Rebecca Haworth hurrying through the archway that separated first and second quad, on her way to a lecture or a party or a date with handsome, cocksure Adam Rowley. The dark, wintry day meant that lights were on in most of the rooms overlooking the grassy quads, and the paths where we walked were crisscrossed with shadows. Not usually over-sensitive to atmosphere, I couldn't help shivering. It felt for a moment as if we were intruding on a haunt of ghosts as we walked under a bare-branched climber that grew over the entrance to third quad, which turned out to be the largest of them all and elegantly colonnaded in the warm golden stone that was a great part of the city's charm.

"Staircase sixteen," my guide said, stopping at a doorway where a wooden board listed four names prefixed with Doctor or Professor, including the one I wanted. "Professor Westcott's room is on the first floor, on the right. His oak will be open if he's expecting you."

I had absolutely no idea what he meant, but I couldn't be bothered to ask since it would mean another lecture. I started up the dusty wooden staircase, feeling nervous in spite of myself. The vice-principal had been terse on the phone and so plummy when he did speak as to be almost incomprehensible. The principal, I had been told, was away. Professor Westcott would speak to me on his behalf. I couldn't wait.

There was a heavy, dark-varnished outer door standing open when I got to the top of the stairs, with a more conventional white-painted panelled door closed behind it. I looked from one to the other, realising that the porter had probably been talking about the dark door when he'd mentioned the oak. It was no wonder I was feeling unsettled. It was like being in another country without a guidebook and only the haziest grasp of the language. I knocked on the panelled door and pushed it open after hearing a muffled, "Come!" from inside.

Professor Westcott's room was large, dark, and infinitely cluttered. I stopped just inside the door to squint at the floor, afraid to knock over one of the piles of books or papers that were littering the carpet. A single desk lamp with a very bright bulb was the only source of light apart from the tall windows, but heavy curtains cut off most of the slate-grey daylight. The books that lined the walls seemed to absorb light too, and gave off a fusty smell. At least, I hoped the smell was from the books.

"Ah, the policewoman." The voice came from the darkness beyond the lamp. "You must forgive me the disorder. I am lost in the arms of Virgil at the moment, preparing a new edition of the *Georgics* for the university press, and the research has rather taken over my room. Are you familiar with Virgil, DC Kerrigan?"

"Not personally. But your work sounds fascinating," I said politely.

"I doubt that." He came out from behind his desk, stooping slightly, and revealed himself to be a tall man with a grey-fringed bald head and the thick-lensed glasses of the compulsive reader. "But how kind of you to say so."

He was a lot more congenial than I had been expecting from his telephone manner. I was aware that he was determined to put me at my ease as if I was a nervous undergraduate, and I had to remind myself that I was not, in fact, a timid eighteen-year-old, but fully ten years older and a detective constable in the Metropolitan Police at that.

A small crimson-covered armchair loaded with books and papers stood near the door and he pointed to it. "Please. Sit. Just throw those things anywhere."

It took me a minute to move the clutter from the chair, discovering in the process a single khaki-coloured sock, which I draped gingerly over the top of the pile of books at my feet. I sat down and found that Professor Westcott had drawn an upright chair into the centre of the room and was sitting on it, peering at me keenly.

"Sorry for being short on the phone. I hate the bloody thing. Never rings at the right time. You wanted to ask about a student."

I scrambled to get out my notes, wrong-footed by his rapid-fire delivery. "Two students, actually. They were undergraduates here seven or so years ago — I don't know if you'd remember . . ."

He flicked a long hand as if to imply that seven years were a mere moment, and I did appreciate that if you spent your days and nights thinking about the literature and history of Ancient Rome, you probably had a different perspective on what counted as recent.

I explained briefly that I was investigating Rebecca Haworth's murder and that I was interested in finding out more about what had happened to Adam Rowley.

"Rowley," Professor Westcott repeated. "Yes. The boy who drowned. Such a sad accident."

"I've just been talking to the DCI who investigated that case. He told me he had suspicions that it was murder."

"Suspicions but no proof," Professor Westcott said, and I had the feeling his mind was elsewhere. "I remember him too." He crossed his legs and smoothed his bottle-green cords over his bony knee. "I'm afraid I can't help you. The senior common room cooperated fully with the police investigation, and it was the coroner's decision to record an open verdict. Of course, the boy had been drinking, as the young folk tend to do on that night. It's quite a bacchanal. The roots of the celebration go right back to pagan times, not that the students care about that, but it's all dressed up as a quasi-religious ceremony now, in the Christian tradition. You know about what goes on in Magdalen Tower, I take it? No? The choristers from the college choir sing the *Hymnus Eucharisticus* in celebration of the day, not that you can hear much from down on the ground. In my day, the thing to do was to take a punt on to the river and listen from the water, but they've stopped that now. There's nothing for people to do but drink, which I think is always a mistake."

"That's very interesting," I said feebly, trying to take a grip on the interview, though conversation with the vice-principal was like manhandling an eel. "I understand that Adam's body wasn't found immediately."

"Indeed not. The Isis flows swiftly here." He squinted at me. "That's the local name for the Thames, my dear. From the Latin, *Tamesis*. I find it a much more beautiful nomenclature for such an important body of water."

"It must have been a difficult time for the college," I persisted. "Very unsettling for the students."

"And the SCR. It was a tremendous shock." He stood up and beckoned me over to a window on the other side of the room. "This is the Garden side of the college. That sweep, from the bridge over to the willow on the right, all belongs to Latimer. It's quite lovely for nine months of the year, but you can't expect to see it at its best in December."

I agreed, staring out at the dark river oozing between sodden banks, overhung with bare branches and defeated-looking shrubs. The flowerbeds that would bring the scene to life later in the year were standing empty, dark-brown cut-outs from yet another impeccable lawn. A fence ran along the edge of the river from the bridge to the tree the professor had indicated. It was made of narrow palings about six feet high.

"The fence was added following Mr Rowley's tragic death. I must say, it seemed a shame to me that we couldn't simply learn from what happened to him, rather than defacing one of the loveliest outlooks in Oxford. But of course the implications for our

258

insurance couldn't be ignored; the bursar was most persuasive. And it formed part of the coroner's recommendations, which we followed to the letter."

He sat down again and waited for me to return to my armchair. "We also conducted our own investigation to find out if he had acquired the drugs he had taken within these walls. He had spent the evening in the college bar, you see, and we were suspicious that there might be someone distributing drugs within the student body. The dean and I found to our great sadness that there was a graduate student — a chemist, perhaps unsurprisingly — who had been manufacturing certain hallucinogens, and although he hadn't sold them to Adam Rowley as far as we knew, he was sent down immediately. We couldn't tolerate that sort of behaviour. The college is quite clear on that front in the material it provides to matriculating students."

"Adam had taken sedatives," I said. "That's not what you'd go for if you wanted to have a good time."

He spread his hands. "I am unfamiliar with the pastime of taking illegal substances, my dear. But I am led to believe that you can't always be sure what it is you are taking. I'm afraid that Mr Rowley was misled about the pills he took. But there was no suggestion that he obtained them from a member of Latimer."

"Do you know anything about what happened with Rebecca Haworth?" I said, changing tack. "She dropped out for a year — had a nervous breakdown, I believe."

"I remember her," Professor Westcott said, nodding. "She was a very pretty girl. Of course, they are very

259

young, the undergraduates, and getting younger all the time." He allowed himself a little chesty laugh. "They feel things terribly deeply. One understood that she wasn't in a position to tackle Schools."

I looked quizzical.

"Schools is another term for the final examinations that the undergraduates sit. Also known as Finals."

So why, I found myself thinking, *didn't you just* say *her final exams?*

"Of course the college was concerned that she shouldn't suffer simply because of what had occurred with her fellow undergraduate. On the other hand, we were reluctant to allow her to avoid Finals because there was the danger that others would take the same route, and we couldn't allow the entire year to defer. She was fortunate that she had a champion in the senior common room — her tutor was very persuasive."

"Her tutor being . . ."

"Dr Faraday. He's no longer a fellow here."

It was not my imagination that a dark look came over the professor's face at the mention of Caspian Faraday.

"You don't seem to be a fan of his."

"Not at all," Professor Westcott said blandly. "A most able historian."

"When did he leave?"

"Oh, it must have been five years ago. Maybe six. He's based in London now, I understand."

"I'm sure I'll be able to track him down."

The professor raised his eyebrows. "Really? You think it's necessary?"

260

"I'd like to hear what he has to say, yes." I decided to push my luck. "Do you mind me asking why he left Oxford?"

"You may certainly ask."

There was a small, awkward pause. Professor Westcott gave a shallow cough.

"I do apologise. Force of habit. It's one of the turns of phrase I encourage my students to drop."

"I'll try to avoid it in future." I leaned forward. "I do still want to know why Caspian Faraday left Latimer College, Professor Westcott. From what I understand, he would have needed a pretty good reason to leave." And I also had a fair idea what might have happened courtesy of Rebecca's university friends. I wondered if he would confirm what they'd told me — that the friendly relationship between student and tutor had gone a bit too far.

Professor Westcott stared past my right ear for a long moment before replying, and when he did, he managed not to answer my question directly. "You know, when Adam Rowley died, it was a difficult time. With the guidance of the principal, we embarked on a close examination of this institution and its members. We were satisfied, when we had finished, that Latimer College could stand up to any amount of scrutiny. We were sure that we had nothing to hide. So while I am enjoying this conversation tremendously, I'm afraid that I can't think how I might provide you with any further assistance."

I could take a hint. The interview was drawing to a close, whether I liked it or not. Before leaving the professor to his books, though, there was something I wanted to know. "Do you remember Rebecca's best friend? Louise North. She studied law."

The professor thought for a moment, then shrugged. "I'm sorry, but no. If she was a lawyer, she probably spent most of her time in the law faculty or the college library. I doubt she was seen in the hours of daylight. Jurisprudence is a most demanding degree."

And Louise had not been a very pretty undergraduate with a nice line in handwringing, it went without saying. Poor Louise, always in Rebecca's shadow. I might have been bitter about that, if it had been me.

Professor Westcott had got to his feet and was replacing the chair he'd been sitting on against a wall. "I apologise if I'm rushing you, but I do have a tutorial in five minutes."

"No, I'm sorry for delaying you. Thank you for seeing me." I gathered my things together in a hurry, shook his hand, then turned to go. At the door, I hesitated and looked back. "Before I leave, do you mind telling me when your close examination of the college ended and you were satisfied you had nothing to hide?"

"Oh, it must have been five years ago. Maybe six," the professor said, and behind his thick lenses, one eyelid drooped in what might have been a wink.

LOUISE

Gil exerted himself to be charming on the drive back to London and a shamefully short distance down the road I found myself laughing at something he'd said, and then it seemed easier to talk than to say nothing, and almost too soon we were drawing up outside my house.

I sat where I was for a moment, reluctant to open the door. Inside the car was a different world; outside it, I would never talk to Gil with the relaxed intimacy we had fallen into on the journey. I didn't care if he was playing a game — I had enjoyed myself. I hadn't ever seen what Rebecca liked about him when they were together, apart from his looks, but then he hadn't bothered to show me how he could be: warm, funny, likable. I found it helped that he couldn't look at me as he concentrated on the road, so I could watch him unobserved. He hadn't seemed to notice that I was staring at him, or at least he hadn't cared. I had tried to work out why it was that he was paying attention to me, and came up with nothing; I didn't believe his story about being more interested in me than in Rebecca, not for a second.

Gil had turned the engine off and was very still beside me. I had to move; I couldn't sit in the car all night.

"Thank you for the lift," I said politely. "There was no need to drive me to the door, but it was very kind of you."

"We had that argument hours ago. Besides, driving you was my pleasure." He tweaked the end of my ponytail. "You should wear your hair down."

I shook my head. "Untidy."

"Liberating," he countered. He reached over and picked up my hand, studying the back of it, then turning it over so he could examine the palm. "You have a long lifeline. Lucky you."

"Do you have a crystal ball as well? Or do you use Tarot cards?"

"Shh." He frowned. "I'm starting to get something. Tomorrow night, I see you having dinner with a dark-haired man."

"You are ridiculous." I took my hand back and started to hunt through my bag for keys.

"You are hard to pin down." He was watching me when I looked up, and my breath caught in my throat when I saw the expression on his face. I wouldn't have said that he even liked me at that moment, but the next second he smiled ruefully and the darkness I had seen was gone as if I had imagined it. "It's going to be a fight all the way with you, isn't it?"

"All the way to where?"

"Dinner. Tomorrow night. I would like the pleasure of your company," he said in a mock-formal tone of voice.

I should have said no — I knew I should have said no — but I found myself agreeing to it, and to being picked up at half past seven.

"Where are we going?"

"I'll tell you when we get there."

"I hate that." I glared at him. "How will I know what to wear if you won't tell me where we're going? It's patronising and controlling."

"I thought it was romantic." He grinned and I knew he wasn't going to back down.

"Fine. Seven thirty, here, tomorrow night. But you have only yourself to blame if I turn up in a tracksuit. Or pyjamas."

"You won't be needing pyjamas, whatever happens tomorrow night."

"Nothing is going to happen." I opened the car door and started to get out. "Dinner. I agreed to dinner. That's it."

"We'll see."

I shook my head at him and slammed the door, walking up the path to my front door and letting myself in without turning around to see if he was still there. But it took all my self-control to do it.

It felt late, but it was just after six, I found, checking my watch. Gil hadn't kissed me goodbye. But he was seeing me the following night. Maybe he hadn't wanted to kiss me. But if it hadn't been as amazing for him as it had been for me, would he have wanted to take me out to dinner? I wandered around the kitchen, biting my thumbnail edgily. I could make no effort for him, or I could pull out all the stops. He would expect me to

265

dress down. I wanted to look pretty. I wandered into the unlit hall and stared into the mirror, my face an oval glimmering in the darkness. I said, out loud: "What would Rebecca do?"

I was lucky; my usual hairdresser had just had a cancellation and they could fit me in the following morning, first thing. I took the stairs two at a time and went through the fitted cupboards in my bedroom, sliding hangers back and forth. All these clothes and nothing to wear.

The problem was settled for me early the following day by a courier who delivered a large box tied with a tulle bow. In it, I found a simple black dress with a label that made my eyebrows shoot up; it must have cost a fortune. I tried it on and found that he had chosen the right size without needing to check what that was. Clinging without being tight, it hugged my body, the skirt narrow to just above the knee, the neckline dipping low at the front and the back. He had bought shoes as well, high with a spindly heel and scarlet soles. There was a damson-coloured silk shawl too. It was, I discovered, the precise shade of the bruise on my neck. I wondered if he had chosen it deliberately and decided that he probably had — it was a typical Gil tease.

As I lifted out the shawl, a box of perfume dropped into my lap and I felt my mood darken a notch. I recognised it immediately. It was the scent Rebecca had always worn, the one I had taken from her flat. Why he wanted me to wear it, I could only guess, but it unsettled me.

266

On the other hand, two could play at that game. My frown cleared and a slow smile spread across my face in its place. The outfit needed something more, and I knew exactly what that something should be. And I was looking forward to dinner, I acknowledged to myself with a tiny shiver of pleasurable anticipation. Whatever happened, it was going to be interesting.

CHAPTER
NINE

MAEVE

It absolutely didn't surprise me to discover, via the
DVLA database, that Caspian Faraday drove a black 1971
Aston Martin DBS V8, a car-collector's dream that was
worth a good six figures. Nor was it a shock that he
lived in a six-bedroom double-fronted house in the
serene and leafy exclusivity of Highgate Village. He had,
after all, made a lot of money from three well-regarded
and popular history books, not to mention the television
series that had accompanied his last, currently available
in hardback and on display in the window of every
bookshop in the interminable run-up to Christmas. And
Google had informed me, in loving, breathless detail, of
the good marriage he had made with the daughter of a
convenience-food magnate. I had been expecting well
heeled; I had even been expecting ostentatious. What
did surprise me, however, when I trekked up to Highgate
on a bright, cold afternoon to interview him, was that
he had invited his solicitor to come along too. And if
that was a bad start to our conversation, things were
going to get a lot more awkward before I was finished.

The historian had seemed nervous on the phone, and
defensive, two emotions that I generally enjoyed in an

interviewee. Nerves and defensiveness were excellent indicators that someone had something to hide, and I was in the luxurious position of having a fairly shrewd idea what that something might be. The best questions for a detective are the ones where you already know the answer, because a lie can be far more revealing than the truth.

It didn't look as if I was going to be hearing much of either when I strolled into Caspian Faraday's comfortable, elegantly furnished sitting room to find an overweight middle-aged man scowling from the depths of an armchair. He had dewlaps like a bulldog.

"My lawyer, Avery Mercer," Faraday said from behind me, and I detected a note of smugness that had not been there when the historian opened the front door and practically dragged me into the house. Heaven forbid the neighbours should notice the policewoman on the doorstep, even if I was in plain clothes. And heaven forbid that lovely, rich Delia Faraday should get back from her shopping trip before I was finished. I was quite certain that she hadn't been told I was coming to see him, or why, and equally certain that he wouldn't tell her about it once I had gone if he could get away with it. There were things no wife needed to know. Especially if she was the reason Caspian could divide his time between the house in London, the villa in the south of France, the mansion in the Lake District, the duplex in New York and the Parisian apartment that had featured in *House & Garden* and overlooked the Place des Vosges. History didn't pay *that* well.

I attempted to look wounded. "I thought I made it clear on the phone, Mr Faraday, this is just a casual conversation. There's no need for you to have legal representation. You aren't a suspect." I waited a beat. "At the moment, anyway."

The bulldog stirred. "My client asked me to join him as he wasn't certain why you were interested in speaking with him. I am sure you know better than to draw any conclusions from the fact of my presence."

I threw the lawyer a meaningless smile and concentrated on Caspian Faraday, who had sat down in a chair by the window so the light was behind him. That old trick. It might have been habit, however, rather than guilt, because the first thought I had had when he had opened the front door was that he had aged considerably since his author photograph was taken. The close-cropped fair hair had silvered and was receding inexorably in the classic M shape; he had had a high forehead in the picture I'd seen previously, but time had tipped it beyond that to straightforward, undeniable balding. He had a deep tan that did nothing to hide the wrinkles around his startlingly blue eyes, and the intellectual's black poloneck was not quite managing to camouflage the softening of his jaw and an incipient paunch. Too much good living, I diagnosed. For all that, he was still attractive: he was tall and broad-shouldered, he had beautiful hands, and his voice was deeply resonant. He was forty-four, I knew from his driving licence, which also told me that he liked to drive faster than was legal and had nine points to show for it. That meant he could be reckless, and

270

impulsive, and that was what I had been hoping to use against him. Avery Mercer, however, was showing every sign that he would take pleasure in applying the brakes on his client's behalf, and I stifled a sigh as I looked around, working out where to sit. There was a small chair near the door and I picked it up and placed it by the window, closer to Faraday than he liked.

"Do you mind? I need good light so I can read my own writing," I said with a wide grin.

He struggled with himself for a moment, looking around the room at the many places I could have sat that would have done just as well. Politeness won out, as I had known it would. "Please. Sit wherever you like. There are probably more comfortable chairs, though."

"This is fine," I said, shifting my weight and feeling it give very slightly as I did so. "Is it old?"

"Regency. But if it's survived this long, it should make it through a — what was it you said? — casual conversation."

"I'll be careful."

Faraday smiled politely, then shot a covert look in his lawyer's direction. Checking to see whether he should be worried, I thought, and took my time about asking my first question.

"I'm here to talk to you about Rebecca Haworth. Can you tell me how you met her?"

"The first time we met was when she was applying to Oxford. I interviewed her. That would have been the December before she came up — so over ten years ago." He looked startled for a moment. "I hadn't realised it was so long ago."

"What were your first impressions — do you remember?"

"She was obviously very bright. Very well informed and well read. She had an active and questioning mind, which is what we were looking for in our undergraduates. You can teach someone the facts, but if they don't have the intellect to draw their own conclusions, there's very little point in them being at Oxford."

"But Rebecca did?"

"Certainly. I remember being impressed with her confidence, but also her speed in responding to a new idea as soon as I suggested it to her. A lot of young people break down if you challenge their views, but she enjoyed the discussion. There was no question in my mind that she should be admitted to Latimer College, and when she came up the following October she seemed to settle in quickly."

"And you were her tutor."

"One of them. There were three history fellows and we shared the teaching between us. She also would have had tutorials in other colleges, in the subjects where we didn't have a lot of expertise between us. And of course the history faculty arranged a programme of lectures. I'm afraid I don't know whether she was good at attending them — they are essentially optional."

His manner was pleasant and open, as if he had nothing to hide, and for a moment a worm of doubt squirmed at the back of my mind. But I had heard enough to know that there was more to the story than he was letting on at the moment.

"What was your relationship with Rebecca?"

272

"I taught her. I provided her with support and guidance, when it was appropriate."

"You stood up for her when she wanted to defer her exams, I understand."

"As I would have done for any of my students." His voice was still calm, but now he leaned forward in his chair, his elbows on his knees, his hands clasped together.

"According to the person I spoke to at Latimer College, you had quite a battle on your hands."

"Who was that?"

"A senior member of the college," I said blandly, not seeing why I needed to tell him anything more.

He sighed. "They were being completely unreasonable. Rebecca was a very good student — first class, in my view. She was having a difficult time. They couldn't expect her to sit finals three weeks after the death of one of her friends, and do herself justice."

"Did you know Adam Rowley?"

"Who? Oh, the boy who died. No. I'd never noticed him. He wasn't one of my students. I had completely forgotten his name until you mentioned it."

It was apparent to me that Adam had been a bit-player in the drama of Caspian Faraday's life. There was only room for one hero in the cast, and as far as he was concerned it was Caspian himself.

"You said Rebecca wouldn't have done herself justice if she'd taken her exams then, but she didn't get a first in the end, did she? She got a 2.2."

He made a dismissive gesture. "It's very hard to come back after a year and sit Finals. I wasn't surprised that she struggled. Especially given that it had taken her a long time to recover from her breakdown."

"You gave her some extra tutoring, I believe."

He looked at his lawyer before answering and I suppressed a smile; we were sailing into dangerous waters now.

"I saw her a number of times, yes. Not formally — the college was quite clear that she shouldn't receive any extra tutoring as a result of having deferred. But I thought she deserved more than that, and I wasn't prepared to toe the line. That was one of the many reasons why I found Latimer College to be a stifling environment. They were obsessed with rules, regulations. They didn't seem to be able to look past tradition and see the students as people."

"But you did see her as more than a student, didn't you?"

"What's that supposed to mean?" There was an edge in the velvety voice now.

"I've been informed that you and Rebecca became very close when she returned to Oxford. I understand that you began a sexual relationship with her. That's not usually considered appropriate, is it?"

"I wondered if you'd know about that." He was still trying for casual and relaxed, but his hands were clamped together so tightly that the strain he was under showed in the white sheen over his knuckles. "Technically, we weren't doing anything wrong. She was an adult, and no longer my student, officially. There was an attraction, I will admit, but nothing

274

happened before her return to Oxford to sit her exams. And when it did, she was the one who started it."

I had heard a different story from Rebecca's friends in the pub. According to them, Faraday had groomed her, gaining her trust, inviting her to come to the house he was renting in Cowley for dinner and long drinking sessions, keeping her away from the friends she still had at Latimer. And Rebecca, still unsettled by the events of the previous year and star-struck by her brilliant, handsome tutor, had gone along with what he had so obviously wanted.

"How long did the relationship last?"

"A couple of months. I was going to teach at a summer school at Berkeley, and she was planning on leaving Oxford as soon as she'd sat her exams anyway. I don't think she liked being there much. Too many memories." He looked at me. "We both knew it wasn't going to be a longstanding affair. It was a fling, but a highly pleasurable one for both of us."

"I'm sure." Debs, when she hadn't been staring adoringly at Leo, had had a nice line in invective about Caspian Faraday and how he had dumped Rebecca unceremoniously and without warning, packing his bags and catching his flight to California on the same day. Rebecca, abandoned by someone she had trusted and admired, had floundered, not surprisingly. But there was no point in challenging Faraday about it now. It wasn't a crime to break someone's heart. I didn't have to like him for it, though. "What happened then?"

"I don't know what you mean." He was looking wary.

"Well, you went off to the States, and Rebecca left Oxford. Did you stay in touch?"

"I had an email from her when the results came out. Of course, she was disappointed with her class of degree. It wasn't a true reflection of her capabilities." He shrugged. "It was still better than nothing. I don't think she found that the result held her back, in the long term. An Oxford BA is worth having, whatever the class."

"And that was the extent of your contact with her? An exchange of emails?"

"I'm a busy man. More so now than I was then, but at the time I was committed to many hours of teaching a week as well as my own research. I didn't have the leisure to keep track of my students — or my ex-girlfriends, if it comes to that."

"And you went back to teaching at Latimer College."

"Yes. But I left at the end of the following year."

I looked at him limpidly. "I heard that you left halfway through the year."

"It might have been the end of Hilary term. I really can't recall, I'm afraid."

"Why did you go?"

"Lots of reasons." He was back to looking tense again. "I was finding my responsibilities to be excessively onerous. I didn't think I was doing justice to my work or my students. I made the decision that I would be better off giving up teaching and concentrating on my writing."

"You had a bit of help with making that decision, didn't you?" I smiled pleasantly. "Who was it who told the college authorities about your — fling, I think you said it was — with Rebecca?"

His lips thinned to a line. "I never found out."

"They took a rather different view of it, didn't they? They felt that the relationship was inappropriate."

"As I said, I found the atmosphere at Latimer to be quite stifling. They were too focused on rules for me to be happy there." He tried a smile. "I've always been one to push boundaries, but on this occasion I really didn't see that I had done anything wrong. I left Oxford because I felt I had spent as long there as I really wanted to. There were other opportunities to be explored. And I think we can all agree that it was a decision that worked out nicely for me."

"From what I understand," I said silkily, ignoring the self-satisfaction, "you were asked to leave Latimer College and it was made clear to you that you shouldn't apply for any other teaching positions within the university. You haven't taught since — are you blacklisted?"

"That is unfounded conjecture. I chose to pursue other avenues. There was no question of anyone not employing me because of what happened." His voice had risen and the solicitor, who had been maintaining a Buddha-like silence, cleared his throat. It seemed to recall Faraday to himself, I was disappointed to see.

"So you didn't apply for any other teaching positions." I had no way of checking whether he had or not, short of contacting each and every third-level institution in the English-speaking world, but Faraday didn't know that.

277

"I did consider a few, but on the whole I felt I had reached the end of that particular part of my career. It was a case of going through the motions while I decided what I was going to do next. I wasn't surprised not to be offered another teaching job. I'm sure it was clear to everyone that my heart wasn't in it." His pride was still wounded, I could tell; he had been cast out of the tribe and it hurt, wealth and fame notwithstanding.

"When was the last time you saw Rebecca?"

"In person? God." He thought for a second. "It must be three — no, four years ago. She came to a book signing I was doing and we chatted for a minute or two — you know, just catching up. I signed her book, told her she was looking gorgeous, and that was it. Next in the queue, please."

I smiled at the historian. "That's not true, is it? Do you want to have another go?"

"I don't understand," he said flatly, and looked over at Mercer again. The lawyer was studying his hands.

"I happen to know that you met Rebecca again. Quite recently, in fact. Make that five months ago, not three years."

"That's not right — I didn't —"

"Oh, you did. You took her out to dinner, to a little Spanish place in Marylebone." And Rebecca had written it in her desk calendar, luckily for me. "It was in July, wasn't it? A Thursday. Where was your wife that night? Or should I ask where your wife thought you were that night?"

Faraday had slumped in his chair and was gnawing his bottom lip. The low winter sun highlighted the sweat that was beading on his forehead and dampening his hair. "OK. OK, you got me. We met for dinner. But it was just once."

I shook my head. "It wasn't, I'm afraid. That was the first time. Then you met her again two weeks later. And again the following week. You sent flowers to her office on the fifth of August." Jess had passed on that little tidbit.

"If you know all this, why are you asking me about it?" Faraday was close to shouting now.

"Because I want to hear what really happened between you. Who got in touch with whom? When did you start having an affair?" I looked down at my notes, giving him time to think that was all I knew, before I hit him with the killer punch. "And why did you transfer ten thousand pounds into her bank account two months ago?"

"My client is only speaking to you on the understanding that this remains confidential. You are right to think that a crime was committed, but it was Mr Faraday who was the victim," Avery Mercer said ponderously.

"Is that a fact?"

"It's true." Faraday was looking defiant; Mercer's interruption had given him time to regroup. "Look, I didn't want to tell you about what happened between me and Rebecca in the last year because I'm not proud of it. I never meant to cheat on my wife — I certainly didn't intend that anything was going to happen between us. I was pleased when Rebecca got in touch, because I'd always liked her — we had had a real connection. It was good to see her. I enjoyed our dinner. It just seemed natural to see her again. And then — well, the situation just got a bit out of control."

"Why did she get in touch with you?"

"She'd just had a bad break-up, she said. She told me she was going back over all the major relationships in her life to see where she'd gone wrong. But I thought it was a bit of an excuse, to be honest."

Honest was the one thing Caspian Faraday wasn't. "So in July she asked you to meet up."

"Yeah. We had dinner a couple of times after that. We started sleeping together in August — I sent those flowers after the first time. It was crazy, and wrong, and I knew I shouldn't be doing it. I mean, someone as well known as me can't go sneaking around without being caught eventually. But that was part of the thrill too."

"What was Rebecca getting out of it?" I asked drily.

Faraday looked past me, as if he couldn't meet my eyes. "That's the question, isn't it? I thought she was getting a buzz out of being with me again. I mean, the sex was great. Mindblowing. It reminded me of the good old days. But I realised later that she'd been working to a plan all along."

"What happened?"

"She started blackmailing me. She said she'd tell my wife what had been going on." Faraday's jaw was clenched. "I realised that getting money from me must have been her intention from the start."

"Very upsetting for you," I said, without bothering to sound sympathetic. No one had made him cheat on his wife, after all. "How much did she ask you for?"

"She wanted five thousand pounds."

"But you gave her twice that."

"I made a deal with her. I'd pay her double what she was asking, but she was never to contact me again, for any reason, and she was certainly never to attempt to make contact with my wife. I mean, it's not as if I was short of cash. It was easy to give her more just to make her go away."

"Do you really think she would have kept her side of the bargain?" I was genuinely curious.

"Yes. I do. You have to understand, Rebecca was basically a good person. The blackmail thing — it wasn't like her. She said she needed money quickly and she couldn't think how else to get it, but I didn't think she *enjoyed* it, if you see what I mean. Not once we'd made an emotional connection again."

Mercer and I exchanged a sceptical look. He could think that if he liked. There was no blackmailer in the world that was satisfied with one shot at their target. Caspian Faraday would have been a walking cashpoint for Rebecca.

"I told her she was playing a dangerous game. Delia would have killed us both if she'd found out about it."

"That's a turn of phrase," Mercer said quickly. "He doesn't mean it literally."

"Where was Delia on the twenty-sixth of November?"

"Out of the country. I think she was in New York." The lawyer again.

I made a note. "We'll check on that. Does she drive?"

Faraday shook his head. "She doesn't have a licence. Anyway, she didn't have a reason to kill Rebecca. I paid her off and Delia never found out about it."

As far as he knew, anyway.

"The frustrating part is that I'd have given Rebecca the money if she'd just asked me for it. I liked her — I liked her a lot. She understood me." He looked at me again. "Are you married, DC Kerrigan?"

"No."

"Well then, you probably won't understand, but I *needed* Rebecca. I needed something outside my marriage. It wasn't just sex — it was the lack of *fuss*. Seeing her was fun. Being with her was fun. It was like a holiday from the real world."

I found myself wondering what Delia Faraday was like. Hard work, I imagined. There was a silver-framed photograph at Caspian's left elbow that I recognised from my Internet research as being a close-up of his wife. She looked groomed, glamorous and very slightly sulky, and I doubted she had ever voluntarily tasted any of her father's convenience foods, even if she had enjoyed the proceeds.

"Rebecca took you for a fool, didn't she? Are you seriously saying you're not bitter about it?"

"I was angry at the time," he said quietly. "I called her every name I could think of. But I thought, in the back of my mind, that one day we might meet again in different circumstances and I could forgive her. I never, ever thought she would die before that could happen."

"You realise that you have a motive for her murder."

His brow crinkled in puzzlement. "But she was murdered by that serial killer. The Burning Man, isn't that what they call him?"

"Maybe she was. Maybe not." I let him think about that for a moment. "Is there anything else you want to tell me about Rebecca?"

"I don't think so." He got up and looked out of the window, his arms folded, and when he spoke, he sounded a million miles away. "You know, she was one of those people who was more alive than everyone else. She just glowed. When I heard she was dead, I immediately thought of those lines from *Cymbeline*. They're such a cliché, but it's true. Are you familiar with the play?"

"I can't say that I am. Why don't you enlighten me."

He gave a rueful smile. "I would, but at heart, I'm still a pedagogue. I'm going to give you the classic teacher's line and tell you to look it up. It's the funeral song from Act IV."

The lawyer had got to his feet and guided me out into the hall, glaring a warning at Faraday to stay where he was and closing the door firmly behind him. He breathed heavily, staring at me with bloodshot eyes for a long moment before he spoke.

"You don't need me to tell you that he's not a killer. He's an idiot, but he couldn't have murdered that girl."

"I haven't made up my mind about that."

"You have, but you won't tell me." He smiled wolfishly. "Let him have his little indiscretion, DC Kerrigan. I'm sure it will be his last."

"Are you? In my experience, they don't stop at one little indiscretion. It becomes a habit."

He shrugged. "That's between man and wife, isn't it?"

I was about to answer when sharp heels sounded on the path outside and a key twisted in the front door. I stepped back against the wall instinctively as the door opened to reveal Delia Faraday, looking even thinner and more beautiful than I had expected. If her face had been capable of moving as nature had intended it to, it would have been twisted into a sneer.

"Who the fuck is this?"

Mercer was too smooth to look tense. "No one you need worry about, Delia. One of the accountants."

"Well, what the fuck is she doing in my hall, then? Get out of the way." She pushed past me and went into the room we'd just left.

I thought for a second about following her, taking out my warrant card and explaining exactly why I was there, but I couldn't, in the end, be so brutal for no reason.

"Thank you," Avery Mercer mouthed silently and I nodded without warmth, then turned to go.

I left Caspian Faraday's house with the absolute conviction that I was not going to bother looking up Act IV of *Cymbeline* just so I could see how bloody clever he was. You can't go against your nature, though. At twenty to two the next morning I was out of bed, hunched over my computer, searching for the funeral song with very bad grace but an overwhelming need to know. And when I found it, I understood what he had meant.

> Golden lads and girls all must,
> As chimney-sweepers, come to dust.

The lines were still on my mind the next day as I sat in the incident room, twirling a pen in my fingers and staring into space. *Come to dust.* Dust to dust, ashes to ashes. Back to burning in two easy steps. Could I picture Caspian Faraday battering Rebecca to death? Could I imagine him methodically arranging the scene to match the Burning Man's *modus operandi*? I was surprised to find that I could, particularly the second part. There had been something stagey about the Highgate house, something self-conscious about the way the furniture was all from the correct period and lovingly arranged as it would have been in the good old days when men were men and women knew their place. He was meticulous in his professional life, attentive to detail, and I thought he would have enjoyed creating a show for the police. He would have liked fooling us as well. And whatever he alleged about his agreement with Rebecca, he certainly had a motive for wanting her dead.

"You look busy." Rob threw himself into the chair next to me and stretched.

"I'm thinking. This wouldn't be familiar to you," I said primly.

"From what I've heard, it's overrated." He handed me a few sheets of paper that were stapled together. "You wanted Gil Maddick's PNC print. I'll say this for you, you know how to spot them."

I was skimming the pages at top speed, and the smile on my face was getting wider by the second. "Oh, my God. His ex-girlfriend took out a restraining order on him four years ago."

"I know," he said patiently. "I've read it. Then he breached it — turned up at her flat and got arrested."

The magistrates had taken a generous view, though; he had pleaded guilty and paid a fine, rather than having to do any time. I put the pages down. "I knew he was trouble. It looks as if he has form for being violent. I bet I was right not to be convinced by his story about how Rebecca fractured her cheek."

"It's certainly worth finding out more. I think we should go and see Miss Chloe Sandler, don't you?"

"Definitely."

The address that was listed on Gil Maddick's PNC printout was still current for her, and a quick phone call confirmed that she was in, and happy to speak to us, and generally keen to cooperate. She was even keener, if possible, when she opened her front door and clapped eyes on Rob, who was just the right side of scruffy that day and looking all the better for it. This was one interview where I would be taking a back seat. I sat on a chair by the door, leaving Rob to sit beside Chloe on the squishy white sofa.

While Rob explained who we were and what we wanted to talk to her about, I took the opportunity to look around her living room. Chloe was thirty-one going on thirteen judging by the collection of rom-com DVDs on her shelves and the clutter of cutesy ornaments on every available surface: an orchestra of kittens playing tiny musical instruments on the mantelpiece, a *cloisonné* frog crouching on the windowsill beside a crystal-studded lizard of surpassing hideousness, a family of tiny cut-glass penguins that marched across the top of the television. She was lovely, with huge wide-set brown eyes in a heart-shaped face that was set off by a Louise Brooks bob. Her voice was breathy and soft, and I had to strain to hear her when she spoke.

"I haven't spoken to Gil in years. I mean, I did call him after the court case, just to apologise for getting him in trouble, but apart from that, I haven't had any contact with him."

"They don't hand out non-molestation orders for no reason," Rob said gently. "There must have been some reason why one was granted to you. Do you mind telling us about what happened?"

She blinked at him, her eyes trusting, and I wanted to tell her to hurry up.

"I probably overreacted. I mean, these things happen, don't they? But my flatmate at the time was very politically active — a real feminist. You know, she went on Reclaim the Streets marches and stuff. She was completely supportive and made me report him."

"What happened?"

"We'd been going out for a few months." A tiny smile. "Everything was going really well. He was so attentive and kind, and he's unbelievably clever. I mean, I still think that. I really liked him."

And I doubted he had disliked the unquestioning adulation she had offered him.

"We were still getting to know one another. We had met in a bar — we got chatting when the barman ignored him and asked me for my order instead. I got so flustered, but he was lovely about it. He was usually such a gentleman." She sounded as if she still couldn't quite believe what had happened. I dug the tip of my pen into the crease down the centre of my notebook, whiling away the time while I waited for her to get to the point.

"Basically, I didn't know any of his friends or colleagues, so I had to go with my instincts when he asked me to go out with him. I really liked him, but I wanted to take things slowly, you know. I didn't want to rush into anything, but I didn't want him to lose interest either."

"Of course not." Rob was nodding as if he was familiar with the difficult choices faced by twenty-something single women in a hostile dating environment. And maybe he was. He tended not to go in for tales from his private life — or at least, he didn't share them with me.

"We hadn't — you know."

"Slept together?" I couldn't help being blunt; I was getting tired of her edging around the subject. She looked affronted for a moment, then nodded.

"This was after you'd been going out for how long?"

"Three months." She blinked at me innocently. I was willing to bet she had a heap of self-help books in her bedroom, and the most frequently consulted would be *The Rules*. She had all the hallmarks of the rabid husband-hunter. If you want someone to buy the cow, you don't give the milk away for free.

"He'd gone out with his friends, on his own. It was a lads' night out. I stayed in and did girly things like painting my nails." She extended a hand in Rob's

288

direction so he could admire her perfect French manicure. "It's really hard to find the time to do stuff like that when you're in a relationship." A pause. "I'm single at the moment, so . . ."

"Very nice," Rob said gallantly. "He came around, did he?"

"At about two o'clock in the morning." She pulled a face. "I wasn't expecting him to come that late. He banged on the door and yelled, and I freaked out. He really frightened me, and he woke up my neighbours. Sonia, my flatmate, was furious. It wasn't even the weekend — it was a Tuesday night. You don't do that kind of thing on a school night."

"What did you do?" I asked.

"Well, I let him in." The searchlight eyes were turned on me for a second. "I mean, it's not as if I didn't know who it was. I took him straight into my bedroom, because I wasn't sure if Sonia was going to go back to bed. I was a bit worried that she might come in and make a scene if he was in this room or the kitchen. She was so pissed off with him, and to be honest, they didn't get on that well. Anyway, as soon as I shut the door, he grabbed me and tried to get me onto the bed."

Her voice had dropped; I could tell she was genuinely upset as she relived the experience, and I felt somewhat ashamed of myself for having been impatient.

"He wouldn't take no for an answer. I mean, he *was* drunk, so he probably didn't really know what he was doing. He wasn't violent, exactly, but he just kept pushing me back, and I screamed at him to stop, leave

289

me alone. He was so much stronger than me. I couldn't get away. He was calling me names, saying I had made him wait long enough and he was tired of it . . ." She closed her eyes and pressed the back of her hand against her mouth, struggling for composure. Rob looked over at me and raised one eyebrow.

"Take your time, Chloe," I said. "We're not in a rush."

She flapped a hand, her eyes still closed. "Sorry. It's just so hard. I mean, it was over in seconds, but it took me months to recover." She squeezed her eyes tight closed and then opened them wide, her long wet eyelashes standing out like petals on a daisy. "Where was I? Oh yeah. Obviously Sonia heard what was going on. She came running in. Luckily for me, she was a really serious hockey player, and she'd picked up her stick on the way. She hit him with it a few times and then basically kicked him out of the flat. She wanted to call the police, but I wouldn't let her. I didn't want to make a formal complaint about it. She talked me into getting the restraining order the following week."

"You must have been very frightened of Maddick to do that."

Instead of answering me straightaway, she wriggled in her seat. "Um. Yes. I mean, I suppose so. It was really that Sonia wouldn't drop it. She kept printing out stories from the Internet about women who were murdered by their exes. I'd come home from work and find them pushed under the door of my room. Girls who'd met men on dating sites and got stalked by them, and the police didn't do anything to stop the stalkers until it was too late and the women had been raped or killed or whatever. It was really upsetting."

"I'm sure it was." Rob was doing his manly, reassuring bit. Chloe gazed at him adoringly. If he wasn't careful, she'd be sitting on his lap soon.

"In the end, I did go to court to get the restraining order. Gil was there too, to put his side across, and I felt really sorry for him, actually, because it was hugely embarrassing. He explained that he'd just been incredibly drunk. Then he said he thought I might have overreacted." Her eyes narrowed as she recalled it. "I mean, that was *it* as far as I was concerned. I wasn't going to back down after he'd said that. If Sonia hadn't been in the flat that night, I don't know what would have happened, and neither does he."

"So the order was granted. When did he breach it?"

"Three months later." She was looking uneasy again. "To be fair to him, it wasn't completely his fault. I hadn't realised how seriously the police took non-molestation orders."

They had become a top priority thanks to the sort of cases she had just mentioned. The bosses in the Met had got tired of making excuses for the fact that so many women had died at the hands of their harassers. You treated domestic violence as a minor concern at your peril. It was a hard lesson we'd learned, at the expense of some vulnerable people who had deserved better.

"What happened?"

She peeked up at Rob through her long eyelashes before replying in a small voice. "He'd sent me a really lovely letter apologising for what happened that night and asking me to forgive him. I put it away in a drawer as soon as I'd read it, but I couldn't forget about it — I just kept going back to look at it again and again. Eventually I rang him up and asked him to come over to pick up the stuff he'd left here. I'd put it in a box under my bed, because I didn't think it was right to throw it away. Sonia wanted me to take his clothes to the charity shop and burn everything else." She giggled, then became serious again. "That was just an excuse. I wanted to see him. I didn't want to leave it on such bad terms. I was feeling a bit embarrassed about the restraining order, and I wanted to clear the air. I thought it would be OK."

"But it wasn't." Rob sounded resigned.

"No, it was. Well, it would have been. Sonia was out for the afternoon, but she came back sooner than I was expecting. She saw his car outside and called the police. I think everyone thought that he'd made me agree to him coming over — that he'd brainwashed me, or manipulated me. But that wasn't it at all. He left as soon as the police came, and I told them nothing had happened, I hadn't been threatened or anything. They seemed to listen to me. I didn't know that he'd have to go to the magistrates' court anyway."

"Did you go along?"

She shook her head violently. "No. I couldn't face it. But the police told me he pleaded guilty. The fine was a bit of a slap on the wrist. I mean, I think they must have known he wasn't doing anything wrong by coming here."

"Have you seen him since?"

She coloured again. "It was too awkward. I felt really bad about what happened, but it was his fault originally. I mean, everyone tells me I don't have anything to apologise for, but I can't help feeling like I have to take some responsibility too."

"You live and learn," I said. "Try not to worry about it."

She tore her eyes away from Rob's face for a moment. "Thanks."

"You're welcome." I stood up. "I think we've got all we came for. I'll just head out to the car."

Rob had twisted around to look at me, consternation on his face, but I didn't break stride. If he wanted to be DC Charming, he had to take the consequences. And that included extracting himself from Chloe Sandler's living room without any help from me.

I had only had time to check my mobile phone — another voicemail from my mother, which I didn't feel strong enough to play back — before the car door opened and Rob sat into the driver's seat. His ears were tinged with red.

"Trouble?" I asked sweetly.

"Nothing I couldn't handle."

"I'll bet. I think she was quite keen to be handled, actually. But only up to a point."

"Are you thirsty? Do you want me to stop on the way back and get you a saucer of milk?"

I purred, then got serious. "What did you make of that?"

He scratched his jaw absent-mindedly. "Could be something. Could be nothing. I know she said it was her idea to invite him round, but —"

"But she's not the most forceful person in the world," I finished for him. "She's a classic victim, isn't she? He nearly raped her and she thinks it was all her fault."

"Yeah. But I don't know if that makes him our killer." He shot a sidelong look at me. "I do know that I wouldn't want to bump into Sonia down a dark alley, with or without her hockey stick."

"You would definitely come off worst," I agreed. "I liked the sound of Sonia. She had common sense."

Sonia had stood between Gil Maddick and poor little Chloe. She hadn't backed down. She hadn't been too polite to make a fuss.

And she just might have saved her flatmate's life.

LOUISE

The effort I had put in was all worth it as soon as I opened the door and saw the surprise on Gil's face. He didn't say anything for a second, just stared.

"Well? Smart enough?"

"Looking for a compliment?" He laughed, taking the sting out of the words. "You're beautiful."

"Hardly." I stepped out and locked the door behind me. "But good enough for dinner."

In fact, I knew I looked better than good enough. I wore my hair loose, curving around my face and swinging over my shoulders, and my hairdresser had taken great delight in making it two shades blonder. The plain black dress, so deceptively simple, looked perfect. And the peridot earrings that had been Rebecca's brought out the green in my eyes. I might not have felt confident, but I looked it, and that was all that mattered.

"How's your neck?"

I turned my head to show him, lifting my hair.

"You can hardly see it." He sounded almost disappointed.

"That's because I covered it in make-up." I could feel it, though, every time I turned my head, a sharp little reminder of something I still couldn't quite understand.

"Where did you get those?" Gil reached out and tapped one of my earrings gently, and I put my hand up to stop it swaying.

"They were a present from Rebecca."

I saw his eyebrows draw into a frown for a second and suppressed a smile of triumph. He had noticed them, as I'd known he would. And I had also known he'd bought them for her in the first place. I let my hair drop back down, hiding them from view again, and smiled.

"Should we go? I don't want us to be late."

Gil drove along the river as far as Chelsea, where he parked in a back street outside a grey, unpromising door. He opened the car door for me and waited for me to get out. I looked up at him warily.

"Is this where we're going?"

"Certainly is."

"It doesn't look like a restaurant."

"That's part of the charm." He took my hand and pulled me out of the car, holding me against him for a moment with his nose in my hair. "Mmm. Nice scent."

"Favourite of yours, is it?"

"I thought it would suit you."

"Funny. I always associate it with Rebecca."

"I don't." He moved back a couple of inches, his hands by his side, and I felt cold all of a sudden, the wind cutting through the fine silk shawl as if it wasn't there.

"She always wore it." I knew I should drop it but some devil made me go on. "Or she did after she met you."

"Don't be like that."

"Like what?" I felt suddenly nervous.

"Jealous, I suppose." He was looking down at me with a remote expression on his face. "I can't stand that sort of thing. You know better than to act that way. And I shouldn't have to pretend that you're the first girl I've ever taken out to dinner."

"I'm sorry," I began, and he shook his head.

"Don't be sorry. Just — I just want to be honest with you. I don't want to bother with the usual rubbish that you get into when you start seeing someone. Let's agree now that if we're going to do this, we're not going to mess each other about."

"I only agreed to have dinner with you," I pointed out. "It's not a lifelong commitment. It's just a meal."

"It was just dinner, but then you opened the door looking like that." He stared down at me. "I'm not going to let you go, Louise."

I followed him into the restaurant with a feeling of unreality that grew stronger when the grey door proved to have been hiding a small room with just eight tables, all with a tiny spotlight overhead that threw the diners' faces into shadow. The tables were immaculate, the maitre d', who recognised Gil and welcomed him as an old friend, attentive without being obsequious. With an enquiring look to me, Gil ordered champagne and it came quickly, creamy pale in tall flutes. I popped bubbles on my tongue as I read through the menu.

"Is there anything you don't eat?"

"My words." I relented. "Not really. Tripe, I suppose. And I'm not keen on oysters."

"I love them. You'll have to get to like them."

"I don't think I will."

"We'll see." He returned to studying the menu and I frowned at him.

"You never accept a no if it's not the answer you want to hear, do you?"

"Not often. Anyway, it doesn't matter because oysters aren't on the chefs menu, and that's what I think we should have. Six courses. Are you up for it?"

I didn't even look at it. I recognised the question as the challenge it was, and the only possible answer was yes.

It may have been six courses but the portions were mercifully small. Tiny plates appeared in front of us, introduced by the waiter, little works of art. Plump white scallops, round and sweet, on a bed of pale-green courgette purée. A scoop of pearl-coloured mushroom risotto. A wince-making grapefruit sorbet in a frosted cup. Tender beef, rose-pink in a rich dark sauce, nestling against a cloud of mashed potato. A swirl of vanilla mousse in a sea of bitter chocolate. Sunshine-yellow lemon tart with fat raspberries.

I ate with true enjoyment, forgetting to be nervous, forgetting that I had always been wary around Gil, and why that had been the case. He was quiet much of the time, and when I looked up I often found his eyes on me. I felt he was trying to work something out, something about me, and I left him to it.

We had got as far as coffee, tiny cups of nightblack espresso frothed with mink-coloured foam, when I said, "Did you ever come here with Rebecca?"

298

"What?"

"You've obviously been here a few times. I was just wondering if you'd been here with her."

"No, as it happens." He leaned back in his chair, playing with his coffee spoon. "Why? Would that matter?"

I laughed. "There's no point in pretending she's not on my mind. If it wasn't for her, we wouldn't be sitting here together."

"People meet in lots of different ways. I wouldn't place too much importance on her role in bringing us together." He looked away from me, scanning the room as if he had lost interest in the conversation.

"I can't let you get away with that. It's not like she introduced us at a party. Besides, I want to talk about her."

"What is there to say?"

"You could tell me what you meant when you said you were intrigued by me, which was why, according to you, you were horrible to me." I could feel my pulse beating in my neck. I took a sip of water, concentrating on not letting my hands shake.

"Horrible isn't the right word," he protested. "I just didn't spend that much time talking to you. There's no mystery about it. You weren't exactly available. I couldn't switch from Bex to you. You'd never have considered it for a second."

"But now that she's dead . . ."

"It gave me an excuse to get in touch with you. That's all."

I shook my head. "I just don't believe you. I'm sorry."

"Why not?"

"Because no one ever noticed me when Rebecca was in the room." I said it simply, without self-pity.

"More fool them." His eyes swept over me again. "They obviously didn't see what I saw."

"And what was that?"

"Your promise." He leaned forward. "You are beautiful, Louise. Really, truly beautiful. Especially now that you're not hiding behind your friend any more. Rebecca was pretty, and fun to be around, but she was basically boring. You worshipped her so you didn't notice it, but I had run out of patience by the time we split up."

"You have high standards, don't you?"

"I just got tired of her always trying to please me. What I like about you is your independence. You don't need to be liked. You go your own way."

I laughed. "The cat that walked by herself."

"I've always liked cats." He reached across the table, and I let him take my hand.

It was time to listen to the common-sense voice in the back of my mind that was warning me, with increasing urgency, that I had had my fun, that I should avoid seeing Gil Maddick again. And I think I might have managed it, too, if he hadn't been holding my hand. The touch of his skin against mine made me shiver with wanting him, and common sense didn't stand a chance.

300

CHAPTER
TEN

MAEVE

I sat at my desk like a cat at a mousehole, waiting for the superintendent to return from the daily press conference. Ideally, I would have spoken to him before it. The press conference now tended to consist of belligerent questions from journalists who'd learned all about murder investigation from re-runs of *Prime Suspect* and couldn't understand why we hadn't found the killer yet. Godley was committed to good communication and keeping the public well informed, so he went through with it. That didn't mean he enjoyed it.

He strode back into the incident room with Judd at his heels. Their matching expressions told me that things had not gone well. I hesitated for a second, then hurried over. *Now or never.*

"Sir, can I have a word about Rebecca Haworth?"

They had been looking at the big noticeboard that occupied one wall of his office, where a macabre gallery of victims hung beside a giant map of the city marked with black crosses where each girl had been discovered. Dates, names, places — all written out neatly, as if by bringing order to the events Godley could find the pattern that eluded all of us and use it to predict where and how the murderer might be trapped. He turned and raised his eyebrows.

"Now, Maeve?"

"If you don't mind."

"Fire away."

Judd threw himself down in a chair by Godley's desk, as if to make it absolutely clear that he wasn't going to go anywhere. I cleared my throat.

"It's just that I think we were right to be concerned about this victim. There were some odd things going on in her life. I've found a few reasons why someone might have wanted her dead. Taking into account the differences in the murderer's MO, I'm inclined to think that this is a copycat crime."

"I don't want to hear this," Judd said, his voice harsh. "You're trying to draw attention to yourself, DC Kerrigan, but you could end up jeopardising the whole case when we get to court."

I felt myself redden. "Believe me, I wanted more than anything to find out that she was a victim of the serial killer."

"We can't ignore the evidence," Godley pointed out. "It might not suit us but we've got to play it out and see where it leads us."

Judd turned to his boss. "If she's right and this is a separate case, at least hand it over to another SIO so you don't have any distractions from the current investigation."

He shook his head. "I want to hold on to it. I don't want to draw attention to it in case we get a shitstorm from the media. Besides, it might be useful to have this murder attributed to our guy. It might frustrate him into showing himself to prove he's the one and only. Carry on as we were, please."

The inspector stood up abruptly. "I can't agree." He looked at me. "But you might as well waste your time on this as on anything else."

I bit my lip, managing not to snap back at him before he left the room. His refusal to use me for anything else was a sore point. Preoccupied though I was with what had happened to Rebecca, I was not too absorbed to miss the preparations that were being made for the undercover operation that was to take place over the following two nights. I wanted to be in on it. And I knew very well that I had no chance whatsoever of being included if Tom Judd was left to allocate resources.

"Try not to worry about Tom. The tension gets to him now and then. Especially when we aren't making much progress."

Now that I had a chance to look at him at close range, I could see the superintendent was exhausted. His eyes were rimmed with red, and blue-grey shadows underneath them looked like bruises. He had lost weight — the collar of his shirt was loose. But opportunities to speak to him like this were vanishingly rare, especially since the entire squad knew we were on a countdown to the next murder.

I gestured to the map. "Do you think we're getting anywhere?"

"Not really. I spent today listening to a criminal psychologist telling me our murderer hates women. Not exactly a stretch, is it? I think I might have guessed that myself."

"I heard we're doing an undercover operation over the weekend. Is that the area the UCs are working?" The map had been marked with a red line that cut through Lambeth and along the Walworth Road, down as far as Camberwell Green, then across Stockwell to Nine Elms and back up the river along the Albert Embankment.

"That's the one. According to the geographical profile, that's the territory he's likely to see as his own. The psychologist thinks he's on foot because the bodies aren't dumped far from where we know the victims were walking. That narrows the field a bit. And he obviously feels confident in this part of the world. Local, they think. We've borrowed officers from Clubs and Vice to be our bait."

They had the training for it; I was rather glad I didn't. I had never been tempted to pursue that branch of policing, not when it meant standing around on street corners in revealing clothes trying to look enticing.

Godley looked grim. "We've got to try it, but I can't help thinking we're unlikely to find him this way. We've just run out of alternatives."

"He's very clever," I said softly, and flinched as the superintendent glared at me.

"He's very lucky, that's all. I thought I'd made it clear that no one was to think this serial killer is anything other than a selfish, perverted individual who acts impulsively and violently and has been exception-ally fortunate not to be spotted in the act of committing his crimes. If we knew how he was getting them to trust him, we'd have arrested him by now. But that's the only remarkable thing about him. We aren't hunting some master criminal."

I mumbled something, feeling stupid. Godley hated the fact that the media had given our killer a nickname. It turned him into a celebrity, it granted him notoriety, it let him join the select club of killers whose crimes had passed into infamy. It was what the killer wanted. And it was, according to the superintendent, highly dangerous.

Godley had returned to contemplating the map. Almost to himself, he murmured, "We just need to know how he's doing it. Whatever it is, he's got it down to a fine art." He gave me a sidelong grin that made my heart flutter a little, because even if I swore blind to everyone else that it wasn't true, I couldn't deny to myself that I had a huge crush on my boss. "Maybe he is cleverer than us."

"I doubt that. We'll get him," I said with total confidence, as if confidence alone would do it.

"Did you want to tell me the details of what you've found out about Rebecca Haworth?"

I wavered. "There's a lot to say — it might take a while. If you want to go home I can tell you about it tomorrow."

"I want to hear it." He sat down and gestured to a chair opposite him. "Come on. Talk me through it. You must know the real Rebecca by now."

I thought about that for a moment before answering him. I'd spent days listening to people talk about Rebecca Haworth, but I was starting to accept that I would never understand her completely. What I had learned from those who had known and loved her was the shape of the space she'd occupied in their minds. Everyone had known a different version of Rebecca and believed it to be the real one.

"I think the truth about Rebecca was that even she didn't know who the real Rebecca was. She was lost. That's the best way I can put it. She'd lost her way. And she was getting further and further away from where she should have been. I think it was only a matter of time before something went catastrophically wrong. And I still haven't worked out exactly why she died."

Godley laced his fingers together and leaned back, the expression on his face thoughtful as I recounted the sad story of how Rebecca Haworth had lived through her twenty-eight years.

"I think she was desperate," I said, as I got to the end of it. "The first major disaster was when she was upset by Adam Rowley's drowning — she had what seems to have been a fairly major nervous breakdown, dropped out of university temporarily, developed an eating disorder and, from what her friend Tilly said, she seemed to think that she had to bear some responsibility for what happened to him. But she got it together again. She got a good job and did well at it. She was back to being the golden girl, a star, everything her parents wanted her to be. And then it all fell apart. First her relationship broke up in traumatic circumstances, then she lost her job, then the affair with Faraday happened, followed by a little bit of blackmail. She was addicted to drugs with no way to pay for them. She seemed to be trying everything she could to hang on to the illusion that her life was a success. And then she died."

"Not murdered by our man, you think."

"No. Someone dressed it up to look like his work, and even if I think I know who, I can't prove it."

"Who do you think did it?"

The question was asked in a casual way, but I didn't make the mistake of thinking that Godley wasn't taking me seriously. I hesitated before I answered, knowing that to get it wrong would be a critical mistake.

"The ex-boyfriend, Gil Maddick."

"What makes you say that?"

I shrugged. "I don't have any evidence, but that's the feeling I have. I'm still trying to work out how it all fits together."

"I'd take it chronologically and start ruling some of these things out. Right at the beginning, you've got the drowning. You need to know what she knew about it. You've talked to some of her friends from Oxford, haven't you? Talk to them again and see what you can shake loose this time."

"I haven't spoken to her best friend about it. She might know something." I hadn't yet had a chance to pin Louise down.

Godley made a note on the pad in front of him. "I think we need to put some pressure on the ex-boyfriend. I'll get Tom to get a search warrant so we can send the forensics team around to look at his flat, check out his car — bother him, basically. You can re-interview him and see if he's rattled by it. You might even get a confession."

"He's pretty self-possessed. I doubt it."

"Well, at the very least he might make a mistake." The superintendent grinned at me. "I know I can count on you to spot it if he does."

"And if he doesn't?"

"You might have to wait and see what happens next. Sometimes the breaks don't come where you think they will. But I'm sure they'll come." He glanced up at the noticeboard again, almost as a reflex, then pushed back his chair in one quick movement. "Is that everything?"

I hesitated, then rushed on. "Actually, I was wondering if I could get on one of the surveillance teams tomorrow night. I've done the course and I'd really like to be involved. I know I'm supposed to be concentrating on Rebecca, but I don't want to lose touch with the main investigation completely. And DI Judd didn't seem to be that interested in including me."

A tiny vertical line creased the skin between Godley's eyes. He turned away and started to fiddle with a pen on his desk. "We'll see."

I cringed inwardly, hoping I hadn't offended him by complaining about the inspector. The audience was over anyway. I thanked him and scampered back to my desk to go over the conversations again in my mind. I tried to make myself invisible behind a heap of files as the superintendent left. His footsteps slowed, then stopped beside me.

"Make yourself available for duty tomorrow night and I'll make sure you're included in one of the surveillance teams."

I mumbled something incoherent but grateful and he went on his way, head bent, the weight of the world on his shoulders. Superintendent God at his best; he knew how to take care of the details — even one as unimportant as me.

Louise North's Victorian terraced house was, predictably, in immaculate order. I had phoned so she knew I was coming, but somehow I didn't think she'd spent the half-hour before my arrival tidying up. The small front garden to the right of the geometrically tiled path was covered with raked white gravel, and the only plants were two round boxes in zinc containers on either side of the front door. I was still looking at them when the door opened, before I even had a chance to ring the bell.

"DC Kerrigan. Come in. Would you like a cup of tea?"

"I would, but if you're making me tea you should definitely call me Maeve."

"Maeve, then. Follow me."

It was the first time I had seen Louise on home territory, and I was instantly intrigued. There was something different about her — something softer. Her hair was loose and hung down around her face. It looked blonder than I remembered. She was wearing old faded jeans, stripy socks in rainbow colours and a sky-blue sweatshirt with worn cuffs and a dusting of flour down the front. It had LATIMER written across the back, I noticed when she led the way through the narrow hall to the kitchen, which was small but cosy, with yellow-painted walls and herbs growing in little pots on the windowsill. The sweet smell of baking hung in the air. Beside the cooker there was a collection of the sort of culinary gadgetry that only a really serious cook would need, and I looked at Louise with renewed respect.

"Don't tell me you make your own cakes."

"Now and then. There's one in the oven at the moment, but I've got homemade brownies that are ready to eat if you'd like one."

I had missed lunch. The thought of a brownie had me positively drooling. "Why not. Thanks."

"Sit down."

A round, well-scrubbed table and four ladder-backed chairs occupied the centre of the room. I threw my coat over the back of one and sat down in another, resting my chin on my hand and watching Louise bustle around the kitchen.

"I didn't think you'd be the domestic-goddess type."

"I'm not, really. But baking is easy."

"If you say so," I said dubiously, thinking of the leaden, airless sponge cake and bullet-hard scones I had made in home economics class, which was the last time I had attempted to make anything that could be bought for loose change in a supermarket. In my view, life was too short to measure ingredients, and I'd never met a recipe I couldn't foul up. But Louise was the sort of person who enjoyed that sort of thing. Painstaking.

Efficient. Everything I would have liked to be and wasn't.

Looking around the kitchen, I noted two mugs on the draining board, two plates in the rack, two wine glasses waiting to be put away. On the way through the hall I had seen a man's coat hanging on the newel post. Unless I was very much mistaken, Louise was single no longer. I recalled the love bite I'd seen on her neck at the memorial service with mild distaste. Not that I thought there was anything wrong with romance in and of itself, but there was something gruesome about the circumstances if that was where things had started. I would not leave without finding out more, I promised myself, while giving Louise an innocent smile.

The brownie was meltingly delicious and I ate it quickly, chasing the last crumbs around my plate before I sat back with a sigh.

"Gorgeous. If you ever get tired of the law, you should open your own bakery."

"Don't think I haven't thought of it. I've set my heart on starting up a teashop in some nice town where there are lots of thirsty tourists to serve. Somewhere on the south coast, probably."

"What about somewhere like Oxford? Plenty of tourists there."

"No. Not there."

I had just been making conversation but her voice was strained, and when I looked up I saw that she had retreated behind the mask of reserve again.

"I thought you were happy there."

"I was. But you know what they say, you can't fish in the same river twice."

"Why not?"

"I don't know." She laughed a little. "I've never really thought about it. The water's always flowing in a river, I suppose. It never stops moving. So it's not the same river even if you're in the same place. Does that make sense?"

"Sort of," I said dubiously. "Actually, that's what I wanted to talk to you about."

"Oxford?"

"Yes. More specifically, the river. What happened to Adam Rowley, Louise?"

She was too self-possessed to bite her lip or fidget, but she couldn't do anything about the colour that drained from her face before she answered. "I don't see what that has to do with Rebecca. He drowned. It was an accident."

"It might have been. But from what I've heard, it might also have been murder."

"Who told you that?" She sounded amused, not alarmed, and I could tell she was back in control, the lapse so fleeting that I might have imagined it.

"Various people. What about you — what do you think?"

"Adam wasn't murdered. He was out of his skull on booze and drugs the night he died. He fell into the river, and frankly, I was just surprised no one had done it before. The banks of the river were completely open at the time; there was no barrier to stop anyone from falling. Typical Latimer College. As long as it *looks* nice, that's the important thing. Never mind *safety* or common sense." The venom in her voice surprised me.

"You liked Oxford. You told me you did the first time we met. You're even wearing the college sweatshirt," I pointed out.

She shrugged. "Yeah, I liked it, but I saw it for what it was. The senior common room is basically a retirement home for perpetual schoolboys. They don't like to deal with the real world. And they don't have to, most of the time. I thought it was heaven to be so remote from reality when I was there. Now I'm not so sure. You only have to look at how they reacted to Adam's death to see what they're like."

"And how was that?"

"They went on a witch hunt. They were determined to prove that they weren't responsible. Some evil influence had come in from outside like shit on a shoe. You'd have thought they were looking for the bloody serpent in the Garden of Eden. And anyone who didn't fit in was automatically a suspect."

The cut-glass accent was faltering a little, consonants dropping here and there as Louise talked more quickly.

"Like you?"

She laughed. "Me? They didn't notice me. No, a friend of mine was sent down. It ruined his career. Alex was a brilliant chemist. He could have gone into research, done something really important. He never went back to it after what happened at Latimer. He's never had a proper job since, just done temping here and there to make ends meet. He didn't look right and he didn't sound right and they hung him out to dry to make themselves look better."

"Rebecca struggled too, didn't she?"

"Only because she wanted to. She was in love with the idea of suffering. She wanted the attention." She must have seen the shock on my face because she gave me a quick half-smile. "Oh, I loved Rebecca, but she was a bit of a drama queen. She was highly strung anyway — she was worried about Finals because work hadn't been going so well for her, and she hadn't been eating or sleeping much so she was getting into a right old state. And then Adam died. It was her way out — a good enough excuse for not sitting her exams when she was supposed to. She had her tutor wrapped around her little finger and he let her get away with it."

"Are you saying she wasn't genuinely upset about his death?"

"She was sincere, don't get me wrong. Rebecca always meant what she said. But it was all very convenient too. She'd completely convinced herself that Adam was the love of her life and now he was gone for ever, when actually he was a nasty little prick who had very little interest in her, apart from seeing her as easy. He was absolutely no loss to anyone, and certainly not to her since she didn't have the sense to stay away from him."

"Ouch."

Louise looked at me defiantly. "I didn't like him."

"No kidding." I was beginning to get the impression that Louise had never thought any man good enough for her friend. I thought for a second, trying to decide

314

how to approach it. "Louise, why would Rebecca have said that she was responsible for what happened to Adam?"

"She said *what?*" I had shocked her out of her composure again.

"One of her other friends told me that Rebecca had told her she had been involved in something dreadful, and because of it, she was sure she was going to die young. The exact phrase was that she owed her life in payment for someone else's. I can only assume she was talking about Adam — unless you know something I don't."

She shook her head, mute.

"Why would Rebecca think that Adam's death had anything to do with her? She wasn't even in college when it happened. She had an alibi."

"More of the same self-dramatisation. I wouldn't put too much faith into what Rebecca said about it. She was the sort of person who couldn't look at the front of the car after a long drive in the summer in case there were dead butterflies stuck in the radiator grille. She was too sensitive for her own good, basically. She took responsibility for everything, whether she could control it or not."

"Did you ever hear her say anything about Adam? About feeling guilty? Or anything that might relate to how he died?"

"Not that I recall. But she wouldn't have spoken to me about it anyway. I told her to pull herself together when she had her breakdown after he died. I said I wasn't interested in hearing about how upset she was.

I thought it was the only way to snap her out of her state of mind. But she took offence. We didn't speak for a few months."

"Just because you weren't sympathetic about her breakdown?"

"Because I didn't back her up. I wanted her to do her exams and graduate at the same time I did. I knew she wouldn't do as well if she came back after a year away. And I was right. She tried to run away. You can't run for ever. Sooner or later, you have to do whatever it is that frightens you."

"Sometimes fear can be useful," I said softly. "Sometimes you have to run away for your own good."

"It didn't help her," Louise insisted. "And no one helped me to get her back on track. If her parents had supported me, she would never have had to go back and creepy Caspian Faraday would never have molested her — which is basically what he did, by the way."

"I know."

"Well, then." Louise seemed to run out of steam. She stared at me. "You know about Caspian and Rebecca?"

"I've interviewed him."

"Oh. What did he say?"

"This and that." I knew she would be annoyed by my non-answer; I also knew that she wouldn't ask me anything further. She could take a hint, could Louise.

Louise's eyes narrowed. "I don't see why you're focusing on what happened to Rebecca at Oxford anyway. It's got nothing to do with what happened to her."

"Doesn't it?"

"Obviously not. She was murdered by a serial killer. That's just bad luck. Being in the wrong place at the wrong time."

I decided it was time to show some of my cards. "Actually, we aren't sure that Rebecca was murdered by the Burning Man. We think it might have been someone she knew trying to make us believe that she was killed by the serial killer. Maybe someone she was blackmailing. Maybe someone else. She was in a lot of trouble when she died, and there were quite a few people who might have wanted her gone."

"Like who?" Louise asked, and I could barely hear the words, she spoke so softly. She looked absolutely terrified.

Before I could answer her, I heard a sound from the hall behind me and I turned in my chair to see Gil Maddick standing in the doorway. He looked very handsome, and very angry, and I had no idea how long he had been there or how much he had overheard, but I noticed that his feet were bare. Considering how rumpled his hair was and his overall demeanour, I was quite sure that he had just got out of bed.

"Well, well, well, look who it is. WPC Nosey making a house call."

"That rank doesn't exist any more," I said calmly. "The title is just PC for everyone. And as it happens, I'm a detective constable, so it's DC Nosey, if you don't mind."

"I beg your pardon." He folded his arms. "Fancy meeting you here."

"I'm surprised to see you too, as it happens." I was trying to recall what I had just been saying. I hadn't mentioned his name yet, that was one thing. But what the hell was he doing in Louise's house?

As if to answer me, he strolled around the table to stand behind her, sliding one hand inside the collar of her sweatshirt as he bent to kiss her cheek. He kept his eyes fixed on mine throughout and I felt as if I was intruding, then became irritated that he'd made me feel that way.

"You shouldn't have let me sleep so late, Lulu. It's almost three o'clock."

She was looking embarrassed but also oddly triumphant, and the glow I'd noticed when I arrived was back in full force.

"I thought you needed a rest. And I wanted to talk to DC Kerrigan on my own. I didn't need any distractions."

The hand inside her collar moved once, then stilled. "Shall I shoot off, then?"

"I think we're finished." She looked at me and raised her eyebrows.

"I think we are too." I was feeling sick; it was like watching someone running towards the edge of a cliff, all oblivious to the danger they were in. "But I wouldn't mind a word with you, Mr Maddick, since you're here. In private, preferably."

"Use the sitting room," Louise said promptly. "I want to tidy up here. Put a couple of lamps on, Gil. It'll be gloomy in there now the sun is off the front of the house."

I followed him into a small room that was dominated by a huge abstract painting over the fireplace, hazy blues and greys that suggested a seascape at first glance. The rest of the room was straightforward IKEA, as if she'd torn a page out of the catalogue and ordered everything on it. Practical, comfortable, unexciting furniture that looked as if it was never used. I remembered what she'd said about spending evenings and weekends in the office and thought the spare time she had was probably spent in her lovely kitchen. This was an impersonal space, indefinably dead, and against that backdrop, Gil Maddick looked very much out of place.

"What are you doing here?"

"I could ask you the same question," I said. He hadn't bothered to switch on any lamps and I flicked down the wall switch by the door. The harsh overhead light scored lines around his mouth and put shadows under his eyes; he looked less handsome, more hooded, and though I knew better than to think criminals looked like what they were I found him flat-out disturbing and I hoped it didn't show.

"Isn't it obvious? Louise and I have made up our differences. You should be happy for us, DC Kerrigan. You brought us together."

"How do you work that out?"

"It gave us something to talk about." He gave me a half-smile that made my skin crawl. "We're very happy — Louise is very happy. Please don't do anything to threaten that."

"What, like telling her one of your exes took out a restraining order on you?"

"What are you talking about?" Then, "How did you know about Chloe?" He looked baffled, though there was a hint of anger there too. "Have you spoken to her? Did she explain it was all a misunderstanding?"

"I've spoken to her, yes. I've drawn my own conclusions about the incidents in question, though."

"Not this shit again. I've been through all this. It was nothing. Don't blow it out of proportion."

"I think Louise should know that you have a history of violent behaviour towards your partners. I think she should know that Rebecca fractured her cheek while she was in a relationship with you."

"I told you before. She was pissed. She fell over, didn't put out her hands to save herself and hit her face. It was nothing to do with me, except that I was the one who sat with her in the waiting room at the hospital and looked after her while she was convalescing. You can tell Louise about that if you like. I don't think I come out of it too badly. And if it had been my fault, don't you think she would have told her best friend about it?"

"Not necessarily. It's well documented that victims of domestic violence can try to hide it. They feel ashamed. They blame themselves."

"Why are you so determined to prove I'm a criminal?" He took two steps towards me, getting too close for my comfort, leaning in so his face was only a few inches from mine and I had to work hard not to flinch. "Is it because you think I know more than I'm saying about what happened to Rebecca?"

"Don't you?"

"As it happens, no, I don't. Get a new theory, DC Kerrigan. This one is getting tired." He spoke softly but the effect was menacing enough. I almost wished he would go further though — try to hurt me — so I could have an excuse for arresting him. I wanted more than anything to get him out of Louise's house, to show her what he was really like and save her from falling for the blue eyes that were staring into mine. If I wasn't too late already.

"I'll be honest with you, Mr Maddick. I don't like the way you talk about Rebecca, and I don't like the attitude you have taken since the beginning of this investigation. Some people don't like the police. I can understand that. But when someone is hostile from the very start, with no apparent reason for it, that makes me interested in them. And at the moment, I'm interested in you."

He stepped back. "I don't know why you're so convinced I'm a bad guy. I'm not who you're looking for. I'm just unlucky in my choice of girlfriends."

"They don't seem to have too much luck either." I closed the gap between us again. *Let's see how you like being on the receiving end of some aggression.* "I'm watching you. And if anything happens to Louise — if she so much as breaks a fingernail because of something you do or don't do — I will come after you and I will not rest until I make sure you've paid for what you've done."

"Don't tell Louise about Chloe." The words came out fast, as if what he said was unpremeditated, and he didn't try to disguise the worry on his face. "Please. Not yet. She won't understand."

"If you're serious about her, and about your relationship, shouldn't you tell her about it anyway?"

He looked more hopeful. "Will you let me tell her in my own time?"

"If by that you mean immediately, yes."

"Great." His voice was bleak.

"It's not going to be any easier to deal with it if she finds out later."

"Except that by then she might have learned to trust me," he said bitterly. "Which is not the case at the moment."

"Good for her," I said crisply, and ducked out of the room before he could respond.

I went looking for Louise, to say goodbye. The front door was ajar and I found her outside in rubber gloves and wellies, washing a silver BMW Z3.

"Very nice."

"Thanks, it's new." She blushed. "I know it sounds weird, but I suddenly felt that I should do something crazy. Something that Rebecca would have approved of. My old car was far too sensible."

"What was it?"

"A fourteen-year-old Peugeot 306. Navy blue. Very practical." She grinned at me as she pulled off the gloves. "I mean, I like driving, and I could afford a flash car, so what was stopping me? I sometimes think I'm too careful for my own good."

322

"There's a time and a place for being reckless." I moved closer to her and lowered my voice. "But Louise . . . don't be stupid, OK? The first time I met you, you were worried about Gil and what he might have done to Rebecca. You need to trust your instincts; you felt that way for a reason. Suddenly you're letting him get close to you, and it worries me."

She wouldn't meet my eyes. "I know what I'm doing."

"Do you? Like your friend did?" She bit her lip and I pressed home my advantage. "I'm not saying that Gil killed Rebecca, but he's not off the hook by any stretch of the imagination, and until I can tell you absolutely, definitely that he wasn't involved, I'd really like you to stay away from him. He has a history of leaving a trail of damage behind him, Louise, and I don't want to see you get hurt. Whatever he did or didn't do, he's bad news, and you don't need him."

"You don't know him." She looked up at me, and there was pure stubbornness in her eyes. "And you don't know me. You don't need to worry. I'll be fine."

I made a snap decision and dug in my pocket for a card. "Right. Well, here's my mobile number. Call me if anything happens."

"What are you, my mum?" She was holding on to the card with the tips of her fingers, as if she wanted to drop it there and then.

"I'm just worried for you, Louise, and there's not a lot else I can do. Think of it as friendly interest."

She looked mildly bemused. Then she smiled. "Thank you, Maeve. It's a long time since anyone has bothered to check up on me."

"It's my job," I said simply. And I didn't want to have to watch Glen Hanshaw conducting an autopsy on Louise too. "If you feel threatened at any time, don't call me. Call 999. They'll get to you quicker."

"I really doubt that's going to be necessary." She was struggling not to laugh. "Thanks for the advice anyway."

I had done my best. I nodded to her before walking away to where I'd parked. As I drove off, I saw Louise standing in the road, watching me go, getting smaller and smaller in my rear-view mirror, until I turned the corner and she disappeared.

LOUISE

I went back into the house, calling Gil's name as I headed down to the back door to put the bucket and sponge in the garden shed. He didn't answer me. I checked each room on my way back and found him in the sitting room, on the sofa. He had his arms folded and was staring into space. I sat beside him.

"What's the matter?"

"Nothing." The tone was a warning. *Leave it alone.*

I knew it was stupid, but I persevered. "Was it something Maeve said?"

"Who? Oh, the copper. I didn't know you were on first-name terms."

"Since today. And look, she's given me her mobile number." I waved her business card at him.

"Why?"

"In case I need to call her to tell her you've battered me to death." He didn't smile and I felt my own falter, then disappear. "Gil . . ."

"It's not funny, Louise." He got up and walked around the room, restless, picking things up and putting them down without really thinking about it. "She's got it in for me. She thinks I'm a violent person."

"Don't be silly." I stood up too and reached out to hold his arm, to stop him pacing. He pulled away and glared at me.

"You don't understand, Lou. There are things you don't know about me."

"I'm sure there are things you don't know about me too."

"Obviously," he said with irritation. "But what I'm talking about is serious. At least, it wasn't, but she made it sound as if it was."

"What are you talking about? Look, do I have to ring Maeve up and ask her what's going on or are you going to tell me?"

"That's what she'd like you to do." He was back to the pacing. "She's making me tell you — but promise me it won't affect your opinion of me."

I spread my hands out helplessly. "How can I when I don't know what it is?" He shook his head, staring down at the carpet and I tried again. "Gil, for God's sake, stop walking around and tell me what you're so worried about before I imagine something really dreadful."

Instead of coming back to sit on the sofa, he folded himself into one of the armchairs, and without looking at me, he told me the sad, stupid story of what had happened with Chloe Sandler.

"The whole thing was a nightmare, and the more I tried to fix things, the worse it got. Do you know what really bothered me? I couldn't remember what had happened the first night, the night I supposedly tried to attack her. I was drunk — seriously, really drunk — and

326

I have a total blackout for two hours before and after I was in the flat. No memory at all. There was nothing I could say to contradict her story, and her flatmate's spin on things, except to say that I'd never done anything like that before, and I didn't think I was capable of it, no matter how much I'd had to drink."

"And the police didn't believe you?"

"I think they did." He looked up at me for a moment, then back at his interlaced fingers. "The guy who was dealing with it as good as told me he thought it was bullshit, but they had to go ahead with the restraining order because his boss was obsessed with them at the time. And I did breach it. I shouldn't have gone to see her. It was beyond stupid, but I thought we could deal with what had happened like mature adults. I think she felt bad about it too." He risked another look in my direction, trying to gauge how I was taking it. "Now Chloe really was a birdbrain. Pretty, but a nitwit. Looking back, I think it was just as well it ended when it did. It was just a shame that I ended up with a criminal record."

He was obviously starting to recover. The wicked glint in his eye was more like the Gil I knew.

"And you weren't going to tell me any of this." It was a statement, not a question.

He hesitated, choosing his words carefully. "I didn't think you needed to know at the moment."

"So you were saving it up for the right time. How nice." I had turned the sarcasm up to ten; he couldn't have missed it.

"I wanted to wait until our relationship was stronger. There isn't enough trust between us yet." He shrugged. "And I didn't think you'd want to hear too much about my ex-girlfriends."

"It will be very hard to trust you if I don't know about your past," I pointed out, standing up. "I can understand why you didn't tell me straightaway, but I don't want to find out anything else you've been keeping from me just because the police happen to know about and think you should share it with me. I'm starting to see why Maeve was so worried for my safety."

"She thinks I hurt Rebecca too, because she fell over once. Do you remember when she busted her cheekbone? It was just an accident." He shrugged. "One of those things. That policewoman can make it look as if I'm the devil incarnate, but she's wrong about me. And she doesn't know me. You do." He got up and moved towards me.

"I thought I was starting to know you," I admitted, turning away.

"Nothing has changed."

"No. Except . . ." I hesitated.

"Except nothing." His arms slid around me and I felt his breath on the side of my face. "You know the truth. She doesn't. And I don't care what she thinks of me — beyond the fact that it's a bore to have to explain myself because the Met's pet giraffe seems to think I'm a threat to you — but I do care about what you think." He laid his face against mine and drew me closer to him. "So tell me."

"I think," I said, keeping my voice steady though feeling his body against me was making me shake, "I think it would be easier to show you." I started to move towards the door and he held on to me more tightly.

"Show me here."

I looked over my shoulder at the window. "But it's the middle of the day. Someone will see."

"That's part of the fun."

I turned to face him, not sure if he was serious. He grinned down at me.

"Take a chance, Lulu. I dare you to."

I wanted to say no, but I had a feeling Gil wouldn't accept it. He was testing me again — testing how far I was prepared to go. Rebecca would have done it without thinking, just because he'd asked, and even then she hadn't managed to keep him.

In the end, the decision was easy. When it came down to it, I wasn't ready to let Gil go yet. I made myself smile back and say what he wanted to hear.

"I never could resist a dare."

CHAPTER
ELEVEN

MAEVE

Even though the superintendent had promised me I'd be able to take part in the surveillance operation, there was a tiny part of me that was convinced it wouldn't be permitted. I sat at the back of the room during the briefing, trying to look inconspicuous. For once I wasn't the only woman present, and I certainly wasn't the most eye-catching in my jeans and sweatshirt. The undercover officers fitted the victims' profile — young, attractive women with long hair. They wore high heels and above-the-knee skirts, party outfits that were accessorised currently, incongruously, with uniform jumpers. The detectives sitting directly in front of me were not put off that the women were their colleagues, but were enjoying a long and speculative discussion about them in terms that made me blush — even though I was used to it and I wasn't particularly thin-skinned.

The room was overheated and overcrowded, and if the buzz of excitement was tempered by cynicism about our chances of success, it didn't do much to keep the noise level down. It gave me more than a little pleasure to watch Judd bouncing on the balls of his feet at the front of the room, sweeping the assembled cops with a withering glare while he waited for a silence that didn't come and his face became redder and redder. Only when Godley himself stood up and raised a hand did a hush come over the group.

"Right, this is the briefing for Operation Mandrake. You all know why we're here," Judd began. He sounded even harsher than usual, his voice rough-edged with tension. "We're being proactive in our search for the serial killer currently operating in the Kennington area. There is a good chance that he will be out there tonight, according to the profile that Dr Chen has written for us."

The criminal psychologist was sitting at the front of the room, facing us, her head on one side and her eyes cast down as she listened to Judd. There was a pained expression on her face, which was triangular like a cat's, with wide cheekbones and a pointed chin. She had painted her small mouth scarlet, like her fingernails, but sat with her lips pressed together so the colour was only visible as a line. I had met her a couple of times, but looking at her across the room, it struck me that I had never actually seen her smile. Her legs were crossed and I wondered what she would make of her swinging foot if asked to analyse her own body language. Dr Chen was not among friends, and she knew it. I admired her for having the guts to sit in such an exposed position, even if I didn't warm to her as a person.

"We know that so far he's been active on Thursday, Friday and Saturday nights. We are very concerned that he's likely to be out there again tonight. Obviously, the surveillance teams on this operation are crucial backup for the UCs who are going to be on the streets. You will need to be discreet, but attentive. You're going out in twos and I don't want both of you to have your eye off the ball, by which I mean the UC officer, at the same time — no toilet breaks or food runs together." Judd looked around the room. "Remember, ladies, you're not pretending to be prostitutes tonight. His victims are nice young girls on nights out, minding their own business. We don't want to scare him off, do we?"

The UCs looked unimpressed; if this was their first encounter with the chief inspector, he had just told them everything they needed to know about him, i.e. that he had the natural charm of a ten-day-dead mackerel. Judd ploughed on.

"We'll have a dedicated radio channel but try to keep communication to a minimum. I'll have thirteen teams to keep track of, I don't want you chatting for no reason. The UCs will be using earpieces and covert microphones. The forecast is for rain, but I want you covering your area, not standing in doorways or sitting in the back of the car, please. We know he takes women as they are walking towards their homes or public transport. We also know that he doesn't move them very far from where he finds them so we believe him to be on foot. Pay particular attention to pedestrians, especially if you see them more than once. Dr Chen tells me he's likely to spend a lot of time moving around his territory, watching what's going on before he acts, so we're looking for anyone who seems to be

332

too interested in what's going on. Anyone who tries to strike up a conversation with you, ladies, treat them with caution until you are sure they aren't a threat. This is a violent man who acts quickly and although you might think his MO is reckless, he hasn't come close to being caught yet so we have to assume that he's good at what he does."

Dr Chen leaned forward. "May I interrupt? My profile suggests we are looking for a highly competent and controlled individual, someone who is prepared to take calculated risks to achieve satisfaction. He doesn't exhibit a great deal of sophistication in his methodology, but the level of violence he uses is significant and increasing, and he is highly dangerous. We think he encounters his victims by chance, but that doesn't mean the murders are the indulgence of a spur-of-the-moment whim. He plans, he prepares, he is confident and he will not stop unless we stop him." Her small hands were bunched into fists in her lap and although her voice was soft, her tone was emphatic. I could understand her being tense. Her reputation was staked on the killer being out on a wet, cold night, looking for a victim.

Judd had been waiting for her to finish, impatience in every line of his body.

"Surveillance teams, please be aware that you might have to take up positions that don't give you a full view of your designated area. I want you to be careful not to be observed. These are the teams. Listen up. Team one: Pollock and Dornton in the car, UC is Rossiter, and you're to concentrate on area A, that's Myatt's Field and the surrounding streets. Your callsign is TA61. Team two: Elliot and Freebody in the car, UC is Fairchild. Area B. Callsign is TA62."

I listened idly, waiting to hear my name. When it came, I was somehow not surprised to hear that I was to team up with Sam Prosser, or that the area we had been assigned was the recreation ground where Alice Fallon's body had been found.

Katy Mayford, the young UC who was supposed to work with us, was not happy. "Is there any point in concentrating on areas where he's already been? He's not likely to go back there, is he?"

"On the contrary," Dr Chen said, "he's quite likely to return to somewhere he has been successful — if not to hunt, to relive the experiences of the previous murder. It's very common for serial killers to return to the scenes of their crimes, particularly if the location holds some significance for them. In this instance, I would expect the killer to derive great pleasure from revisiting the locations in question, particularly since there are still signs of his work visible in some of them — scorch marks on the ground, damaged shrubbery and trees. Don't forget that there is probably a sexual component to these crimes, even if it's not immediately clear to us. You should pay close attention to anyone exposing themselves or masturbating in these areas."

A ripple of laughter went through the room at that and Dr Chen looked irritated. Judd clapped his hands.

"All right, that's enough. You heard the doctor. If you see any flashers and perverts, we have a couple of uniformed crews in the area who can make arrests

334

without jeopardising the undercover op. Call it in and leave it up to them, please."

He went on with the list of teams and locations, carving up the chosen area into neat little parcels. It was a comprehensive operation, lots of resources committed, and even if it was all likely to be a huge waste of time it was effective window dressing. Word would leak out to a friendly journalist about it — no details, just enough to make the task force look dynamic and imaginative. And everyone could go home happy, knowing that they'd done their best, while we did what we couldn't admit we were doing and waited for another body.

When Judd at last finished, Godley gave us his final blessing in the manner of a high priest officiating at a sacrificial ritual. Once it was over, I got up along with everyone else in the room and shuffled towards the door, intent on making a few final preparations before collecting Sam and Katy and heading out. I was planning to read through the briefing notes somewhere quiet and grab a sandwich. For the detectives who had been in front of me in the briefing, final preparations consisted of a fag, a slash and a cup of vile, bitter coffee, which was all that was available in the South London police station where the briefing had been held. Each to their own.

The corridor outside the briefing room was crowded. I threaded my way through, trying not to bump into anyone or, worse, rub up against any of the older detectives. Fragments of conversation struck me as I passed.

"This woman is convinced her husband is having an affair . . ."

". . . stops him for not wearing his seat belt . . ."

". . . nice little arse, too . . ."

". . . comes home early, thinking she'll catch him in the act, but he's just sitting on the sofa, watching the football. But she's still suspicious. She searches the whole house, top to bottom, under every bed, in every cupboard, attic, cellar, the works . . ."

". . . checks the boot and there's a fuck-off great bag of coke. So he hauls the driver out of the car, cuffs him, puts him in the back of the area car . . ."

". . . gagging for it . . ."

". . . the woman has a massive heart attack, keels over and dies. When she gets to heaven, the first person she sees is her next-door neighbour . . ."

". . . he has a look under the seat and finds a sawn-off shotgun, fully loaded. He gets back in the area car and says to the bloke, you're in a lot of trouble, mate."

"Cynthia, she says, how did you die? I froze to death, she says. What about you? So she tells her the whole story — coming home early, searching the house."

"He says, never mind about the gun, am I going to lose my licence?"

". . . until she couldn't walk in a straight line."

"Cynthia goes, shit, what a shame. If only you'd checked the freezer."

Seeing a detective roughly the size and shape of a fully grown rhino moving in my direction, I dived sideways and fetched up beside a back I recognised.

"All right, Rob? Which area did you get?"

He turned around and the expression on his face was pure embarrassment. "Oh. Maeve. Um . . . hi."

I looked past him to see the two DCs he'd been talking to, Harry Maitland and Ben Phipps, killing themselves laughing. I only knew them slightly, but what I knew of them made me think that their amusement was at my expense. A phrase I'd heard moments before floated back into my mind and repeated itself in Rob's voice. *Until she couldn't walk in a straight line* . . . and I knew without the least doubt that the first part of the sentence would not bear repeating in polite company. It shouldn't have been a surprise to find out that he was just like the others, but it was, somehow, and I wondered which of the UCs had caught his eye.

"Not dressed yet, Maeve? Thought you'd be getting all dolled up like the others." Maitland grinned at me, baring yellow teeth in what he obviously thought was a winning smile. "You're disappointing us."

"Sorry about that," I said. "You know I live for your approval."

The smile widened. He had white gunge that might have once been bread wadded between two of his molars. "Langton here tells us you look good half-naked. Maybe we can persuade you to dress down for us later on."

My usual non-confrontation policy when it came to suggestive remarks was just not going to cut it. "Yeah, or maybe you can get stuffed." While Maitland thought about his comeback, I turned to Rob, who was looking acutely uncomfortable. "Can I have a word?"

"Sure," he mumbled, and walked beside me down the hall, away from the others.

"What the fuck was that?" I was still smiling, still looking serene. No one would have known I was shaking with rage.

"What do you mean?"

"I really don't care if you want to join in with the sexist bullshit directed at the UCs — that's your business, nothing to do with me — but I do mind that you let Maitland insult me and said nothing."

"I didn't really get a chance to say anything." Rob sounded injured. "You were pretty quick off the mark."

"And what was that about me being half-naked? Did you tell them about coming over to my house? Were you talking about what I was *wearing*, for Christ's sake?"

"Not really. No. I just — it just came up." He rubbed his hand over his head, ruffling his hair and smoothing it back down. "Shit. Look, Maeve —"

"No, you look. You shouldn't have said anything about that night. It was out of hours, we were off duty, you were a guest in my home and I was entitled to expect that you wouldn't brag about it to anyone." I looked at him, puzzled. "And God help you if you think it was worth bragging about anyway. What, we shared a pizza and that's gossip? Did you tell them about my boyfriend coming home while you were there?"

Rob looked over my shoulder and grimaced. In spite of my best intentions, my voice had risen and the calm

338

demeanour I'd been struggling to maintain had gone by the wayside. We were attracting attention of the wrong sort. He grabbed my arm and dragged me another few yards down the corridor and around a corner where we wouldn't be observed.

"Look, I didn't mean to say anything. They were speculating about what you'd look like in a short skirt, OK? No one here has ever seen you in anything except suits and trousers, and I know it's deliberate because you want to be taken seriously but it does a damn good job of hiding your figure. Phipps said he thought you probably didn't have good legs — tall birds never do, according to him. I was just telling them that he was wrong. You have amazing legs." The lighting wasn't particularly good in the corridor, but I was fairly sure that he had gone red. "Sorry, but I couldn't help noticing."

"For Christ's sake," I said again, but the heat had gone out of my anger. In spite of myself, I started to grin. "So I should say thanks for the compliment, is that it?"

"No." He gave me a look that was simultaneously shy and cheeky. "I owe you an apology. But would you take a coffee instead?"

I checked my watch. "We don't have time."

"Not now. Later. We're not going to be far from where you've been posted. I'll come over around two o'clock."

"Better bring three coffees," I said. "Sam and Katy won't be pleased if I'm the only one who gets a caffeine fix."

"No problem. I really am sorry. I'd better go." He was walking backwards away from me, still with the cheeky grin on his face, looking about nineteen years old with his hair all ruffled and his T-shirt half-tucked into his jeans. "It is a shame, though. You had the best legs in the room. None of the UCs were even close."

"Get on with it, Langton," I said in as repressive a tone as I could manage, even though I felt a strange fluttering sensation in my abdomen that might have been my stomach flipping over when he grinned at me. I watched him walk away and my smile turned into a frown.

It couldn't be that I fancied him. It wasn't that. It was something else. Nerves about the undercover op, or the ongoing tension of hunting Rebecca's killer as well as the Burning Man. It was something completely unrelated to DC Langton, of that I was completely sure.

It had to be.

I couldn't swear that Judd had deliberately chosen the most depressing, bleakest and most godforsaken area on the map for our surveillance team to monitor, but if he'd wanted to find the worst place in the world for us to spend the night, he couldn't have done any better than our current location. Sam had parked in a side street overlooking the recreation ground, which I recognised from the scene-of-crime photos of Alice Fallon's body. It was nine weeks exactly since her corpse had been discovered by the wall on the far side of the park from where we sat, and as I surveyed the scene through my discreet infrared binoculars, the scorch marks were still faintly visible on the breezeblocks. In the children's play area, a swing dangled uselessly, one side detached from its chain, and the plastic slide was splintered at the bottom, a semi-circular chunk broken off leaving an edge that made it too dangerous to use. There were more dead leaves on the ground now, and heavy rain had churned what grass there was into a lake of mud. Otherwise, nothing had changed.

"Better put them down. Don't want you giving the game away." Sam had reclined his seat as far as it would go and was squinting out through the windscreen, his massive arms folded across his chest. He was wearing a black sweatshirt that had seen better days, and now performed a useful function as the unofficial archive of what Sam had had to eat recently. Egg yolk (from a midnight snack of a breakfast butty) and crisp crumbs featured extensively.

"Yeah, because we look so unobtrusive."

"I don't know what you mean. It's completely normal for a fat old bloke to spend the night with two beautiful girls. In a car. In the middle of winter. Fully clothed, but freezing my knackers off nonetheless." He leaned forward and flicked the heater on.

"You're steaming the windows up again." I slid down my window an inch and icy air struck in at me along with a scattering of sharp raindrops. I buried my chin in my chest, pulling my scarf up around my face to try to keep my nose warm. I had a down-filled jacket wrapped around me, but after hours of sitting still in the car, the cold seemed to have seeped into my very bones.

"Adds to the overall effect, doesn't it? Looks as if you're giving me some reason to steam the windows up."

"Yuck." Katy was sitting in the back of the car, a rug over her knees, shivering. "This is the worst job ever. Remind me why we're doing this?"

"Proactive policing," Sam and I said in unison.

"Total bollocks," the detective said, and I had to agree with her.

"Two more minutes and then you'd better get out there again." Sam tapped the clock on the dashboard. "You shouldn't be spending all night in the car. You heard what Judd said. You might miss your big chance."

"I bet Tom Judd has never had to wander around a park in fishnet tights and a mini," Katy said lugubriously. "Not in the middle of winter, anyway."

"I bet he has worn that kind of thing, though. In the privacy of his own home."

We sat in silence for a minute, reflecting on the image I had conjured up. Sam spoke for the three of us. "Jesus."

A rattle of rain splattered the windscreen and Katy flinched. "Is that sleet?"

I busied myself in checking the surveillance log on my knee, letting Sam break the bad news.

"It is indeed. More where that came from, I'd say. I wouldn't send a dog out in weather like this, would you, Maeve?"

342

"Shut up, Sam," I said calmly. "Katy, do you think you could stand to have another wander around? It has been a while."

"Yeah, why not." She gathered up her bag and checked her make-up in the rear-view mirror. Under her breath, she added, "I was just starting to get the feeling back in my feet. Wouldn't want to get used to that or anything."

"Never mind, darling." Sam stretched and then scratched his belly. "I can think of a few ways to warm you up when you get back."

She slammed the door hard enough to make us both jump and I scowled at her as she walked away, hoping that she hadn't woken anyone up in the houses on either side of us. It was an odd area, a mixture of housing and industrial units, and owed much of its character to having been bombed to smithereens during the Blitz. The odd half-terrace of townhouses hinted at a prestigious past but most of them had been converted to flats, and not well-maintained ones at that.

"No one about. Not surprising, given the weather," Sam observed.

"Yeah, and the serial killer. Don't forget about him. He's probably putting off a fair few of the locals from taking a nice nocturnal stroll."

Katy wandered across the recreation ground as if taking a shortcut and stopped halfway to light a cigarette. The microphone she was wearing picked up the rasp of the lighter and every rustle from her clothes. She took a long, slow look around while she dragged on the cigarette, and while her hand was still covering her mouth, whispered, "Still nothing."

We watched her move away, walking slowly.

"What's this?" Sam sat up straight for once and pointed at a car that was creeping along the street on the other side of the park, going at about five miles an hour. "One occupant, silver saloon car — Ford Focus, something like that. What's he up to?"

I lifted the binoculars again and focused on the driver, feeling my heart thudding. There had been plenty of silver saloons on the CCTV I'd watched over the past few weeks. Maybe we'd missed something. He was poking at his sat nav, his face illuminated eerily. I estimated he was in his mid-forties, white, with thick greying hair and a heavy beard. After a moment, the car started to pick up speed and took one of the other streets that led off the park, driving towards Stockwell.

"Nothing doing," I said, putting the binoculars down again. "But you could get on the radio and mention he's driving around, in case someone else sees him acting suspiciously, I suppose. I don't think he even saw Katy, to be honest with you. He didn't seem to look at the park at all."

The wind gusted again, tossing the bushes that lined the recreation ground and setting the broken swing to twist uselessly. The rain that had been speckling the windscreen suddenly gathered strength and the world outside the car blurred. Sam swore quietly and flicked on the windscreen wipers. One of them dragged on each pass with a squeak that set my teeth on edge. Katy had made it to the other side of the park and was wandering down the street, head bent, with only a brightly coloured umbrella to protect her from the elements. She flickered in and out of sight as she passed behind the bare trees. *Now you see me, now you don't.*

I jumped about a mile as the car door behind me suddenly opened with a blast of cold air. It was tinged with the scent of coffee, and as Rob sat into the back seat, balancing a little cardboard tray in one hand, I twisted around to look at him. Rain was dripping from his hair and down his nose. He was wearing a navy-blue windcheater that was slick with water and his jeans looked soaked.

"Wet out, isn't it?"

"Just a touch," he said pleasantly and handed me a cup. "Black coffee for you. Sam, black or white?"

"White, two sugars."

Rob rummaged in his jacket pocket and produced a handful of packets of sugar, little cartons of UHT milk and a couple of coffee stirrers, which he dumped into the coin tray behind the handbrake. Sam looked at them and raised an eyebrow. "Didn't realise we had a branch of Starbucks in the back seat. Any chance of a blueberry muffin?"

"Just be grateful for what you've got. Do you have any idea how hard it is to find a coffee around here at this hour of the morning?"

"Not very? These came from the garage down the road," I pointed out. "Must have taken you all of three minutes to walk there."

"Yeah, but it was raining, in case you hadn't noticed, and cold."

"Poor angel."

"To what do we owe the pleasure?" Sam said. "Bored, are you?"

"I promised I'd do a coffee run." He caught my eye for a second and gave me the ghost of a wink and my stomach flipped over again — what was *wrong* with me? "And besides, Andrews keeps farting. I had to get out of there or I'd have passed out."

"We're having the same trouble. Sorry, Maeve, but it's true. I warned you not to have baked beans for dinner."

"Fuck off, Sam," I began, but before I could say anything else, Rob's hand came down on my shoulder and gripped me, hard.

"Wait a second. What's that?"

The silver car was back, cruising past the end of the street with its lights off. As we watched, the brake lights glowed and it ground to a halt, engine throbbing. The driver was a silhouette but I could make out the beard and the streetlight struck a metallic gleam on his hair. All of his attention was directed towards the other end of the recreation ground, where a brightly coloured umbrella was bobbing along in time to the staccato stride of a very cold UC officer. I picked up my radio.

"Katy, we've got a man in a four-door saloon car, silver, no licence plate yet, parked on the west side of the park. He seems to be watching you, but we'll leave him be for a minute and see what he does."

Her voice was muffled as she whispered a quiet OK. Not far away, a moped engine whined. The sound came through the open car window and was echoed by

Katy's microphone; it had to be at her end of the park. I could see now that the silver car was indeed a Ford Focus.

"We need the index for a PNC check."

Rob had already opened the car door and was easing himself out, keeping low to the ground. "I'm on it. Back in two." He stopped. "My radio is buggered, by the way. Can you run the check for me?"

"Will do," Sam said. "Off you go."

The moped engine changed note, sounding like a stuttering hornet, and it sounded louder through Katy's microphone as it neared her. I watched Rob move cautiously down the street until he reached a point where he could see the back end of the Ford but remain unobserved. He started back towards us after a couple of seconds and Sam lowered his window, holding his hand out for the bit of paper Rob lobbed to him.

"MP from Tango Alpha Six Five," he muttered into the radio.

"MP receiving, go ahead." The controller in the main Met control room sounded harassed, as if it was a busy night.

"Would you oblige me with a vehicle PNC check." Sam gave the controller the car's location and the licence-plate number, sounding as calm as if it was routine. My throat was aching with tension.

"Wait one." The controller went off the air for a few seconds. "Comes back to a Ford Focus, silver, MOT current, insurance good, registered owner is the *Sunday Courier*. No reports. All received?"

"Tango Alpha Six Five, all received, nothing further." Sam turned to Rob, who was crouching beside his door. "He's a fucking hack, out trying his luck. Do you want to go and have a word, or shall I?"

"I'd be delighted to speak to the gentleman if you don't mind me doing it."

"Be my guest," Sam said, and Rob ghosted back down the street, almost invisible in the shadows. This time, he moved to the back of the car and along the passenger side, stopping halfway along. He knocked on the window with the back of his hand, two sharp raps that carried over the sound of the rain clear across the quiet street to where we sat. They must have been shockingly loud inside the car where the journalist had been completely oblivious to Rob's presence. I saw him jump, his head whipping around so fast it was almost funny. Having given him enough time to panic, Rob bent down and held his warrant card where the man could see it, then pointed down meaningfully. *Window down, tosspot.*

A muffled voice spoke over the radio and I picked it up, holding it to my ear to try to make it out.

"Hi," Katy said, with a laugh in her voice. She sounded amused. I could only hear her end of the conversation clearly and I held up a finger to shush Sam, who had been embarking on a long commentary on the state of the reporter's trousers after Rob's interception.

"Yeah, it is late. I'm waiting for my boyfriend — he's supposed to be meeting me, but he's running late." Katy delivered the cover story beautifully, sincerity ringing through every word. "He's just texted me to say he'll be another twenty minutes."

More muffled sounds. The rain was pummelling the roof of the car as if it was about to bore through it. Rob had hauled the reporter out to pat him down, which seemed a bit keen.

"I know. Freezing."

Mumble mumble mumble.

"I do like pizza." She laughed. "I'm not hungry, actually. But thanks,"

Mumble.

"Really, I'm OK. But thanks for asking."

There was a pause. Rob was shining his Maglite into the back of the silver car while the man stood beside him, gesticulating angrily.

The moped engine revved a couple of times, then trailed away into the distance. Katy laughed into her microphone. "Did you hear that? The delivery guy wanted to give me a free pizza. Said it had been ordered but there was no one in when he went to deliver it. It was his last run of the night and he was feeling generous."

There was something about what she'd said that made me feel uneasy. Distracted, I followed the thread of thought back to my conversation with Rob earlier — what had he been saying about me to the other detectives? I keyed the radio. "Shame. We could have done with a snack."

"If he comes back, I'll nab it."

"How are you doing?"

"OK. I'm a bit cold and wet, not surprisingly." Her voice sharpened. "What happened with the guy in the silver car? I saw it driving by."

"Reporter. One of the other DCs is having a word." Katy made a sound that might have been a word, something I couldn't quite catch, anyway. "Say again?"

The radio hissed quietly, one step above white noise as I waited for her to respond.

"Katy, can you repeat your last?"

Dead air.

"Katy, can you hear me?"

There was a rustling sound, and then a dreadful choking noise filled the car. I was reaching for the door handle before it died away, and without consciously deciding to move I had sprung out of the car and was racing through the rain without waiting for Sam to follow. It was a couple of hundred metres along the side of the recreation ground to the place where I'd last seen Katy and I covered the distance in seconds that felt like hours, without noticing anything except that my radio had fallen silent again, apart from the faintest clank of metal on metal. All of my attention was focused on where I expected to see her, and as I swung around the corner, I saw three things that shocked me to a standstill for an instant.

An umbrella, still open, wheeling in lazy circles on the wet pavement at the whim of the wind.

A small moped with L-plates, a red container mounted on the back and a notch missing from the top left corner of the number plate, parked at the end of the street.

The gate to the recreation ground standing open.

I stood for a second, taking it in, as realisation after realisation slotted into place in my mind.

First of all, the umbrella was Katy's, and there was no reason on earth why she should have dropped it when the rain was still pattering on the bare branches above me, still ringing music from the metal lamp standards.

Secondly, I had seen the moped countless times on the CCTV I'd watched from the area, and thought nothing of it; if I'd noticed it at all, I must have discounted it immediately. What could be more commonplace than a delivery bike? They were part of the backdrop, all but invisible, out at all hours in all weathers. I had seen it, though, that particular bike with the distinctively damaged plate, and too many times. And what could be better for gaining a potential victim's trust than the offer of a free pizza? It was all starting to make a horrible sort of sense.

The last thing I noticed, the most important, was the gate to the recreation ground — the gate that was now standing wide open — had been securely chained when I'd last seen it, and even if I didn't want to do it, even if I was afraid, I had to go through it. At the thought, I gathered myself together and moved again; I had probably only stopped for a couple of seconds, but it was long enough. With one hand I took the CS canister out of my coat pocket, with the other I hit the emergency button on my radio. Pressing it overrode all other communications on that channel with a call for immediate assistance; it was the policeman's 999 and I didn't like to think why Katy hadn't been able to get to hers, unless she hadn't needed it, unless she was OK, unless I had completely overreacted.

But if I wasn't overreacting, I couldn't hang around waiting for backup. I looked through the gate, stretching my eyes wide to peer through the darkness, but all I could see was the cracked concrete path, slick with water, disappearing as it passed out of the streetlight's reach. Laurel bushes with biliously speckled leaves clustered around the entrance, cutting off my view of the rest of the park. I checked that the nozzle for the gas was pointing away from me and stepped through the gate, wishing I hadn't left my extendable baton in the car, along with my handcuffs. I was stuck with the sodding CS. Even if I managed to spray it in the right direction, I'd learned during training that not everyone is affected by it, and knowing my luck, the Burning Man would be immune. It was about as much use as — I shook myself. *Concentrate.* My mind was racing, filling the darkness with inconsequential images, throwing off thoughts like sparks. The bright light in the briefing room shining pinkly through the jug ears of the detective who'd sat in front of me. A trace of Dr Chen's lipstick, sticky on her teeth. Sitting in the car, eating one of Sam's vile cheese and onion crisps against my better judgement. I could still taste it. I bit down on my lower lip, hard, and kept moving, seconds passing, searching, searching.

One foot after the other. Fast as you can. Careful, though. Don't slip. Don't make too much noise. Left or right, pick a path. Which way? Stop. Listen . . .

Somewhere in the distance, I could hear heavy breathing as someone pounded along a path, making no effort to be silent.

"Maeve! *Maeve!*" It was a hoarse whisper, incredibly loud in the silent park, and immediately identifiable as Sam's voice. I rolled my eyes to heaven and willed him to shut up. If I could only hear Katy . . . if I could only see her . . . if I could only be sure I was looking in the right place . . .

I had reached the middle of the park, where a small, bleak brick building housed public toilets. If I had thought about it, I might have realised that the building offered a bit of protection from the weather, and that if you were intent on battering someone to death and burning their body on a wet night, shelter might be one of your priorities. As I scurried past it I heard a sketch of a sound that might have been a whimper, shockingly close, and from quite a long way behind me, a shout. I whipped around, pivoting on one foot, and as I moved I sensed rather than saw something cutting through the air, aiming for my head. I wasn't conscious of feeling any pain when the blow landed, just a dizzying sensation of utter weakness. I knew that I had to keep moving, I had to get away, but my legs wouldn't carry me and someone was still shouting, shouting at me, shouting my name. I fumbled for the CS spray and felt it slide out of my hand, clattering to the path and now the pain was coming, as if from a long way off, and I was aware of more blows landing, and pain bloomed along the side of my head, and I fell to my knees, thinking that I should do something, thinking that my parents would be so disappointed in me, thinking that Ian had been right, thinking that Rob would be furious. I'd wanted to do better. I'd hoped to do better. The world was receding but my thoughts kept spinning irrationally as the ground came up to meet me and my cheek hit it and I opened my eyes to see a boot swinging towards my face and that was the thing, in the end, that just

made everything

stop.

LOUISE

Gil was attentive after Maeve left — almost too attentive. He followed me around from room to room, watching what I did. I felt claustrophobic, crowded in my own home where I was used to being on my own. It was a relief the following afternoon when he left. He had to sort out a few things, he said. I hadn't asked what. I was too glad to have some time to myself to think, to breathe.

I had needed to be alone, but as I moved around the house I felt happiness bubbling up inside me. There was evidence of Gil everywhere, and I sang to myself as I tidied up. I ran a bath scented with roses and lay in it for a long, languorous soak, a glass of ruby-red Australian Shiraz at my elbow. It was quiet without him and I felt myself start to relax. Almost dozing, I floated in the warm water and allowed my thoughts to roam where they would, dwelling on Gil, and the things he'd said to me, and the things he'd done . . . Inevitably, I found myself thinking about Rebecca. She had brought Gil and me together, but he was right — alive, she would have kept us apart. Her death had freed us. And I had changed too, since her death. I had come into my own. I was more at ease with myself than I had ever been.

I lifted the glass of wine off the edge of the bath and held it up. "Here's to you, darling Rebecca. Thank you for everything."

It smelled like blackberries and tasted like heaven, and I sipped it slowly until the glass was empty and the bathwater tepid.

By the time Gil let himself into the house using the key I had given him, I had got dressed again and started to make dinner.

"Something smells good." He came into the kitchen looking arrogant and as pleased with himself as if he'd won a prize. He walked straight over to where I was standing, chopping broccoli. I dropped the knife to twist my hands in his hair as he spun me around and kissed me greedily, as if we had been apart for months, not hours.

"You've been drinking."

"I opened a bottle of wine." There was a glass waiting for him on the table.

"How decadent." He slipped his knee between my legs, easing them apart, sliding my short denim skirt up my thighs. "What's for dinner?"

"Shepherd's pie." He was kissing my shoulder, pulling my top down to touch my bare skin and I leaned back against the counter, feeling myself start to melt.

"Turn the oven off." He pulled away abruptly. "I've been thinking for hours about the things I want to do to you and I don't want to have to rush."

"Nobody wants that," I assured him, abandoning dinner for the time being. It could wait.

As I followed him out of the kitchen, I noticed a small black bag on the table, square and shiny with black silk braided handles.

"What's that?"

He frowned, not pleased at the diversion, then changed his mind and laughed. "That wasn't fair of me. I shouldn't have expected you to walk past a bag from a jeweller's."

"A jeweller's?" I picked it up. "What is it?"

"Have a look."

"Is it for me?" I was holding the bag warily.

"You and only you." He leaned against the doorframe and watched me shake a little leather box into my palm. I flipped up the lid carefully.

"Oh, Gil. They're beautiful." Two diamonds sparkled against the black satin, fat and round as peas, with a tear-shaped pearl dropping below each of them. "Can I try them on?"

"Be my guest." He watched indulgently as I scampered into the hall to the nearest mirror. I pulled my hair back, turning my head from side to side to get the full effect. The pearls were a particularly warm shade, almost pink, and the diamonds glittered like fireworks as they picked up the light.

"I can't believe it. Why, though?"

"I wanted you to have something for yourself." He moved so that I could see him reflected in the mirror behind me. "Not a hand-me-down. Do you like them?"

"I love them."

"Well, then, they're yours. On one condition."

I felt my smile stiffen on my face. "What is it?"

"Give me back Rebecca's earrings. I don't like to see you wearing them."

I turned around so I could look at him more closely. "Why not?"

He looked irritated. "Does it matter?"

"Yes, actually." I put my hands on my hips. "Come on, Gil. They're just a nice way for me to remember Rebecca. Why can't I keep them?"

"Because Rebecca's dead." He stared down at me, his face unreadable. "And you aren't her."

I started to walk away and he grabbed my arm, pulling me back to him.

"You aren't her, Lou, and I don't want you to be. I want you to be you. I know you want to remember Rebecca — she was your friend. But please, let her go. She's dead." He shook me a little, not hard. "She's gone. Let her be."

"I know she's gone. I don't keep talking about her. If it comes to that, you're the one who just brought her up," I pointed out, not unreasonably.

He exploded, shouting, "For fuck's sake, just do as I ask for once. It's not difficult."

"Gil!" I stared at him, shocked, and it seemed to annoy him more. He was still holding my arm and now he yanked me off balance, dragged me along the hall and threw me at the stairs where I sprawled inelegantly.

"Go on. Go and get them."

I lay there for a second without moving, tasting blood on my lip and feeling the heat of a carpet burn

358

above my right eye. Then I rolled on to one elbow and looked at him.

"No."

"What did you say?"

"I said no. No, I won't go and get them." It wasn't about the earrings — I knew that. It was about control. And I couldn't or wouldn't give in.

He stood at the bottom of the stairs, breathing hard, his hands clenching and unclenching slowly at his sides, though I doubted he was aware he was doing it. His hair was dishevelled, his eyes glazed, and I felt he wasn't really seeing me. When he moved I was expecting him to hit me, but he slipped his hands up under my skirt instead, holding my hips and pulling me down towards him. I started to twist away but he was too strong. He had worked my underwear down and now he used one hand to hold on to my wrists so I couldn't push him away or claw at his eyes. I couldn't break free, no matter how I struggled. Under his breath he was saying, "Why do you have to fight all the time? Just stop fighting me."

I did stop fighting. I had to. He would have hurt me, I thought, feeling sick as he pushed himself on top of me. And this was Gil. Gil who had shared my bed. I had willingly screwed him in a variety of places and ways. This was no different.

But it was different. It was a demonstration of force, a show of strength. I stared up at the hall light, trying not to think about what he was doing as he drove into me, panting in my ear, his sweat cold against the side of my face as he finished with a grunt and collapsed on top of me. He had hurt me, forced himself into me, and now it stung as he slipped out again, leaving a wet smear on my thigh. The stairs dug into my back, my hip, and my arm was trapped underneath him; I was glad when he moved. He rolled off and sat beside me, his breathing still ragged.

"God, Lou. That was incredible."

I could tell he was looking at me, trying to gauge my reaction, trying to see if he'd upset me.

I didn't make a scene. I didn't say anything at all. I smiled instead, feeling my lip twinge as the cut pulled apart. Because the only way to win — the only way to defeat him — was to show him that I didn't care.

ROB

In theory, it was all very exciting to be involved in an undercover operation aimed at trapping a highly dangerous, prolific serial killer. In reality, I could think of a few things I'd have preferred to be doing than standing in the rain in the middle of the night, catching pneumonia. Things like cleaning out a blocked drain bare-handed. Watching snooker on a black-and-white TV. Being doorstepped by a Jehovah's Witness early on a Saturday morning while suffering from the mother and father of all hangovers. The surveillance op was a pain in the arse to begin with; having the *Sunday Courier* turn up didn't help. And the weather was the last straw. I was soaking wet already from wandering around South London in the dark, which didn't improve my mood as I came up behind the silver Ford. The only thing to be said for the rain was that it made me almost invisible — and the reporter was looking in the wrong direction anyway. I knocked on the passenger window twice, hard, and had the pleasure of watching him jump out of his skin. I held up my warrant card where he could see it and pointed to the ground until he got the message and the window slid down.

"Good evening, sir. Can I help you with anything?"

My tone must have confused him. I could see the wheels turning inside his skull as he tried to think of a reason for being there. "No — er — I was just looking for an address. Trying to get my sat nav to work, you know. It keeps sending me back here."

"Where are you trying to get to?"

He opened his mouth and closed it again, flummoxed. I could see his problem. It had to be somewhere in this general area, which he evidently didn't know particularly well, but it couldn't be anywhere too well known or he wouldn't need sat nav to get there. Before he could come up with anything specific, I shook my head at him.

"Don't bother. We know you're a journalist, and we know what you're doing here."

His shoulders sagged for a moment. As I had expected, it didn't take him long to rally. "Since you know all that, you know I have a right to be here."

"Yeah, but here is in the middle of an operation which you might be about to compromise. I'm going to ask you nicely. Please leave."

"It's a public street. You can't make me go."

"Fine," I said. "Out of the car."

"What?"

"Step out of the car, please. And if you have your driver's licence on you or any other form of photo ID, I'd like to see it."

"Why?"

"It's the middle of the night and you're driving around on your own. You haven't given me a valid

362

reason to be here. I suspect you may be in possession of stolen goods or prohibited items so I'm going to search you and your car under Section 1 of PACE." It was straight out of the textbook on stopping and searching, totally legal, and entirely invented as an excuse to annoy him. And he knew that as well as I did.

"You can't do that."

"If you obstruct me, you will get nicked." I said it like I meant it. The only sound was the rain tapping on the roof of the car.

"For fuck's sake." With extreme bad grace he opened the door of the car and got out, fumbling in his pocket. "NUJ card. Driver's licence. What else do you want?"

I walked around to where he was standing and moved him back two paces so he had his back to the wall, away from his car. "Stay there, sir."

In the light of my torch, the cards showed me a younger version of Spencer Maxwell, crack reporter. The bearded, paunchy reality was less impressive. He had an address in Hackney and I raised my eyebrows. "On your way home, were you? Decided to take a detour?"

"I was doing some research. I wanted some colour for a piece I'm writing about the murders. The atmosphere here." He waved a hand vaguely, indicating the street and park. His hair was beginning to flatten against his head and the shoulders of his suit were dark. Another couple of minutes and he would be nicely soggy, I calculated, and went on searching the car in a cursory manner while he rambled on about it being ridiculous and harassment and how he wanted my name and number. I might have done a PNC check to round off his evening, but an experimental poke at my radio confirmed it was totally dead. I settled for checking under the seats and in the boot, staring without comment at the pile of junk he had in there until he felt moved to explain that he wasn't the only one who used the car; he hadn't even known that stuff was there.

"Not stolen, is it?"

He looked wildly at the rat's nest I had uncovered: plastic bags, a tow rope, a leaking container of engine oil, empty water bottles, crisp packets, sandwich wrappers and a few old, torn copies of the *Courier*. "N-no. I mean — it's rubbish, isn't it?"

"So it would appear." I shut the boot and turned, shining the torch in his eyes. "Just thought it was odd you were claiming you didn't know it was there, that's all."

It wasn't that odd. Everyone lies to the police, all the time, about nothing. I wasn't going to arrest him for being a slob, but he still couldn't own up to having made the mess himself. I held up my hand to stop him from gibbering at me any more.

"Right. I've marked your card, Mr Maxwell. Now fuck off, or I'll nick you for obstruction, and you can spend the rest of the night in the drunk tank at the station. I'm sure your paper's expensive lawyer will get you out in the morning."

He looked a bit sick at the thought. "No need for that. I'll go."

"See you do," I started to say, but I was distracted by a noise to my left. I looked around to see Sam running — *running* — down the side of the park, panting into his radio.

"Sam!" He didn't hear me, or didn't look around anyway, just kept going. I threw a wild look in the direction of the surveillance car to see if Maeve or the UC were there but both front doors were hanging open, the inside light shining on empty seats, and all I could think was why the fuck did something have to happen while I was tied up with the world's most decrepit cub reporter?

Late to the party, I didn't hang about. The shortest route to the recreation ground happened to be over the railings so that's how I went, vaulting over them. I hit the ground running, aware now of scuffling somewhere up ahead of me, of a repeated dull thud that sounded very much like something heavy hitting muscle and bone. I cut through the playground and ducked between two trees that raked at me with low branches before I burst into open space and saw a scene out of a nightmare. Propped up against the wall of the toilet block like a broken doll, her head lolling to one side, was the UC officer who'd been assigned to Maeve's team. On the ground nearby was a huddled shape that was, I saw with horror, Maeve herself. And standing over her was a figure in bike leathers. And as I watched, he drew back for a kick that was aimed squarely at her head.

I had been running flat out but now I dredged up an extra turn of speed from somewhere and hurled myself across the grass. It would have been more sensible to hold off until backup arrived, but I'd seen torches bobbing through the trees on the other side so I wasn't going to be on my own for long. Besides, it was an emergency. I was too late, of course. His foot connected with Maeve with sickening force a split second before I cannoned into him, shoving him off-balance and falling on top of him. Training and technique had gone out the window; the only thought in my mind was my intention to leather the shit out of him. I got in a few good short punches to his face and cracked him across the nose with my elbow, but then he started to fight back. He was strong, and desperate, and I found myself in trouble almost immediately, even though I had no compunction about fighting dirty. After a couple of blows to the head that made my ears ring and stars flare in the dark, I stuck my thumb in his eye, then pushed my forearm hard against his throat. I'd have thought that was enough to knock the fight out of anyone, but the next thing I knew, his teeth were trying to meet through my arm. At long last I heard the welcome sound of an extendable baton being racked open behind me, accompanied by wheezing breaths. I had just enough time to be relieved that backup had arrived before I felt a searing pain in my leg.

"Not me, Sam, for fuck's sake. Hit him!"

Second time around, Sam did a bit better, and when two uniformed officers ran up to join in, even my opponent had to admit it was all over. I rolled away when he was face down, hands cuffed behind him, being sat on by the larger of the two PCs. I lay on my back for a couple of seconds, catching my breath, eyes closed against the rain. The most serious damage started to make itself felt. I sat up abruptly. If I felt bad, Maeve had to be worse off. I had been too focused on fighting to think about her — now she was all I could think about.

It could only have been a couple of minutes since the alarm had been raised but two ambulance crews had already responded. One paramedic was kneeling beside the undercover officer, talking to her as he checked her over. Three were gathered around Maeve, who was still on the ground, not moving. There was blood smeared on their gloves, and a spreading pool of it under her head. They were bending over her so I couldn't see her face, or really gauge how badly she was hurt. But she was limp as they handled her, and it came to me with a shock that I hadn't heard her make a sound so far. I swallowed, my mouth suddenly dry. If she was seriously hurt . . .

They had lifted her onto a stretcher. Forgetting about the suspect, I got up to go and check on her, only to be blocked by one of the paramedics. She was short, square and motherly, and she would not get out of my way.

"Do you mind?" I said after the third attempt to sidestep her failed. "I want to check on my colleague."

"Plenty of time for that at the hospital after you've been treated."

"I'm not going to hospital." I was trying to see over her shoulder. They were loading the stretcher into one of the ambulances.

"You most certainly are. You've got a gash in your eyebrow that needs stitching and I don't know what else." She tutted. "What have you done to yourself?"

I looked where she was pointing and saw blood dripping down my fingers. I flexed them and pulled a face as pain darted up my arm. "Nothing much."

"Come on. I'm not taking no for an answer. At least let me assess you properly."

"Look, I promise I'll go to hospital and get checked out, OK? Just tell me where they're taking Maeve and I'll go there." I watched the ambulance take off down one of the paths in the direction of the gate, blue lights whirling.

"Your colleague?" She looked at me shrewdly. "I'll find out for you. But a promise is a promise. You'll go and get yourself checked over in A&E."

"Scout's honour," I said, holding up three fingers.

"You were never a scout." She walked away, shaking her head. As it happened, she was right about that. But I would have made good on my promise if Judd hadn't turned up two seconds later, wild-eyed and quivering with excitement.

"Where is he?"

"Who? Oh." I had almost forgotten. "Over there."

"Have you searched him? Checked his ID? Run him through the PNC?"

"I've been a bit busy," I said mildly. "Maybe one of the others has had the chance."

"Did anyone even caution him?" I let silence be his answer. "Christ, do I have to do everything myself? Come with me."

Why, do you need someone to hold your hand? I didn't say it out loud; I wasn't stupid enough to think that Judd would forget or forgive a smart remark even on the best day of his miserable career.

The suspect was standing by now with one uniform on either side of him, his head hanging down. The officers were holding his arms up a little so he had to bend forward to relieve the pressure on his shoulders. Nothing like being in a bit of pain to make you compliant.

When we got close enough, I could see that he was shaking. It was cold, though the rain had slackened off a bit. But as he glanced up briefly, then looked back down at the ground, I realised that he was much younger than the psychologist's profiles had suggested our killer would be — and that he was absolutely terrified.

Judd pushed forward self-importantly. "Who is the arresting officer?"

Silence. I winced. They had been waiting for me to do the formalities, I guessed, though I hadn't thought of it. I didn't exactly see it as an honour, even if I was the first officer to lay hands on him. Still, time to step up. "I suppose I am."

"You suppose?" He swung around. "Are you telling me you haven't arrested him? And neither has anyone else?"

I shrugged painfully. "They might have. Like I said, I was a bit busy."

"Do it now, and do it properly." Judd was speaking through gritted teeth. I'd never seen anyone do that in real life. As ever, being around the inspector was an education.

"Why don't you do it, Tom." The superintendent's low voice came from behind me. "I think it would be appropriate. You don't mind, do you, Rob?"

"Not at all."

Godley clapped me on the shoulder and I managed not to flinch. "Good lad. Tom, he's all yours. Get it right."

Judd would do it all by the book. He'd even get a kick out of the paperwork. I didn't stay to watch, judging that my work there was done. As I walked away, the motherly paramedic saw me and called, "St Luke's."

I gave her the thumbs up and she frowned at me. "Make sure you go."

"I will." I wouldn't necessarily stop to get treated, but I'd go.

I spotted Sam sitting on a bench a few yards away, hunched over, a picture of misery, and I went over to him.

"Thanks for hitting me. What did I ever do to you? I thought you were going to gas me next. Another time, hit the serial killer."

"Sorry." He looked up. "Do you think she's going to be all right?"

I didn't need to ask who he meant. "I hope so." Then, needing to say it to someone else, "It looked nasty."

"I shouldn't have taken so long to catch up. She was out of the car and halfway down the street before I even noticed there was anything wrong."

He was right, but there was no point in making him feel worse than he did already. "You're not exactly built for the four-minute mile, are you? And Maeve has an unfair advantage with those legs." He didn't smile. "Look, she's a fighter. She'll be OK." I sounded a hell of a lot more confident than I felt.

Sam shook his head stubbornly. "I'll never forgive myself."

"All right, get out the violin. Do you want to do something useful instead of sitting here moping?"

Even in the depths of despair Sam was too much of a cunning old fox to say yes straight out. "Depends. What is it?"

"They've taken her to St Luke's. Any idea how we could get there?"

He got up, looking a sight more cheerful. "I've got the car."

"I wondered when you'd remember." We started to walk out of the park together. The path took us past the spot where the young man was being systematically searched as the inspector and Superintendent Godley looked on.

We both stopped at the same time.

"Christ. Look at that lot."

In front of the young man was a pile of belongings — a wallet, house keys, a mobile phone. So far, so normal. Not so normal: the small black plastic rectangular object with two metal prongs that I recognised from briefings as a stun gun, the crowbar, the bolt cutters, a roll of green gardening twine, the brick hammer with a black rubber grip.

"I suppose that means it is him," Sam said blankly.

"Yeah. You know you're getting old when the serial killers start to look like kids."

The suspect was down to a white T-shirt and his trousers. They had taken his boots off to search inside them and his feet were bare and bluish on the cold wet concrete. He looked up at us, his face woebegone, a dappling of acne livid and inflamed on his chin. He had red marks around his eyes and across his nose where the struggle had bruised him. He was tall and heavily built, but from his face he could have been a teenager. Surely not, though. Not when you thought about what he'd done. The violence he'd used. The women he'd killed.

I turned away and after a moment Sam followed me. We walked out of the park in silence. The Burning Man was in custody, but somehow neither of us was in the mood to celebrate.

The hospital was like the end of the world. The waiting room had been decorated with some sagging green tinsel and gold paper stars, which in no way lessened the wall-to-wall horror, just reminded me that it was almost Christmas and there was little enough to be joyful about. The plastic seating was packed with walking-wounded survivors from festive parties, drunken office workers, filthy tramps and lads who had rounded off a good night out with a bloody fight. A warm fug of vomit-tinged air met us when we came through the doors and I stopped, revolted.

"Jesus."

"Even He wouldn't bother with this lot." Sam, who had recovered much of his bounce, barrelled over to the glassed-in reception desk. Behind it I could see at least five members of staff who were doing a fine job of ignoring the queue. Sidestepping everyone who was waiting, much to their irritation, Sam tapped on the glass and held up his warrant card. It would be an exaggeration to say the receptionists hurried to find out what he wanted, but a heavy-eyed dark-haired woman came to the window eventually and listened to what he had to say. She disappeared, and Sam looked around. "She's gone to see."

"I'm going to clean up a bit. Don't go anywhere without me."

"Never."

After a quick look at the state of the men's room, I went into the disabled toilet instead. It had the great advantage that it was private. I risked a look in the mirror and saw the cut that had bothered the paramedic, right through my right eyebrow. Blood had run down the side of my face and my neck; I looked about as good as the lads out in the waiting room. I dabbed at my skin with some wet toilet paper, trying to make myself appear a bit more human. I had the makings of a black eye and a sore patch on my jaw where he'd caught me with a left hook, but otherwise it wasn't too bad. I peeled off my soaking jacket and dropped it on the floor, then took off the sweatshirt I had worn underneath, swearing under my breath as it caught on the drying blood from my arm. The bite was not good; even I could see that. He had gone right through the skin, gouging two semicircular arcs in my arm that were still oozing blood. A livid mark in the centre was a bruise, and the whole thing ached. I couldn't remember if you needed a tetanus shot for a human bite but I had a vague suspicion it wasn't a good thing to neglect. I really needed to get it seen to, I thought vaguely, without making any firm plans to do so.

I yanked off my T-shirt, pulling my arm through the sleeve gingerly, and twisted to the left, then the right, checking for any more damage to my torso. I had a few bruises developing on my ribs and chest, but no more cuts. Superficial damage only, so no big deal, nothing to get too excited about. But I was tired, and cold, and I leant on the sink for a minute, feeling like death, trying to gather the energy to get dressed again.

The T-shirt was wet and pink around the collar from where the rain had diluted the blood that had run down my neck. I wadded it into the bin but put on the sweatshirt again as it looked reasonably decent. I checked my jacket pockets, transferring my phone and Maeve's into my jeans. I had used hers to call Ian from the car on the way to the hospital. I'd thought I should; I would have wanted to know if I was him. He'd gone all the way from irritated through concerned to the kind of wrenching anxiety I was feeling myself. But then again, I reminded myself, he was entitled to feel that way. I was not.

I went out, carrying my jacket, to find that Sam had disappeared. Thinking evil thoughts, I went up to the reception desk myself and attracted the attention of the heavy-eyed woman.

"Your friend's gone in already. Go to the door and I'll buzz you through."

So much for waiting for me. The scene in the business end of A&E wasn't much better — too few staff, too many people on trollies. I wandered through a couple of areas without seeing Sam, then grabbed a passing nurse, who was thin, middle-aged and harried.

"Police, love. I'm looking for one of my colleagues that was brought in just now from Kennington — she's been attacked."

"Oh yeah. She's over there." She pointed at a cubicle in the corner with the curtains drawn around it.

"Is she OK? I mean — can I see her?"

"She's fine. We just drew the curtains to give her some privacy. It's mad in here tonight."

Relieved was not the word for how I was feeling. I grinned down at her. "I'd have thought you'd be used to it."

"You never get used to this." She raised her eyebrows at a man being led past us with a pair of antlers on his head and a white gauze pad held over one eye. He was wearing white knee-socks and green underpants, and nothing else. I could see her point.

I wished her luck and went over to the cubicle, pulling back the curtain gingerly. "Knock, knock."

It wasn't Maeve in the bed, or sitting beside it. The undercover officer — Katy, I recalled — was lying down with one hand to her head, looking pale. Another of the

UCs was beside her, holding a glass of water. Katy sat up on her elbows at the sight of me.

"How's Maeve? Is she OK?"

"That's what I'm trying to find out." I remembered my manners. "Er — how are you feeling?"

"Like shit," she said, and lay back down again.

"She's covered in bruises," her friend said. "But he didn't get the chance to do too much, thankfully."

"Not to me, but he did enough to other people," Katy pointed out. She looked back at me. "When you find Maeve, let me know how she's getting on."

"Will do."

I went back out and walked straight into the nurse I'd spoken to before. Her name tag read "Yvonne". "Different officer. Have you seen another one?"

"No, but I've seen you. Come with me." She had got a cubicle ready and before I could so much as complain I was sitting on the bed with my head back and a bright light shining in my eyes. "You need a stitch in that. The doctor will have to see it."

Yvonne cleaned up the cut and I closed my eyes, feeling exhausted.

"How did you do this, may I ask?"

"I was arresting someone."

"Fighting them, did you say? And who came off worse?"

"I did," I admitted. But then, I wasn't looking at a life sentence or two, so I didn't have my opponent's added incentive.

"Now, you'll feel a sting."

She was right; the disinfectant hurt more that the cut. "Ow."

"Be brave. Almost done."

"Can you find out what happened to my colleague? Her name is Maeve Kerrigan." I peered at her. "Please?"

A nod. "What else did he do to you?"

I reckoned I might as well own up. I pulled back my sleeve and showed her my arm. "Just this."

She frowned over it. "Oh dear. I'll get the doctor."

"Can't you clean it up for me and stick on a plaster?"

"We take human bites very seriously. When did he do it?"

I had no idea. "An hour ago, probably."

"You'll need to go to theatre to have it washed out and tidied up. Don't worry, you won't feel a thing."

I was regretting showing it to her at all. "Look, I'd love to stick around for that, but I'm a bit busy, and —"

A large, jowly head poked through the curtains. "What are you up to in here, my friend?"

"Sam, where the hell have you been? How's Maeve? Did you find her?"

"Yes and no. I haven't seen her, but I know where she is. Down the hall in resus. They're still working on her." He looked grey, as if he'd aged ten years since the last time I'd seen him. "Fractured skull, they think. They're worried about internal bleeding."

"Is she going to be OK?"

He shrugged helplessly. "They're doing their best for her."

I removed my arm from Yvonne's clutches and stood up, grabbing my jacket.

"Where do you think you're going?"

"To see her."

"You need to get your arm fixed."

Sam leaned in for a closer look. "Ooh. You don't want to take any chances with one of them. I know a fellow got bit in a fight outside a club in the East End. Nearly lost his hand."

"Yeah, all right, Sam, point taken." I turned to the nurse. "Look, how long is it going to take to sort this out? I mean, you need me to go to theatre. That isn't going to happen straightaway, is it?"

She shrugged. "As soon as we can manage it. I'll try and get you in quickly."

"It's not going to be in the next quarter of an hour, is it?"

"No," she admitted.

"If I promise to come straight back, please may I go and see how my colleague is doing?"

"I can't stop you. But I want you back here in five minutes so the doctor can see you."

"Ten minutes." She looked stern and I did my best pleading look. "Please, Yvonne?"

"If you promise."

I was gone before she'd finished saying the last word.

Yvonne proved to be a total pushover compared to Dr Gibb, who had absolutely no interest in hearing why I needed to see Maeve. She was small, dark-haired, serious and implacable, and she had just emerged through the double doors that led to the resuscitation area — in other words, between me and where I needed to be.

"There's no visiting in this area. We will keep the patient's next of kin informed about her condition but if you are just her colleague —"

"I'm not just her colleague. I'm her friend." It was as if I hadn't spoken.

"— it would be infringing her privacy to tell you about her treatment."

"I want to know how she is."

"I'm sure you'll be kept informed by her family."

Desperate, I dug a smile up from somewhere. When all else fails, try charm . . . "Look, you understand how it is. I was there when she got attacked, I really care about her and I just want to make sure she's OK. Please?"

A shake of the head. "I can't help you. I suggest you stop wasting my time and your own."

"For fuck's sake," I snapped, irritated beyond endurance.

Sam plucked my sleeve. "Come on, mate. Give up. Back to your cubicle like a good boy."

I had to go; I had run out of time and a promise was a promise. Swearing under my breath, I walked away, Sam bobbing along at my right elbow.

"Never knew you felt that way about Kerrigan."

"What? Oh, that. You know better than to take that at face value. I was just trying to convince the doctor to let me see her."

"Course you were." He gave a wheezy little laugh and I glared at him.

"Feeling better, are we? You should — there's no need to feel ashamed of breaking your own land speed record by taking twenty minutes to run two hundred metres."

"Don't be like that. Just because I heard what you said back there —"

"I've already explained to you that I didn't mean it. And if you repeat it to anyone — anyone, Sam — I'm going to find that guy with the antlers, borrow them, and put them somewhere that'll have you walking funny for a week."

"Easy, easy, no need for violence . . ."

I got to the cubicle first and pulled the curtain across to stop him from joining me. I had had about as much as I could take of Sam for one evening. I sat down on the edge of the bed, feeling like death, and waited for the next fun thing to happen to me.

Yvonne was true to her word. It was only another couple of minutes before the doctor came to assess my arm. It was somehow typical of the way my night was going that when the curtain went back, the doctor in question turned out to be Dr Gibb.

They let me go once they'd finished sorting out my arm, sending me off with a bandage up to the elbow and a plastic bag that contained some really quite decent painkillers that I didn't intend to touch. Most people would have gone home — I should have gone home — but instead I found myself heading for the police station, and I didn't want my edge to be dulled by pain relief, no matter how welcome it might have been. There had been no word on Maeve's condition and I thought I might be able to find out more at work. Besides, I couldn't rest, knowing that she was in trouble. The thoughts just kept squirreling around in my mind. *If I'd been a bit quicker . . . If I hadn't been tied up with the journalist . . . If she'd just called to me before she ran to help Katy . . .*

I was also reasonably interested to find out what had happened with the young man I had so nearly arrested. From what I'd seen earlier, there was no question but that he was the killer we'd been hunting. And we had been way off. The belief is that serial killers don't come out of nowhere — there's a pattern of offences before they escalate to murder. But the lad I'd been fighting didn't look as if he'd had time to commit many crimes, and I didn't recognise him from the rogues' gallery of local perverts that we'd spent many hours tracking down. I was pretty sure he hadn't come to the attention of the enquiry before now. So either he was very clever, or, which seemed more likely, we were very mistaken in what we'd been searching for.

Given what had happened before he was arrested, I wasn't expecting him to have been passed for interview by the doctor. I wouldn't have been; I was exhibiting the alertness and tensile strength of overcooked broccoli. Apparently he was tougher than me, though, because when I got to the nick at six, the first thing I saw was Chris Pettifer being lectured by Judd in the corridor. Pettifer was one of the squad's trained interrogators and his presence there at that hour of the morning could only mean that the suspect was fit and healthy and ready to talk. I went past without interrupting, noting that Judd was looking even more intense than usual. I was very glad I didn't have the responsibility of securing a confession.

I found Peter Belcott in the interview room when I went in, which wasn't a surprise. He had a trick of turning up when things got interesting.

"Fill me in, mate. Who is he?"

"I'm not your mate." Belcott relented. "His name's Razmig Selvaggi." He rolled the syllables around in his mouth, enjoying the sound of the name. "Twenty-four years old. His mother's Armenian, father's Italian. He lives in Brixton with his family, who run a takeaway. He does deliveries for them. No trace PNC. That's it."

"Has he confessed yet?"

"They're just going to talk to him now. There'll be a live feed from the interview room, if you want to watch it." Belcott nodded towards the small meeting room where the light from the TV flickered.

"I might just do that." I started to walk away.

"I heard Kerrigan stopped him with her face. Wouldn't be the first time she'd had that effect on a man."

My hands clenched into fists before I could stop them. "She got injured going to the assistance of another officer, so I wouldn't joke about it too much if I were you. And where were you last night? Hot date with *World of Warcraft*, was it?"

"Fuck off."

"Delighted to."

I went into the meeting room where a couple of the lads were already sitting, waiting for the show to start. I stood behind them, leaning against the wall. My arm throbbed dully and I felt wretched, on the whole. I wanted to see Selvaggi again, but I was glad of the distraction too.

On screen, the door opened and Pettifer walked in, Judd right behind him. The sound was off but I could see the inspector was still talking. Obviously he didn't trust him enough to let him do his job. Pettifer looked fed up and I didn't blame him. One of the detectives who was sitting in front of me booed loudly and threw a balled-up piece of paper at the screen. He might have made the arrest, but Judd wasn't going to be winning a popularity contest any time soon. The two of them took their seats at the table, Pettifer with a look back over his shoulder at the camera. He knew we were watching and I wondered if it was a help to know we were rooting for him, or if it just put him under more pressure.

The next time the door opened, it was to allow Selvaggi and his lawyer to enter the room. A couple of other officers had come into the meeting room by now and there was a low rumble of comment at the sight of him. The bruises on his face were darkening nicely. His shoulders were hunched with tension and he looked distinctly unimpressive as he sat down at the table.

"Young, isn't he?" Colin Vale voiced what I had been thinking. He looked younger than twenty-four, especially when he started biting his nails.

His solicitor was young too. I guessed she was on call for one of the local defence firms — it being the weekend, she had to be one of the most junior lawyers. She had long, straight red hair with a heavy fringe. Under it, her face was pale, which wasn't surprising given the early hour. Her suit looked creased and I thought she was nervous as she sat down beside Selvaggi, leaning over to mutter something in his ear. That wasn't a surprise either. Crimes didn't come much more serious than this.

I became aware that everyone in the room was leaning forward. "Turn it up, Colin."

The sound came up on Pettifer running through the formulaic preamble that began every interview: stating the time, the date, the location and who was present for the benefit of the tape. Asked for his name and date of birth, Selvaggi gave them in a voice that was so low and husky I strained to hear it. He had a soft South London accent that made his words run together. The solicitor's name was Rosalba Osbourne. She sounded absurdly matter-of-fact, as if what she was doing was all in a day's work and nothing to get excited about. Technically, it was, but it was clear to me at any rate that she was hoping no one would notice the nerves that had her fidgeting with her pen. Pettifer cautioned Selvaggi again before launching into the interview. Everything by the book. Nothing open to question.

"Right," Pettifer said once the formalities were out of the way. "Mr Selvaggi, do you know why you were arrested this morning?"

"Mistaken identity."

384

"What do you mean by that?"

He cleared his throat but it didn't make much difference; his voice was still hoarse when he spoke. "You've got me confused with someone else. That serial killer."

"You were arrested in Campbell Road recreation ground, weren't you?"

He nodded, then after a nudge from the solicitor said, "Yes."

"What were you doing there?"

A shrug. "Just walking around."

"Walking around. Do you often go for a walk in the middle of the night? In the rain?"

"I'd been working. I needed a break."

"Do you often attack women while you're taking these walks?"

He looked to his solicitor, who shook her head. "No comment."

"You were caught in the act of attacking two this morning, weren't you? Both police officers, as it happened, but you didn't know that."

"No comment."

"When we searched you, we found these items on your person." Pettifer waited for Judd to lay the evidence bags on the table in front of Selvaggi. "A stun gun. A hammer. A crowbar. Twine. Bolt cutters. What's your explanation for that?"

"I found them." It was stupid of him to be tempted into an explanation and I thought Rosalba looked annoyed, but she let him speak. "They were on the ground and I picked them up."

"Was this before or after you attacked the women?"

"I never. They were on the ground too."

"Who attacked them, Mr Selvaggi?"

"Someone else."

"Did you see someone else? Because we were running a surveillance operation in the area and I think we would have noticed if anyone else had been there."

Another shrug.

"For the record, Mr Selvaggi shrugged." Pettifer took a sip of water. It wasn't going badly, all the same. But it was hard to see how he could get out of it when I'd caught him red-handed.

Judd obviously felt he could do better than Chris. "Do you really expect us to believe that you just happened to come across the crime scene by chance? How do you explain the petrol can in the carrier of your moped?"

"It's in case I run out of petrol," Selvaggi deadpanned and the room around me erupted into guffaws; Judd had picked pretty much the only thing that Selvaggi could explain away.

"We're going to search your house," Judd snapped. His ears had gone bright red. "We're going to go through everything that belongs to you, and everything that belongs to your parents, and everything that belongs to your sisters. We're going to rip the place apart. And then we'll see if you have an explanation for what we find."

"Better hope we find something," one of the older detectives said mordantly. "Or that won't be much of a threat."

Selvaggi's face was hard to read, but the quality of the footage and the angle of the camera made it difficult to see the details anyway.

"When are they searching the house?" I asked, hoping someone would know.

"Right now. We've just got the warrant." I hadn't noticed him arrive, but Superintendent Godley was leaning in through the door. "Rob, I was hoping you might be here. Do you want to come?"

"Definitely." I peeled myself off the wall and followed Godley out to the car that was waiting to take us to Brixton. I recognised it was his way of thanking me for getting Selvaggi under control; it was typical of him to think of it and I appreciated it. I also appreciated the distraction from my concerns about Maeve, because even seeing Judd doing battle with Selvaggi wasn't enough to keep my mind off her.

"There's no news," Godley said abruptly as we got into the car. "About Maeve. I've just rung the hospital."

"Oh. Right. Thanks for letting me know."

"I'll tell you if I hear anything."

"Very kind," I said, not managing to sound anything other than embarrassed. Godley took out his phone and called the commissioner's staff officer to bring him up to date. I stared out of the window at the streets, wondering if everyone on the squad had worked out how I felt about her, wondering if they'd known it before I did.

Selvaggi's home turned out to be a modest Victorian house in the middle of a terrace. Deceptively narrow, it went back a long way, which explained how there was room for him, his parents and his three sisters to live there. Skylights in the roof were a giveaway that they had done a loft conversion and it was there, Kev Cox told us, that Selvaggi lived, in what was effectively a self-contained flat.

"We've moved the family out already. They weren't pleased, needless to say, but they've gone to stay with relatives in Carshalton."

The house was uninhabitable already. Kev had arranged for tarpaulins to be hung on frames in front of the windows on the ground floor, and screened off the family car that was parked in the street nearby. Like the rest of the search team, Kev was wearing a white hooded boiler suit and blue gloves. Godley and I ducked behind the tarpaulins to change into paper suits and gloves before we went into the house — there was no way we'd be allowed across the threshold if there was the least chance of us compromising any evidence. The neighbours had been busy getting in touch with the press, and a helicopter whined overhead, filming the search that was going on in the small garden. A cordon was in place at either end of the street so we didn't have to worry about the media getting too close, but every resident within eyeshot of the house was recording anything they could see. It would all be on the news channels before too long. Riveting it wasn't, as far as I was concerned, but the news that there had been an arrest was sensational stuff and they needed some sort of visual entertainment to go with the reports. Kev, his face crinkled with tension, was trying to sort out tents to cover the search areas in the garden so he could work unobserved. Godley and I left him to it, stepping gingerly in through the front door, anonymous in our hooded suits and masks.

"Can I help you?"

The voice belonged to Kev's second-in-command, Tony Schofield. He was tall and gangling and not normally forceful, but Kev seemed to have given him the job of keeping the crime scene under control.

"Superintendent Godley and DC Langton," Godley said with just a trace of impatience. "Kev knows we're here."

"Sorry — I didn't know — I mean —" Schofield's eyes were wide with horror. "I thought I'd better check."

"Quite right. Can you show us around?"

"Of course." He scrambled to put down the box he was carrying and gestured into the front room. "We've started down here but to be honest we're not expecting to find that much. It looks as if he kept most of his things in his room upstairs."

"The loft conversion? Let's start there."

From the hall I could see into the kitchen where officers were opening every jar and checking every container in the freezer. It looked like it had been a tidy house before we'd got there. Mrs Selvaggi was not going to be pleased when she got home, whenever that might be.

I followed Schofield and Godley up the stairs to the second floor. There was just enough room for all three of us to stand upright in the centre of the room, but the ceiling sloped down sharply. There was a single bed, a chest of drawers and a few built-in shelves, but most of the storage was in cupboards built into the eaves. The doors hung open, showing where the search team had swept through the room like a tornado. It felt cramped in there but it was private, away from the rest of the family, and there was even a small bathroom with a shower in it.

"He lives up here, pretty much. Eats here. Sleeps here. Spends a lot of time here during the day. Keeps to himself, according to one of his sisters. They don't even know if he's in the house a lot of the time. He spends hours at the gym in the health centre too — lifts weights. He doesn't have a job, officially — just a bit of casual carpentry for cash-in-hand and pocket money from the family business when he does deliveries. We found his work boots and tools. They've gone off to the lab."

"What else?" Godley sounded edgy. We had caught him in the act but juries were unpredictable; we needed more evidence that he couldn't explain away.

"On those shelves" — Schofield pointed — "he had true crime. Lots of material about serial killers, specifically ones who killed women — two about the Yorkshire Ripper, a few about the Wests, one about the Suffolk Strangler, one about the investigation into Rachel Nickell's murder, and then a few about foreign killers — Bundy, the Green River Killer, Andrei Chikatilo, Ed Gein, the Hillside Strangler, Charles Manson."

"All the top names," Godley commented.

"You've got to aim high," I murmured.

"I suppose he was looking for tips," Schofield said seriously. "He had a set of memoirs by an FBI profiler and a book about forensic investigation too. He'd done the research. How to do it and how to avoid getting caught. Looks like he should have spent longer thinking about the second part. He had a few books on the occult, too. Aleister Crowley and that kind of thing. Amateur Satanism."

I was getting bored with the discussion of Selvaggi's reading habits. "What else?"

"Under the mattress we found a collection of porn magazines and a few adult DVDs, mostly with an S&M theme — bit more specialised than your usual top-shelf material, I'm led to believe. In this drawer here," and he indicated the bottom one in the small chest of drawers by the bed, "there was a cardboard box with women's jewellery in it."

"The missing jewellery from the victims?" Godley asked.

"I couldn't say. But it's gone off to be photographed and examined for DNA. We checked with the sister before she went and she said it didn't belong to her or her sisters or her mother, as far as she knew, but we're getting that confirmed."

"That's good," I observed. "Anything that ties him to the other victims is what we need."

"Might be able to help you out there." Schofield's eyes were bright above his mask. "In that cupboard behind you, right at the back, there was a plastic bag containing a shirt, complete with bloodstains, and two hammers. Looking at one of them, we could see staining that was almost certainly blood, and a couple of longish hairs still attached. I'd like to see him explain that."

"I would too." Godley sounded pleased, but also weary, as if he'd finished a marathon at long last. "Thanks, Tony. Is there anything else?"

"We're checking the shower trap and waste pipes from the bathroom in case he washed off any other evidence. Other than that, it's just a case of going through the property and making sure we haven't missed anything."

"Good. Keep up the good work," Godley said.

Schofield nodded. "If there isn't anything else . . ."

"You get on with what you were doing. Thanks for the tour."

He scuttled off back down the stairs and Godley looked at me. "What do you think?"

"I think even the most suspicious juror should be convinced by the hammer and the jewellery. Some of it is totally circumstantial, like the porn and the true crime. I'm pretty sure some of the team have similar libraries at home. But Dr Chen will be all over it."

"It'll give her something to do while she's trying to think of reasons she got the profile wrong."

"How right you are." I looked around the room, at the cupboard doors hanging open, the stripped bed with its mattress askew, the empty shelves. It was all so pathetic, so meagre. "From nothing to murder in one step. No previous offences. How does that work?"

"Maybe he just didn't get caught. Or maybe he could imagine enough to keep himself happy."

"And then he reached a point where imagining wasn't enough."

Godley straightened up incautiously and banged his head. "Ow. Right. Let's get back. We'll see what Pettifer can do with the new evidence. I'm betting we get a confession by midday."

The superintendent was out by an hour and ten minutes: Selvaggi confessed to all four murders at 10.50 precisely. I had slipped out for a bit of breakfast (coffee and a bacon roll that I abandoned after one stomach-churning mouthful) and I got back just in time to see him cave in. His solicitor had moved her chair back during the preceding hours of questioning and the gap between them was now noticeable. She was taking notes in red pen as if her life depended on it, her concentration focused on the pad in front of her rather than her client. Judd was still leaning forward, every muscle tensed, but Pettifer was relaxed in his chair, calm, encouraging Selvaggi to trust him.

"Tell us about the first murder. Nicola Fielding."

"Back in September," Selvaggi said with a faraway look in his eyes. His voice was quiet. "It was a warm night. Nice night for a walk." He gave a little high-pitched giggle. "That's what she said. I just saw her and stopped. You know. Chatted for a while. I'd done that before a few times. Stopped, I mean, if I saw a girl on her own."

"You did more than chat," Pettifer pointed out. "What was different about this one?"

"Nothing, really." He looked down at his feet. "Except I'd been thinking about it before I saw her. And I'd brought the stuff with me, you know. The things I needed. I was just going to talk to her but we were right beside the park, and I'd taken out the stun gun when I saw her. I was just going to hold it while we chatted, to imagine, like, what it might be like, and then I just did it." He still sounded amazed at his own audacity. "It was like something took over my body and I saw myself put out my hand with the stun gun in it. She didn't even notice me do it. One minute she was telling me about her night, the next she was on the ground."

"You didn't stop with her on the ground, did you? You moved her into the park and you beat her until she was dead."

"It was what I'd been wanting to do for ages. And I got to do it. And no one saw me." There was a strange mixture of shyness and triumph in his tone, as if he knew what he'd done was wrong but he was still proud of it.

"Was it what you'd hoped it would be?" Pettifer sounded genuinely curious. "When you planned it, I mean? Did it live up to your expectations?"

"Killing her?" Selvaggi stared across the table with eyes like stars. "It was better. Much better."

Nauseated all over again, I turned away. It was a solid case. He would plead guilty and get a whole-life

394

sentence; there was no chance he'd ever see freedom again. Justice done.

But I thought about what had been sacrificed to get that far, and somehow I couldn't persuade myself it was worth it.

CHAPTER
TWELVE

MAEVE

I stuttered back to life by the grace of God, with the help of the angels. Real-life angels, like the paramedics who kept me breathing through the siren-filled ride to hospital, the doctors who deliberated over me, and the nurses who kept watch over me during the critical hours when no one was sure if I'd survive until the morning. All the angels and saints in heaven, if you asked my mother, who took refuge in decade after decade of the Rosary, her trust placed in the Blessed Virgin Mary and the various ranks below her in the celestial hierarchy. Later, Dad told me that she had had everyone running scared, from Superintendent Godley down to Ian, who spent most of his time in the waiting room, out of range.

I knew none of this at the time, of course. I knew nothing except the pain in my head and body, and the strange confusion that comes from waking up in the sensory deprivation of a hospital room with no real recollection of how you ended up there. I didn't know what I was doing or what had happened to me, whether it was night or day, whether I would live or die, and mostly, I was too miserable to care.

When I came back to proper consciousness for the first time, I opened my eyes to the sight of a doctor in surgical scrubs leaning over me. He had peeled back one of my eyelids to shine a bright light in my eye.

"Ow." My voice was rusty with lack of use and thirst and I coughed a little, painfully.

"Welcome back. Can you tell me your name?"

"Yes, I can. Can you tell me yours?"

"I'm going to need to hear it, I'm afraid."

"Maeve Áine Kerrigan. Your turn."

He laughed. "Nothing wrong with you, is there?"

"What is wrong with me? Why am I here?"

"Do you remember what happened?"

I wanted to answer him, if only to make him go away, but when I opened my mouth to tell him, there was nothing there. I frowned.

"Take your time."

"I don't need time." I plucked at the blanket that was spread over me, feeling a quiver of fear that spread from the pit of my stomach all the way up my spine. "I'll think of it in a minute."

"Hmm." The doctor straightened up and took out a pen to make a note on my chart. I felt as if I had failed an important test.

"My head hurts."

"I'm not surprised. You have a fractured skull."

"Oh."

That didn't sound good. I closed my eyes again, trying to remember how and why that had happened to me. A car accident? I had been in a car; I remembered turning around to look at someone in the back seat.

But it hadn't been moving, I thought. That couldn't be it.

When I opened my eyes again, the doctor was gone. But in his place were my parents, one on either side of the bed. They looked tired and a bit crumpled around the edges. Dad was wearing a cardigan with the buttons done up wrong, and Mum's hair had gone flat — most unlike her usual array of brown curls.

"What are you doing here?" I sounded better, I was pleased to hear. Stronger. Less croaky.

"You're awake." There was an expression of pure relief on my mother's face for an instant and I saw it mirrored by Dad when I turned my head.

"How are you feeling, love?"

"My head hurts, Dada." The childish name slipped out before I could catch it, but then I felt childish, like I wanted to be petted and soothed and looked after. Then I remembered. It was important to tell them what had happened to me. "I have a fractured skull."

"We know. The doctors told us. You've been in and out for the past thirty-six hours." Mum was back to her usual tartness, I was slightly relieved to see. I couldn't be *that* ill. "They said they'd have to wait and see how things would turn out. There might be some degree of impairment, apparently."

"Impairment?"

My father clicked his tongue in irritation. "Ah, Colette. Don't upset her."

I turned to him. "What happened?"

"Do you not remember?" Dad looked at me worriedly and I made a special effort to recall, for him.

"I was at work . . ."

"Indeed and you were," Mum snapped. "Work. Do they pay you extra for putting yourself in danger? You should never have been there in the first place."

"It was a surveillance op." It was starting to come back. "I was in the car, watching."

"You ran to help another officer and you were attacked." Dad's voice was gentle but his words still made me jump.

"Who was I helping? What happened? Was it the serial killer who attacked me?"

"You saved another policewoman from being killed. And yes, they think it was the fellow you've been looking for."

"Was he arrested?"

"I think so." Dad sounded vague. "We haven't seen the news. We've been here."

"Waiting to see if you'd be all right." Mum leaned back in her chair, as if she was exhausted. "Maeve, I'm sorry. I just don't understand what would make you want to be a police officer. I never have and I never will. You're a bright girl, you could have done anything. You still could. Have you thought about teaching? Or what about becoming a lawyer? They're always paid well."

Mum had been a doctor's receptionist for thirty years. Dad had worked in insurance. My spirits plummeted at the thought of trying to explain to them what I loved about my job — especially in my current state — but I tried anyway.

"There's nothing like being a police officer, Mum. Especially a detective. I get to investigate the biggest crimes, the worst things that can happen, and if I do my job properly, the people who commit the crimes are taken out of society. It's not even about justice being done — it's about making sure that ordinary decent people don't have to live in fear." And there was the adrenalin rush; mustn't forget that. "It's an important job. A really important one. It saves lives. If we've caught the Burning Man —"

"He won't kill anyone else," Mum finished tiredly. "But Maeve, he nearly killed you."

There was a little silence. All I could think to say was to point out that I was still here, despite his best efforts, and I didn't think that would go down too well. Eventually I asked, "Is Ian here?"

A look flicked between my parents. "He was here," Dad said, his voice carefully neutral. "He waited with us for a while. But he had to go."

"He said he'd come back tomorrow," Mum added.

I stretched, feeling the drip pull in my arm. "He wasn't too worried about me, then."

"He was worried enough."

If Mum was desperate enough to give Ian credit for something, she had to be serious about it. I hated to see her upset, but I'd fought hard enough to become a police officer in the first place. There was no way I'd give it up now.

Always assuming that I didn't have too severe a degree of impairment, obviously.

The following day, I didn't consciously wait for Ian to show up, but I was aware I hadn't seen him yet as the

400

day drew to a close. I had persuaded my parents to take the evening off and go home. There was nothing on TV that I wanted to watch, and my head still hurt too much for reading. I sat and thought instead, and reached some interesting conclusions. I must have drifted off, because I resurfaced to find Ian standing by my bed, watching me.

"How do you feel?"

"With every nerve-ending." He was wearing a dark-blue pinstripe suit and a white shirt, collar open. "Hi."

"Hi yourself."

"Were you at work?"

"Yep."

"Where's your tie?"

"In my pocket." He showed me. "You never stop trying to work things out, do you?"

"I like to know what's going on." I paused for a second. "It's still Monday, isn't it?"

"Still Monday." He checked his watch — a Rolex Oyster that had cost him a fortune. A rich boy's toy, when I had a cheap Sekonda that my parents had given me for Christmas one year. I'd seen his watch a million times, but suddenly I couldn't take my eyes off it. "It's twenty past seven. Visiting hours are over at eight, I'm afraid, so I won't be able to stay for long. I got here as soon as I could."

I gave a one-shouldered shrug. "You had to work. I understand."

"Yeah. You know all about needing to work, don't you?" He was looking at me with a strange expression on his face. He ran a finger down my cheek. "Pretty."

401

"You always say that when I'm looking hideous," I said, suspicious.

"Not at all. All the colours of the rainbow."

"Oh. My face."

"Yeah." He stood by the bed, his hands in his pockets. "Do you want anything?"

"Like what?"

He shrugged. "Grapes? That's the traditional gift, isn't it?"

"Not hungry." My mouth was cotton dry. "Actually, is there any water?"

He poured a glass from a plastic jug on the bedside locker, and helped me sit up a little to drink it. The effort made the room spin and I collapsed back onto the pillows with a groan.

"Are you OK?"

"Not just at the moment, but give me time."

He was looking concerned and I felt a rush of affection for him — he was a good person, really.

"You were right, weren't you? Policing did turn out to be a bit dangerous."

He laughed. "Is now a good time to say I told you so?"

"There's no good time to say I told you so." I gathered my courage and plunged on. "Just like there's no good time to say it's over between us. It's just not working out, is it?"

His smile faded away. "Maeve . . ."

"You're not going to say it because I'm weak and injured, but it's true. What we had was great, as far as it went, but it's not going anywhere. We're too different. We want different things."

"When did you decide this?" His expression was neutral and I couldn't tell what he was thinking.

"I've had a bit of time to think, for once, but it's been coming for a while. And you feel the same, don't you?" I knew the answer was yes; he didn't even have to say it. And I knew I was doing the right thing.

"Is this because of your near-death experience? Life's too short not to look for Mr Right?"

"Honestly, no. It's more that I think we both deserve to be happier than we've been lately. And I don't think I can make you happy, Ian."

He didn't argue with me. Instead, he said, "You don't have to move out straightaway. You're in no condition to go flat-hunting."

"You don't want me convalescing in your flat — I'd just get in your way. Besides, Mum and Dad want me to go home."

He pulled a face. "If you're OK with that . . ."

"It's fine. Really. It will be relaxing," I lied. I really couldn't make myself sound convinced, though.

"Right. Well, there's no hurry. Take your time. Let yourself get better before you start dashing around again. You push yourself too hard."

I smiled. "I'm glad you don't mind."

"I didn't say that." Ian's voice was gentle. "I'm sorry it didn't work out. But I can't say you're wrong about it."

"I'm sorry too. No hard feelings."

"Definitely not," he agreed.

I put out my hand and he took it, holding it for a moment in both of his. There was a knock on the door before it opened a few inches and Rob poked his head around. He saw us holding hands and immediately began to reverse.

"Sorry. I'll come back."

"Wait!" Ian and I said at the same time and Rob stopped.

"I'd better go." Ian laid my hand back down on the bed. "I'll see you soon. Do you want me to make a start on packing up your stuff?"

"Don't bother. My mother will love the opportunity to have a good snoop through my things," I said sleepily. "I might as well get her to do something useful."

He winced. "Right. I might arrange to be out while she's there."

"Wimp." I grinned. "I don't actually blame you. Every time she comes to see me, my blood pressure goes up. The doctors are always convinced I'm having a relapse."

Ian bent and kissed my cheek lightly, his lips barely grazing my skin. "Feel better soon." He turned and walked quickly to the door, saying something to Rob in a low voice as he went by. I saw a grin light up Rob's face like a flash of lightning. It disappeared just as quickly, too; I might almost have thought I'd imagined it if I hadn't been watching him closely. The door closed and Rob came over to the bed, standing in the spot Ian had just vacated.

"Sit down, would you? Looking up is giving me a crick in my neck."

"Can't have that." He looked around and found a chair, drawing it forward and sitting down with a sigh. Even in the dim lighting of my hospital room, I could see that he was pale, with bluish shadows under his eyes and a dark bruise on his jaw under the stubble. He had a cut in one eyebrow too.

"You look like hell," I said. "What's going on?"

"What makes you think anything is going on?"

"You're the first copper I've seen since I've been in here. That makes me think everyone else has somewhere better to be."

"It was family only for the first bit," Rob protested. "I came as soon as I could."

"Well, now you're here." I eyed him. "Do you want to fill me in on what happened the other night?"

"If I had a pound for every woman who's ever said that to me . . ."

"For God's sake!"

"OK, OK. Keep what's left of your hair on."

I put my hand up to my head without thinking and encountered bandages. "You can't see if they cut any of it off, can you? The nurse promised me that the surgeon didn't shave my head."

He was laughing. "Sorry. I couldn't resist it. I'm sure you're like a Vidal Sassoon ad under those bandages."

"I don't know why I'm getting so upset," I said wonderingly. "It's not as if I care about that sort of thing usually."

"Maybe that knock on the head has changed your personality. You might become a proper girl if you're lucky."

"I'm already a proper girl," I said with dignity. "You just don't know it."

"You keep it well hidden." I must have looked hurt again, because he leaned forward and patted my hand. "Only joking, Kerrigan. You're all right."

"Anyway, get back to what you were saying about what happened the other night." I looked at him expectantly.

"I'm not supposed to talk to you about work."

I made a noise that was pure frustration and he held up his hands. "OK. You've convinced me. What do you remember?"

"Katy," I said instantly. "Is she —"

"Fine. Better than you, actually. Bumps and bruises and a burn mark from the stun gun."

I breathed out slowly. I hadn't dared to ask anyone else, not that I'd thought they would tell me anyway. But Rob was telling the truth, I was pretty sure. "So it was him, then."

"Oh yes. Most certainly. The Burning Man in all his twenty-four-year-old glory."

"You're kidding."

He shook his head. "Remember all those briefings from the psychologist about how he was in his late thirties to mid-forties, lived alone, likely to have a history of violence, blah blah blah? Not quite right."

"Who is he?"

I listened, rapt, as Rob told me all about Razmig Selvaggi.

"He's his mother's darling — can do no wrong. She lets him get away with doing whatever he wants, according to his sister."

"I have literally no idea what that would be like," I said seriously.

"Razmig has what amounts to a self-contained flat in the loft conversion and the rest of the family aren't allowed to go up there. Plenty of privacy. The parents work until all hours in the takeaway and the sisters don't keep track of where he is or what he does. And of course the scooter belongs to the business so he doesn't even have to pay for his own petrol."

"Just what you want if you're out a-murdering."

"Indeed. And he uses the pizza as his opening gambit — offering free food is a good way to get girls to stop and chat."

"Did he confess?"

"He didn't have much choice," Rob said frankly. "The search of his house turned up items of jewellery that match the missing pieces belonging to the victims, not to mention a bloodstained hammer."

"Everything that we were looking for."

"Exactly. Even his solicitor didn't have much to say when they whacked the photographs of what they'd found on the table in the interview room. When you're that screwed, there's nothing much to do but talk, and good old Razmig did."

My mind was racing. "Did he confess to all of them? What about Rebecca Haworth?"

Rob leaned back and grinned. "Nothing wrong with that brain of yours, is there? No, he didn't confess to Rebecca's murder. He's got an alibi. His cousin got married the day Rebecca died, and Razmig was at the wedding reception all evening and into the night. There's a video of it and everything. Not only was he very, very drunk by about nine o'clock, but the wedding was in Hertfordshire. He'd have to have mastered bi-location as well as murdering women in five easy stages."

"I *knew* it."

"He was a bit fed up with whoever stole his MO. Couldn't wait to tell us it wasn't him."

I was still stuck on his age. "Did you really say he's twenty-four?"

"Yep. Never had a girlfriend." Rob leaned over to reach into his back pocket and produced a colour print-out of a picture. "There's the custody image. That's Razzi."

It was a close-up of a thick-necked young man with soft, woebegone dark eyes and a slack, wet mouth that was startlingly red, like a child's. He had short black hair with an inch-long gelled fringe that was combed forward over a low forehead, and his nose was long and narrow. Not by any stretch of imagination could he be described as attractive, but he wasn't hideous either — except that somehow, you had the sense that there was something missing when you looked at him. But then, anyone would look a bit dispirited when they were arrested for four murders.

"He lifts weights in his spare time," Rob observed, reaching out for the photo. "That explains the neck. You should see his arms."

I was more interested in Rob's. As he stretched to take the picture, his sleeve slipped back and showed a white bandage that was wrapped around his forearm from the wrist back to the elbow. "What happened to you?"

He grimaced. "It's no big deal. They got a bit over-excited when they were bandaging it."

"What did you do to yourself?"

"You know how my radio wasn't working the other night? When you interrupted Razmig's big night out, I didn't hear you press your red button. The first I knew of it was when I saw Sam waddling past at warp speed, puffing like a walrus. He headed around to the gate you'd gone through, and I hiked over the railings to come at it from the other side."

"Did you gouge yourself on them? Ouch."

He shook his head. "It gets better. So I'm running around in the dark, trying to find you without making too much noise, and when I finally spot you, you're on the ground and there's a lad in motorcycle leathers standing over you. You'd curled up into a ball, which was sensible. I legged it across the lawn and jumped on him. Not in time to stop him from booting you in the face, though. Sorry about that."

I waggled my fingers dismissively. "It's the least of my troubles. Apparently it's looking quite pretty today."

"Mmm," he said. "You haven't been looking in any mirrors lately, have you? Best to keep it that way."

"You still haven't told me what happened to your arm," I reminded him.

"Yeah. Well. Before the uniforms caught up with me, I got in a few good punches. I was a bit annoyed, to be honest. Katy looked to be in a bad way, and you were lying there —" He broke off and shook his head. "I thought I was too late."

"Poor Rob."

"I know. Get out the violin. So I was having a bit of a wrestle with Razzi, and the next thing was, he *bit* me." He sounded totally disgusted. I couldn't help laughing. "I'm glad you think it's funny."

I stretched, feeling a tiny amount of energy coming back into my arms and legs. "Thanks for rescuing me."

"Any time." He saw me looking sceptical. "I mean it. If you're ever out on an op again, I want you to be paired up with me. If it had been up to Sam to intervene, you'd be in the mortuary now. As it was, he had to have a little sit-down once all the excitement was over. Someone even made him a cup of tea."

"I'll ask specially for you. But I like Sam."

"Sam is the reason there should be a compulsory annual fitness test," Rob said bluntly. "The sooner he retires the better."

"Everything worked out fine in the end." I shut my eyes again, but not for long. "Wait a minute. I can't believe I forgot. What happened with the Haworth case and putting pressure on Gil Maddick? Did they search his house?"

"Yep. Nothing strange popped up. They found a few items of women's clothing, a hairbrush, some cosmetics

— but nothing's come back to Rebecca. Bit of a ladies' man, isn't he? Is he good-looking?"

"If you like that sort of thing. Is Louise OK?"

"Fine, as far as I know."

Now that Selvaggi was under arrest, there would be time for the focus to shift from the Burning Man murders to Rebecca's death, and I hoped the extra attention would gather the evidence we needed to arrest Gil Maddick. I didn't feel as if I was Louise's only line of defence any more, and that, frankly, was a relief.

A nurse poked her head into the room, saw Rob and tapped her wrist meaningfully.

"I'd better go before they kick me out."

I put out my hand without thinking. "No. Stay."

"You need to get some rest, and I have to get to work." His voice was gentle but firm as he stood up. "We're following up on a few things — making sure the case is watertight. The CPS don't want anything to jeopardise this one."

"Right. Of course not." I found myself blushing. We were colleagues, first and foremost. We had been talking about work. Rob probably didn't see me in any other light. Of course he would assume I wanted to keep talking about the job. "If you have to go, you have to go. I wish I could join you."

"Time enough for that. When are they letting you out?"

I shrugged. "No one tells me anything."

"Are you going back to Primrose Hill?" Rob's voice was deceptively casual, but I saw the glint in his eye.

"As you probably noticed, Ian was saying goodbye. We've broken up. I'm going home to my parents to recuperate."

"That should be nice. Comforts of home."

"I'll get better quicker because I'll be desperate to leave."

"When they discharge you from here, let me know. I'll give you a hand with moving to your parents if you like."

I was thinking about something else. "Rob, what did Ian say to you when he was leaving?"

A slow smile spread across his face. "I'll tell you some other time."

"Rob!"

He patted my hand. "Don't get excited. Think of your blood pressure."

"You utter tosser, Langton."

He stood up and stretched. "Proper Gurkha, aren't you?"

It was police slang for officers who never made arrests. I frowned up at him. "Because I didn't collar Razmig Selvaggi?"

"No. But it is because you take no prisoners." He leaned over and surveyed my face. "There is literally nowhere to kiss you that isn't bruised." In the end, he settled for a peck on the tip of my nose. And before I could think of an adequate response, he was gone.

I had a steady stream of visitors the following day, but even so I was heartily sick of being in hospital by the time I was discharged. I left with my mother clucking in attendance on me, half a pharmacy's stock of pills, and a file under my arm. It was the gift Superintendent Godley had given me when he came to see me, sitting by my bed and chatting easily with my father as if he had known him for years instead of having met him when he went to my parents' house on Saturday morning to tell them what had happened. He had driven them to the hospital himself. I wasn't altogether comfortable with my two worlds colliding like that. My mother, from the black look on her face, couldn't understand why Godley was asking me to spend my sick leave working on a case file. But there was nothing I wanted more than a chance to help find out what had happened to Rebecca Haworth, and the file was the best get-well-soon present I could have imagined. It would help me to feel useful, and it would stop me from trying to return to work before I was fully fit. Godley knew his man-management.

"We'll get everything else boxed up and sent over to you. And I'll come and see you," Godley had promised. "Give me a call when you've got something you want to discuss. If you want anything followed up, Peter Belcott is available to do it. You know this case better than anyone on my team. I want your knowledge of the players, your understanding of their characters. I know you have your own suspicions about who killed her, but if you can, put them from your mind and start looking at the evidence with an open mind."

"DI Judd was in charge of the investigation into Rebecca's death," I began, but the superintendent shook his head.

"Don't worry about Tom. He's busy with other things. I didn't get the impression that he was giving this as much attention as you were, anyway. I have a feeling you've got the answers, Maeve, if you just give yourself a chance to realise it."

"I appreciate your faith in me, but I'm not sure I do," I stammered, feeling anything but insightful.

"You might surprise yourself." He caught my mother's eye. "Don't work too hard, of course."

I had promised not to tire myself out, but I was determined not to let him, or myself, down. If that meant having to sit on the file in the car and sleep with it under my pillow so Mum didn't get a chance to spirit it away — well, that was just what I had to do.

Back at home, in the inhumanly tidy surroundings of my parents' semi-detached house in Cheam, I took over the mostly unused dining room. I spread out the contents of the file on the table, organising things into neat piles as if that would help to make sense of them, as if by making a pretty pattern I could see the truth. Two boxes arrived a day later, delivered by Rob, who watched me rifle through them with a resigned expression on his face. He thought, and said, that I shouldn't be trying to work, for which my mother absolutely adored him. I sent him off to have a cup of tea and indulged in an orgy of organising. One pile was interviews that Judd had ordered other officers to do with Rebecca's neighbours, her ex-clients and a couple of old flatmates. One pile dealt with Oxford. I wavered over it — I still wasn't sure it deserved to be so prominent — but in the end, Tilly Shaw's words, and her serious face, came back to me. "She said she owed her life for someone else's and she'd have to pay sometime." If Adam's death had set Rebecca on a path that led to her murder, I wanted to trace her footsteps. One pile was the material from the investigation into Rebecca's death: forensic reports, the autopsy notes, photographs, CCTV logs, witness statements, mobile phone records, financial documents. Lastly, there were my own notes from the interviews I'd done. I needed to review it, all of it, in case there was something I'd missed, something someone else had noted and not understood. Godley was right. If I couldn't find the answers he needed, no one would.

Rob poked his head in halfway through. "I'm going to head off."

"Oh." I sounded far too disappointed. I forced myself to smile. "OK. I thought you might have had enough by now. Prolonged exposure to Mum will do that for a person."

"What are you talking about? She's a poppet," he said with a grin.

"Oh yeah? If you ever see Ian again, ask him about her. He'll tell you the truth."

"I'll make up my own mind, thanks. Good luck with the work and take it easy." He waved from the doorway and disappeared.

I caught up with him as he unlocked his car. "You still haven't told me what Ian said to you at the hospital."

"No, I haven't." He looked down at me for a moment, then leaned in for a kiss that took me completely by surprise. I managed not to splutter but

415

couldn't stop myself from turning when it was over to check whether anyone in the house had seen us.

"Don't get cold," Rob said, as calm as if nothing had happened. "You aren't dressed for being outside." He sat into the driver's seat and turned on the engine.

I wrapped my cardigan around myself more tightly, trying to match his composure even though I was tingling all over. "I'm fine. Tell me what he said. I mean it, Rob."

"If you must know, he wished me luck. He told me I'd need it."

I didn't know what to say, and Rob didn't help me. With a raised eyebrow he shut the car door and reversed out of the drive, speeding away leaving me with a million unanswered questions and a stack of paper to read through.

It took days to get through all of it, scribbling notes as I went, fuelled by endless cups of tea and diverted by occasional spats with my mother, purely from habit. Dad took refuge in the front room where there was a vast TV and Sky Sports, and for a little while, it was just like being a teenager again. The effect was heightened when Mum enlisted my brother Dec to help her retrieve my belongings from Ian's flat. My life amounted to pathetically little when it was in bags and boxes. Dec carried the lot up to my old bedroom where it sat in a heap, because I refused to unpack.

Dec being Dec, of course, he attempted to persuade me to stay. "Mum and Dad would love you to be around more. They don't see enough of you."

He was four years older than me but seemed middle-aged already. He had got married when he was twenty-five and already had two kids, girls. He lived in Croydon, not far from Mum and Dad, but I knew — because he had told me — that he thought I should pull my weight more where they were concerned. He had responsibilities, after all. I, it seemed, did not.

You would have thought that the grandchildren would have been distraction enough for my mother, but she managed not to lose her sense of grievance if I didn't call her often enough. I had a feeling that Dec was hurt that his devotion wasn't recognised as it should have been. But then, he'd never really learned the lesson that life wasn't fair. I ignored Dec's comments. Being at home was temporary, I promised myself. I would be off on my own again soon, even if I didn't know where I was going to go.

This wasn't the only thing on my mind, of course. Generally, the things I didn't know vastly outnumbered the things I did, both personally and professionally, but the difference was that police mysteries didn't make my head hurt. But all the time, my mind was working away on what I had read, what I had seen, what I had heard. And when I pushed the last pile of paper away from me on the third day of reading, I had a sheet of paper in front of me that was dense with notes and scribbled questions, and a growing conviction that I was tantalisingly close to a definite answer. I had a list of suspects who had clear motives to kill Rebecca Haworth: she had many more enemies than the average twenty-eight-year-old. I knew that some of them had lied, and lied again — I could prove it. But I couldn't yet prove which one of them had murdered her.

I dug through the boxes I hadn't yet unpacked until I unearthed DCI Garland's fat dog-eared folder of notes on Adam Rowley. I sorted through it until I found the inspector's account of Adam Rowley's life up to its early termination, specifically his family background, and read it with renewed interest before picking up my phone. Belcott answered on the second ring.

"Belcott."

"Peter, it's Maeve Kerrigan. I understand you're working on the Haworth murder. I've got something I'd like you to follow up." I was at my silkiest, knowing that it would irritate him almost beyond endurance to be working for me.

"Of course," he said stiffly. "What do you need?"

"A twenty-year-old man named Adam Rowley" — I spelled it — "drowned in Oxford in 2002. I want to trace his older brother. I don't have a first name or any other details but he would have lived in Nottingham and his parents' names were Tristan and Helen Rowley. Tristan Rowley was a doctor, if that helps."

"Not a lot, as it happens. Any idea if the parents still live in Nottingham?"

"Nope," I said cheerfully. "And call me back when you find out about him. If you get hold of him, I'd like to talk to him." I wanted to find out who else might have mourned for Adam, apart from Rebecca. I wanted to know who might have wanted revenge.

He hung up without saying goodbye, which I didn't mind. I was occupied with searching through my notebook for what I'd taken down during my interview with Caspian Faraday when he rang back, surprisingly quickly.

"Adam Rowley's brother Sebastian is thirty-one, married, and lives in Edinburgh. I've just spoken to his wife. Seb is in surgery, apparently, but he will call you when he's free, she said. He's a vet. Small-animals practice."

"You found out a lot." I was actually impressed.

"Mrs Rowley junior likes to talk. Was there anything else?"

"Yes. I want you to find out everything you can about Delia Faraday, Caspian Faraday's wife. Specifically, where she was on the twenty-sixth of November and in the days leading up to it, and what kind of car she drives. And anything else I might be interested in."

"Right." He hesitated. "Do you really think she was involved?"

"I want to rule a few things out." I was deliberately vague; I wasn't ready yet to tell anyone what I was thinking, let alone Belcott, who would hijack my ideas in a heartbeat.

"I live to serve," he said, and hung up.

A pleasant-sounding Seb Rowley called me a couple of hours later, cheerful, intrigued and not a little surprised about being contacted by the Metropolitan Police. I asked him a few questions about his brother's death and got no new information from him, except

419

that Adam had been a difficult child, inclined to sulk, and that he and his brother had never got on.

"Three years is a big gap at that age. Maybe if he'd lived longer we'd have got to know one another a bit better as adults." The shrug travelled down the phone line. "Never happened."

I persevered. "Was Adam particularly close to anyone in the family? A cousin, someone like that?"

"No. We don't have a big extended family. My parents were both only children, so no cousins." He sounded puzzled but unguarded and I had to believe he was telling the truth. He didn't know anyone named Gil Maddick. Dead end.

Belcott had left me a voicemail, I discovered on winding up my conversation with Seb Rowley. Delia Faraday didn't have a UK driver's licence, but there was a black Range Rover Vogue registered to the Highgate address in addition to the Aston Martin.

I headed back to the table, to the CCTV logs. We had searched far and wide for clues and there was a lot of CCTV, pulled in from the surrounding streets. Colin Vale, a tall, cadaverous detective who looked as if he hadn't seen daylight in years, had spent weeks running the plates from all of the Operation Mandrake CCTV through the PNC and DVLA databases and then following up, tracing drivers, ruling them out because they had alibis for Burning Man murders. Then he had to do it all for Rebecca's murder in the light of Godley's decision to run the enquiry alongside the main investigation. If there was one thing DC Vale was good at, though, it was organising information. The spreadsheets he'd produced were things of beauty. I had looked through them already in my trawl through the file, but now I looked again, and this time I concentrated on the cars that had been tagged as "not of interest/untraced", looking for the Range Rover. About halfway down the fourth page, I saw something completely unexpected, something that made my heart jump with shock. A make and model that I recognised. One occupant.

Godley, or whoever had assembled the file on his behalf, had been thorough enough to include three disks of CCTV, and Vale had lovingly cross-referenced each entry in his log with a timestamp and location. It was simple to find the right disk, slightly harder to persuade Dad to part with the remote control for five minutes — "Why? What is it? Is it a film? I'll put it on for you" — and the work of seconds to select the right part of the recording. It was a tape from a petrol station near the New Covent Garden market, the angle acute enough to show the traffic passing for a second or two. I held my breath as the car I wanted to see crossed the bottom of the picture, one occupant visible in no great detail, but clearly enough, especially on Dad's giant TV, that I could guess at the features and know who I was looking at. It might not have been enough to convince a jury, but it had convinced me.

And it changed everything.

LOUISE

After the incident on the stairs, I made up my mind that I had to end it with Gil. Not because I couldn't forgive him for what he'd done — strangely, I took it for granted that he would treat me that way: it was his nature. I'd known he was as dangerous as a naked flame; I had only myself to blame for acting the part of the moth. Belatedly, I'd learned my lesson, grateful for the reminder that came in time to stop me from trusting him or even falling in love with him. Not, I assured myself, that there had been any danger of that. I had just been doing a good impression of it. But I was tired of playing a part, tired of being the version of Rebecca that he could have loved for ever. The novelty had worn off. And I was a little bit ashamed of myself that I'd let it go on for so long. Fun though it had been to try out being his girlfriend, it was past time to call a halt.

I gave him twenty-four hours, though. A whole day to think that I had been brought to heel. Mastered. Taught a lesson. He believed it, too. I found him in the spare bedroom, sanding the window frame as if it belonged to him, whistling through his teeth. He was doing it the old-fashioned way, with a bit of sandpaper wrapped around a block, getting into every crevice of the old frame so all the traces of yellowing paint had been removed.

"What are you doing?"

"Finishing this off for you. You haven't exactly been making much progress."

He was right. I had shut the door on the room after stripping it bare. There was nothing left of it as it had been, just gaping bare floorboards and the off-white, bumpy old plaster on the walls. The redesigned interior only existed in my head.

"I haven't had a chance to get back to it. I've been busy."

"Haven't you, though." He half-turned to grin at me. I didn't smile back. "Are you OK?"

"Fine. Look, leave that, would you? I'll get round to it some time myself."

"No time like the present." He kept sanding and I felt anger start to burn through me. How dare he behave as if it was his house? How dare he ignore me when I told him to stop?

"You look good," he said without turning around. "I like that colour on you. You should always wear blue."

I plucked at the sky-coloured T-shirt I was wearing. "Glad you like it. This was Rebecca's favourite colour."

That got his attention. He set the sandpaper down on the windowsill with deliberate lack of haste and turned to face me. "I thought we talked about that. Why do you keep bringing her up?"

"She's on my mind," I said simply.

"Well, she shouldn't be. She belongs to the past. You should only be thinking about the present, and the future." He walked over to me and tugged up the hem of the T-shirt, pulling it over my head. "You should only be thinking about me."

I let him take my top off — not that he would have stopped if I had resisted him, I could tell. Instead of dropping it to the floor I held on to it, hugging it to my chest. "Actually, I have been thinking about you. And the future."

"Really." He had a quizzical expression on his face, guarded, as if he wasn't sure where this was going.

"I'm sorry, but I don't think you're going to be a part of it. My future, that is." The direct approach seemed best.

"What do you mean?"

"I mean I'm finished with this. I don't want to play any more."

His face darkened. "Is that what we were doing? Playing?"

"Sure." I shrugged. "You weren't taking it seriously, were you?"

It was absolutely impossible for Gil to believe that I might be breaking up with him. "You're very funny."

"I'm not laughing," I said softly. "And I've made it easy for you. I've packed up your things." I took a step back, wary of what he might do.

"What?" He folded his arms. "What the fuck are you talking about?"

"While you were in here, I was collecting your things," I explained. "They're in a bin liner outside the

424

front door. I'd hurry down if I were you; it would be terrible if someone mistook the bag for rubbish." I had thought that putting his things outside might make him leave, and quickly.

"Why are you doing this?" He took a couple of steps towards me and I put out my hand to stop him, showing him the pepper spray I had ordered from the Internet. I almost hoped he'd give me an excuse to use it. He looked down at it, stunned, but he didn't come any closer.

"It seemed the best way to make sure we had a clean break." I threw him the T-shirt. "Here you go. When you find the new girl you want to make into another Rebecca, give her this with my love. And wish her luck. She'll need it."

I turned and walked to the door, leaving him standing in the middle of the room, at a loss.

"You can't do this," he called after me. "I won't let you."

I stopped at the door. "No, Gil, I really can. You don't get a say in the matter, I'm afraid. You had your fun; I had mine. Now take a hint and get lost."

He was a bully, and a coward. The pepper spray was enough to make him think twice about trying to argue with me. He wasn't the sort who'd risk being hurt. I thought he was pathetic. I wished I'd never allowed him into my life in the first place. But having made that mistake, I wasn't going to make another now. I didn't stay to hear what else he had to say.

I heard him walk past my bedroom door while I was putting on another top.

"Gil."

"Yeah." There was an undertone of hope in the single syllable.

"Make sure you leave the key when you go."

I heard the front door slam a couple of seconds later, and the rustle of the bin bag as he picked it up. Under my breath, very softly, I said, "Goodbye."

CHAPTER
THIRTEEN

Maeve

Godley had told me to give him a call if I had anything to discuss, but I hadn't expected him to come to see me that day. It was flattering and nerve-racking in equal measure. He stood in the dining-room doorway, looking too tall in the context of my parents' house, and surveyed the scene in front of him.

"Plenty to look at. I wondered how long it would take."

"I'm not saying I've worked everything out," I warned him. "But I'm pretty sure we have enough to warrant an arrest, if not to get a conviction. It's circumstantial, mainly, but I just don't think there's any other way of explaining what I've found out."

He took off his coat and jacket and threw them over the back of a chair, then sat down opposite me, rolling up his shirtsleeves and drawing a blank piece of paper towards himself so he could take notes. "Start at the beginning, then, Maeve. And don't leave anything out."

"OK. Well, as you know, when we looked at the crime scene we weren't sure if Rebecca had been a victim of the Burning Man or not, because of the way her body was left. It was a by-the-numbers imitation of his manner of killing and disposal of the body, but it didn't ring true. There was something tentative about it. It wasn't him, but it was someone trying to be like him. And that person is Louise North."

Godley didn't so much as twitch a muscle, but I could sense doubt emanating from him and I went on quickly to explain what I had found out.

"I couldn't find any trace of Rebecca Haworth in the twenty-four hours before she died. No one saw her or spoke to her — not her neighbours, not her friends, not her family. She didn't show up on any of the CCTV we checked. She didn't use her oyster card on public transport. We got in touch with taxi firms all over the capital and no one recalled giving her a lift. In fact, the last trace of her that I could find was her mobile phone signal. It went off the air on the Thursday night by London Bridge, in the vicinity of her flat — so the phone was switched off or was destroyed then. But before that, it was in Fulham — within a hundred yards, give or take a few, of the mobile phone mast nearest Louise's house."

"She could have been visiting her friend."

I shook my head. "Louise said she hadn't seen her for months."

"OK, she could have been visiting someone else."

"Who? She didn't have any other friends in the local area, as far as I can tell. We can go door-to-door and see if anyone remembers seeing her in the neighbourhood on the Wednesday evening or the Thursday. But I think Louise lured her to her house on Wednesday night, with the intention of keeping her there until Thursday. I saw the lab reports; the body fluids that Dr Hanshaw sent for toxicology came back positive for sedatives. What if Louise kept her there, knowing that she probably wouldn't be missed since she didn't have a job or a flatmate or a boyfriend? What if she drugged her? And what if she killed her?"

"Evidence, Maeve. Cell-site analysis isn't going to be good enough in a built-up area. The signal bounces around from mast to mast; you can only narrow it down to a quarter-mile radius at best."

"Take it as an indication of where we should be looking, then. That's not all." I quickly outlined how I'd found Louise's car in the CCTV logs, and checked to see that she was driving it. "She had no reason to be there at that time of the morning. She didn't mention being there to me, even when she heard where Rebecca's body was found. I can't believe that she wouldn't have made some comment about the coincidence if it had been innocent. And since then, she's got rid of her car and bought a new one. A present to herself, I believe. Maybe a reward for a job well done."

"OK. That's better. I like that we can put her in the relevant location at the correct time. But if she's got rid of the car, we're not going to have any forensics."

"I imagine that was the idea. She left a few false trails for us here and there — she'd thought of leaving voicemail messages on Rebecca's phone to make it look as if she was trying to get in touch with her after she was already dead. She even left one on Rebecca's old work number. But Louise knew that Rebecca had left her job. She'd helped her to tidy out her desk.

429

Rebecca's assistant remembered the name when I rang her today and prompted her. Why would she call a number she knew wasn't going to be answered unless she wanted to make us think she was out of touch with Rebecca? And don't forget that she turned up in Rebecca's flat when we went to check it out. She was tidying the place to make sure there were no tell-tale clues that she'd invited her to dinner the day before she died — no notes Rebecca had left that might give us a clue to her motive. She said that Rebecca was untidy in her personal habits. Everyone else I've spoken to has said how meticulous she was, how organised. I thought it was a sign of the strain Rebecca had been under, but if you turn it around and look at it the other way, Louise lied to us."

"You mentioned motive — what could hers be?"

"I'm not sure. But maybe it's as simple as finally getting fed up always being in Rebecca's shadow. Though Louise was also there in Oxford when Adam Rowley died, and she didn't like me asking about it. She got really uptight. I thought she was scared of Gil Maddick overhearing us, but now I think that perhaps she was worried for herself because I was getting too close for comfort."

"Maddick." Godley pulled a face. "That's part of the problem for me. I don't see how you've gone from thinking she's a potential victim to being sure she's the killer."

"I was supposed to see her as a victim. And I was so busy thinking of her in that light, I forgot to consider her as a suspect. That was the plan. She's been pushing me towards Gil Maddick all along — he's the ex-boyfriend, he has a history of violence towards his girlfriends and his break-up with Rebecca seemed to act as the starting gun for her decline into catastrophic personal circumstances, including the loss of her job and the intensification of her drug use and eating disorder. Louise wasn't the only one of Rebecca's friends to tell me that Maddick was possessive. It seems as if he tried to keep her away from them — that's classic controlling behaviour. But it's not proof that he wanted her dead. I can't find any evidence of them being in touch before she died — no emails, no phone calls, no texts. I honestly think he'd moved on."

"But you were absolutely sure he was guilty, Maeve." Godley's voice was gentle. "That's hard to explain away now that you're equally sure about Louise."

"I thought he was an abuser who resented his ex starting a new life, but that just didn't fit in with the facts. He's in line to get her life insurance money, but he's wealthy anyway, and I don't think he had the least idea he was the named beneficiary. Then I thought he might have been looking to get revenge on Rebecca — he does bear a startling resemblance to the boy who died in Oxford, the one Rebecca felt so guilty about. But I think that's truly a coincidence. It's not really a surprise that she'd find the same things attractive in another man; she was obsessed with Adam Rowley."

"How does Rowley's death fit in?"

"I'm not sure about that either," I confessed. I had called DCI Garland before Godley arrived. He had been in a pub but if he'd been drinking, it hadn't dulled his edge in the slightest.

"I was wondering if I'd ever hear from you again. What did you make of it? Get any closer to working out who did it?"

"I don't think you'd ever be able to get enough evidence for a charge — not at this stage, anyway — but I do have some idea as to what happened to Adam Rowley, yes."

"Go on, my love. I'm listening."

I had told him my suspicions: that Rebecca and Louise had known more than they'd let on about Rowley's death. Either Rebecca had killed him herself and Louise had helped her to cover it up, or Louise had played some part in his death with Rebecca's support and connivance. Louise had been able to cope with the pressure of the subsequent investigation but Rebecca had cracked. That was why they had fallen out.

"Louise was in a good position to know that Adam was very drunk and vulnerable because she had been serving him all night in the bar. Either of them could have given him a nudge and sent him into the river."

From the other end of the line, there came a long, low chuckle.

"Well done, girly. That was where I ended up too, a long time ago, but I didn't have a hope of getting the CPS to take it any further. I was always wary of Louise North. Cold, she was. I couldn't fluster her, and believe me, I tried."

432

"Interesting that DCI Garland didn't like her," Godley commented when I recounted our conversation. "But he didn't find any evidence to link her with the boy's death, did he?"

"No, but he didn't get a chance to treat it as a murder enquiry once the coroner had ruled the death accidental. There was a possibility Adam had been drugged without his knowledge so that he was somewhat incapacitated. But he could have taken the pills voluntarily. There was an abrasion on the back of his head that might have been caused by a blow, but it was also consistent with drowning. He didn't seem to struggle when he fell into the water — he was a young, fit, healthy man and he made no attempt to climb back out onto the bank. He was drunk at the time, but I still think it's strange he didn't try to save himself. I think whatever happened that night it gives Louise a major motive to want Rebecca dead, though."

"Go on."

"Rebecca's life was teetering on the edge of disaster at the time she died — she had lost a job that she was desperate to keep, so desperate that she offered to sleep with her boss to convince him to change his mind, and if you'd seen him, you'd know that was not the easy way out. She was trying to hide the fact that she was unemployed from her family and friends, so kept on her very expensive flat and tried to maintain her lifestyle. She had a ruinously expensive drug addiction to manage and her romantic relationships were complicated to say the least. We know that she blackmailed one lover, getting ten grand for promising not to tell his wife what he'd been up to. I can't say he didn't deserve it, and worse, but I wonder if Louise got a fright when she heard what Rebecca had done. She couldn't take the risk that Rebecca would think of blackmailing her."

"There's no evidence that she did, is there?"

"No. If she did give her money, it was cash. And I seriously doubt she could afford to pay her off, unlike the other victim, because even though she's well paid, she's got a mortgage to pay on an expensive house. Besides, there's the threat to her reputation to consider. Louise has worked very hard to get to where she is now. I don't think she'd be too pleased about seeing it all disappear because her best friend is an unemployed cokehead."

"So you think they entered into a pact together to murder Adam Rowley, which we can't prove. And we don't know why. You think Louise was afraid of being blackmailed about it, which, again, we can't prove. You think Louise drugged Rebecca, hid her away for twenty-four hours, murdered her and dumped her, on the strength of some CCTV and mobile phone cell-site analysis, and we might be able to prove some of it, but she's had enough of a head start to get rid of most of the evidence."

"That's about the size of it."

The superintendent sat for a long moment, his eyes hooded, and I began to wonder if I had fouled up spectacularly, if I had missed something obvious and embarrassed myself beyond redemption. I knew I had little evidence to prove my theory, and what there was was circumstantial. Just as the silence was becoming unbearable, he looked up, his eyes very blue, and smiled.

"It's patchy. But there's something there. And I don't want to see her get away with it if you're right." He stood up and pulled on his jacket. "Are you fit to come with me? I want a council of war. We'll see if we can't find a way to out-think Ms North once and for all."

I said yes, of course; even if I felt wobbly and exhausted, I wasn't going to miss out. Godley drove back to the nick in what had to be record time, having phoned Judd and told him to round up a few of the key members of the team.

We were just coming into central London when my mobile phone rang. I looked at the screen and froze.

"Boss, it's Louise. Why would she be ringing my phone?"

Godley frowned. "Don't answer it. If she leaves a message, we can all listen to it."

It felt like hours until the ringing stopped. A few seconds later there was a beep: new voicemail message. I let out the breath I hadn't realised I was holding and put the playback on speakerphone.

"DC Kerrigan — Maeve? I just wanted to let you know that I've broken up with Gil. I saw on the news that you'd been injured . . . and I know you've been in hospital so I'm sure you don't care too much, but I wanted to tell you." She sounded more hesitant than usual. "I wanted to say . . . I just thought you should know, when I tidied up Rebecca's flat, I found a pen on the coffee table. It had Gil's initials on it — GKM. It made me wonder if he'd been there, before she died.

He said he hadn't, but . . ." There was a pause, and then a sigh. "I just don't know what to think any more." *Click.*

I looked at Godley, my eyebrows raised. "What do you think?"

He was concentrating on the road. "I think you're an excellent police officer and your instincts are sound."

"You're not convinced that we should go and arrest Gil Maddick?"

"Are you?"

"No." I was definite about it. "This just makes me more confident that she's guilty."

"Then let's work out how to catch her."

Before we could do that, Godley had to convince a room full of highly sceptical policemen that we would be able to construct a legitimate case against Louise North. It was easier said than done. As the superintendent explained what we were doing there, I looked around the table, all too aware of the fact that I was in jeans and a jumper rather than my usual suit, and that my face was still bruised from my encounter with Selvaggi. DI Judd was sitting beside Godley and looked tired, but not hostile, which was more than could be said for Peter Belcott. Rob was there too, sitting down at the end of the table, with an encouraging expression on his face. After my first glance in his direction I didn't dare look at him again in case I got distracted. Ben Dornton and Chris Pettifer were there because they were the team's expert interviewers; Sam, Kev Cox and Colin Vale made up the remainder of the group. And none of them seemed completely convinced as Godley finished explaining what we knew, what we thought and what we needed to find out before handing over to me.

"Is that it?" Peter Belcott's upper lip was drawn back in a sneer that revealed his abnormally long incisors.

"I can't see there's any other explanation for this footage. Louise North drives a very smart BMW sportscar, bought the week Rebecca died. She traded in her old car, a car she told me was a fourteen-year-old blue Peugeot that had seen better days."

I picked up a remote control and pointed it at the DVD player behind me. I had cued the disk to start in the right place.

"This is two hundred yards from where Rebecca Haworth's body was found. These images were recorded at two fifty-seven on the morning of Friday the twenty-sixth of November. This" — I pointed — "is a blue Peugeot with one occupant, a female, driving towards the waste ground where Rebecca's body was dumped. You can see the side of her face." I stopped the DVD and moved forward to the view from a different camera taken around a minute later, showing the back of the car as it braked at traffic lights. The driver was just a silhouette, unidentifiable. "Here it is again. You can get a partial on the registration number in this image though the car behind blocks some of it. I've checked Louise's old car registration and it matches the partial plate here." I skipped forward again. "This is twenty minutes later, footage from the second camera. The car is coming back from the direction of the body dump. This time, we can see the driver quite clearly." I

437

paused it, letting everyone look at the slightly blurred but completely identifiable image of Louise North. "If you were wondering, she lives in Fulham. She told me the first time I met her that she had been at home the night of Rebecca's murder. She certainly didn't mention a walk on the wild side south of the river in the middle of the night."

Colin Vale was shaking his head. "It didn't fit the profile. If I'd known . . ."

"You had no reason to look at this car and think anything of it," I said comfortingly. "I would have missed it if I hadn't seen it in your log. And I was looking for a different car at the time. It just so happened that Louise told me about changing her car and mentioned what make and model it was, and I happened to spot it."

"It was lucky," Godley said from the head of the table, causing everyone's heads to turn towards him like compass needles swinging to the north. "But it was also good police work. And as Maeve has pointed out, if it hadn't been noted in the first place, we'd have missed it."

"We could examine those images," Colin said. "See if the car is more heavily laden going in the direction of the body dump."

"Yeah. That's all we can do, I'm afraid, because according to Louise, the car was scrapped."

"Well, that's something else we could do," Kev Cox observed. "Trace the car. Find out where it went and where it is now. We might still be able to recover trace from it, even if it's been compressed."

438

"That's a long shot," Judd said. "And the defence would have a field day pointing out how the evidence might have been compromised."

"In the absence of a better idea, let's try it anyway," Godley ordered. "Colin, that sounds like a job for you."

The cadaverous detective nodded. He didn't look excited at the prospect, which was fair enough. It would be a tedious job to do, especially when the chances of recovering anything were so slim.

"What were you looking for when you noticed her car in the logs?" DI Judd was frowning.

"When Rebecca was a student, she had an inappropriate relationship with her tutor. It started up again a few months ago, but this time she blackmailed him."

"Academics don't have any money," Judd pointed out.

"This one does. Caspian Faraday."

"I've got his books. I've watched him on TV." Colin Vale sounded shocked. It wasn't often that I got to witness the fall of an idol and I felt a twinge of sympathy for him.

"He's married to an heiress, Delia Waynflete. I got the distinct impression that his priority in life is to maintain his relationship with his wife — I don't want to accuse him of seeing her as his meal ticket, but she definitely makes a big difference to his standard of living. I could imagine him deciding that he couldn't stand to live with the fear of his wife discovering his extra-marital affair. I could also imagine him staging Rebecca's murder. I couldn't quite see him killing her, but in the right circumstances, maybe he would have found some reserves of brutality within himself. His wife, however, would have the funds to hire someone to kill a rival even if she didn't do it with her own hands. And Faraday himself seems to have had some doubts about it; their lawyer lied to me when I asked if she'd been in the country at the time of Rebecca's death. DC Belcott did some digging and found agency pictures of her at a charity ball in London the night before Rebecca died, and at an art gallery the day after the body was found. I was looking for her car, or her husband's."

"You'd think for the sake of the money alone he'd keep his cock under control," Ben Dornton commented.

I pulled a face. "I didn't spend a lot of time analysing him, but I'd have to guess that he finds it a bit emasculating to be in such an unequal relationship. He's done well enough for himself, especially given that basically he's a disgraced academic, but she's astronomically wealthy. It must be hard to give up the kind of lifestyle he currently enjoys — that doesn't mean he likes himself for it."

"Let's get rid of Dr Chen and have Maeve do her bit instead."

I glared at Rob. "Thank you for the suggestion, DC Langton. It's just conjecture, as you know."

"This is all conjecture," Belcott complained. "Why did you decide the academic and his wife were out of the picture?"

"Rebecca was Faraday's walk on the wild side — he didn't want her dead. And I don't think that Delia would have bothered with having her rival killed. She'd just have reminded her husband who was in charge and made him live in a different city for a while." I pointed at the screen. "With hindsight, Louise's behaviour has been suspicious from the start, when we found her in Rebecca's flat. We never found Rebecca's address book, an appointments diary or the notebook she always carried. I have a feeling they walked out the door in Louise's Prada bag." I turned to Sam. "Do you remember her bursting into tears all of a sudden and needing to pay a trip to the bathroom to recover her composure? What do you want to bet that while we were talking in the living room, she was hunting through the rest of the flat to make sure she hadn't missed anything?"

"Wouldn't be surprised," Sam said. "We missed it."

"Comprehensively," I agreed. "But if we hadn't been there in the first place, we'd never have known she was in the flat at all." I managed not to look at Godley as I said it. He had already apologised to me for bollocking us; Sam's apology would presumably come after the meeting.

"Why take the risk of trying to make it look like a Burning Man murder?" Judd asked.

"I think she thought she could get away with it. She must be extremely arrogant to have taken the risk of going to Rebecca's flat and cleaning it up. Remember, if I'm right about all this, she got away with murder once before. And there is something flashy about this crime, something that I, for one, was convinced fitted in with the flamboyant confidence that Gil Maddick has in spades. From the first, Louise tried to point me in his direction. She had him lined up to take the fall if we weren't convinced Rebecca was one of the serial killer's victims. That was before she started a relationship with him, of course. I have to assume becoming involved with him wasn't part of her initial plan, because it seems foolhardy in the extreme. Rebecca was always the dominant one when they became friends — she was the pretty, popular girl, and Louise was more in her shadow. I get the impression that with Rebecca gone, Louise has a chance to shine, and she's taking it, no matter how unwise it may be."

"I'm still missing something," Judd said. "You've told us how. You haven't said why."

"Because I can't be sure about it until we talk to her, and that's assuming she'll cough to it, which I doubt she will. She is a lawyer, after all. And she's very proud of that fact. She has a lot to lose if her reputation is damaged. That's why, I think, Rebecca had to die."

"Because she threatened her reputation?" Colin Vale asked.

"Because Louise couldn't take the risk that she would. Her only insurance was if Rebecca had been sufficiently involved in killing Adam Rowley to make it impossible for her to blackmail her friend without dropping herself in it. But Rebecca was broke and desperate, and she'd exhibited some fairly appalling judgement all along. Louise couldn't trust her. If she got away with murder seven years ago, why not perform the same trick now when she had so much more to lose if she didn't?"

"Are we taking this to the CPS on the strength of a voicemail message and some CCTV?" Judd asked Godley.

"We've got enough to make an arrest. Whether we can charge her with murder depends on the interview. We need a confession." Godley looked down the table. "Ben and Chris, were you taking notes? It's going to be up to you now to get this case off the ground."

Dornton and Pettifer nodded, looking thoughtful. I wished them luck with facing down Louise when she was brought in; I wouldn't have wanted to try. I was gathering up my notes, so tired I could barely see straight. Godley's voice called me back to attention.

"Maeve, stick around. We'll get things organised for the arrest and go straight into the interview. I'm going to need you to watch it with me. There's that chance you might spot something we'd miss, like you did with the car."

"Oh. Really? I —"

"It'll be a couple of hours before we move on making the arrest. So get some food or something. Relax. Take things easy."

"I was going to —" I broke off. Godley wasn't listening to me. He had already moved on to talk in a low-pitched mutter with Judd about briefing the CPS. I stood there, swaying with fatigue, wanting more than anything to go home.

Out of the corner of my eye I noticed that Rob was standing up, stretching, then sauntering towards me. Rob, whom I had known for over a year without being remotely ruffled by his presence. Rob, who had sat beside me in countless cars and interviews and briefings, his shoulder against mine. Rob, who had surely never made my heart beat in such an infuriatingly erratic way just by standing near me and saying my name. I turned and smiled, hoping that he wouldn't notice the colour that had risen in my cheeks.

"Are you OK?"

"Just tired."

"You must be. All that talking."

"And thinking. Don't forget the thinking."

"Unaccustomed as you are to it. Want to go for a coffee? You've got time if it's going to be a few hours yet before she's interviewed."

I shook my head. I couldn't think of anything worse than coffee for my state of mind. I was already feeling jittery, nervous about Louise being arrested, worried that I'd missed something or invented something that wasn't there. I had that sort of fatigue that comes at the end of a long-haul flight, when the world seems to recede down a narrow tunnel. Even Rob was suddenly very far away.

"I'm OK." I looked around the room piteously, as if a bed would materialise in front of me if I wished for it. "What I'd really like is a rest."

"We can manage that." He dug in his pocket for car keys. "Let me take you home."

"To my parents' house? Too far to go. We wouldn't even have time to get there and back before the interview starts."

"So I'll take you somewhere else. Come on."

"Where to?"

He didn't answer, just smiled and walked out of the room. I followed, too worn out even to be curious. I didn't even particularly care if anyone saw us leaving the building together. No one would think anything of it. We went places all the time together. And Rob wasn't acting as if there was anything to hide anyway.

He interrupted my train of thought by stopping on the steps outside and looking at me assessingly. "We'd better get a cab. You look as if you couldn't walk to the corner without keeling over."

"You're not driving?"

"No parking," he said succinctly, and hailed a black cab, leaning in through the driver's window to give the address so I didn't hear where he was taking me. The traffic was, as usual, horrible, and it took a while to get to our destination, even though it proved not to be too far away. Rob looked out of the window, his face turned away from me, and instead of second-guessing him as I usually would, I leaned my head back against the seat and closed my eyes, drifting a little. Somewhere, Louise was going about her life, oblivious to the effort that was building up to take her into custody, more or less on my say-so. I felt a wave of nausea and fought it down. If I was right, she deserved it. If I was wrong . . . but I couldn't be wrong.

Where Rob took me turned out to be a tiny hotel tucked between shops in a Knightsbridge back street, a hotel that made up in luxury for what it lacked in size. He made me sit in a wing-backed armchair by the fire in the minuscule bar while he dealt with the receptionist, and the warmth revived me to the point where I was ready to tackle him when he came back.

"You can't do this. We can't just check into a hotel because I want a rest."

"Can. Have." He dangled a key in front of me. "Want to see if there's a minibar?"

"We're on duty," I said automatically.

"Spoilsport."

"This is ridiculous." I allowed my arm to be taken as I was helped out of my chair and escorted to the lift, past the reception desk where two immaculately made-up girls were standing, eyes cast down discreetly as we went by. "And what must they think?"

"They can think what they like," Rob said firmly, summoning the lift. "If you want to go back to the nick, tell me and I'll get you a cab. But I'm staying."

I grumbled all the way into room 4, where I abruptly stopped, because it was a jewel of a room with rose-coloured walls, a claw-footed bath in the black-and-white tiled bathroom, big windows veiled in layers of curtains that muffled the sounds of the traffic below and, dominating the room entirely, a vast bed with fat pillows and a satin coverlet.

"Wow. How did you know about this place?"

He laughed. "Do you really want to know?"

I had time to experience a spasm of pure jealousy in the split-second before he relented.

"It's not what you're thinking. I used to be on the Met hotel crimes squad. I arrested someone here. The assistant manager was part of a gang from Kosovo who had a nice little thing going, thieving from the guests.

446

He got four years, I seem to recall. And I got a discount card from the very grateful manager which I hadn't had a chance to use before today."

"Oh. So not a regular romantic hang-out, then."

"No. I haven't brought anyone else here. Just you." He turned and prodded the bed. "Decent mattress, I hope. Do you want to lie down?"

I did. But I did not want to lie there on my own. Before I could think of a way to convey my feelings without sounding too cheap, he had knelt down in front of me and started undoing the laces on my trainers, whistling under his breath in a particularly unromantic way.

"I feel like a horse at the blacksmith's," I said as he lifted my foot to slide my trainer off.

"Whoa there, Bessy." He pulled the other one off and stood up, very close to me, and again I experienced that wave of excitement and nerves that had so unsettled me earlier. I stared at his mouth, thinking about leaning forward and letting my lips brush his . . . I edged forward a little, close enough to feel the warmth from his skin.

He cleared his throat. "Maeve."

I snapped out of my reverie and looked up at him, aware from the blood beating in my cheeks that my face had gone the colour of the walls.

"I thought you might just want to rest. Don't think I haven't realised that you may be suffering from brain damage because of your head injury."

"I'm fine. I feel much better. Really, apart from being tired, I'm back to my old self," I gabbled and he laid a finger on my lips to stop me talking.

"Don't think I won't take full advantage of your weakened condition, then. If you want me to."

I took his hand and moved it away from my mouth. "How might you do that?"

"I thought I might start like this." He bent his head to kiss me, and it was wonderful and strange and completely right all at the same time.

"The only part of me that is weak," I observed presently, "is my knees."

"Really?" Rob sounded interested. "Let's have a look."

The easiest way to do that, it seemed, was to take off my jeans. And before long, we had moved beyond the initial awkwardness, the laughter, the playing around. It was serious, what we were doing. But more than that, it was right.

And it was better than I could have imagined.

"Again?" he asked some time later as we lay side by side, facing each other, no more than three inches apart. He was trailing his finger down the length of my spine and back up in an unhurried rhythm.

"Yes. No. Not yet." I struggled to open my eyes, lulled into a daze by the overwhelming feeling of well-being. "Rob."

"Maeve." He matched my tone, sounding and looking absurdly solemn. I poked him in the chest.

"Take me seriously. We need to talk."

"Now?" He rolled onto his back and threw his forearm over his eyes, shutting me out. "Really?"

"Really." I sat up, pulling the sheet up around me. "We shouldn't be doing this. It's just going to complicate a good working relationship. And if you tell anyone on the squad, I'm not going to be able to show my face in the incident room."

He moved his arm so he could glare at me with one eye. "Why do you think I would talk about this?"

"'Maeve's got great legs and a nice little arse too. She's gagging for it. I'd shag her until she couldn't walk in a straight line,'" I mimicked. "That was it, wasn't it? I haven't forgotten anything? I only heard bits of it, but I think I got the gist."

"That was completely different. That was just talk." He reached up and drew me down to him. "Let me see if I can do it, though."

"For God's sake," I protested, half-laughing, half-cross. "We have to work together. We can't possibly do whatever it is we're doing here without jeopardising everything. At the very least, one of us will probably have to leave the team, whether this goes anywhere or not. I mean, I'm jumping too far ahead here. It's not like I'm trying to see into the future. But we should be responsible about it."

Rob frowned, looking down so I couldn't see his eyes. "Why don't you stop thinking about what's going to happen and concentrate on the here and now?"

"Don't you even care about what I'm saying?" Did that mean he saw what we were doing as a one-off?

He thought for a second as his hands moved, sliding under the sheet I still held around me. "No. Now I appreciate your efforts to wrap yourself up as my Christmas present, but I've been a very good boy and I'd like to open it a few days early."

It was easier, somehow, to push the doubts to the back of my mind. Easier to allow myself to be folded into his arms again. Easier to run my hands over his skin, learning every inch of it, shutting out the real world as it rattled on, far below our windows.

Easier just to let go.

The room was dim when I opened my eyes, wondering what had woken me. A small lamp on the table by the window was the only source of light. I turned my head, disorientated for a moment, and looked into Rob's eyes. He was standing by the bed, hovering over me. From where I was lying, he seemed to be showered, fully clothed and ready to go.

"You're up already," I said, starting to sit up, feeling groggy and somehow at a disadvantage for being still in bed.

"Yeah. Sorry, pet, but you need to get moving too." He opened one hand to show me a mobile phone: my own. I reached across and snatched it from him, checking the screen. One voicemail.

"It's from Godley."

I looked up, ready to snap at him for listening to my messages. He held up his hands.

"I didn't touch it. I heard it ringing and his number came up on the screen." He shrugged. "I thought you wouldn't want me to answer it for you."

"You thought correctly." I shushed him then, listening to the superintendent's mellow voice murmuring from my phone, pulling me back to the real world.

The message was a short one, and when it finished, I looked at Rob, reluctant to be the one to speak. He knew already though.

It was time to get back.

LOUISE

I risked a covert glance at my watch under the table and almost groaned. It was ten past six and the client meeting had been going on for over three hours. Not that I was surprised. The sale of Pientotel's UK subsidiaries to Kionacom was the most important deal I'd been involved in, and as the senior associate, this should have been a big thrill. I looked around the table at the assembled bigwigs from Kionacom who were frowning as Preyhard Gunther's heads of tax, real estate, finance, pensions and employment reported on the due diligence we had done on Pientotel's assets, and wished I was somewhere else.

The conference room was on the top floor of the Preyhard Gunther offices; the wind cut around the building at the best of times, but it was blowing a gale now and I could hardly hear the senior partner who was chairing the meeting. From the shuffling of papers and fidgeting around me, I wasn't the only one who was keen to get on with my day. I had a frightening backlog of work in my office, things I should have done weeks ago. It wasn't like me to let things slide, but then it hadn't been like me to embark on a passionate,

452

wrong-headed relationship with a highly unsuitable and demanding man. My stomach turned over at the thought of Gil. The pressure had been getting to me. I'd made some questionable decisions but that was all over. I was back on track.

I shook myself mentally, forcing myself to sit up properly and concentrate as best I could, only to discover that, at long last, the meeting was drawing to a close. I started to draw up a list of tasks to tackle in order of priority, but found myself drifting again after number six (update the company searches on each of the subsidiaries to verify current directors and shareholders). Another scintillating night in the office lay ahead of me. I had wanted it — needed it, in fact, if I wasn't to get in serious trouble at work. Even though I didn't miss Gil — not at all — I was missing having a life already.

Pathetic.

I went back to the list, scribbling points as I recalled jobs undone, emails unwritten, documents to check. It was a petrifying prospect, far more than one evening's work.

The one good thing about being in the office all the time was that I was inaccessible. The presents had started the day after I broke up with him — expensive, lovely trinkets: a pearl and gold pendant in the shape of a flower; a rough-hewn chunk of amethyst that looked like a purple pansy frozen in ice; a tiny eighteenth-century portrait miniature of a girl with fair hair and a small red mouth; an ivory netsuke in the shape of a donkey, presumably because I was so stubborn. I had collected them in a box under my desk, tantalisingly close to the bin. If one of the cleaners happened to make a mistake and threw them out, I wouldn't shed too many tears. There were flowers, too, every day. I had told Martine not to show them to me any more. I wasn't interested. I didn't care.

My foot tapped under the table. *Come on, Louise. Concentrate.*

"I think that concludes our business for today. Unless anyone has any other business they'd like to discuss." The senior partner looked around the room expectantly.

On cue, there was a rattle from the door handle. Like everyone else in the room, I craned to see what was going on, and saw with some bemusement and not a little shock that Martine was at the door, her face tragic.

"So sorry to interrupt," she began, "I wanted to speak to Louise."

I was already on my feet and moving around the table, concerned but a little irritated that she hadn't been able to wait. The meeting was almost over. It was embarrassing to be called out of it. I couldn't think why. What had Gil done now?

And then I saw, behind her, the unmistakable tall figure of the policeman who had been in charge of the Burning Man murders, and of Rebecca's case. I recognised him from the news. I was still walking, still closing the distance between us, but it was as if time had slowed, as if the carpet I had to cross had suddenly stretched out for miles, as if my feet wouldn't move quickly enough. I had to get to the door before he spoke. I could take him to my office and close the door and no one need ever know what he had wanted with me; I could make something up. And maybe I didn't need to. Maybe he was just here to tell me what was happening with the investigation. Maybe there was nothing to worry about.

The last flickers of hope died when he came to meet me, shouldering past Martine as if she wasn't there.

"Louise North," he began, "I'm arresting you on suspicion of the murder of Rebecca Haworth. You do not have to say anything, but it may harm your defence if you fail to mention when questioned something which you later rely on in court." He went on with the caution, the familiar warning about my words being taken down as evidence, but I wasn't really listening. I had turned where I stood to see my colleagues, the firm's heads of group, the senior partner. I wanted to see their faces. They were frozen, mouths hanging open, an identical expression of shock from one end of the room to the other. It was almost funny.

I turned back to the silver-haired policeman who was waiting for me to move. He put out his hand to take my arm and I shook my head; I would walk out myself, no handcuffs, no manhandling. The end of my career was turning out to be pretty dramatic. The best I could do was to make it a dignified affair too.

CHAPTER
FOURTEEN

MAEVE

I hadn't imagined that Louise would fall apart in her interview. I hadn't been naive enough to imagine that she would confess, no matter how expertly the questions were directed. But on the other hand, I hadn't anticipated that she would take the option chosen by every obviously guilty career criminal I had come across, and answer "no comment" to each and every question.

"Did you murder Rebecca Haworth on the twenty-sixth of November this year?" Chris Pettifer asked in his usual level tone, the opposite of confrontational.

"No comment."

"Did you murder Adam Rowley on the thirtieth of April 2002?"

"No comment." She answered the same way each time, in a conversational voice, as if it was all a game.

"Did you try to stage the scene where Rebecca was found so that it looked as if she had been the victim of the Burning Man?"

Not a flicker of distress. "No comment."

I sat beside the superintendent, watching the television screen that relayed live footage from the interview room. Godley was completely still, hardly blinking, totally focused on the interview. Behind us, other detectives came and went, standing for a few minutes or hours to watch Louise North defeating the efforts of our best interviewers, specially trained to deal with people accused of the most serious crimes. And as they took turns to try to break down the reserve of the woman in front of them, they couldn't make her break a sweat.

"She's tough," Bill Pollock commented from behind me, "Not a hair out of place."

"She's always like that," I said without looking around. "This is what she does."

Godley took his eyes off the screen for a half-second to glance at me, having picked up on the bleak tone of my voice. "Don't doubt yourself, Maeve. You may have been taken in by her initially, but you found her out in the end. The evidence is there. The facts don't lie. And even if the rest is conjecture, it's convincing."

It was nice of him to sound so positive, but I knew the arrest had gone ahead with only lukewarm encouragement from the CPS. I didn't know the lawyer who had been assigned to the Haworth case once Rebecca's murder was positively, definitely and permanently removed from the list of Razmig Selvaggi's alleged crimes. Her name was Venetia Galloway and her first name was the only flourish about her well-scrubbed, mid-forties person; otherwise she was strictly no-nonsense and as far as I knew, utterly lacking in a sense of humour. I had seen her in the distance, standing in Godley's office with her arms tightly folded and her mouth puckered like the top of a drawstring bag as the case we were constructing began to fall apart for the lack of a confession.

And we weren't going to get one. Louise's manner was pleasant. Not even the most personal, borderline offensive questions seemed to ruffle her. Her solicitor sat beside her, massive in a pinstriped suit, a heavy gold signet ring on the little finger of his right hand, with the air of a man who hadn't had to sit in a police station for quite a long time. He was the head of a large practice of criminal solicitors, generally regarded as the best in the business and certainly one of the greatest beneficiaries of legal aid cash in the country. The fact that Louise had got Thaddeus Sexton himself to sit by her side showed that she knew what she was doing. His reputation was as formidable as the man himself. Not, it had to be said, that he was doing much to earn his pay at the moment. Looking like a walrus who had spent some time and much money on Savile Row, he sat back with his eyes half-closed and let his client deal with the questions.

"Were you jealous of Rebecca?" Dornton was taking a more forceful approach than his colleague had tried. It had much the same effect on Louise.

"No comment."

There was a definite sneer in his voice as he asked, "Isn't it true that you've been sleeping with her ex-boyfriend?"

"No comment."

"Everyone loved her, didn't they? Didn't anyone love you?"

"No comment."

Training meant that Dornton and Pettifer didn't show their frustration with Louise's intransigence, but outside the interview room they were able to give vent to their feelings, and did. The frequency of breaks must have been one indication to Louise and Sexton that we were running out of ideas, especially since the clock was ticking. We had to charge her or free her within twenty-four hours of making the arrest, and either option had its risks.

"We aren't going to get anywhere," I observed once the screen had gone blank for yet another interview suspension. I looked at Godley, who had a thoughtful expression on his face.

Before he could respond, the door opened. Chris Pettifer was the mildest of men usually, but his face was red as he came in. He pushed the door so hard that it banged against the wall and a few tiny flakes of plaster slipped down to frost the carpet. "The fucking cow."

"All right, Chris," Godley said. "Sit down and have a break."

"She's sat in there smiling at that tub of lard. Makes me sick."

Dornton trailed in after him, too worn out even to swear. "I've had it, boss. We've done everything now, haven't we? Tried the lot. She's not going to say anything."

"That's what Maeve thinks too." Godley stood up and stretched. "Right. Well, if we're wasting our time, we should stop. What time is it?"

"Twenty to four," I said after a glance at the big clock on the wall.

As if on cue, Judd poked his head into the room. "A little over two hours left, boss. What do you want to do?"

"Not sure yet. Is Venetia around?"

"Coming over in half an hour. She's just been on the phone." Judd grimaced. "Not happy."

"Good," Godley said absently, and I suspected he'd stopped listening once he'd heard she was on her way. "Right. Here's the plan. We'll ask Venetia what she wants us to do. Whatever she says, we're going to charge Louise North anyway."

"How are you going to get away with that? What if she says we have to let her go?"

"Leave her to me, Tom. I'll convince her."

The look on Judd's face spoke volumes — disbelief, awe and concern. "I don't even want to think about how you might be planning to do that."

"You don't have to think about it," the superintendent said. "You just have to wait until I've done it and make sure everything's in order for us to charge Miss North."

"Are you sure?" I was starting to panic again. "I mean, we really needed her to say she'd done it, didn't we? That was something we'd all agreed. You said it yourself. We need a confession."

"And *you* said just now we weren't going to get one. As it happens, I agree with you. But I also feel very strongly that the young woman in our interview room is guilty, and I dislike letting people like that go." He shrugged. "The trial is a long way off. Anything could happen. If we can charge her, we'll get her into the system and see if being on remand makes an impression on her. Holloway is a bit different from the comforts of Fulham."

I thought of the house I'd visited, the warm sunny kitchen, the cold living room. "We'll see. But I wouldn't be too sure that prison will make any difference to her. I think it'll push her further into herself, even more out of reach. And I don't know how we'll get her back."

"With luck," Godley said, and grinned. "With a bit of luck."

He whistled as he headed off towards his office, Judd two steps behind him as usual. I watched them go and my face must have shown how surprised I was. Pettifer, now restored to good humour, laughed.

"You didn't know that about Charlie, did you? Give him a risky proposition and he'll always take it. And what's more, it usually pays off."

"I hope so. I really do. But I wouldn't bet against Louise either. And don't forget, he's still got to convince Venetia."

How he got away with it, I will never know, but at twelve minutes past six on the eighteenth of December, Superintendent Godley formally charged Louise North with the murder of Rebecca Haworth. At his invitation, I was among the group of detectives watching from beside the custody sergeant's desk as the superintendent went through the charge against her.

"Louise North, I charge you with the following offences:

"That between the twenty-fourth day of November and the twenty-sixth day of November 2009 you unlawfully and injuriously imprisoned Rebecca Haworth and detained her against her will.

"That on the twenty-sixth of November 2009 you murdered Rebecca Haworth."

As Godley read I was looking at Louise, trying to see any hint of fear or anger. She was totally composed but her face was colourless as she listened. Sexton patted her arm with a fat paw and she moved an inch away from him without acknowledging it. *Touch me not.* She was small beside him, almost fragile, and I recalled with surprise that she was my age. She looked much younger, and totally harmless. Well, appearances could be deceptive. I waited for her to look at me, but she kept her eyes fixed on Godley's face while he spoke, and afterwards she looked down at the floor until she was taken to the cells, as if no one else was there.

I was at Horseferry Road Magistrates' Court early the following morning, nursing a polystyrene cup of watery tea and a headache as I waited for Louise's first appearance. Thaddeus Sexton would be determined to keep her out of prison in the lead-up to the trial; we were equally determined not to allow her out on bail, and this was the first opportunity for battle to be joined. I wondered how she was coping with being in custody. The holding cells at the court made the police station where she had spent the night look like the Savoy. It was noisy down there, and chaotic, and altogether not what Louise was used to.

Up above, things weren't much better. I dumped the tea and went into the correct courtroom to wait for Louise's appearance. It was overheated and crowded, and the CPS prosecutor had a massive stack of files in front of him that suggested it was a busy morning. I crossed my fingers that Louise would feature early in the proceedings; I did not want to have to sit through a procession of drunk and disorderlies or possession of class A or common assaults, the usual fodder for the magistrates.

I spotted Sexton near the front, looking about as cheerful as if he had just stepped in shit. The magistrates' court was so far beneath him I was surprised he had bothered to come himself. But then, Louise was going to be a high-profile client. It was worth his while to be there.

The district judge who was hearing the cases in that court was female, determinedly unmade-up and supremely efficient. She dispatched the first few cases on the list with barely a pause, and the list caller was kept busy, shuttling back and forth between the waiting area and the courtroom. At long last he came back into the room and said lugubriously, "Number seventeen on your list, Louise North, represented by Mr Sexton."

It was a feature of the courts that you could hear the heavy security doors between the cells and the dock opening and closing with a shriek of metal and a jangle of heavy keys. It ratcheted up the tension nicely as the sound of locks turning and doors slamming came closer and closer. I fidgeted in my seat, looking around to see if anyone else I knew was there. At the back of the court I saw a familiar face: Gil Maddick. He looked strained, as if he hadn't slept, and his eyes were glued to the door at the back of the dock. I looked in the

463

same direction just in time to see it open and Louise step through it, flanked by two custody officers. She wore a white shirt and a black skirt, and the expression on her face was entirely neutral.

Her role in the proceedings was limited to stating her name, date of birth and address, which she did in a low-pitched but clear voice; pleas would not be entered until the case reached the Old Bailey. The clerk stumbled a little over the charges and the judge bent her head, listening. As soon as he'd finished, she nodded. The normal routine was to refer the case up to the Old Bailey for a plea and case management hearing, known as the PCMH, and that was exactly what she did.

"We'll have the PCMH in six weeks."

Thaddeus Sexton surged to his feet in response. "We'd like to apply for bail, madam."

The judge turned to the CPS lawyer who gave a brief, not to say sketchy outline of the Crown's case, speaking rapidly and hoarsely so it was sometimes hard to hear him. "The Crown objects to bail being granted on the grounds that Miss North will fail to attend her trial because of the serious nature of the charges and the inevitable life sentence that would apply on conviction. She has no family, no community ties. She has considerable financial resources that are not restrained and would enable her to flee the jurisdiction, and as she has shown considerable ingenuity in attempting to avoid being brought to justice, there is every reason to believe that she would do the same to avoid the risk of conviction at trial."

"Madam, my client is of good character — she's a respectable solicitor without a criminal record," Sexton countered. "There are other options than custody. She could be under a curfew and monitored with a leg tag. She is prepared to report to her local police station daily; she would surrender her passport and reside only at her home address." He spoke persuasively, rocking a little on the balls of his feet, putting in a fine performance in conveying arguments that the judge considered for all of three seconds before turning them down crisply.

"Bail is refused because there are substantial grounds to believe that the defendant would fail to attend her trial if released. Take her down."

The custody officers moved to take Louise back to the cells, but she stood where she was for a moment, staring across the court to where Gil was sitting. Her face was unreadable. I twisted in my seat to look back at him and saw that he looked distraught. He scrambled to his feet as she was taken away, and hurried out of the court before I could try to attract his attention.

I sat on in the court, thinking, as prisoner after prisoner shuffled into the dock and faced their fate. Gil should have been angry with Louise — he must have realised by now that she had planned to frame him for murder, having heard the outline of the prosecution case. But if anything it looked as if it was the other way round. There was no love on Louise's side — that much was clear. But Gil had looked utterly and completely smitten. I sighed. People were strange. Love was stranger still.

And I hadn't heard from Rob since we'd gone our separate ways two days earlier.

The six weeks between Louise's appearance in the magistrates' court and the next hearing passed quickly. There was Christmas to think about, and New Year's Eve, and one unforgettably riotous night out for Godley's team, when the superintendent put his credit card behind the bar and the lads did their very best to drink to its limit. We were still working to build the cases against Razmig Selvaggi and Louise North, and new jobs were coming in all the time demanding our attention, but somehow the pressure was off. We weren't under scrutiny any more. We had done our bit.

Six weeks was long enough for things to have changed for me, too. I'd found a flat to rent, for one thing, moving into a house in Camden. On paper, it was a step down from Primrose Hill, but it was bliss to be in my own space once again, no matter how small and poky that space may be.

And there was Rob, of course. I still wasn't sure exactly what we were doing and neither, I think, was he. We were both wary of moving things on too far, too fast. Although he seemed to have feelings for me, I wasn't sure — wasn't sure about trusting him, or risking my place on the squad, or getting involved with someone else so soon after Ian. I didn't know what Rob thought about it. I spent a lot of time thinking about him, though. More than I would like to admit, even to myself.

So a lot happened.

But all the time, Louise was on my mind. I had been dreaming about her, waking up panicked and dry-mouthed. Somehow, the events of the night Selvaggi was arrested had got mixed up with my worries about Louise and the shock of finding out I had been wrong about her. In my dreams, I ran along dark paths, wet branches catching in my hair, my clothes, lashing my face. I saw her lying on the ground, helpless, her fair hair streaming on the ground above her head like a candle's flame. A dark figure bent over her, threatening, unidentifiable. Sometimes I couldn't reach her before I woke up. Sometimes I did, and found myself lying on the ground in her place. Once, the dark figure turned and plunged a flick knife into my stomach. Up close, I could see its eyes, silver grey, like Louise's. I felt I had to see her, to remind myself of what she really was.

Guilty, for starters.

As we had expected she would, she applied for bail again at the plea and case management hearing in the Old Bailey. It was the court where she would eventually be tried, and I couldn't help the shiver of excitement that raced through me as I passed through the security check and made my way to Court Number One.

I had never been in the Old Bailey on official business before and the history of the place seemed to echo down every corridor: the notorious, the innocent, the insane and the downright evil had walked there before me through the centuries. I slipped through the double doors into Court One, which was small, oak-panelled and currently home to a long-running trial, so papers and files were stacked up all over the barristers' benches, pushed to one side to make room for the briefs in Louise's case. I sat in the seats by the door rather than going to the other side of the courtroom to sit in the benches behind the barristers and solicitors with the other police. Where I sat was closest to the dock, which was high, but not screened off so I would be able to see her clearly.

Thaddeus Sexton was there, sweat beading on his forehead as he leaned over the back of the barristers' bench to mutter comments to Louise's QC and his junior. I had seen the QC outside the court, tall and red-faced with a scrape of grey hair across his domed head. He seemed totally confident, as if his success was guaranteed in advance, and I couldn't suppress a squirm of doubt that the bail application would be refused. I looked up, scanning the public gallery above. The first person I saw was Gerald Haworth, sitting at the end of the front row, in what would be Louise's line of sight. That, I imagined, had been his plan, and I hoped for his sake that he wasn't planning to make a scene when she was produced from the cells. He was as immaculately dressed as ever, today in a dark grey suit and a sober blue tie. He looked distinguished but unexceptional, and you would never have guessed his relationship to victim and accused, or even that he was emotionally engaged with the proceedings at all. That was, unless you observed the slight tightening of the

468

skin around his eyes and the bunched muscle in his jaw as the court usher bustled around the room, joking with the barristers who were already in their bench. His poise seemed tissue-paper thin, as if it would only take the slightest touch to shred it. I knew, of course — better than most — that what was life and death for one person was bread and butter for another. That was my job, after all — I made a living off other people's tragedies too. And you couldn't expect the court staff to be reverent all the time, no matter how serious the upcoming charge was. The banter was kindly and not offensive, but I felt for Gerald Haworth anyway. It must have been lacerating for him.

The door behind me kept swinging open and I couldn't help but look around each time to see a court reporter or a black-gowned barrister clapping a horsehair wig onto his or her head with a practised sweep. There were other journalists too, shuffling into the well of the court with nods to their colleagues. A hearing such as this wasn't generally considered to be interesting, but Louise North was good copy, Rebecca an attractive victim. It would fill space in the newspapers the next day

The door at the back of the public gallery banged and I looked up automatically, then did the classic double-take as Gil Maddick walked down the steps to the front row. If it was hard to see the strain in Gerald Haworth's face, I had no trouble spotting it when I looked at the younger man. He had lost pounds in the six weeks since I'd last seen him, and his eyes looked sunken in his head. He edged along the row,

469

apologising as he went, until he got to the empty seat beside Gerald Haworth, who lifted his coat on to his lap with a nod of acknowledgement. After a moment, the two men fell into conversation, and I remembered with a slight shock that of course Gil knew the Haworths well, that he had been a guest in their house on many occasions.

The wholly ordinary door at the back of the dock now opened, and I felt a flutter of nerves under my ribcage. The two men in the gallery leaned forward as Louise was led out. Her hair was tied back in a ponytail, but not tightly; loose waves of it were softly swept back from her face, making her look sober, serious and somehow younger. She had lost weight too, refining her appearance to something quite ethereal with eyes that looked huge in her narrow face. She wore a slate-grey wool dress that hung down in folds around her like a nun's habit, and the only adornments she had allowed herself were tiny stud earrings and something on a silver chain that hung down under the high neckline of the dress. The chain glinted over her sharp collarbones, catching the light. Her skin was luminous, but with soft pallor rather than the glow of good health, and I found myself thinking of Mary Queen of Scots, whose complexion was said to be so translucent that onlookers could see red wine passing down her throat as she swallowed it. The expression on Louise's face was grave but dignified. She stood for a moment and looked around the courtroom, meeting curious stares without any loss of composure, until she saw the two men in the public gallery. Haworth had half-risen to his

470

feet and Gil put out a hand to restrain him. Louise stared at them, looking stricken, and one tear rolled down her thin cheek unheeded. It ran down onto the neck of her dress, where it made a charcoal stain on the fabric. I suppressed the urge to applaud. As a piece of theatre, it was sublime. It was her bad luck that the judge, still in his chambers, had missed it, worse luck that there was no jury to impress, and most unfortunate of all was the split-second change in her face when her eyes cut away from them and fell on me. Cold loathing was the kindest interpretation I could put on it, and I sat back in my seat, satisfied that I had done my job well.

There was a sudden, sharp rap on the judge's door, and a simultaneous, "Court rise," from the clerk of the court, thin and stooped in his black robe and wig. His Honour Judge Horace Fentiman bustled onto the bench, small, stout and peering through thick glasses. He blinked myopically around the room, looking as if he was surprised to see anyone in front of him as the clerk asked Louise to stand and confirm her name. But when he spoke, the impression of bumbling vagueness was immediately dispelled.

"Yes, Mr Barlow," he said to prosecuting counsel while opening a large red notebook and unscrewing the cap from a fountain pen. His voice was deep and well modulated, and his approach was direct. He obviously wanted to get the hearing out of the way and he wasted no time once the prosecutor had introduced his opponent.

"Are we ready for arraignment?"

Louise's QC half rose from his seat and answered, "Yes, my lord." He had lost a lot of his loud assurance now that he was actually in court, I was pleased to see.

It took a minute or two for the clerk to read the indictment and ask Louise how she pleaded; her "not guilty" was clear each time.

"When can the trial be fixed? What's the time estimate?" the judge asked testily.

"Three weeks," said the prosecutor, after a whispered conversation with his opponent.

"Really, Mr Barlow? I have read the papers and I must confess I can't think what you're going to ask most of these witnesses. What is the defence case here?"

Louise's QC looked slightly sick for a second before recovering his poise. "A complete denial of involvement, my lord."

"I gathered that from the fact that your client pleaded not guilty. What, I asked, is the defence?" To give him credit, Hughes succeeded in speaking vaguely for several minutes about circumstantial evidence and the uncertainties of cell-site analysis without coming near to answering the judge's question. I was quite impressed. And even if the judge wasn't, he didn't press the point.

Once the administration was out of the way, the judge asked, "Any other matters?"

"I understand that the defendant wishes to apply for bail," replied the prosecutor, managing to sound surprised, as if it was a completely bizarre idea.

The judge looked penetratingly at Louise's QC before turning back to the prosecutor. "Well, Mr

Barlow, I suppose you should outline the facts and the Crown's objections. You do object, I assume."

Barlow laughed a little bit more heartily than the joke might have deserved before putting forward the prosecution's objections.

"The serious nature of the elements of this murder — premeditation, sophisticated planning, imprisonment of the victim — are likely to result in a substantial minimum term of any life sentence imposed after conviction."

And rightly so, I found myself thinking. It was wicked, what she had done.

Louise's QC tried to argue, but the judge was having none of it. She was going nowhere, I was pleased to see. Relieved, too. I quite hoped the judge would be the one who heard the trial.

I slipped out of the courtroom before the proceedings had quite come to an end. I ran around the side of the building and up to the door that led out of the public gallery, where I waited for Gerald Haworth and Gil Maddick. Rebecca's father looked shattered as he walked towards me, his hair slightly dishevelled as if he had run his hands through it without thinking. I held out my hand.

"Mr Haworth, I don't know if you remember meeting me last year at the memorial service for Rebecca, but . . ."

I trailed off, startled by the look on his face. He ignored my hand and I closed it into a fist as I let it drop to my side.

"I do remember, yes. You spoke to my wife and me about our daughter. We trusted you, DC Kerrigan."

"And I appreciated that trust." I flicked a look at Gil Maddick, who was still standing shoulder to shoulder with Rebecca's father. "Am I to understand that you don't think the correct person was arrested?"

"Of course not." Haworth shook his head. "The whole thing is ridiculous. And keeping her in that prison for no reason — I don't understand it."

"Murder is a very serious charge." I used the word deliberately and saw the two syllables hit home like blows. "And the trial date isn't far off."

"It's too far. You saw her. She's finding it terribly difficult."

"Have you been to visit her?" I couldn't believe that he would have braved Holloway to see the woman who killed his only child, but he nodded.

"Just once. I wanted to tell her that Avril and I know she didn't do it." He was shaking a little, tremors quivering through his hands. "We told you she was like a second daughter to us. How could you be so cruel as to take her away too?"

"Mr Haworth, I wanted to believe Louise wasn't Rebecca's killer, believe me. Unfortunately, the evidence doesn't lie." *But she does, fluently and constantly*, I managed not to say.

"That's to be decided by the jury," he snapped. "And if I have anything to do with it, they'll see she couldn't have killed Rebecca. She loved her. What you've suggested is hurtful and vindictive and I can't understand why you are doing this, unless it's to further

474

your career. It certainly hasn't helped Avril or me, and that was what you promised to do, wasn't it?"

"I promised to find out the truth," I said without heat. "And I think that's what I've done."

He shook his head and walked away, muttering to himself.

I looked hard at Gil Maddick. "What about you? Have you seen her? Have you told her you believe her story?"

He looked pained. "No. No, I haven't. I wanted to, but — I didn't know what to think, to be honest with you. If you're right, then she tried to frame me."

"That's right." I was intrigued. "But you still want to see her?"

"I love her. At least, I thought I did. But then, I've heard about the evidence you've got, and I can't explain it. I'm not saying I agree with your version of events, but I want her to tell me what really happened. If she'll agree to see me. You know she broke up with me."

"Do you mind me asking why?"

"That's something else I'd like to know myself." He looked grim. "I still don't understand it. One minute she was behaving as if she felt about me the way I feel about her. The next, she was throwing me out."

"You do seem to have difficulties with women, Mr Maddick." I was thinking of Chloe Sandler and her restraining order, and from the way he flinched, he knew exactly what I meant.

"Yeah, well, they don't usually break up with me." He sounded like a sulky teenager. "I still haven't got to the bottom of that one."

"Maybe you had a lucky escape."

"I don't think I was in any danger." He frowned at me. "Do you think I should go and see her?"

"I couldn't advise you either way. But if you did . . . you know she gave no-comment interviews to the police. She hasn't given any explanation for what she did. I'd like to believe she's innocent, but she doesn't trust us enough to talk to us."

"Do you blame her?"

"Not really." I met his gaze squarely. "But if she did talk to you, could you see your way to telling me what she says?"

"Absolutely not." He sounded completely determined, but I persevered.

"If she gives you the idea that she's guilty, presumably you won't want her to be released. And if you're convinced she's innocent, I promise you, between now and the trial I will devote myself to investigating whether someone else murdered Rebecca."

"I have to think."

He walked away a couple of paces with his head bent and his arms folded, and I watched him wrestling with himself, afraid to interrupt. After a minute or two, he turned back to me. "I can see why you would want me to do it. And I can see why I would want to do it. But I don't know that I could like myself very much if I did. It feels like a betrayal."

"You could think of it that way. But the only thing I want — the only thing you should want — is the truth. And if she's innocent, then she has nothing to fear."

"What if she won't see me?"

"She'll see you," I said with confidence I didn't really feel. "Why would she say no?"

"Why would she break up with me?"

I could think of a million reasons but as he obviously regarded it as a mystery on a par with the fate of Atlantis, I settled for a sympathetic shrug.

"Will she have to know about it? Afterwards, I mean?"

"Probably not. But look at it this way, if it gets her off the hook, she'll be nothing but grateful to you. And if it incriminates her . . ."

"I won't care anyway," he finished. The long seconds dragged out as he stared at me, considering. I held my breath. Finally, he sighed.

"I'll do it."

"Fantastic."

"It's the right thing to do, isn't it?"

"Absolutely."

His face was bleak. "So why do I feel like Judas?"

Judging correctly that it was a rhetorical question, I looked sympathetically at him until he got tired of that and went off in the same direction as Gerald Haworth. I sighed, watching him walk away. If we were relying on Gil Maddick to provide the *coup de grâce,* we were in trouble.

After court, I went back to the nick to report on what had happened. Superintendent Godley spotted me the moment I walked in and came to the door of his office.

"Maeve, you're going to want to hear this."

There was a small gathering in the room, I discovered — DI Judd, Colin Vale, Peter Belcott. All of them looked cheerful, remarkably so, and it was distinctly out of character for Judd and Vale to be so jolly. I turned to the superintendent.

"What's going on?"

"Colin found the car." Four words that changed the whole case.

"How did you manage that?"

"I got in touch with all of the scrapyards in the Home Counties and found the one Louise North used. It's a smallish one in Kent, near Ashford."

"But weeks ago she said she had got rid of it."

"Ordinarily, the car would have been scrapped within a couple of days, but it was in such good condition he let his son have it."

Belcott took over. "I went down to retrieve it and apparently it hadn't even been driven. The lad is only sixteen — just about to start lessons on his birthday, which is in a few weeks. The Peugeot was just sitting there in the yard, parked beside the office. We've had Kev Cox look it over and he found blood."

"Where?"

"In the boot. He sprayed the area with Luminol and it lit up under UV light. There was quite a significant amount of it even though you couldn't see it with the naked eye. It had soaked into the material lining the boot. Looks as if Louise tried to tidy up but didn't go to too much trouble. I suppose she thought it would be gone before we caught up with it, if we ever did."

"Nice one, Colin." I couldn't bring myself to congratulate Belcott. He hadn't really done anything — he'd just been the one who went to get it. I couldn't believe he was getting a share of the glory, but that was him all over. The right place at the right time, as usual.

"There were a couple of hairs, too. And Kev said we might be able to match fibres from the carpet in the boot to ones that were found on Rebecca's dress. The colour looked right."

I turned to Judd and Godley. "There's no innocent explanation for that, is there? And no break in the chain of evidence — Rebecca was dead days before the car changed hands."

"No. We've got her." Godley's face had lit up with triumph.

"Have you told Venetia yet?" I couldn't resist it.

"Just about to." He lifted the phone. "That'll teach her to trust me."

Judd was shaking his head. "You had no way of knowing we'd find the car. It was a total fluke."

"It was good luck and good policing. And if you have enough of one, you don't need the other." He nodded to the rest of us. "Nice work, all of you. We'll wait for the forensics to be confirmed before we spread the word too widely, but I don't mind if the squad hears about it first. It's definitely worth a drink or two."

I went back to my desk and sat there, staring into space in a haze of self-satisfaction tempered with anxiety. I couldn't see how Louise would get out of this one. Even the most thick-headed juror couldn't fail to see the point of the evidence. But I just couldn't believe it was going to be that easy.

And then the door banged as Rob walked in. He saw me, raised his eyebrows and smiled, and I forgot all about Louise North all over again.

LOUISE

Against my better judgement, I agreed to see Gil. Blame it on the tedium of prison, the desire for anything to break the mind-numbing routine. Blame it on a need to see someone from the outside world who wasn't a lawyer. Blame it on simple curiosity about what he could want. When they told me he had come I left my cell and walked without haste through narrow halls to the room where he was waiting, slipping through the door silently thanks to the trainers on my feet. He was sitting still, lost in thought, incongruously handsome against the backdrop of breezeblock walls clotted with bland pink paint. My first sight of him was in profile and in spite of everything I couldn't help but respond to him as I always responded to beauty — that shiver of simple pleasure at the happenstance of natural perfection. He turned his head and saw me then and moved abruptly, awkwardly, half-rising to his feet.

"Don't get up." I stayed by the door, ignoring the chair that was placed on the other side of the table from Gil.

"Lou. My God."

He was staring at me, seeing the changes in my appearance that I didn't like to think about. The pallor. The weight loss. The shadows under my eyes from not sleeping. He had all the same signs of strain, and more — a muscle twitched in his cheek and I thought he was fighting to keep his composure.

"It's been a long time."

"Almost two months." He leaned forward across the table. "I wasn't sure if you'd see me."

"And yet here we are." There was little warmth in my manner.

"I didn't know if I could bear to see you." He said it like it was a challenge, and watched me for a reaction.

"I see. You think I did it," I said pleasantly.

He looked wretched. "I honestly don't know what to think. Why don't you tell me what really happened?"

I felt a laugh bubbling up. "Tell you? Why would I?"

"I think you owe it to me."

I did laugh at that, the sound harsh and jarring even to me.

He put out his hand. "Come on, Louise. This is hard for me. I hate seeing you here, like this. I hated seeing you in court. It's all wrong."

"So why did you come?"

"Because I needed to see you. I needed to know that it was real. It just feels like a horrible nightmare."

"Poor Gil. How you must have suffered." Ice frosted every word.

"Of course it's harder for you," he said quickly. "Shit, I just can't get this right, can I? I'm trying to explain, it wasn't that I was convinced you were guilty; I just

482

didn't know what to think. I've been trying to decide if you could have done it, for God's sake, and if you did, if you were trying to frame me for Rebecca's murder — that's a hell of a tough one."

"And what do you think?"

"I don't know." He stared at me, puzzled. "What is the truth, Louise? What's your story?"

"The truth is . . ." My voice trailed away. "The truth is that I don't have anything to say to you about it, or anything else. Just leave me alone. Forget about me if you know what's good for you." I turned to the door and rapped on it a couple of times.

"Don't go yet," Gil pleaded, stepping forward. "I haven't even touched you, and I miss you so, so much — I still wake up in the middle of the night and reach out for you. I don't understand what happened between us. I feel as if you were playing a game with me and I just can't work out what it was."

"I'm sorry." I had wanted to see him humbled; I had wanted to make him beg. I had got what I wanted, in a way. Oddly, it gave me no pleasure. Given the circumstances, though, maybe it wasn't so odd.

The door opened and I moved towards it, then stopped. "One day, I'll tell you about Rebecca and me and how things really were. One day, I'll tell you what really happened. But not now."

He called my name as I walked out, but I didn't stop. I didn't even look back.

CHAPTER
FIFTEEN

Dear Gil,

By the time you read this, I will be dead. That's how a suicide letter is supposed to start, isn't it? A clear statement of intent. And I am perfectly clear on what I want. I want to be gone.

I should start by telling you the truth, as you wanted me to when you saw me a few weeks ago: I did it. I murdered Rebecca. You were right, I'm afraid; I had every intention of framing you for it, if my attempt at copying the Burning Man didn't come off. I wonder if Rebecca would have been amused to see you convicted for it. I can't think it would have been completely unfair. You are morally responsible for her death, believe me, even if you don't know it. But that was my plan — I thought it was what you deserved. The more I got to know you, the more I realised you needed a far harsher lesson, one about betrayal. I went to great lengths to be perfect for you, to make you fall in love with me, and I think it worked, as far as you're capable of loving anyone but yourself. It's almost worth getting caught to show you how stupid you've been, how wrong about me. You've always underestimated me, you know.

I'm sure you're wondering what's prompted this. I've just had a meeting with my solicitor, to discuss the prosecution case summary he's received. He didn't say it outright, but I could interpret it easily enough. I don't have a hope of being acquitted. The car is the problem. I thought it would be OK. I thought it would be dismantled, untraceable, gone. But you can't rely on anyone to do their job, can you? I should have dealt with it myself — dumped it in a canal or burned it out, but I was too clever for that, too subtle. Too bloody stupid.

Thaddeus thinks I should plead guilty. There would be a certain poetry to that, since I am, but I don't want to. Pleading guilty would mean a life in prison, or most of it. I could be looking at thirty years. All the good years. Missing out everything that makes a life meaningful — travel, work, new experiences, maybe even children. No stability. No normality. No domesticity. No thank you. I'd rather make my own choices and opt out. I don't want to be part of the legal system any more. I've had enough of it, and everything else.

But before I go, I want to tell you what happened, and why. I don't want your forgiveness. I don't want you to grieve for me — don't you dare pretend to be broken-hearted when we both know you don't have the equipment. I want you to understand because I want to know you have had your eyes opened to what you really are. You have money, and charm when you want to use it, and a pretty face, but all that is just window-dressing. It made me laugh every day that we were together to see you try to manipulate me. DC Kerrigan thought I was at risk from you, but it was the other way around. You thought you were the dangerous one, but you don't know what dangerous is. You're just a misogynist with a predilection for forcing women to have sex. You raped me, and I'm pretty sure you raped Rebecca — that story about the fractured cheekbone that was just an accident didn't ring true for me either, I'm afraid. That doesn't make you special, Gil. It doesn't make you clever. And it doesn't make you worthy of me, or of Rebecca, or any of the other women you've tried to control over the years.

I have no idea when you're going to read this letter, or if they'll even allow you to. I'm going to leave a note for DC Kerrigan too, when I'm ready to go, asking her to make sure you get it. I have a feeling she'll do that for me. Or for you, if it comes to that. She probably feels bad about suspecting you. I wouldn't blame her for it. I was very plausible. I am good at lying, as you might have noticed.

I'm trying to write clearly. "Nothing extenuate, nor set down aught in malice." Isn't that it? I don't remember a lot of *Othello*, but that bit always stayed with me. In the end, there's nothing left but the truth. There's no point in trying to hide any more. Just a few more days and I'll be able to take the antidepressants I've been hoarding. I can't wait until after the trial; they'll be watching me then. Now is the time to do it. I've devoted a lot of time to making the guards trust me. They never search my cell. Amazing what saying "please" and "thank you" can achieve. Being on

486

remand is stressful and I didn't have any trouble convincing the prison doctor that I needed to be prescribed antidepressants. The hard part was not taking them — now that really did require an effort of will. But I have a lot of self-control, especially when there's something I want. Just as, briefly, I wanted you.

I didn't want to kill Rebecca, though — I need to make that clear from the start. It wasn't a thrill for me. It wasn't fun. I had to do it, to save myself. Rebecca was weak. Too weak to know what she knew about me. Too weak to be trusted. Too weak to be a friend to me like I was to her.

If you're going to understand, I have to start at the beginning, and that's not easy. I don't talk about my childhood; I never have. Since I left the town where I grew up, I haven't been back, and I won't tell you where it was. It's not relevant to who I became.

I lived with my mother and grandmother. No father — don't ask me where he went, but he was never around. I didn't miss him. Mum was a wreck, barely functional most of the time, a manic depressive who was either flying high or flat out and I never knew what I'd find when I got out of bed in the morning. I have no idea how I survived until my grandmother came to live with us when I was four. She brought a bit of order. She made sure there was food in the cupboard and sheets on the bed, and that my clothes were clean even if they weren't new or nice or what I would have wanted. But I was clean, dressed and fed, and I actually didn't mind that I had to share a room with Nana.

Not then, anyway. I'd wake up in the middle of the night and hear her breathing and know that someone was there. It was only when I was older that I grew to hate the sound of her huffing and groaning in her sleep. I could never get away from her, never have any space of my own. She was always there, watching me, commenting on what I was reading or wearing or saying. She had a mean mouth, Nana, and you never knew what she was going to find objectionable, but when she did, there was no mistaking it. I spent a lot of time trying not to attract her attention. That meant I spent a lot of time in the local library, or at school. There was nowhere else to go. It made me into a reader, a hard worker. It made me achieve more than I might have otherwise, so thanks, Nana, I suppose.

The other thing about Nana was that she was a total hypochondriac, never out of the doctor's. She must have been up there twice a week for something or other. She had prescriptions for every painkiller known to man, as well as something for her nerves and other tablets to help her sleep and a few to help her wake up . . . Eventually, she got a new GP who diagnosed her with polymyalgia rheumatica and she was delighted, telling everyone about her polly-molly-what's-it and how the old doctor hadn't known what it was. I looked it up once, on the Internet. Do you know what it is? Unspecific aches and pains. *My back. My knees. Ooh, doctor, it's in my hip. My neck. I can barely stand today.*

Never mind. Have some painkillers.

Oh, well, if you insist.

I never thought of making use of Nana, not until Steve Wilmot from two floors down tried to mug her on the stairs. Steve was as thick as a brick and about as dynamic, and he hadn't reckoned on Nana being more determined to hang on to her handbag than he was keen to steal it. He'd put a scarf around his face but she knew who he was. It wasn't difficult. He wore the same Russell Athletic sweatshirt every day. It never occurred to him to change it before he jumped on her. She told him she'd tell his mother on him and he ran a mile. He was a bit older than me but I knew him to nod to, and the next time I saw him playing football outside the flats I asked what he'd been trying to do. He knew as well as I did that Nana didn't carry much cash.

"Drugs. She's got plenty, hasn't she?"

"You don't take them, though." It was true. He fancied himself as an athlete and kept the illegal substances to a bit of hash now and then.

"I was going to sell them on. Make good money if you can get the right stuff to the right people."

"Like what?"

Steve, who had never been known to remember anything other than football stats and his usual order at the Chinese takeaway, became suddenly fluent. "Uppers. Downers. Jellies — you know, Valium, that kind of thing. Anything with codeine. Tramadol. If they've given her proper morphine, that, obviously."

I thought of the locker beside Nana's bed, the army of small bottles with a handful of pills in each, the cardboard packets with foil-backed blister strips poking out. She had tried everything that was available and never threw anything out. I had seen it just as more old-lady clutter but now it looked more like an untapped resource.

I started taking a few pills here and there — not enough for her or the doctor to notice, but enough to put by a bit of cash. I'd pick up prescriptions for her too and lift a bit here, a bit there. I got very helpful all of a sudden, running to get her pills for her if she was watching TV. She got used to it. She liked having me fetching and carrying for her. And I liked doing it, for obvious reasons. Steve took a percentage off the top but I didn't mind; it made it less likely that I'd get caught. I had an old envelope full of cash that I kept in my room. It was the most precious thing I owned. I'd get up in the middle of the night and move it to a new hiding place, holding my breath in case I disturbed Nana. I'd find myself thinking about it in school, and used to hurry home to check no one had found it. I never spent any of it. Not a pound. And even though it was only small amounts now and then, it added up.

Say what you like about drug dealing, but that's how I was able to afford to go to Oxford for my interview. I would never, never have thought that someone like me would be able to go to somewhere like that, but I had a teacher, Mr Palmer, who took me to one side after maths one day and huffed sour coffee breath in my face while he told me about Oxbridge and how I should apply and not let anything hold me back. He went to Cambridge, himself. Told me all about it. The Backs. The Cam. The fens. That made up my mind for me; I didn't want to go there. Mr Palmer had not gone far enough, in my view. And you can't apply to both in the same year; you have to choose. Oxford it was.

And Oxford chose me, too. I was pushing an open door, did I but know it. They were bending over backwards to improve the ratio of applicants from a state-school background. I could have doodled all over the exam papers and I'd still have been invited for interview. I was terrified when the letter came in November. Interviews at the start of December. Accommodation arranged in Latimer College, though I would have interviews in two other colleges as well. Advice on how to get to Oxford, what to bring, how long I would need to stay, when I would hear if I was successful. Mr Palmer offered to lend me some money himself so I could go, realising, I think, that there was no point in me even asking Mum or Nana for help. I told him no, I would manage, thinking of the rolled-up envelope that was currently living in one half of an old pair of trainers under my bed, right back against the wall. It was soft with handling, the paper creased into a million tiny wrinkles, the ripped edges fluffy like velvet, and it had almost nine hundred pounds in it.

I didn't even tell them where I was going, and Mum didn't ask. Nana was more interested, but I managed to fob her off with a geography field trip. She didn't seem to know I wasn't even doing geography for A-level. Small rebellions — tiny lies — made life bearable. Homeopathic deceit. What they didn't know wouldn't hurt them. I spent some of the money on an interview outfit, a plain black dress with thick tights and flat slip-on shoes, and packed the rest of the money away in my backpack. There was no way I was going to leave it behind. I caught a coach to London, then changed for Oxford, getting there just as the sun was setting. It was one of those winter sunsets where the sky is completely clear, the sun dark red, and the light coming through the leafless trees by the river made my heart jump when I saw it. I had never seen anything as fine as the time-worn carving on the faces of college buildings, the arc of the High Street that had the perfect curve of a strung bow, the river running grey-green under Magdalen Bridge. Nothing was mean, or meagre, or glaringly new. I wandered around for a while until the light had faded and the gold stone turned to grey, then found my way to Latimer College and stepped in through the wicket gate that was cut into the huge, heavy oak doors. The stone beneath my foot was worn to a shiny hollow by generations of students that had passed that way, and I promised myself that I would be one of them, not just a candidate bleating nervously at the porters' lodge that I was here for interview, and receiving in return a key with a round metal fob that made my sweating hands smell like coins.

My room was in Garden Building, overlooking the river, with a high window and empty bookshelves over the bed. I sat on the edge of the bed and looked out at the bare trees that clustered around Angel and Greyhound Meadow, and Magdalen Tower standing sentinel over it all, bleached pale by floodlighting. There was noise in the corridor, other candidates talking loudly, confidently, making plans to go out and try their luck at getting served in the nearest pub. I stayed where

I was, too shy to speak to anyone. Besides, I didn't want to. I wanted to take in every detail of where I was, of the smells and sounds and feel of the place, in case I never got to experience anything like that again. I didn't even dare imagine it was my room, and how I would live in it. The undergraduate who used it in term-time had cleared out all evidence of her presence except for the tiny luminous stars that I discovered dotted all over the ceiling when I turned out the light.

My first interview was at ten the following morning and if it had been up to me I would probably have avoided breakfast, but the girl next door banged on my door at eight and asked if I wanted to go with her to hall. She needed moral support, she claimed, and chattered all the way there as if she had been there many times before, as if she belonged. She was a candidate for history, with a wide face scattered with freckles, and I can't now remember her name. She didn't get in, anyway, for all her confidence. I was silent, trying to see everything between Garden Building and hall, and once we got in there I was too busy to talk, staring at the oak panelling, the great gold-framed portraits on the walls, the long massive tables. Hundreds of people were sitting on benches along the tables, talking at the tops of their voices, though there was a fair proportion who were silent with nerves. I choked down some toast and lukewarm tea while I listened to . . . we'll call her Joan, since I really can't guess what her name was . . . telling me about her friends and her hobbies and how she really didn't think she wanted to go to Oxford because it was too much like hard work and all her mates had laughed at her for applying in the first place.

I managed to shake Joan off after breakfast on the grounds that I needed to get ready for my interview, and wandered through the college taking in everything from the chalked-up rowing results above doorways in second quad to the smell of brass polish outside the college chapel. It was a bright, cold day, the sky clear and blue overhead, and all the colours were especially vivid. I was in love with the place already — painfully so — and went to my interview with a feeling of rising panic; they couldn't invite me here and show me what was, to me, heaven, and then take it away again . . . Looking back, I realise that I was given an easy ride in the interview, nothing like the mouth-drying questions that some of the other candidates were asked, like "define reason". The last thing the law tutors wanted to know before they let me escape was simply why I wanted to study at Latimer. I looked out of the lead-latticed window at golden chimneys as sharp against the blue sky as if they were paper cut-outs. I needed an answer that would convince them, something that wasn't trite or pleading. But what came out was the truth.

"I didn't know anywhere like this existed, but it's all I've ever dreamed of."

I went down the little wooden stairs from the law tutor's rooms, past the next candidate, a boy in a suit who looked through me when I tried to smile at him, and I knew I hadn't done well enough to get in. I went through the rest of the interviews mechanically,

494

nodding and smiling until my cheeks ached, answering questions in a soft voice that had the tutors leaning forward, asking me to repeat myself more often than not.

"No chance. No chance. No chance," beat in my brain as I packed up my things on the morning of the third day, dragging myself away from the little room with one last look at the view before I went.

And home was that bit greyer, uglier and harder to endure when I got back.

You know what happened next: against all the odds, probably because I fitted the correct demographic, they offered me a place. When the letter came I locked myself in the bathroom to get some privacy and just stared at the envelope, knowing that I was either going to be completely delirious with happiness or totally crushed after I looked at it. My fate was decided but I didn't know what it was going to be, and I remember the way my heart fluttered and my sight darkened around the edges as I eased the envelope open and took out the folded sheet of paper inside. It would have been better all round if I hadn't got a place — if I'd never gone further than the Co-op supermarket where I'd got a part-time job. But I got a place, and a generous entrance scholarship to go with it so I didn't have to worry about fees, or paying for books, or kitting myself out with a gown and mortar board and all the other little bits of Oxford paraphernalia. I realised very quickly, though, that I did need cash — more than I had at my disposal — to buy everything else, like clothes that didn't make me stand out. I'd seen what the undergraduates wore when I was there, and no, Oxford wasn't the most fashionable place on earth, but they still looked different from me.

I didn't ask Nana for much. I knew she had money — I'd seen her savings book. I told her I needed a loan, but not for what. And she didn't even ask me why before she said no.

"You'll get money from me when I'm dead and not a minute sooner."

She put the idea into my head, so it was really sort of her own fault, wouldn't you say?

Calm down, I'm only joking. About it being her fault, that is. But I did justify it to myself on the grounds that she was in a lot of pain, all the time, as well as moon-faced from steroids, shuffling around the flat like a little grey-haired troll, snapping at the world. It didn't take me long to make up my mind.

I had a few months in hand until I needed the money, so I devoted myself to stockpiling drugs. I stopped passing on everything to Steve — just kept him going with a bit here and there. It was useful to have a reserve, in case I needed a bit of pocket money. And besides, I'd discovered that people started to be nice when they thought I could help them out with a mood-altering substance or two. I had a feeling it might be good to have some available when I got to Oxford too. Nana never noticed a thing, even when I swapped out her Tramadol for aspirin. I'd encourage her to go back to the doctor when she complained about how she was feeling. She worked her way through two or three of them in the local practice. And the drugs kept coming.

Two months before the start of term, and just before bedtime, I made Nana a lovely cup of tea and gave her a dose of painkillers, just like she'd asked me to. Except that I told her that the dosage had changed and she needed three times what she'd had before. Oh, and these. The pharmacist said you should take these with the others to make them more effective. Down the hatch.

I wasn't totally sure that it would be enough. I stood outside the door of our room and listened to her breathing, shallow and slow, hoping that each quavering exhalation would be the last. But the old bitch kept going. I resented it; I resented that I'd given her an overdose that should have pushed her off her branch within hours, but there she was, wheezing away. In the end, I went in and took a pillow off my bed, putting it over her face and holding it there while I tried to remember all of Madonna's UK number ones in order. It's weird, the things that go through your head at a time like that. I don't even like Madonna.

When the GP came to do the death certificate, he was a bit dubious about Nana. He thought she might need an autopsy. Very suspicious man, Dr Considine. I told him that I was worried she might have got confused about what medicine to take. I showed him a load of empty bottles. Maybe she'd been prescribed too much over the years. What did he think?

He thought he'd sign the certificate, funnily enough.

Mum got the money, in the will Nana left. I got a cameo brooch that I'd never liked. It didn't matter to me; I'd already lifted Nana's bank card before she tragically passed, and I'd helped myself to a nice chunk of her savings over the previous couple of weeks. Poor Nana, she'd been a bit out of it on the extra tranquillisers I was giving her — too confused to notice that I'd nicked her stuff. As soon as I left, she'd have come out of the fog and worked out what I'd done, so I had no choice but to get rid of her. I sort of missed her, in a strange way — like I would wake up and listen for her snoring before I remembered. Mum was in pieces. They took her into the local loony bin for a non-optional "rest" and I took the opportunity to pack up and go. I didn't tell her where, or why, but I did leave a note saying I was all right. She could have found me through the school, if she'd thought of asking, but I suppose she didn't think of it. Anyway, I haven't seen her since. I don't even know if she's still alive. I'm not going to try to find out, not at this stage. It's strange. I was always ashamed of her. Now I'm afraid she'd be ashamed of me.

The start of term was beautiful, warm and sunny during the days, cool in the evenings. Thinking about it, it would have been the end of September when I went up, but it had been one of those Septembers that give you a last taste of summer. Every patch of green space was occupied by students lazing on the grass, calling hellos to one another and comparing stories about their travels in the long vac. I wandered through it in a daze, still unable to believe that I was really there, that I was allowed to sit by the river myself, that I had a timetable of tutorials and my first essay to write. I had a day or two before the reading list appeared in my pigeon hole and spent it working out where things were in the college and the city, putting things to rights in my room and not really talking much to anyone else. It wasn't my way to go up to people and introduce myself. Everyone else seemed to be making friends as if that was their first and only priority. I avoided most of the college events — the drinks parties, the pub crawl organised by the JCR, the meeting and greeting. I liked being on my own. I liked the silence. I liked not speaking, letting time trail through my fingers as the river flowed.

And that was the one thing that worried me. I wasn't in Garden Building in a neat little self-contained cell as I'd hoped I would be. I was in third quad, one of the older parts of the college, in a set — two bedrooms, a large sitting room and, wonder of wonders, a bathroom all of our own. They were sought-after rooms; anyone who managed to find out where I was living told me how envious they were. But I was furious. The other person hadn't arrived yet, but what if I didn't get on with her? What if she was loud? Or liked loud music? Or loud sex, even? What if we had nothing in common? What if she didn't like me?

As the days slipped past and the other room remained unoccupied, I started to dare to hope that she wouldn't come. Something must have been wrong, I thought. Maybe she was ill. Maybe she had decided Oxford wasn't for her. By Friday, I was almost certain that she would never come, that I would spend the year in blissful solitude. I moved one or two things out of my bedroom — a pink cushion with a gingham border that I'd bought after seeing other people's rooms made different with their own possessions, a poster of Klimt's *The Kiss* (I was nothing if not predictable in my tastes), trying to add some colour to the institutionally beige furnishings in the sitting room. I sat down in one of the armchairs, trying it out. I didn't have a television or a stereo, but I didn't miss them. I could hear conversation floating up from the quad below, and the ticking of my watch, and my breath, and for a moment, I felt total peace.

And then, footsteps on the stairs. Several people, coming quickly and firmly, carrying heavy things that scuffed against the walls. A man's voice rumbling, answered by a quicksilver exclamation.

"This one!"

I stood up, not knowing where to go (run? Hide in my room? The bathroom? Too late . . .) and so it was that the first time I met Rebecca was when she stumbled in through the door, laughing at having tripped, her skin tanned gold and her hair a mass of shining curls. She stopped laughing when she saw me standing with my hands folded in front of me, as if I had been waiting for her.

"Sorry. Typical me. I'm Rebecca."

"Louise." I freed one hand for an awkward wave, which I regretted as I did it — nothing could have looked more gauche. But before I could recover, Rebecca's father came through the door with a large box, followed by her mother who was carrying garment bags over her arm.

"Isn't this lovely? Rebecca, you've got such a nice room. And who's this?" When I knew her better, I understood that Avril was always ready to be sociable; I'd never met anyone like her before and was frankly terrified of Rebecca's glamorous mother, slender in white jeans and a striped Breton top. She looked as if she'd just stepped off a yacht, which was accurate as it turned out, because they had been sailing in the Greek Islands and that was why Rebecca came up late.

"This is Louise," Rebecca said after the tiniest pause to allow me to answer. I was too tongue-tied to try.

"Louise. How are you going to put up with Rebecca? You poor darling. Have you just arrived too?"

I looked around the room and could see why she was asking. I had not made it my own. Rebecca was already moving the furniture, unrolling a rug, dumping a plant on one of the two desks in the room, making it alive as I had not. "I've been here for a little while," I said in the end, not wanting to admit that I'd had almost a week of solitude. My voice was rusty and sounded flat to my own ears.

"God, don't you just hate college furnishings?" Rebecca held the pink cushion up at arm's length. "Look at this. Shall we dump it?"

The appeal was to me, the first joint act of living together, and I made the decision on the spot not to react, not to admit by so much as the flicker of an eyelid that I had picked the cushion myself and thought it pretty.

"Definitely dump it."

"Brilliant." It sailed through the air and landed beside the bin in the corner. I didn't look at it again. It had nothing to do with me any more.

"I do pity you." Avril threw an arm around her daughter's shoulders. "She's tough to live with. She likes everything to be just so."

"I bet Louise does too," Rebecca said, flashing a smile at me and I managed to smile back, feeling panic flutter beneath my ribcage. There was no way she would like me. No way I wouldn't be forgotten once she got to know everyone else in college — and she would know everyone; she would sweep them up and carry them along and charm them as she was charming me.

The Haworths got on with unpacking Rebecca's belongings, pounding up and down the stairs with unfailing energy and good humour. I joined in, carrying a few bags and boxes at Avril's direction.

"Did your parents help you to unpack?" Gerald was having a breather on the landing, sitting in the window seat after delivering another load of Rebecca's belongings.

"No. But I didn't have much stuff."

"Did they drive you?" I could tell he was curious about me, my background. That didn't mean I had to tell him anything. Let alone the truth.

"I came by coach." I slipped through the door and looked around the frankly unrecognisable room. "Wow."

"More like it, isn't it?" Rebecca stood with her hands on her hips and surveyed the room. She had tied back her hair and in her pale-blue fitted polo shirt and denim mini she looked utterly, unself-consciously gorgeous, all long limbs and tanned skin. "I've taken this desk because it's nearest my room — is that OK?"

"Fine by me."

She had already put up a series of black-and-white photographs — details of architecture mainly — and shelved books in the little bookcase beside her desk. A sleek steel-cased laptop and a stack of multicoloured notebooks sat on the desk beside the plant, a miniature rose. It was well organised, almost intimidatingly so, and also somehow pleasing. I wanted it for myself. And I wanted parents who were devoted to me, beautiful wealthy parents who supported everything I did and were proud of me.

Gerald pulled Rebecca into a bear hug and I turned away from them, afraid that they would see how I felt.

Gerald checked his watch. "We'll take you out to dinner before we go. Make sure you eat something decent before you get started on fast food and too much booze."

She thumped him affectionately. "You know I won't. Not all the time, anyway."

There was a tiny pause. I went into my room, mumbling about needing to check something. I opened the top drawer of my chest of drawers and stared into it, waiting for them to go.

"Louise, would you like to come with us?" Avril was in the doorway behind me. "We'd love you to join us for dinner."

I could see Rebecca over her mother's shoulder, not looking at me but listening. I said what I thought she would want to hear. "Oh, thank you. But I couldn't. It's your last night together."

"Don't be silly. I get to talk to them all the time." Rebecca took her hair out of its ponytail and shook it out, then tied it back up again, smiling at me with uncomplicated warmth. "Please come. If you've been here for a bit already, have you found anywhere nice to eat?"

I shook my head, miserable again. Failure.

Her father said firmly, "We'll ask the porter. There's always Brown's. Or at least, that was the place to go in my day. But I was up at that end of town."

I fell into step behind the Haworths as they wandered out of third quad, listening to Gerald reminisce. I had fallen for them, from a height, and all I could do was hope against hope that Rebecca might let me be her friend. If I did enough for her — if I put her first, if I earned it — then maybe she would. And it was worth it because I would benefit from it; I could learn from Rebecca, from her parents. I could become someone else with her as an example to follow.

You know as well as I do that Rebecca wasn't the sort of person who craved attention. She wasn't my friend because I sucked up to her. She didn't care about being looked after; it had always happened to her and she neither expected it nor demanded it. She took me for granted, in the nicest way possible, as part of the backdrop of her life, and I never actually needed to work to stay there. But old habits die hard. Old ways of thinking, too. I never quite managed to shake off the feeling that if I didn't worship at her shrine, she would move on to someone who would. Maybe that's because I would have been that way, if I'd had what she had and been what she was. Rebecca was a lot nicer than me. Maybe that goes without saying.

Being friends with her was an amazing experience, though. It took me a long time but I started to trust her. I let her choose clothes for me, borrowing from her wardrobe rather than buying, mostly. It had hurt but I had told her I was too poor to go shopping, and she never made me feel self-conscious about it for a second. Nana's money was dwindling and now I realised I had bought the wrong clothes, the wrong shoes, the wrong everything. Eventually I got a job in the college bar that paid for some of my expenses, and later I worked in the city as a tour guide during the Easter and summer vacations, moving into flats while their usual inhabitants were off travelling and didn't want to have to cover their rent. Plus I made a bit on the side from selling Nana's drugs. I was the most unlikely dealer imaginable, above suspicion, a meek law student who barely spoke. I let a couple of the more free-living graduates know what I had available and used them for distribution; as before, I didn't get my hands dirty if I could help it.

Rebecca knew nothing about it. She dressed me up and dragged me around with her to college bars and student parties and the dismal nightclubs that were the best Oxford had to offer. I was her audience, her coat-holder, her general dogsbody. And at Christmas, every Christmas, she took me back to her home, to spend the holidays with her parents in a house that was all holly on mantelpieces and mistletoe in the hall, a huge fir tree and candles everywhere — the great English Christmas that doesn't really exist, except in tiny pockets of privilege here and there. It sounds fake but there was nothing pretentious about the way the Haworths lived. They were the real thing and I couldn't get enough of them.

We spent the first year in the greatest harmony, as I got used to Rebecca's compulsive need to keep everything neat and organised; we lived together in a house in our second year, and in our third year when we were back in college, in separate rooms this time, she spent hours drinking tea curled up on my bed, her eyes glittering as she spun tales. I stood in her shadow, even when she tried to draw me into the light. I preferred to watch, anyway. She broke hearts without meaning to; everyone adored her. It makes her sound like Pollyanna, but she wasn't, not at all. She was brilliant and funny and a little bit mad. There was a vulnerability too, an innocence, a desire to be liked that was almost childish. The only person who got under her skin — the only one who ever made her really doubt herself — was the one person who seemed to be immune to her. He had worked out that the best way to bring her to heel was to pretend he didn't like her, and it baffled and intrigued her until she became hopelessly obsessed. If there was one thing Adam Rowley was good at, it was making women crazy, and Rebecca was no different. I might not have been particularly experienced myself but I was born cynical; I tried to tell her that how she was feeling was all part of the game he was playing with her, but she wouldn't listen, or couldn't. By the time we were in our last year, she was unguardedly open about her feelings for him, utterly reckless.

You never knew Adam, and I doubt Rebecca ever told you about him, but you have a lot in common. He was beautiful on the outside and vile on the inside. The university was littered with his rejects, the girls he'd pursued and slept with and dropped as soon as he'd got what he wanted from them. It wasn't sex with him; it was power. He'd find out where your limits were and then devote himself to pushing you beyond them. He was a bully and a misogynist, and if he hadn't been charismatic — more than that, cult-leader standard — I don't think he would have had many friends. He wanted to take what was best from people and leave them with nothing. There was a rumour that he had hepatitis, that he had passed it on to a few girls in the full knowledge that he should have been more careful, but no one ever knew for sure. I suppose none of the victims would have wanted to admit it was true.

With Rebecca, he saw her innocence, her trust in goodness, and I think he wanted to take that away from her, just to see if he could. He made her silent and watchful, nervous around him, stepping carefully, trying to please. It was painful to watch, but worse for her, because she couldn't understand what he was doing. I knew. I could always read people like that. It takes a user to know a user, maybe. I got what I wanted from Rebecca, but I left her whole. Adam took her soul.

507

You probably think I'm exaggerating, but you didn't know her before. Not before I killed him. Before what he did to her. You know, you should be grateful to him; he broke Rebecca in for you. She liked you because she'd loved him, and you reminded her of him, physically at least. Does it hurt to know you weren't the first? To hear that Rebecca was using you to revisit the bad old days? Adam Rowley was much worse than you, if it helps. He was imaginative in his cruelty, for one thing. Rebecca didn't see the danger until it was far too late.

It was Trinity term, the last term before Finals — almost the end of our time at Oxford, and everything seemed bittersweet, or at least it did when I had the chance to lift my head from my books. Law students don't get out of the library much and I was desperate to get a good degree. It was my ticket out of my old life. For the first time I had lost focus on what Rebecca was doing. I saw her, every day, and usually had one meal with her at least, but I wasn't aware that she was drifting ever closer to Adam, or that she was prepared to do whatever he wanted to prove how she felt about him.

It happened one Saturday night. He was living in college but he had friends — acolytes — in the year below who had a tiny house in Jericho. He wanted privacy for what he was planning, and he got it. They went out for the night, obediently, while he invited Rebecca to join him for dinner. She must have thought it was a dream come true. I have no doubt that she didn't tell me about it because she knew I would disapprove. The first I knew of it was a feather-light scratching at my door in the early hours of the morning, and a tiny whimpering sound that I somehow knew to be Rebecca, though I'd never heard her make a noise like that before. I opened the door and she fell into my arms, shaking uncontrollably, sobbing so hard I couldn't understand what she was saying at first. But I got the story, in the end. They hadn't got as far as dinner. He'd poured her a tumbler of whisky when she got there, watched her swallow it too fast because she was nervous, poured her another, and a third, and Rebecca never drank spirits. Then he took the glass from her, and raped her on the living-room floor. He raped her again upstairs, in one of the bedrooms. He raped her and he told her she'd asked for it. No one would believe her, he said. She'd followed him around for too long. She was drunk; he could tell anyone who asked that she'd agreed to have sex with him and then regretted it when he didn't want a relationship with her. He told her she was ugly, and that it was a pity fuck anyway because she'd made herself so pathetic over him, and no one would ever want her if they knew what she was really like.

She got away when he was in the bathroom having a shower, though I don't think he would have minded her leaving. He'd been careful to use just enough force to make her do what he wanted. She had bruises, yes, and she was bleeding, but it was just — *just* — within the bounds of possibility that the sex had been consensual, though rough. Oh, he'd judged it well. I don't think it was the first time he'd done it. He knew what would work.

Rebecca had spirit, though. She wanted to go to the police, or at the very least the d, and make a formal complaint against him. She wanted him to be sent down. She wanted him to be punished. I had the horrible job of explaining that if she told the police and it got as far as a trial she'd be savaged by any decent defence barrister. He would get off, just as he'd said. She had told anyone who would listen that she was obsessed with him. She had gone there willingly. She had drunk more than a little. He was well spoken, handsome, charming and credible. She had very little chance of securing a conviction even if she did manage to get it to court. Basically, it would blight her life for years.

"Move on," I advised her. "Get over it in your own time and put it down to experience. There's nothing you can do legally to punish him. He's too clever."

"But it's not fair." That's all she kept saying. "It's not fair." And it wasn't. She was so bewildered. Doing that to her was like kicking a kitten — she hadn't expected it, or known to be afraid, and now she was petrified. She had to go and get tested for STDs because he hadn't used a condom, naturally, and she had to get treatment. She was on the Pill, so there was that, at least — a pregnancy would have killed her. She couldn't be around him — couldn't stand to be in the same room with him. He had primed his friends to think it was hilarious. They made comments about her, under their breath but loud enough that she could hear

510

them, about what a miserable shag she'd been, what a stupid bitch she was. I could see him enjoying it, feeding off her distress, getting a thrill from the power he had over her.

And I didn't think he deserved to get away with it.

It was my good luck that Adam was a thrill seeker, the sort who loves to experiment and feel they're doing something outside the law, preferably demonstrating their own heroism. For once, I broke my own rule about dealing. I approached him directly and asked if he'd be interested in buying something to make May Morning go with a swing. I pretended he was the only person I knew who was edgy enough to want to do drugs. I quoted him a price that was laughable, making him believe I didn't know the value of what I was selling. It was speed, he thought. Something to put a spring in his step. I promised I'd meet him after the bar closed, by the river, but he had to promise he wouldn't tell anyone. That was the risky bit. He could have told anyone that he was meeting me, and why. But he loved the secrecy. And he was too arrogant to think twice about why Rebecca's best friend would even be talking to him, let alone doing him a favour.

I watched him all night from behind the bar, pouring him drink after drink, seeing him flirt and freeze alternately, throwing out negative remarks to make the girls try harder to impress him. Sarcasm had never done it for me but Adam Rowley could have had most of the girls in the bar that night by clicking his fingers. That was why, I suppose, he didn't bother. Too easy.

511

Much more fun to make them give him what he wanted in spite of themselves.

He shook off the friends who usually followed him around, as I'd told him to. He came down to the river as I'd planned. He took the pills I gave him without really looking at them, and he let me talk to him, a shade desperately, until they kicked in. I'd calculated that he would think I was trying to chat him up, and his amusement at my temerity would hold his attention. I was right about that. And then I asked him about Rebecca — knowing that he knew we were friends. He laughed in my face. She'd deserved it, he said. She'd enjoyed it, in the bit of her soul where the bad girl lived. He'd thought she was enjoying it a little bit too much at times. It almost spoiled it for him.

He was slurring his words and repeating himself, and I hoped that the combination of diazepam and alcohol would dull his reactions. I let him start to walk away from me and I whacked him on the back of the head with a champagne bottle I'd taken from the recycling bin behind the bar. It was reinforced glass, so it didn't shatter, and it was heavy enough to do the job. Adam dropped like a stone. It was child's play to roll him into the river, with just the fear that he might come back to consciousness when he hit cold water. The drugs took care of that. He slipped out of sight and the river washed him away. I didn't stand around to watch him die, or curse his spirit, or gloat, or whatever it is murderers are supposed to do. I didn't waste my time. I was back in my room within ten minutes, rinsing out the socks I'd put on over my shoes when I left the path so I didn't leave footprints on the riverbank. I had gambled that Adam, who was exceedingly drunk, wouldn't notice in the dark, and I had been right. The bottle had been wiped clean and was back in the recycling bin; it was due for collection the following day, I happened to know. I took the money he'd given me and burned it, flushing the ash away down the lavatory in a different staircase.

I slept well, afterwards. It was a victimless crime. I'd saved other women from the same fate Rebecca had endured, and besides, he had deserved to die.

The big mistake — the huge great fucking mistake that has landed me here — was to tell her what I'd done. I knew it was stupid. I knew I should have said nothing. But I couldn't stand the conjecture. Maybe he drowned himself. Maybe he felt guilty about what happened. Maybe he would have apologised one day. Maybe maybe maybe.

The ridiculous thing was that I thought she'd be pleased. I thought she'd thank me. But I told her what I'd done — how clever I'd been — and she looked at me as if she didn't know who I was. And Adam had his revenge, even from face down in the Thames, because it was only when I told her what I'd done that the light truly went out of her eyes. They were as dull and unreflective as mud, and they stayed that way. (I didn't see them sparkle again until she met you, which just proves she hadn't learned her lesson.)

Rebecca and I obviously fell out over Adam. I was annoyed that she couldn't appreciate what I'd done for her. She was upset that I'd killed him, I suppose. It was the best gift I could think to give her and she threw it back in my face. Anyway, we didn't talk for a while. She had her little breakdown and opted out of her exams. I got on with mine.

The following year, Avril and Gerald persuaded us to meet up together in London. We sort of picked up where we'd left off. Things weren't quite the same — how could they be? — but we were on good terms. She was disappointed with her degree but it was OK; it was good enough to get her into PR, and that suited her down to the ground. Enthusiasm, organisation, persuasion, charm — the role was made for Rebecca. The new Rebecca, who had energy to burn and was always cheerful. It was entirely fake, but no one else would have noticed. She was acting all the time, pretending to be happy, pretending to be fulfilled when really, her life was empty.

I was starting to work my way up at PG, impressing the right people while I was doing my training contract, working out where I wanted to specialise. Mergers and acquisitions, the fun bit, the high-powered late-night deal-making bit. It absorbed me. I saw Rebecca, but only about twice a month. We emailed. I phoned her, now and then. She was out a lot in the evenings, for work. She seemed to be finding her feet. She got tired, after a while, and someone gave her a bit of coke to help her out.

She liked cocaine. She liked it a little bit too much. Weak, you see.

And she knew too much about me.

As I said, there was a beautiful symmetry in trying to frame you for Rebecca's death, because if you follow it back far enough, it was your fault. If you hadn't split up with her the way you did, she wouldn't have been broken-hearted. Maybe the rejection reminded her of Adam. Maybe she thought you were special, or something. I wouldn't have wasted any time crying over you, but Rebecca was different. If you hadn't made her feel like shit, she wouldn't have let her little cocaine habit get out of hand. She wouldn't have lost her job. She wouldn't have been struggling to pay rent and bills. She wouldn't have been desperate for money to stop her parents and friends from finding out she was broke. I was the only one who knew, at first, and I was the last person she should have told, because I was already worried about her. I was going up the ladder and she was sliding down a great big snake. The evil bit of me enjoyed it, a little — it was proof that she wasn't perfect after all — but mostly I was just worried for her.

Then she got money out of Caspian Faraday (who got such a kick out of it, from what she told me. The *drama* of being blackmailed by his beautiful young lover . . .). The alarm bells really started to ring in my mind. She was brooding on the past, on Oxford, and she said she was thinking about getting in touch with Adam's parents, just to talk to them. I could read between the lines. She knew what I'd done, and I knew that the investigation into his death could be reopened easily if there was new evidence. She was desperate; she was bound to ask for money sooner rather than later. And I didn't want to give it to her. It was my money, and my life she was in a position to wreck by telling someone what I'd done. No way.

For someone who doesn't take drugs, I know a hell of a lot about illegal pharmaceuticals. I ordered Rohypnol from an Internet pharmacy, using my secretary's credit card, and had it sent to a PO box I'd hired in the same name. (I also bought flights to Lagos and a flat-screen TV, just to muddy the waters a bit more. No need to worry; the card company noticed those and she didn't have to pay for any of it.) I asked Rebecca to come to dinner on the Wednesday night. She was so trusting, so grateful to me for feeding her. She'd lost a lot of weight, I thought. I could see her shoulder blades jutting through the wool of her jumper. She wasn't looking her best, truth be told. You wouldn't have been impressed, put it that way.

The plan was so simple. I dosed her drink with the Rohypnol and she passed out, like a good little victim. I kept her in my spare bedroom for the next twenty-four hours. Every time she stirred, I gave her a drink that knocked her out again. She never knew where she was or what she was doing there. I stripped out the room completely afterwards. You know how I never got around to redecorating? Changing the decor wasn't exactly the point. Trace evidence was what worried me. Fibres. Hair. Skin cells. Fingerprints. I'd cleaned the room, but it wasn't enough. I couldn't be sure. And I like being sure.

On the Thursday night, late, I went to the room. I made sure she was out of it — she had no idea what was going on. I put make-up on her. I dressed her in expensive clothes, the kind she would have worn to see you. I made her look beautiful, and then — well, I did it.

I don't want to talk about killing her. It was horrible. I was just focused on imitating what the serial killer was doing. He was a bit too violent for my tastes, a bit too physical. I'd done my research but I sort of knew I might get some of it wrong, even though the fire should hide any mistakes I'd made. That was all right. I had already lined you up as my suspect of choice.

I went to Rebecca's flat the next day. I hadn't planned to. But lying in bed, I started thinking about how she'd always written things down. *Dinner with Louise.* It was probably on a calendar somewhere. On a Post-it note. Or in her diary. I didn't want it there. I didn't want any recent contact between us. So I went over and I started searching. At the same time, I cleaned the whole place, so there was no evidence you *hadn't* been there. I took a pen with your initials on it. Rebecca bought it for you but you broke up with her before she had a chance to give it to you. I don't know why she kept it. Wishful thinking, perhaps, in case you came back. You might not remember this, but I showed it to you after the memorial service — got you to hold it so your prints were on it. I thought I'd show it to the police at some stage, worriedly, and say I'd found it in Rebecca's flat but not thought twice about it at the time. *Nudge nudge. Investigate Gil. Don't focus on me. I'm not important.* But when I got around to it, I was too late.

517

It was a bit of a sickener when the police turned up at the flat before I was ready. I was so close to leaving, too. I had to come up with a story about how untidy Rebecca was — when she would have been the last person to leave something out of place — and pretend to be overcome with emotion so I could finish checking the flat for giveaway hints to where Rebecca had been. I thought I'd been pretty convincing, for a spur of the moment lie. Not convincing enough, maybe. I should have pretended to have OCD or something. But I knew Rebecca's friends thought I was her slave. They would have told the police as much. I thought I'd get away with that one.

I threw out Rebecca's clothes that she'd worn to dinner with me. I got rid of anything I'd worn while she was in my house, and of course what I'd been wearing when I killed her. The same went for my car. Bye bye, old car, with your DNA particles and fabric fibres that might link me to Rebecca. Hello, sporty new car, clean and evidence free. As a manifestation of grief, it was a very nice one. Quite understandable, too, that I would devote myself to living it up now that Rebecca was gone.

But all along the line, I've made mistakes. Talked too much to the wrong people. Tried to be too clever. That's something I've always done. I can get so far but no further. I got into Oxford, and I got a 2.1 in the end, but by the skin of my teeth — absolute rock bottom of the class. And I worked hard. God, I worked. Then, when I started at PG, I worked more than anyone else. I worked more than anyone should. I didn't want anyone to have an excuse to get rid of me. It's sad, but I would never have made partner. I certainly won't now.

Then again, there are lots of things I won't do now. I've lost everything I'd worked for. Everything I wanted. All gone because of Rebecca. So you could say I deserve it.

I've had enough, Gil. I've said what I wanted to. I've owned up to my crimes; the punishment is up to me too. There's nothing the state can do to rehabilitate me. And prison would not have suited me — all those people, and no prospect of any peace, ever. Most of the women here are addicts and prostitutes, mentally ill, unstable in various ways. It's the world I took great pains to leave behind me, but I'm beginning to realise that I never truly got away. You can change everything about yourself — the way you look, the way you talk, the way you behave — but you can't escape what you truly are.

I'm sorry my plan didn't work out. I'm sorry I won't get another chance to make you pay for what you've done.

I won't miss you, and somehow I doubt you'll miss me.

And now it's time to go.

L.

Maeve

I was asleep when the phone rang, not unreasonably given the time of day. Ten past four, according to the clock on my bedside table. No one ever called me at a sensible time, I found myself thinking as I scrabbled for the handset, answering just before it switched to voicemail.

"Maeve?"

"Sir." I was awake instantly, recognising Superintendent Godley's voice.

"I'm sorry to wake you. I've just spoken to the governor at Holloway. They've been trying to get hold of both of us for the past couple of hours. It's Louise North. She's back in the prison infirmary now, but she was rushed to hospital." I knew what he was going to say before he went on. "She's taken an overdose."

"Jesus. I knew she'd try something to get out of the trial but I didn't think of suicide. How did she manage that?"

"I haven't been able to find out yet." He paused. "She wrote you a note, Maeve. And what seems to be a confession."

I was already out of bed, hunting around for clothes. "I'll come to the prison."

"They're expecting us. I'll see you there."

It didn't take me long to get ready, though I skipped breakfast and closed my front door on a scene of devastation. Living on my own wasn't good for me. I needed the discipline of sharing a space with someone else to make myself be tidy, and I found myself wishing Rob was there to put his arms around me and tell me what had happened wasn't my fault. I made myself focus on getting to the prison instead, wondering what was waiting for me. I headed out into the cold, dark morning to the sound of plaintive birdsong that matched my mood.

Godley was there before me, sitting reading in the governor's office with a pile of pages in front of him. He handed me an envelope with my name on it in the firm writing I recognised as Louise North's.

"You might want to start with that. I haven't opened it."

I slit the envelope carefully along one side, habit making me preserve it from damage as far as I could, and skimmed through the brief contents.

"It's just a note to ask me to make sure Gil sees the letter in the bigger envelope." I looked up and realised that the A4 envelope in front of the superintendent was what she had meant. "What is it? Interesting reading?"

"Very." He turned over the pages and handed me the fat sheaf of lined paper written in a biro that tended to blotch. She had only used every other line so it was mostly legible. "I'm nearly finished. When you've caught up, let me know."

I nodded, already reading, already absorbed in Louise's letter. We read in silence, the superintendent passing me the pages he had finished as he went along. When I finally got to the end, I looked up at him. He was sitting with his fingers steepled in front of his face, his expression set.

"That's it, then. She did it. She did it all."

"That's what she wrote."

"And I was right about Gil too. I knew there was something off with him."

He winced. "Knowing it doesn't mean we can do much about it."

"But he raped her."

"She's not going to be a brilliant witness, is she? You can't have it both ways, Maeve. She has lied and lied about murdering Rebecca; she can't be credible in a case where she's alleging rape. It's hard enough to prove at the best of times."

"Don't you believe what she wrote?"

He smiled. "I wouldn't assume anything she said was true, up to and including 'hello'."

"I disagree. I don't think she'd lie in these circumstances."

"You got to know her. I didn't."

I pulled a face. "I wouldn't say I knew her. I saw more of her than you did, that's all."

"And do you want to see her now?"

I did not. I wanted to say no, more than anything. But I nodded, and followed the superintendent out to where a guard was waiting. He led us down airless corridors to the prison infirmary, where we spoke briefly to the doctor. Godley hung back to ask him a few more questions and motioned to me to go on alone. I walked down to the end of the room, and there, small and vulnerable under a white sheet, lay a motionless figure. She didn't look like a murderer. Her eyes were closed, her hair limp and dirty as it fanned out on the pillow. They had given her charcoal to drink, the doctor had said, to absorb whatever remained of the drug in her stomach, and her lips were blackened where the skin was dry. There was no colour in her face, none at all, and I looked down at her feeling something like sadness.

And then she opened her eyes and looked straight at me.

I didn't say anything, I just waited for her to know me. It took a moment. Then, in a weak, thready voice, she spoke.

"I wrote you a letter."

"I read it."

"I wrote one for Gil."

"I read that too." I watched her to see her reaction, the flicker in her eyes as she registered what I knew, what she had said. "I think you might regret writing that, to be honest."

Her face crumpled and she closed her eyes, shutting me out. A tear slid down the side of her face, slipping into her hair. I thought about what had happened to her — what Gil had done to her — and I tried to feel sorry for her. But thinking about what she'd done herself made it hard. When she had regained control of herself, she took a deep breath.

"I thought the pills would work. Why didn't they work?"

"A pipe leaked in the cell next door. The guard came in to check that yours was still dry, and found you."

She nodded and turned her head away. "I wish it had worked. I don't want to spend the next thirty years in prison."

"No one ever does." I leaned down, so no one else could hear what I said. "I'm glad you didn't die."

She looked back at me, surprised — not a little pleased, I think. I leaned an inch closer still.

"You took Rebecca's life to safeguard your own. You picked over what she'd left behind and you borrowed what suited you from it. You took the man she'd loved. You took her place in her parents' lives. You dressed like her. You copied the way she spoke, the way she wore her hair, her make-up, her jewellery."

Louise's eyes were fixed on mine, her pupils wide and dark. She ran her tongue over her lips nervously, and it was black too, as if she was rotting from the inside, the evil festering within her.

"I hope you live a long life, Louise. And I hope you don't know a minute's peace from now until the day you die. You took Rebecca's life," I said, one last time. "The very least you owe her is to live it."

Outside the prison, I stopped by Godley's car.

"So that's it, then? We can't go after Maddick, even with this?"

"Pass it on to the sex crimes unit at the Yard, if you want. Let them follow it up with his ex-girlfriends — see if there's anyone else who wants to make a complaint. But I think you're going to have to let it go, Maeve."

"That's not right. If we walk away from it, we can't be sure justice will be done."

"You don't think that's our job, do you? Making sure that justice is done?"

I frowned. "Isn't it?

"We're just trying to hold back the tide, Maeve. For every killer we catch, there's another we don't. Murderers who are clever enough to find victims who don't count. Rapists who are plausible enough to get off every charge. Abusers whose crimes don't come to light for decades. We can only do something about the crimes we know about, and half the time, even if we get a conviction, the punishment isn't fit to be called justice."

I shook my head, bewildered. "If you're so cynical about it, why do this job at all?"

"Because it's better than not even trying." He sat into the driver's seat and looked up at me. "Maddick will come again, Maeve. His type always does. And when he does —"

"I'll be ready," I finished for him.

The Burning Man "Will Never be Released"

Razmig Selvaggi will spend the rest of his life in jail for murdering four young women in South London.

Selvaggi killed Nicola Fielding (27), Alice Fallon (19), Victoria Müller (26) and Charity Beddoes (23) before setting fire to their bodies. He terrorised the residents of the Kennington area, where he hunted his victims between September and December of 2009.

Mr Justice Cauldwell, sitting at the Central Criminal Court, ordered 24-year-old Selvaggi to serve the maximum sentence. He said: "This was a targeted campaign of murder. It is right you should spend your whole life in prison. You will never be released."

Selvaggi listened without showing any emotion as Mr Justice Cauldwell said he had targeted vulnerable young women. "They were out late at night, walking home alone. But they should not have been at risk from harm. You killed them, burned them and left them, by your own account because you enjoyed it." The judge said the case met the legal requirements for a whole life sentence because the murders involved a "substantial degree of premeditation and planning".

Selvaggi pleaded guilty, having confessed to the crimes once in custody. He was caught while attempting to attack an undercover policewoman in December 2009. Analysis by forensic science experts revealed DNA from two of the victims on a hammer that was found at his address, as well as items of jewellery that had belonged to all four women.

Detective Chief Superintendent Charles Godley, who led the investigation, said Selvaggi had committed "despicable acts of violence" that had left the capital in a state of terror.

Selvaggi is expected to be placed on suicide watch and undergo routine psychiatric assessments. His defence team said they would be considering whether there were grounds for an appeal, as is routine in all criminal cases.

The Metropolitan Police will now check outstanding cases in the London area to see whether there could be links to Selvaggi.

Woman Jailed for "Mistake" Knife Attack

A woman has been jailed for two years for wounding a 56-year-old call centre worker "by mistake". Kelly Staples, 20, of Richmond, Surrey, was sentenced at Kingston Crown Court.

In January she pleaded guilty to wounding Victor Blackstaff, but in mitigation her barrister told the court she had believed she was under threat.

"The capital was in a state of hysteria at the time of the incident because of the activities of the serial killer known as the Burning Man, then unapprehended, My client believed her life was in danger. She was considerably inebriated following a night of drinking and admits that her judgement was impaired. She wounded him by mistake."

The judge, His Honour Judge Steven Delaware, said that the two-year sentence reflected her early plea of guilty and also the fact that she had no previous convictions, but pointed out that it was a warning to others not to carry knives. He was also concerned by the serious long-term effects of the attack on the victim. Mr Blackstaff is continuing to receive medical treatment for his injuries and has not been able to return to work.

The Missing

Jane Casey

Casey has created a flawed but likeable heroine and a tremendous sense of suspense that continues until the final page   **Sunday Times**

A most impressive first novel   **lovereading.co.uk**

The Missing is an assured debut by an Irish writer, written with elegance and it delivers more twists than a corkscrew.   **Irish Independent**

When Sarah Finch was a little girl, her older brother went out to play and never came back . . . Not knowing what happened to Charlie has ripped her family apart. Now a teacher, Sarah's back living at home, trapped with an alcoholic mother who keeps her brother's bedroom as a shrine.

Then twelve-year-old Jenny Shepherd disappears and it's Sarah who discovers her pupil's body, abandoned in the woods near her home. As Sarah becomes more involved in the inquiry, suspicions are aroused. But it's not just the police who are watching her . . .

ISBN 978-0-7531-8692-3 (hb)
ISBN 978-0-7531-8693-0 (pb)

Elegy For April

Benjamin Black

As a deep fog cloaks Dublin, a young woman is found to have vanished. When Phoebe Griffin is unable to discover news of her friend, Quirke, fresh from drying out in an institution, responds to his daughter's request for help.

But as Phoebe, Quirke and Inspector Hackett speak with those who knew April, they begin to realise that there may be more behind the young woman's secrecy than they could have imagined. Why was April estranged from her powerful family, the Latimers? And who is the shadowy figure who seems to be watching Phoebe's flat at night?

As Quirke finds himself distracted from his sobriety by a beautiful young actress, Phoebe watches helplessly as April's family hush up her disappearance. But when Quirke makes a disturbing discovery, he is finally able to begin unravelling the web of love, lies and dark secrets from which April spun her life . . .

ISBN 978-0-7531-8774-6 (hb)
ISBN 978-0-7531-8775-3 (pb)

Someone Else's Son

Sam Hayes

TV presenter Carrie Kent can't believe the voice on the end of the phone. Surely it didn't just say that her son — her beloved Max — has been stabbed within his school gates? This sort of thing happens only to the guests on her daily morning chat show. Not to someone like her boy.

But when Carrie arrives at the hospital and learns that Max is dead, she is thrown into a nightmare. No one will reveal what really happened and the only witness, a schoolgirl, is refusing to talk. Carrie must enter an unknown world of fear and violence if she wants to find the truth. But will she be able to live with what she discovers?

ISBN 978-0-7531-8854-5 (hb)
ISBN 978-0-7531-8855-2 (pb)

Also available in ISIS Large Print:

Evil in Return

Elena Forbes

Bestselling novelist Joe Logan walks out into a hot summer's evening in central London. The next day his body is found dumped in a disused Victorian crypt at the Brompton Cemetery. It was no ordinary murder — he'd been tied up, shot and castrated.

Detective Inspector Mark Tartaglia is convinced that Logan's personal life holds the key to his violent death, but unravelling his past proves difficult. Following the overnight success of his debut novel, Logan had become a recluse. Was Logan just publicity shy or did he have something to hide? Then the body of a second man is found in an old boathouse on the Thames — killed in an identical fashion. Can Tartaglia find the link between the two dead men before the killer strikes again? As he soon discovers, nothing in life or death is straightforward.

ISBN 978-0-7531-8872-9 (hb)
ISBN 978-0-7531-8873-6 (pb)

I had help from various legal sources; in particular I would like to thank Philippa Charles for her insights into a solicitor's life. I would also like to mention the policemen who answered my queries promptly and fully, but did not wish to be named here. I am very grateful to them nonetheless.

Readers may wonder if Latimer College is based on the college I attended: it is not. Occupying a part of Oxford which is in reality the home of the Botanic Gardens, it is a total invention, as are the characters who live in it.

I could not have written this book without my friends and family. Special thanks must go to RP for spotting the difference between a glass of water and a cup of tea. Bridget and Michael Norman provided a home from home in Devon and encouragement when it was very much needed. The inhabitants of the snakepit were a tremendous help and inspiration, as ever.

Last but not least, my sincere thanks to Edward for sleeping occasionally, to Fred for his company throughout many long evenings, and to James, for everything.

Acknowledgements

My thanks to all at Ebury, particularly Gillian Green who kept me on the right path from the first synopsis to the final set of proofs.

Many thanks also to Simon Trewin and Ariella Feiner, and all at United Agents. Simon and Ariella are the first readers and the finest; their opinions are always well judged and entertaining, and their support is tremendously important.

Professor Derrick J. Pounder kindly allowed me to quote him; his clear and informative writing about forensic medicine was extremely helpful to me in researching the various murders and their investigations.

I am very grateful also to Janna Kenny, Chris Bowen and Nick Sheppard for their advice and guidance on matters medical, and for letting me have sufficient literary licence to get away with one or two things that might not have been strictly accurate. Nick's help was instrumental in working out key elements of the plot. I particularly appreciate his enthusiasm for answering strange questions in more detail than I had any right to expect.

exaggerated in many places. The trial received considerable media attention because of North's attempt to copy the crimes of notorious serial killer Razmig Selvaggi, dubbed the "Burning Man", who was still at large at the time Rebecca Haworth was murdered.

In spite of her history, North was not considered to be a suicide risk by the prison authorities and was not under special supervision. She was regarded as a model prisoner.

Three women have taken their own lives in HMP Mantham since 2009, despite efforts to improve living conditions for the inmates and the introduction of a counselling service. Sophie Chambers, chief spokesperson of prison reform group Cell Out claimed that there are still serious problems with over-crowding and poor facilities in the Victorian jail, and urged the government to release funding for the construction of new prison buildings as a matter of urgency.

Convicted in May last year, North received a life sentence with a minimum tariff of twenty-five years. She would have been eligible for parole in 2035.

Third Suicide at "Overcrowded" Women's Prison

A third prisoner has committed suicide at HMP Mantham in Northumberland. Louise North, 29, was halfway through the second year of a life sentence for murder. She was returning to her cell on the top landing of the prison yesterday morning after breakfast when she jumped over the railing and plummeted sixty feet. She died instantly. Anti-suicide netting had been removed to allow repairs to take place on the landing below. Prison authorities have launched an enquiry into why North was able to move around the cell block without adequate supervision.

This was North's second attempt to kill herself. She had previously taken an overdose of antidepressants while on remand awaiting trial for the murder of her best friend, Rebecca Haworth, but was discovered in time to receive medical treatment. Her suicide note was a key part of the case against her at her trial, although her barrister argued it was written while she was suffering from depression and should not be viewed as reliable evidence of her guilt. In the witness box, she claimed it was intended to convince her then boyfriend not to mourn for her, and that she had lied or